D0272044

NOBBS/D.

Pratt
of the *Argus*

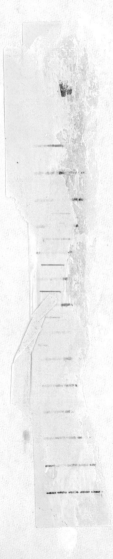

SEP 1991

by the same author

THE ITINERANT LODGER
OSTRICH COUNTRY
A PIECE OF THE SKY IS MISSING
SECOND FROM LAST IN THE SACK RACE
A BIT OF A DO
(published by Methuen)

THE DEATH OF REGINALD PERRIN
THE RETURN OF REGINALD PERRIN
THE BETTER WORLD OF REGINALD PERRIN
(published by Gollancz)

Pratt
of the *Argus*

David Nobbs

F/337816

WEXFORD
COUNTY
LIBRARY

METHUEN

First published in Great Britain 1988
by Methuen London Ltd
11 New Fetter Lane, London EC4P 4EE

Copyright © 1988 by David Nobbs

Photoset by Rowland Phototypesetting Ltd,
Bury St Edmunds, Suffolk

Printed and bound in
Great Britain
by
Redwood Burn Ltd,
Trowbridge, Wiltshire

British Library Cataloguing in Publication Data

Nobbs, David
Pratt of the Argus.
I. Title
823'.914[F]
ISBN 0-413-50520-0

For all the journalists of the provincial press,
and especially for my ex-colleagues
on the *Sheffield Star*. They were kinder to me
than I deserved, and, in gratitude for that,
are spared from these pages,
where all the characters are totally imaginary,
as indeed is the town of Thurmarsh.

Contents

1   A Night to Forget

Henry Pratt stared in disbelief at the first word that he had ever had in print. It was 'Thives'.

The full story read, 'Thives who last night broke into the Blurton Road home of Mrs Emily Braithwaite (73) stole a coat, a colander and a jam jar containing £5 in threepenny bits.'

Henry was twenty years old, pale, rather short, somewhat podgy. He had just completed his first day as a reporter on the *Thurmarsh Evening Argus*, and was sitting with three of his new colleagues at a corner table in the back bar of the Lord Nelson, a brown, masculine pub, tucked away in Leatherbottlers' Row. The back bar was a dark and secret room, popular with barristers, police officers and criminals. It smelt of carbolic and male intrigue. No juke-boxes or fruit machines disturbed the concentration of the drinkers. Trams could be heard clanking along Albion Street, and two elderly ham sandwiches were curling together for comfort in a glass case on the bar counter. You wouldn't have been able to find a slice of quiche this side of Alsace-Lorraine. It was Monday, January 16th, 1956.

He glanced through the paper, pretending that he was interested in it all, not just the one paragraph that he had written. Employment in Thurmarsh had reached a record level, with only 0.3 per cent out of work. Lieutenant-Colonel Nasser was claiming fresh powers for six years under a new constitution in Egypt. King Hussein had pledged Jordan to the cause of Arab unity. Henry didn't fool Neil Mallet. 'Never mind,' said Neil, his round, smooth, incipiently freckled face breaking into a brief, friendly smile. 'I didn't set the world alight on my first day, and look at me now. Half the West Riding hangs on my words.' Neil Mallet, a bachelor, of Pitlochry Drive, Thurmarsh Lane Bottom, wrote a weekly opinion column under the pen-name of 'Thurmarshian'.

Ted Plunkett raised his bushy black eyebrows that might have been purpose-built for sarcasm and said, 'It's true, Henry. From Barnsley to Dronfield, from Penistone to Maltby they're agog for

9

his smug, reactionary views.' He turned to Neil. 'Murderers sent to the gallows by judges who've just read your virulent prose are the only people who hang on your words.'

Neil Mallet smiled benevolently. Henry's heart sank. He couldn't cope with Ted Plunkett. Were the doubters right? Was he unsuited to the hard world of journalism?

He might not have been so overawed if he'd known that Ted wrote the Kiddies Club column. The kiddies were known as the Argusnauts and did good deeds. Ted was known as Uncle Jason.

Henry replied to Neil, as if Ted hadn't spoken. 'I know,' he said, 'but a misprint in my first word! Are they trying to tell me something?' He'd often found self-deprecation useful. At school he'd become a stand-up comedian, Henry 'Ee by gum I am daft' Pratt, in order to mock himself before others did. But now it was his ambition to become Henry 'I was the first British journalist to enter the seething hell-hole that was Dien Bien Phu' Pratt, and he sensed that self-deprecation would no longer be useful to him. He ploughed on through the paper. A floating elevator costing £300,000 had been kept idle in Hull docks for three months because of a dispute over manning levels. 100 shivering people had queued all night to book summer coach holidays to Torquay. Eggs were down to 3s. 9d. a dozen. Would he ever write exciting stories like those?

'Same again?' said the third of his new colleagues, Colin Edgeley, who was writing a novel, had lost two front teeth in a fight, and had kept the gap as a badge of courage.

Henry ought to be getting back for his tea, but how could he, on his first day? One thing he wasn't going to become was Henry 'I'm not stopping. I've gorra get back for my tea' Pratt.

Helen Cornish, general reporter and women's page, breezed in with Ben Watkinson, the football correspondent. Ben was tall and thin and grizzled. Helen wasn't. She said, 'Room for a little one?' and sat beside Henry on the bench seat. Their thighs were touching. He grew excited. She was fair-haired, with pearly grey eyes and pert, delicate lips. Already he found her so attractive that even the sight of the words 'By Helen Cornish' under the headline 'What the stars wear next to their skin' had given him an erection. He wondered what Helen wore next to her skin. This was ridiculous. Ben's left hand had just brushed her right knee. They were probably married. Women did sometimes marry the most unsuitable men. And didn't he have his childhood sweetheart, Lorna Arrow, whose existence had nourished him through two years in the army? He hadn't clung to the thought of her throughout that business in Germany in order to abandon her now. He met Ted's deep, dark, troubled eyes and had an uneasy feeling that Ted could read his thoughts.

They drank halves, which in Thurmarsh were referred to as glasses. You drank more that way, because the beer kept fresher. Henry tried to say, 'No thanks, Ben. I said I'd be back for my tea,' but the words wouldn't come.

Neil had been to London and seen *Waiting for Godot*. Henry said, 'Oh, *I've* seen that,' and Neil said, 'What did you think of it?' Henry wanted to say, 'Magnificent! I think Beckett's a giant, sweeping theatrical realism under the carpets of the bourgeoisie,' but he was frightened of sounding pretentious so he said, 'I quite liked it.' 'I thought it was magnificent,' said Neil. 'Beckett's a giant, emptying the fag-ends of realism into the overflowing dustbins of the middle classes.' Ted raised his bushy eyebrows. 'Go to London a lot, do you?' he asked Henry.

Fleet Street was their magnet. At forty, Ben knew he'd never make it. At thirty-four, Neil suspected he wouldn't. At twenty-seven, Ted still hoped. At twenty-four, Colin had few doubts. At twenty-two, Helen had no doubts at all.

Henry bought his round, fighting his way through a burst of dutiful laughter at a joke cracked by Chief Superintendent Ron Ratchett. Helen was on gin and orange. He longed to kiss her slightly sticky tongue. No! Think of Friday night. Think of Lorna.

'Do you have any good contacts, Henry?' asked Ted.

'Contacts?' he said, puzzled.

'People you know whom you can use to get stories off,' explained Ted, as to a rather dim Argusnaut.

'Oh!' he said. 'Yes. I see. No. Well, I've been away, in the army.'

'Which Thurmarsh United player broke his leg in three places?' said Ben, and although it was apropos of absolutely nothing, nobody seemed surprised.

11

Henry knew the answer, but kept silent. He sensed that Helen despised sport.

'Reg Putson,' said Helen.

'Correct,' said Ben. 'Which three places did he break his leg in?'

'Halifax, Barrow and Wrexham,' said Helen.

'Correct.'

It was like a double act. They *were* married.

'You're keen on football, Helen?' said Henry, carefully hiding his surprise.

'Don't sound so surprised,' said Helen. 'I support Stockport County.'

'I'm a great United fan,' said Henry. 'I know Tommy Marsden.'

They all gawped at him.

'You know Tommy Marsden?' said Colin Edgeley.

'We were at school together. We were in the same gang.'

'Then you do have a contact,' said Ted Plunkett pityingly. 'Tommy Marsden.'

'Rapidly rising star in the Third Division (North) firmament,' said Ben Watkinson.

Tommy Marsden had been Henry's one good social card. He had played it so ineptly that it had become a revelation of his journalistic naïvety. He fell silent, and another half of bitter appeared, just as he was about to go.

'Time I was off,' said Ben. 'Got to go home and give the wife one.'

Joy and fear swept through Henry. Ben Watkinson was married to somebody else. Helen Cornish was free. Deeply though he loved Lorna Arrow, he couldn't help acknowledging that Helen was more beautiful. She was also more sophisticated. She was also nearer. In fact their thighs were still touching, even though there was more room now Ben had gone.

He wanted to start a private conversation with her, but couldn't think how. She did it for him. 'Do you have any brothers or sisters, Henry?' she asked.

'No. I'm an only child.'

'What about family?'

'My mother was knocked down by a bus and my father hanged himself in the outside lavatory.'

Oh no! At last they were talking, and he had produced the conversation stopper to stop all conversation stoppers.

She said, 'Oh, I'm sorry,' and touched his thigh briefly. His leg tingled. He resisted an absurd temptation to say, 'Why? It wasn't your fault.' He floundered on. 'I was brought up by this uncle and aunt. Then he went to . . . er . . . Rangoon, and I went to this other relative.' He asked her about her family and was too aroused to listen to her reply. He became aware that Ted was speaking.

'Sorry, Ted,' he said. 'What was that?'

'I said you seem to be getting on very well with my fiancée.'

Greenhorn reporter in fiancée blunder. Henry was terrified that he was going to blush. 'I am,' he said. His voice sounded small and far away. 'She's a lovely girl. You're a lucky man.'

He inched carefully away from Helen. The loneliness flooded over him again. For two years he had counted the days till the end of his national service. And then, ever since it had ended, ever since Cousin Hilda had met him at Thurmarsh (Midland Road) Station, sniffing with suppressed love like a truffle-hound with a bad cold, how he had missed them. Not only Brian Furnace. Not only Michael Collinghurst. All of them. Taffy Bevin, Lanky Lasenby, Geordie Stubbs. Even Fishy Fisk, who smelt of herrings. He'd been counting the hours till the nakedness of Lorna Arrow, and Cousin Hilda had whisked him away to a boarding house in Bridlington! She'd meant well. The rain had never kept them in all day, Mrs Flixborough had three jigsaws with very few pieces missing, the white horses breaking over the groyne had been really rather spectacular, and Cousin Hilda had been right to rebuke him for his meanness in laughing when the floral clock had flooded. Then, at last, Lorna. Husky, lisping, toothy Lorna. Brief moments in the hay, in Kit Orris's dry-stone field barn. Shyness. Doubts. Climaxes. Anti-climaxes. Desolate rattling train journeys from Troutwick to Cousin Hilda, changing at Leeds. A visit to London to see Paul Hargreaves, his old chum from Dalton College. No Diana. Paul's luscious, chunky sister Diana was skiing at Davos. 'What play would you like to see, Henry?' The sophisticated Hargreaveses had scorned his suggestion of *Separate Tables*. They'd gone to *Waiting for Godot*. Several people had walked out, but Dr Hargreaves had said, 'Beckett is a giant, sweeping theatrical realism under the carpets of the bourgeoisie. Rattigan is only fit to wait at the table where Beckett eats,' and Henry had said, 'Is Rattigan waiting for Godot at the separate tables where Beckett eats?' and everybody had laughed, but not quite enough, at Paul's funny little northern friend. *Waiting for Godot, La Strada*, daube Provençale, and sexual frustration. Then more Lorna. But his two years in the army had begun to institutionalize him, and the loneliness had lurked throughout those last, long months of 1955.

Ted's lovely fiancée bought him a drink, so he couldn't refuse that, and she looked him straight in the eyes, almost as if she were regretting being engaged, and Ted gleamed dangerously under his mass of black hair behind his cool, firm glass of beer. Henry hurried off to the toilet, to read again the letter from Lorna, and relieve himself of his desire for this new, dangerous, unavailable woman.

Podgy Sex Bomb Henry sat in the icy cubicle. On the door a closet wit had written: 'God is alive and well and working on a less ambitious project.' Henry liked that.

> Dere Henry [he read]
> I carn't wate for Friday nite. I'm rite excited. It'll be the first time I've ever done it in a hottel and it'll be nice singing in as mister and misses! It were luvly in the barn but it'll be grate not having all that hay being verry tickellish as you now. I'll be on the 5.40 from Leeds so I'll be their at 6.32 as you said. Eric Lugg's got leave from the Cattering Corpse and wants me to go out with him this weakened. Tuff luck! Sorry Eric I've better things to do! This is quiet a long letter for me so I'll stop now.
> With luv and kisses as ever
> You're Lorna

It didn't matter if Lorna couldn't spell. It didn't matter that all the journalists would laugh if they read her letter. He hated snobbery and it was a luvly letter. 'Oh, Lorna, Lorna,' he moaned silently, but it was no use, it was Helen Cornish whose superb pointed breasts hung down towards his naked body as they writhed in ecstasy on the subs' table, in the vast, empty news-room of his mind.

14

He returned, a little calmer, a little wearier. He sipped his beer. He remembered, with muffled alarm, his waiting tea. Ted and Helen set off for the Shanghai Chinese Restaurant and Coffee Bar, which served glutinous curries, haystacky chop sueys and frothy coffee. Now the lights in the pub seemed dimmer than ever.

He accepted a drink off Neil. Well, if he left as soon as Helen had gone, it would look a bit obvious, it would be a bit rude to Neil and Colin.

'I must go in a minute,' said Neil. 'I've some laundry to do.'

Henry, who had never left licensed premises because he had laundry to do, gave Neil a look of sheer astonishment. 'I must go too,' he said. If he missed that cue, he'd be stuck for the night.

'So must I,' said Colin, 'or Glenda'll kill me.'

'Glenda?'

'My wife.'

Henry was surprised to discover that Colin was married.

Suddenly Colin spoke in a low, tense voice, dramatic and excited. 'Hey,' he said. 'Don't look now, but there's a feller by t'door that got put away because of my evidence. He's sworn revenge. Mick Tunstall. He's gorra knife.'

'Oh I say,' said Neil.

Henry looked towards the door. Two Neanderthal giants with prison haircuts were sitting there. All the police had gone.

'Don't look,' hissed Colin. 'That man is a bonfire of hatred, and he's tinder-dry. One spark, that's all it needs.'

Henry wondered if he looked as pale as Neil.

'Right,' said Colin. 'What we do is, we walk out together, looking normal. We don't look at Mick. Then we walk down the alley into Albion Street, not hurrying. If he sees you're scared . . . and don't worry, kids.' He opened his right fist, revealing a handful of sharp-edged coins. A thin line of sweat had broken out on Neil's forehead. It looked as if it were seeping through a fault in his skin's crust.

They stood up, self-consciously.

'Look normal,' whispered Colin.

Henry tried to walk out normally, at normal pace, with head held high, but not abnormally so. His heart was thumping. He felt sure that they looked so abnormally normal as to be utterly

15

ridiculous. He walked down the dark, narrow alley into Albion Street, longing to break into a run. Then he looked round, with failed nonchalance. Nobody was following them. Nobody saw his failed nonchalance.

'Well done!' said Colin.

Neil hurried off, towards his laundry. Henry and Colin walked down Albion Street. The night was cold. The street lamps cast a dim, mournful light over the dirty stone and brick of the Victorian shops and offices. Above the ground-floor displays, the rows of small, regular grime-streaked windows were dark. Nobody lived in Albion Street.

'How about a quick one at the Globe and Artichoke?' suggested Colin.

Henry tried to say, 'I'm hours late for my tea,' but, since Colin might say, 'In that case a few minutes more won't make any difference' he said, 'What about Glenda?' When Colin said, 'Glenda won't mind. She's all right,' Henry felt that he'd been outmanoeuvred. He was glad he'd been outmanoeuvred.

They turned into High Street, between piles of discoloured snow, and entered a yellow-painted pub. There were dirty red walls, and the frayed flock-paper was almost covered in theatre bills. A few customers were reading the *Argus*. Colin talked about his novel. Denzil Ackerman, the arts editor, had read the first five chapters and thought he could be the second D. H. Lawrence. Henry felt happy, although he was a little disappointed that none of the readers of the *Argus* said, 'Good Lord! Thives have broken into the home of Mrs Emily Braithwaite.' But then none of them said, 'Hello. I see Hussein has pledged Jordan to Arab unity' either. He was also disappointed when Colin said, 'Sorry about that business with Mick, but don't worry. You're all right with me, kid. I'll look after you.' He said, 'I don't want to be looked after, Colin. I'm norra kid.' He talked about when he *was* a kid. He felt vaguely guilty about revealing what should have been deeply private, about feeling pride in relating what should have been purely tragic. Colin got quite excited when he learnt that Henry had drunk with Tommy Marsden in a pub from which his father had earlier been banned for life.

'That's the stuff,' he said. 'Come on.'

16

Henry found himself in the street. Colin yelled, 'Taxi!' A taxi slithered towards them over the crumbling grey town-centre snow.

'The Navigation,' said Colin.

On the one hand, a dried-up tea and duty. On the other hand, adventure, spontaneity, friendship with the second D. H. Lawrence, the Bohemian life, Thurmarsh style. No contest!

The polluted and fetid courses of the River Rundle and the Rundle and Gadd Navigation took a great loop on the south-eastern side of the town, but the main Rawlaston road went straight up out of the valley, past the great fortress of Brunswick Road Primary School, which Henry had once attended. The taxi breasted the rise and slithered down again, past a stranded trolley bus, past the Pineapple and other small, friendly pubs, back towards the river and the canal, back towards Henry's past.

Henry paid for the taxi. It was Monday, and already Colin was broke.

How small the Navigation Inn was. In his memory it had been a world. They stood at the bar, in the little snug, with their backs to the smoked-glass Victorian window. The tiny fire roared. There was the peaceful clack of dominoes. The green upholstery that Henry's father had so resented had gone. The bench seats were red now, and they squeaked.

They ordered glasses of Ward's Malt Ales, and whisky chasers.

'Where did Tommy sit?' whispered Colin.

Henry pointed to an empty seat. Colin sat in it, gave an almost shy, gap-toothed smile, and sighed contentedly. His dark brown hair was receding. His face already bore the coarsening ravages of life, but when he smiled he looked like a child.

Henry recognized Sid Lowson and nodded to him. Sid Lowson nodded back, his face as blank as the domino with which he closed up the game, to the unconcealed chagrin of Fred Shilton, the lock-keeper. Nowhere do we feel such strangers as in our own pasts.

Yet somebody almost remembered Henry. 'Don't I know you?' said Cecil E. Jenkinson, the landlord, towering paunchily over them.

'I'm Henry Pratt,' said Henry. 'I'm Ezra's boy.'

'Get out of here,' said Cecil E. Jenkinson, licensed to remember old grudges. 'You're the bastard who got me banned for allowing under-age drinking. Out! You're banned for life, sunshine.'

Cecil E. Jenkinson lifted Henry out of his seat and began to propel him towards the door. Colin rushed to the rescue. 'Take your hands off my mate,' he said, grabbing the landlord's lapel. 'Nobody pushes my oppo around.'

'Colin!' said Henry. 'It'll be in the paper.'

'Good. I'll write it meself,' said Colin.

Colin began to pull Cecil E. Jenkinson off Henry.

'Barry!' thundered the landlord.

Barry Jenkinson, the landlord's far from brilliant but unquestionably bulky son, was soon at his father's side. They bundled the flailing young journalist out of the pub together, paunchy father and massive son. Henry followed willingly, shaking his head at Sid Lowson, indicating that reinforcements wouldn't be needed. Henry felt no anger, as if Colin were angry enough for both of them. Besides, these were old battles, fought and lost for ever long ago.

The Jenkinsons threw Colin down onto the snow-covered cobbles. They wiped their hands in unison, as if removing contamination. They glared at Henry, and returned to their tiny kingdom.

'Bastards!' shouted Colin. 'I'll get you!'

'Come on,' said Henry. 'Let's go home.'

A thin yellow mist was rising over the valley as they waited for a tram under the great blank wall of Crapp, Hawser and Kettlewell, the huge steelworks, opposite the tiny cul-de-sac of wine-red back-to-back houses, where Henry had been born.

'Dinna thee worry,' said Colin, as they staggered up the narrow stairs of the tram. 'I'll look after you, kid.'

'I've told you,' said Henry. 'I don't want to be looked after. I'm norra kid.'

'OK,' said Colin. 'OK. I'll make sure nobody looks after you. Anybody tries to look after you, I'll punch him on the nose.'

Colin just caught the last bus to Glenda. Henry walked home from the tram terminus, in Mabberley Street. He felt that the sharp, raw air would sober him up. In this he was mistaken.

He weaved his way through the frozen gardens in front of the pseudo-Gothic town hall, Victorian confidence and plagiarism writ large in soot. Puffed up pigeons slept uneasily on ledges coated with frozen droppings. Henry stumbled along the deserted Doncaster Road. A red light warned of a hole in the road. He picked it up. This was another mistake.

'Now then,' said the police officer. 'What's all this?'

'It's dark up my road,' said Henry. 'The street lighting is frankly abdominable. Need the light, see where I'm going.'

'Name?' said the officer.

'Plunkett,' said Henry. 'Ted Plunkett.'

'Address?'

'The *Thurmarsh Evening Argus*, Thurmarsh.'

'A journalist!'

'Your powers of deduction are staggering.'

'So are you. Come with me.'

At the police station, while Henry was again giving Ted's name and address, an emergency broke out. Officers hurried off, their boots ringing on the stone floor. Panic and urgency reigned. Suddenly, Henry was alone. He walked out, a free and forgotten man.

As he approached the Alderman Chandler Memorial Park, he passed a small, whitewashed, detached late-Georgian pub called the Vine. It was set back from the road, and in the rutted snow in front of it three police cars were parked. He wondered whether to go in and say, 'Excuse me. I'm a journalist. What's going on?' He decided against it. He was tired. He was too inexperienced. He didn't want to meet the police again. A shrewd observer might notice that he was slightly inebriated. And it was probably only a late drinkers' brawl, anyway.

He fell over, and realized for the first time how drunk he was.

Number 66, Park View Road was a stone, semi-detached Victorian house, with a bay window on the ground floor. It looked blessedly dark as Henry crunched carefully through the snow on lurching tiptoe.

He turned the lock in the key . . . no, the key in the lock . . . why was he so drunk? He opened the door quietly and entered the dark, cold hall, which smelt of cabbage and linoleum. The wind must have caught the door, although there was no wind, because it slammed behind him. The hall became as flooded with light as a sixty-watt bulb could manage. The barometer said 'Changeable'. Cousin Hilda's face said 'Stormy'. She sniffed, loudly, twice.

'What's for tea?' he said, enunciating slowly, carefully. It was a stupid remark on two counts. It was past midnight, and he knew the answer anyway. Tea on Monday was liver and bacon, with boiled potatoes and cabbage, followed by rhubarb crumble.

'Never mind "what's for tea?",' said Cousin Hilda, her mouth working painfully. 'What sort of time do you call this?'

Henry stared at the barometer. 'Quarter past stormy,' he said. 'Didn't realize it was as late as that.'

He sank slowly to the floor. A stranger inside him began to laugh hysterically.

'Journalists!' said Cousin Hilda grimly.

The headline in next morning's *Daily Express* was 'Four shot dead in Thurmarsh pub massacre'. Henry would have been the first journalist on the scene, by more than half an hour.

F/33786

2   Contacts

Premier House, the *Chronicle* and *Argus* building, was situated on the corner of High Street and Albion Street. It had a curved frontage in lavatorial marble. A large green dome proclaimed its importance. Henry entered with a thick head and a sense of dread.

The news-room was on the first floor. It was large, noisy and dusty. The windows were streaked with grime, and the lights were on all day, bathing the room in the brownish-yellow hue of old newspapers. There was a perpetual throb of suppressed excitement, even when nothing at all was happening. When there was a murder or a big crash, or expenses were being filled in, the excitement became almost palpable.

The reporters sat at four rows of desks. It was like school, and Henry had been to too many schools already.

Terry Skipton, the news editor, sat behind the news desk, facing the reporters as if he were their form master. He admitted no Christian names into his puritanical world. 'Good morning, Mr *Pratt*,' he said, emphasizing the surname, as if it were a judgement.

Henry had hoped that Helen's beauty would turn out to be illusory, but it pierced him like a hard frost. He had hoped that Colin would look as if he too had experienced a heavy night but, perhaps because he always looked ravaged, he seemed untouched. The freshly laundered Neil Mallet gave him a friendly smile. So did the young woman at the desk on his right. She was less beautiful than Helen, rather big, squat-faced. She said, 'Hello. I had a day off yesterday. I'm Ginny Fenwick.' He got an erection simply because she was friendly.

He tried hard to look busy, like everyone else. The phone on Ted's desk rang, and he heard Ted say, 'That's funny. The editor wants to see me. Something about the police.'

Henry's heart sank, but he hurried over to Ted's desk.

'I'd better come too,' he said.

'You what?' said Ted.

They entered the editor's office. It was an airy room, with a wide

WEXFORD COUNTY LIBRARY

window looking out onto the inelegant bustle of Albion Street. On the walls were framed copies of momentous editions of the *Argus* – the abdication, two coronations, the beginning and ending of two world wars, the day the circulation reached two hundred thousand. Mr Andrew Redrobe was small and neat. He looked more like a shrewd businessman than a romantic newspaperman, his nose sharpened for profits rather than elongated for sniffing out scoops. His green-topped desk was large and neat.

'What are *you* doing here?' he asked Henry, giving Ted a questioning look, which was answered with a shrug.

'All this is my fault, sir,' said Henry. Damn that 'sir'. He'd promised himself that he'd never say 'sir' again after he left the army. 'Last night I got rather drunk.'

'Oh?'

'Yes. I . . . er . . . I was . . . excited.'

'Excited?'

Mr Andrew Redrobe hadn't told them to sit down. Henry felt like a naughty schoolboy.

'Yes, sir.' Damn. 'I was carried away by the atmosphere.'

'I'm not with you. What atmosphere?' said the puzzled editor.

'Meeting my new colleagues. Talking. Drinking.'

Ted Plunkett looked almost as surprised as Mr Andrew Redrobe.

'Let's get this right,' said the editor. 'Are you saying you were excited by spending an evening with members of my editorial staff?'

'Yes, sir.' Damn.

'Good God.'

'Yes, sir.' Damn. 'I . . . er . . . I took a red light. I was arrested. Being . . . er . . . slightly . . . er . . . over the . . . er . . . I'm afraid I gave Ted's name as my own.'

'You went to five different schools, covering the whole stratum of public and private education, didn't you?' said Mr Redrobe.

'I did, yes,' admitted Henry, as if it had been his fault.

'What did I say to you last week, Ted?' said Mr Redrobe.

'"English education fails dismally to fit people for real life,"' quoted Ted.

'Precisely. You're the proof of the pudding, lad.' The editor

sounded grateful to Henry for proving him right. 'You're a total mess.'

Henry didn't wish to agree and didn't dare to disagree, so he said nothing.

'I don't think we'll hear any more of this matter,' said Mr Andrew Redrobe. 'We pride ourselves on having a good relationship with the police. *But* I don't want that good relationship endangered by your juvenile antics, Henry Pratt. Do I make myself clear?'

'Very clear, sir.' Damn.

Outside, in the corridor, Henry said, 'I'm sorry, Ted.'

'No! Please!' said Ted. 'I'm flattered to find how deeply I've impinged on your consciousness.'

'Sorry.'

'*You've* impinged pretty deeply on Helen's consciousness.'

Henry went weak at the knees.

'What?'

'She thinks you're attractive. I'll never understand women.' .

Ted stomped back into the news-room, just as Colin Edgeley came out.

'The editor wants to see me about last night,' said Colin grimly. 'Apparently that landlord's complained.'

The editor raised his neat eyebrows neatly at the reappearance of his most junior reporter. He listened to their tale in pained silence, once pushing a hand discreetly through his neat, Brylcreemed hair.

'Well,' he said. 'Luckily for you, which is more than you both deserve, I don't think we'll hear any more of this. We pride ourselves on having a good relationship with the licensed victuallers. *But* I want it kept that way, so . . . no more antics. You've proved yourself a good journalist, Colin. I'd hate to lose you. You haven't proved anything yet, Henry. I'd hate to lose you before you have the chance. I still think it's *possible* you could have a career in journalism.'

Neither of them spoke.

'I'd like to line all your headmasters up, Henry Pratt, and show you to them. You're a walking condemnation of the system. You're a living indictment,' said the editor.

Again, Henry found it impossible to say anything. Colin didn't help him out.

'You must have gone pretty close to the Vine last night, Henry,' continued Mr Redrobe. 'You didn't see anything of the incident? Nothing at the police station?'

Oh god. Don't blush. Don't give yourself away. Show some nerve.

'No, sir.' Damn. But the voice sounded steady enough. 'I think I must have got home just before it happened.'

'Mmm.' Did the editor believe him? Did it matter? His career was ruined. 'You are now going to be educated in the forcing house of the provincial press. In the school of life. In the college of the streets. I expect a vast and rapid improvement. I'll need it.'

'Yes, sir.' Damn. 'Sorry, sir.' Damn.

'Oh, get out.'

'Don't you worry, kid,' said Colin, as they walked back to the news-room. 'You'll be all right. I'll look after you.'

'Mr Pratt?' called out Terry Skipton.

Henry approached the news desk with trepidation. His nerves felt shredded. Terry Skipton had high, slightly humped shoulders, no neck at all, prominent, heavily lidded eyes and a large nose. He looked like a slightly deformed frog. Behind him, to Henry's left, was the great table round which all the sub-editors sat, honing their headlines.

'A man's phoned about a cat, Mr Pratt,' said Terry Skipton. 'Pop in on your calls, and see if you can make something of it.'

Henry's spirits leapt. His hangover was forgotten. The sixth sense of the born journalist visited him for the first time, and told him that he was about to have his first scoop.

On the tram, returning promptly for his tea, Henry tried to read the rest of the paper. A new air-raid warning had been developed by the Home Office, to protect against radioactive dust in the event of an H-Bomb attack. That was reassuring. Billy Panama, American Yo-Yo Champion, had made a personal appearance at Cockayne's in High Street, and Johnny Hepplewhite, aged 14, had become Yo-Yo Champion of Thurmarsh. That was interesting. And yet . . . again and again Henry was drawn back to page 8, as if he feared that his scoop would no longer be there.

Those readers who have lodged at 66, Park View Road will not need to be told that tea on Tuesday consisted of roast lamb, with roast potatoes and cauliflower, followed by spotted dick.

'We had an amazing run on Wensleydale today,' said Norman Pettifer, who ran the cheese counter at Cullen's. He was a slightly stooping, sallow-skinned man whose mouth was set in an expression of disappointment borne with fortitude. He had arrived at number 66 as a temporary measure, while looking for a new job and a house for his wife and family. The wife and family had never materialized. Nor had the new job. This would be his pinnacle, to be manager of the cheese counter at Cullen's, and mothered by Cousin Hilda.

'Did you indeed?' said Liam O'Reilly, the gentle, bewildered, shiny-faced, almost teetotal Irish labourer who seemed to have been at Cousin Hilda's since the beginning of time, and even that degree of conversational initiative caused him to blush with confusion.

'An amazing run? How amazing!' said Barry Frost. Norman Pettifer searched his face for signs of sarcasm. Barry Frost, Cousin Hilda's most recent 'businessman', was a junior tax inspector from Walsall, with smelly feet and a talent for amateur operatics. He was a big-boned man with large features that were not quite rugged. Henry had once met his fiancée, a strikingly attractive PE instructor from Dudley, with smelly feet and a talent for amateur operatics. Henry hoped that they and their feet would hum together through a happy life, but he did wish Barry Frost wouldn't sing the leading role from *The Desert Song* under his breath throughout tea, occasionally referring to the script at the side of his plate. Norman Pettifer spoke of the time he had seen the Lunts in the West End. Barry Frost searched his face for evidence of sarcasm.

It was warm and airless in Cousin Hilda's basement room. A fire glowed merrily in the little blue-tiled stove, but there was nothing merry about Cousin Hilda. She was thin-lipped, thick-scowled. She gave Henry an extra large portion of spotted dick, so he knew that she was still displeased with him. Once he met her eyes, and

25

what he saw there was pain, and it shrivelled him up inside. He knew, as he forced down his concrete pudding, that he loved Cousin Hilda very much, but that he couldn't bear to live here much longer. He turned to page 8 of the *Argus*. 'When Thomas Hendrick . . .'

'Where are our manners, Henry? We don't read at table,' said Cousin Hilda.

'Barry does,' said Henry.

'Barry is paying,' hissed Cousin Hilda.

Barry Frost banged his copy of *The Desert Song* shut, and gave Henry a look that might have abashed a sizeable tribe of Rifs.

'I offered to pay, Cousin Hilda,' said Henry.

'We don't talk about money at table,' said Cousin Hilda. They didn't talk about money, sex, food, drink, pleasure, religion or politics at table. 'Besides,' she continued. 'Mr Frost has his "lines" to learn.' She sniffed as she said 'lines'. Barry Frost had replaced Tony Preece, an insurance salesman who at night became a struggling comic called Talwyn Jones, the Celtic Droll. 'What do people think my establishment is – a theatrical "digs"?' said Cousin Hilda's eloquent sniff.

Soon the three 'businessmen' were gone, and Henry faced his disappointed surrogate mother, across the corner table, among the debris of spotted dick, in the stifling basement room, with its smell of the water in which the greens had been overcooked, which Cousin Hilda, who hated waste, saved for her six sad, overwatered rose bushes.

Henry was determined to say, 'I'm going to find a flat.' He also felt that he should say, 'I'm very sorry about last night.' Why couldn't he bring himself to say either of these things? Why did he say, instead, 'Did you see my scoop about the cat?'

Cousin Hilda ignored this. Her mouth was working painfully as she prepared her words. 'About last night,' she said at last. 'I don't want any repetition.'

'I'm sorry,' he mumbled gracelessly.

'All right,' said Cousin Hilda. 'You were led astray. Journalists! If your poor parents were alive today to see you become a journalist, they'd turn in their graves. They'd blame me.'

'No!'

26

'It's a responsibility.'

'I don't want to be a responsibility,' said Henry. 'I'm not ready for the responsibility of being a responsibility.'

'Mrs Wedderburn thinks you've turned out so well,' said Cousin Hilda. 'Only yesterday I met her in the Co-op. I won't use Cullen's. I don't like Mr Pettifer's cheese counter, it's no use pretending I do, I was never one for pretence, not like some I could mention.' She sniffed twice, once for Auntie Doris and once for Uncle Teddy, with whom Henry had lived before Cousin Hilda. 'So to save Mr Pettifer's embarrassment it's best I go to the Co-op, even if it is further from the tram. "Ee, Hilda," she said. "Hasn't your Henry turned out well?"'

'She makes me sound like a cake,' said Henry.

'Now then, Henry,' said Cousin Hilda. 'There's no call to be rude about Mrs Wedderburn, who lent you her camp-bed in time of need.'

'I really don't see why I shouldn't pay,' said Henry, who didn't want the burden of Mrs Wedderburn's good opinion. 'I'd rather not be indebted.'

'Indebted,' snorted Cousin Hilda. '"Indebted," he says. If I charged you it'd put you on a footing with poor Mr O'Reilly. It'd put you on a footing with poor Mr Pettifer.' Her voice developed an acid coating of disapproval. 'It'd put you on a footing with Mr Frost. You are not my lodger. You are my son.'

Henry blushed and Cousin Hilda looked embarrassed too.

'Well you are . . . now . . . you are.'

He was pleased, of course. He was moved, of course. He was also appalled. How could he say he was looking for a flat, now?

He had to tell her about the weekend.

'Er . . . by the way . . .' he said. 'I'm . . . er . . . going away for the weekend.'

'Away? You'll only have been at work a week.'

'I have alternate Saturdays off.'

'Where to, "away"?'

'London.'

'London?' Cousin Hilda couldn't have sounded more surprised if Henry had said 'Outer Mongolia'. 'London? What do you want to go to London for?'

'I'm going to spend the weekend with Paul Hargreaves.'

'Oh.' Cousin Hilda was rather ambivalent about Paul, the brain surgeon's son, the friend from public school days who had visited Thurmarsh briefly in the summer of 1953. She had disturbingly contradictory feelings about private education, since she believed strongly in standards but despised people who put on airs. 'Well, I've met worse boys, even if he didn't think we were good enough for him.'

'That isn't true,' said Henry, knowing that it was. 'One of the boys I used to fag for, at Dalton, is making his début for England at rugby.' For a moment, Henry wished he really was going to watch Tosser Pilkington-Brick versus Wales, rather than lie naked with Lorna Arrow in the Midland Hotel. But only for a moment.

'Rugby!' said Cousin Hilda, as if it were the apogee of human absurdity. 'I don't know!'

'I feel the same,' said Henry. 'If God had meant us to play rugby, he'd have given us oval balls.' It was out before he could stop it. To his relief, Cousin Hilda didn't seem to understand it. 'I have to go out now,' he said.

'Out?' Cousin Hilda sounded astonished at his geographical profligacy.

'Yes. I have to develop my contacts.'

'Contacts?'

'That's what we journalists call the people in places of influence who can put stories our way,' explained Henry airily, with all the experience of twenty-four hours.

'And what people in places of influence are you seeing tonight?'

'Tommy Marsden.'

'Tommy Marsden!'

'Ace goal poacher of the Third Division North.'

'Aye. Well . . . don't be "late".' For 'late', read 'drunk'. Her mouth was working again, with the tension.

'I won't,' he said, and gave her a quick kiss, which astounded them both. '*Did* you see my scoop about the cat?'

'Cats!' said Cousin Hilda scornfully. 'Scoops!'

They sat in an alcove in the bar of the Conservative Club, of which Tommy was an honorary member. Above them was a portrait of Sir Winston Churchill. The carpet was blue. They could hear the occasional clunk of snooker balls from the back room.

They talked about the Paradise Lane Gang. 'Those were the days,' said Henry. He didn't remind Tommy that it had all broken up in fighting and bitterness when Henry and Martin had gone to the grammar school. He wanted Tommy in a good mood.

'Aye,' said Tommy. 'Does tha see Martin at all?'

'We have a jar every now and then. We sup some lotion,' said Henry. 'It isn't the same. I think becoming a sergeant's made him take himself very seriously.'

'It's age,' said Tommy Marsden. 'I'm twenty-one.'

'I'm twenty. It's frightening. Are you married or engaged or owt?' His dialect was returning, in Tommy's company.

'Chuff me, no,' said Tommy. 'Mr Mackintosh says many a promising career's been nipped in t'bud because a player's shagging himself to death. Same again?'

No, thanks. I must remain sober for Cousin Hilda. 'Yes, please.'

'Same difference wi' supping,' said Tommy, as the waiter brought them two pints, and Tommy discovered that he had no money, and Henry paid. 'There'll be plenty of time for that later.'

Henry judged that the time was ripe. 'Tommy?' he said. 'Will you be my contact from the world of sport?'

'Tha what?'

'Will you put stories my way?'

'Stories? What stories?'

'I don't know. Whatever happens. Transfers. Disciplinary suspensions. Dressing-room arguments. Whatever happens. Stories.'

'What? And be known as Tommy "The Leak" Marsden?'

'No. No one'll know where they come from. Us journalists never reveal our sources.'

'Will I get paid?'

'I can't. I'm only on seven pounds ten a week.'

'I'll think about it,' said Tommy Marsden.

'Hey!' said Henry, judging it unwise to press the matter at this juncture. 'I've only been on the paper two days, and I've had my first scoop.'

He showed Tommy page 8. Tommy grabbed it, and began to read aloud, to Henry's embarrassment, especially as he read very loudly, and very slowly, as if he had only a passing acquaintanceship with words.

'"When Thomas Hendrick, aged 37, self-employed plumber, took a stray cat to Darnley Road police station yesterday,"' read Tommy Marsden, to the surprise of the assembled Conservatives and social-climbing Liberals and socialists, '"little did he suspect that it belonged to his sister.

'"The amazing 5,000 yard journey of Tiddles, aged 5, from the Bagcliffe Road home of his owner, Mrs Doris Treadwell, to the Hendricks' abode in Dursley Rise has puzzled both parties.

'"'I can't think how he came to find my brother,' Doris, aged 36, told our reporter. 'I've only had him ten days and Tom hasn't even seen him as he's been off with his chest. Tiddles can't even have met Tom,' she added,"' read Tommy.

'"And Thomas Hendrick? 'I didn't even know our Doris had a cat,' he said, 'but it certainly must be an animal with a family sense!'

'"A police spokesman commented, 'This is a most unusual case, unique in my experience.'

'"Joked Mr Hendrick: 'I hope Tiddles doesn't try to visit our brother. He lives in Canada!'"'

Henry smiled modestly at the stunned listeners in the bar of the Conservative Club.

'Bloody hell,' said Tommy Marsden. 'Call that a scoop?'

'It *is* a scoop,' said Henry indignantly. 'A scoop is a story that no other paper has printed. No other paper has printed that story.'

'I'm not surprised,' said Tommy Marsden.

Next morning, in the bustling news-room, nobody praised Henry's story, but this wasn't surprising, in that hard world, where men were men and Helen Cornish wasn't and had deeply disturbing bulges in her pale sage-green sweater to prove it. Terry Skipton asked Henry to do a 'Voice of Thurmarsh' that afternoon, and Henry's heart sank.

No scoops attended his rounds of the hospitals and police

stations. The weather was milder, and he felt clammy with sweat. His self-assurance, that occasional visitor who never took his coat off, had hurried away, and he couldn't face them all, in the canteen or the Lord Nelson, witnessing how absurdly nervous he was about his 'Voice of Thurmarsh'. So he lunched alone in the Rundle Café, in Rundle Prospect, next to the Polish barber. It was drizzling, and the cramped little café smelt of damp clothes. The *Light Programme* blared out constantly, and Henry ate his meat pie, chips and beans to the strains of the Eric Delaney Band. His rice pudding with jam was accompanied by *Listen with Mother*. Bank clerks and gas board salesmen pretended not to be listening to the tale of Tommy the Tortoise. Henry wished he were Henry the Hedgehog, and could curl up in a ball that afternoon, after making love, very carefully, to Helen the Hedgehog. In two days and five hours he would be making love, not carefully but with great abandon, doing the only thing in the world he was good at, with Lorna Arrow, his childhood sweetheart. Stop thinking about it, Henry. You'll go blind.

He felt absurdly self-conscious, standing ankle-deep in slush outside W. H. Smith's, his hair lank with sweat and the faint, raw drizzle. He hoped none of his colleagues would pass by. He wished Alec Walsh, the hard-bitten, overweight photographer, wasn't standing there, trying not to look too obviously scornful.

He approached an extremely burly man, whose extreme burliness he hadn't noticed until he'd approached him.

'Excuse me,' he said. 'I'm from the *Argus*.'

'Oh aye?' said the extremely burly man.

'Yes, and . . . er . . .' Why did he think that there were ghosts from his past, watching him from the surrounding windows? Uncle Teddy, Auntie Doris, the slimy Geoffrey Porringer, Diana Hargreaves, Tosser Pilkington-Brick and his effete, ascetic, aesthetic, homosexual friend Lampo Davey? The scornfully superior Belinda Boyce-Uppingham from the big house at Rowth Bridge? All peering at him from the windows of Cockayne's and Timothy Whites and the Thurmarsh and Rawlaston Co-operative Society? 'We . . . er . . . we do a weekly feature which we call "Voice of Thurmarsh".'

'Oh aye?' said the extremely burly man.

'Yes. We ask the public a question about a topical issue and we print their answers along with photos of them.'

'Oh aye?' said the extremely burly man.

'So I wondered if I could ask you the question we're asking people today,' said Henry.

'Oh. Aye,' said the extremely burly man.

'Er . . . do you think Britain is being too lenient towards Archbishop Makarios?' said Henry.

The extremely burly man thought long and hard.

'I don't know,' he said. 'I'm a stranger here.'

A magnificent ruse had freed Henry from the need to go home for his tea. He'd told Cousin Hilda that he was going to the Essoldo, with his new chums, to see Dean Martin and Jerry Lewis in *My Friend Irma Goes West*, and that, prior to the entertainment, they would take solid refreshment at the Shanghai Chinese Restaurant and Coffee Bar.

'Chinese meals!' Cousin Hilda had snorted. 'I don't know.'

Henry wasn't going to see *My Friend Irma Goes West*. He wasn't even going to see Cornel Wilde and Yvonne De Carlo in *Passion*. He was going to drink glasses of bitter with his new chums, and then meet his contact from the world of industry.

They stood by the bar that evening, in the back room of the Lord Nelson, because nobody was staying long. Colin Edgeley had to get home before the kids went to bed. Henry was astounded to discover that he had children. Ginny Fenwick had to review a performance of *Candida* by the Rawlaston Players in the Drill Hall, Splutt Road, Rawlaston. Ben Watkinson was off to Sheffield to see the Wednesday play Charlton. There was no sign of Helen Cornish.

'So how are you enjoying newspaper work?' said Ginny. She was standing extremely close to him. Again there seemed, to his surprise, to be evidence that he was attractive to women.

'Very much,' he said feebly. Her lips were slightly too thick. Nothing wrong with that. Sensual?

'I *love* it,' she said, with an intensity that stirred his nether regions. This was, he decided, an extremely attractive person. Pity about the nose. 'I long to get to Fleet Street,' she said. Large, uneven teeth, slightly yellow, but not repulsively so. 'In about five years, when I'm ready.'

'Really?' he said feebly. 'What? As a fashion correspondent?'

Ginny Fenwick snorted. What a man I am, thought Henry, for making women snort.

'That's stereotyped thinking,' she said. 'No. I want to be a war correspondent.'

'A war correspondent!' he said, feebly. My god, I'm being feeble tonight, he thought. Yes, there was something Amazonian about her. He could imagine her, with her large thighs and broad buttocks, and her well-formed bust, striding round the battlefield, taking shorthand notes as the shells whizzed round her head. He felt a spasm of fierce desire. He had a brief glimpse of her, naked except for army boots and a helmet, holding out her hospitable arms to him. Stop it! Think of Friday night. No. Don't think of Friday night. Talk about work, quickly, before you have an accident. 'So you must feel pretty fed up about covering something like the Rawlaston Players,' he said.

'No! *Not at all.* Every job is important.'

'Well, yes, I . . . er . . . I . . . er . . . yes.' Every time he thought he had scaled the Himalayas of feebleness, he found new ranges of conversational ineptitude above them.

'Think of *them*,' said Ginny. 'Think of *her*.'

'Them?' he said feebly. 'Her?'

'The Rawlaston Players. The girl playing Candida. What is she? A nurse? A teacher? Probably a teacher. They usually are. It's a highlight in her life, Henry. She deserves my full attention. Have another drink.'

'Thanks.'

She was magnificent! She must be fully twenty-five, but he liked older women. And he'd never had a big woman. Mind you, he'd never had a small woman either. Let's face it, he'd only ever had one woman. Tall and slim. 'Cheers, Ginny. That was quick.'

'Cheers, Henry.' Massive eye contact. Blue as a summer's day, shining eyes of a warm woman. 'Come with me. To *Candida*.'

'Yes, I . . . er . . . I very well might, Ginny.'

Colin and Ben interrupted their growing intimacy. Colin

gave Henry a meaningful look which meant 'Get in there, kid.'
Ben said, 'Name the four football league sides that have x in
their names.' Henry glanced at Ginny, uncertain whether she'd
think better of him for knowing or for not knowing. In the
end, he couldn't resist the challenge. 'Wrexham,' he said.
'Halifax. Exeter.' He made a mental tour of the country. 'Crewe
Alexandra.'

'Well done!' said Ben, and Henry felt rather absurd, smiling his
pride. Colin seemed proud of him too. Ginny looked as if she were
trying to hide her amusement.

Neil Mallet entered with Denzil Ackerman, arts and show
business editor. Neil's carroty hair looked windswept, but Denzil
was wearily immaculate. He was in his fifties, had private money, a
mews cottage in Chelsea, a pink bow-tie, a limp, a hand-carved
Scottish walking-stick and a high-pitched voice. He only spent
three days a week in Thurmarsh as he saw it as part of his job 'to
cultivate my intellectual garden and save you from your depressing
provincialism, my quaint darlings.' The middle pages were his
domain. Some readers started at the front and others started at the
back. It wasn't clear how many reached the middle pages, and it
didn't seem to matter very much, in those halcyon days of the
provincial press.

'Ah! A fresh face!' said Denzil Ackerman. He examined Henry
as if he were a doubtful antique. 'Really very fresh. One of those
strange faces that ought to seem repellent but which one finds
oddly attractive because one doesn't find them repellent. Don't
you think so, Neil?'

Neil Mallet, whose sexual proclivities were a closed book to his
colleagues, some of whom believed that he was only a dark horse
because he had never entered a race, blushed slightly at being
included in this assumption of homosexuality. Henry throbbed
with fury. Ginny, with magnificent understanding, touched
him sympathetically and said, 'Denzil's outrageous,' as if this
excused everything. Henry felt that it excused nothing. He was
appalled at the depth of his immediate loathing for Denzil
Ackerman.

'I hear you're one of the eight people in this philistine dump
who've seen *Waiting for Godot*, Henry,' said Denzil.

34

Henry decided that he must fight his loathing and his feeble-ness. 'Yes,' he said. 'And I loved it, which for some stupid reason yesterday I wasn't prepared to admit.'

Denzil gave Henry a warm smile, and began to talk pleasantly and unaffectedly about films and plays. Henry fought his loath-ing so successfully that he actually began liking the man. Ben Watkinson bought a round. 'Pink gin, dear boy, since they haven't *heard* of wine in this *hole*,' said Denzil, and the landlord, Mr Bernard Hoveringham, who had also not heard of lasagne or chilli con carne, smiled.

Denzil talked about art, and Henry pretended to more knowl-edge than he had. Just as Denzil said, 'And who are your favourite artists? Tell uncle,' Ben handed Henry his drink and said, 'Name all the English and Scottish teams that have Athletic in their name.' Henry didn't want to offend his friend of three whole days, who seemed to regard his talking to Denzil as a defection, and he didn't want to offend his new friend of ten minutes, whom he had so recently loathed. Nor did he want to seem an artistic prig to Ben or a sporting lout to Denzil.

It isn't easy to keep two conversational balls in the air at the same time.

'Charlton,' said Henry.

'I don't know him,' said Denzil.

'Charlton Athletic,' said Henry.

Denzil looked bewildered.

'Constable,' said Henry.

'Don't you mean Dunstable?' said Ben, 'and I think they're Dunstable Town anyway.'

'Alloa,' said Henry.

'You're pulling some obscure ones out of the hat,' said Denzil. 'Basque, is he? He sounds Basque.'

'Klimt,' said Henry.

'Not including foreign teams,' said Ben.

'Gainsborough,' said Henry.

'I think they're Town as well and I didn't include non-league,' said Ben.

'Gainsborough, the painter,' said Henry.

'You like Gainsborough?' said Denzil, shocked.

35

'Not much, no, but I couldn't think of anybody else,' admitted Henry.

And then there came a sharp pain in the two balls that he wasn't keeping in the air as Helen Cornish swept into the room, magenta skirt swirling, pert lips pouting. Podgy Sex Bomb Henry gasped with desire, and Ginny knew, and Henry blushed and said desperately, 'Rembrandt. Bournemouth and Boscombe. Botticelli. Hamilton. No, they're Academicals.'

It was his round. Forces which he couldn't control engineered brief physical contact, as he asked Helen what she'd have. Ginny refused a drink. 'I must go,' she said. She didn't repeat her suggestion that he accompany her. 'Nice girl,' said Denzil. 'Pity she's so unattractive.' This was too much for Henry. 'I don't think she's unattractive,' he said, and Helen raised a delicious eyebrow, and Henry blushed again, and Denzil said, 'No, dear, but I find all women unattractive. Present company excepted. Anyway, don't worry your quaint little head over Ginny, she'll make somebody a very good war correspondent.' There was laughter. Henry glared and felt the loathing again. Then he realized that it was all right, because everyone knew that Denzil was outrageous, so he smiled feebly. Ben went off to his football. Denzil sought companions for dinner. Neil said he had to hoover and dust the flat. 'How about the second D. H. Lawrence?' said Denzil. 'Strange ambition. I wouldn't want to be the *first* D. H. Lawrence.' Colin refused. He didn't enjoy eating. Denzil left in a slight huff.

When only Henry and Helen and Colin remained, Colin said, 'Where's Ted?'

'He's covering the man who had his head cut off in a sawmill,' said Helen.

Henry had a vision of a man in a sawmill, blood gushing, with his head lying at his side, perhaps registering a faint expression of surprise. He felt dizzy and faint. 'Are you all right, kid?' said a tiny voice from a vast distance. 'Fine,' he said, as he fainted.

He came round to see Helen's pert lips and concerned eyes staring at him, and behind her Colin. They laid him on a bench seat, and he began to revive. The sweat poured off him. Helen wiped his forehead with a scented handkerchief, and kissed his cheek, and Henry said he thought he had the flu coming. He didn't want to lie, but couldn't admit that he was too soft for this hard world. Helen went to buy him a brandy. Colin said, 'Are you sure you're all right, kid?' and Henry said, 'I'm OK,' rather angrily. Colin said, 'I ought to get home, but I can't leave you on your own.' Henry said, 'I won't be on my own. I'll be with Helen.' Colin said, 'Exactly!' Henry didn't want to leave Colin alone with Helen, but he had to, because a) he'd said he thought he had the flu coming and b) he had to meet his contact from the world of industry.

Martin Hammond was working as an overhead crane fitter at the Splutt Vale Iron and Steel Company. He lived with his family in a pebble-dashed semi in Everest Crescent. He was Henry's best friend, and Henry was beginning to wonder if he liked him.

They sat in the back room of the Pigeon and Two Cushions, a small, quiet, almost sedate pub in Church Lane, with gleaming oblong tables studded with beer mats and ashtrays. On the panelled walls were cheerful sepia pictures of Thurmarsh disasters – the great flood, the great gale, the great snowfall, the great train crash. There were bells at frequent intervals, for waiter service. The waiter had a cold.

How on earth had slow, owlish, bespectacled Martin become a sergeant? They must have been short of candidates for promotion in the Royal Army Ordnance Corps.

'I saw Tommy Marsden yesterday,' said Henry. 'He's going to be my contact from the world of sport.'

'Good old Tommy. What a player,' said Martin, who had only once seen Tommy play.

At a table by the brick fireplace a group of pasty-faced men in slightly shiny suits were discussing breasts and bums. There was something familiar about one of them.

'Will you be my contact from the world of industry?' said Henry.

'You what?' said Martin.

'Will you phone me up with stories?'

'What stories?'

'I don't know! Anything. Impending strikes. Unusual industrial accidents. Lost cockatoos. Anything.' Had Martin always looked so pompous?

'I'm not keen on supporting your rag,' said Martin. 'Its editorial policy is slightly to the right of Genghis Khan. That's what my dad reckons, anyroad.'

Henry realized that he hadn't given much thought to the *Argus*'s editorial policy.

Martin pressed the bell, and ordered two more beers.

'Please, Martin,' said Henry. 'I mean . . . we're friends.'

The waiter brought their drinks.

'Have one yourself,' said Martin grandly.

'Oh, thank you very much, sir,' said the waiter. 'I'll have sixpennorth with you.' He hesitated, feeling that Martin's largesse deserved some social response. 'I've never known a cold like it,' he confided. 'Three weeks I've had it. Can't seem to shift it.'

They sipped their beers slowly. It was very important to Henry to remain sober.

'I thought you were a socialist,' said Martin.

'I am,' said Henry. 'I'm working from within to turn the paper leftwards.'

'With stories about cats?'

'Give me time. I've got to establish me credibility. Give me socialist stories, Martin.'

'Such as?'

'I don't know. Workers with hearts of gold. Stupid bosses. I don't know.'

'They won't print them.'

'I'll resign if they don't.'

'All right, then.'

Henry bought two more pints, to celebrate the recruitment of his contact from the world of industry. The men with shiny suits were talking about arses now. The one who seemed familiar winked. Henry remembered, and went over to him.

'It's Tony Preece, isn't it? he said. 'I'm Henry Pratt. From Cousin Hilda's.'

'By heck,' said Tony Preece, who still had a bad complexion.

'I'm working on the *Argus*,' said Henry. 'Could I have a word with you some time on a business matter?'

They arranged to meet on the following evening. Henry re-joined Martin. 'Sorry about that,' he said. 'A little business matter.' There was an uneasy pause. There was a gulf between them, a hole where his past should have been. 'Got a girl-friend, have you?' he asked.

'No,' said Martin. 'What with work and night school and union meetings and party meetings, I haven't got much time for all that.'

Poor miserable Martin, thought Henry. Poor miserable lucky enviable Martin.

Almost as soon as he'd boarded the strangely swaying tram, Henry realized that he desperately needed food. So he got off at the first stop.

'Boring,' he told the conductor. 'Most boring tram I've ever been on.'

Those were the days before the proliferation of Indian restaurants. Even Chinese restaurants were a rarity in some parts. In Thurmarsh, in January 1956, after ten o'clock at night, the only place where you could get a sit-down meal was the Shanghai Chinese Restaurant and Coffee Bar, in Market Street.

Inside the Shanghai, the lights were dim, the tables were crowded, the cups were of glass, the coffee was frothy, rubber plants abounded, and the most beautiful woman in the world called out, 'Henry!'

'Hello, Helen.' As in a dream, he drifted to his beloved's side. She was sitting beside a brown-haired man with rugged features set in a slightly puffy face.

She introduced them. 'Greetings,' said Gordon Carstairs, who was thirty-six. He turned away from Henry, as from a troublesome fly. 'You aren't really going to marry Ted, are you, Helen?' he said.

'Why not?'

'Why not? Why not?? Helen!!' Gordon Carstairs stopped, as if he had explained everything.

Henry ordered beef curry and coffee. The Shanghai had no licence.

'Make that tea. The special tea,' said Gordon Carstairs firmly.

'Why?' said Henry, bristling.

'Because,' said Gordon Carstairs. 'Because, laddie. That's why.' He had a large, piercing nose, and there were deep bags beneath his bloodshot eyes. When we are drunk, the drunk don't strike us as drunk. Henry had no idea that Gordon Carstairs was as drunk as he was.

He could feel a leg stroking him. He didn't think it was Gordon Carstairs's.

'I thought you had flu coming on,' said Helen.

'I think it must have been one-day flu,' said Henry.

'More like one-hour flu,' said Helen. 'Gordon's been covering a big story in Sheffield.'

'Oh, you're on the paper,' said Henry. 'What big story?'

Gordon Carstairs tapped the side of his nose and said, 'Discretion.' The Chinese waiter brought beef curry for Gordon, sweet and sour pork for Helen, and a pot of Chinese tea for Henry.

'Whisky,' whispered Gordon, and winked. Henry's heart sank. More drink, and more winking. He needed these things like an enema.

He rubbed Helen's leg and got a sharp kick. Had he rubbed Gordon's leg by mistake?

'How did you get the whisky?' he whispered.

'Precisely!' said Gordon Carstairs, and Henry assumed that it was his fault, because he was drunk, that Gordon was making no sense.

Suddenly Gordon stood up and said, 'My bill, please.'

A waiter hurried over. 'You no like, sir?' he said.

'The Great Wall!' said Gordon Carstairs. He drained his last cup of seventy per cent proof Chinese tea, and stalked out.

'What was all that about?' said Henry.

'He's too proud to fight you for me.'

Henry gawped. His beef curry arrived. In the dim light it looked vaguely green. He took an eager mouthful. The meat was stringy. The sauce was slightly sweet, faintly hot, thickly glutinous. It would be many years before he discovered the delights of real Chinese food.

'Fight me for you?'

'He knows he'd lose,' said Helen Cornish.

Henry forgot his tea was whisky and took a big gulp which almost choked him. 'You what?' he said.

'Come back with me,' said Helen.

'You're engaged.'

'I'm not married yet. Frightened?'

Yes. No. Well . . . a little, perhaps, of Ted, who was already an enemy. A little of Helen, perhaps, who was too beautiful. A little of himself, perhaps, who was too drunk. A little, perhaps, of what it would do to his one true love. Oh god! He'd forgotten! He had less than forty-eight hours to wait. What was he doing even thinking of going back with Helen? A wave of relief, mixed with just a little regret, broke over him.

'Of course I'm not frightened,' he said, 'but I can't go back with you.' Suddenly his speech became slurred. 'I'm schpoken for,' he said, and burped.

'Good night,' said Helen Cornish coldly.

He was on his own at a table cluttered with congealing, half-eaten green and orange semi-Chinese meals, yet he didn't feel lonely. He was on the verge of a sexy weekend, and he'd just turned down a beautiful woman. What strength. What coolth. No, there was no such word as coolth. He'd made new friends, tough, enigmatic journalists, limping queers from Chelsea. He was drinking whisky disguised as tea. He was sophisticated.

'Finished, sir?' said the waiter, indicating Helen's plate.

'Finished.'

He heard a familiar laugh, and there were two men walking past, solid, almost respectable.

'Uncle Teddy!'

Uncle Teddy turned pale and gawped.

'It's me. Henry.' Uncle Teddy hadn't seen him since he was fifteen.

'Henry! It's Henry! Good God!'

'Yes.'

'Henry, this is a business colleague, Derek Parsonage.'

Henry tried to stand, tried to seem sober.

'Please. Don't stand,' said Derek Parsonage. He was a big man, and his nose was festooned with blackheads, which puzzled Henry slightly.

'On your own?' said Uncle Teddy.

'No,' said Henry. 'I'm with Gordon Carstairs and Helen Cornish, but they've gone.'

'The selfishness of lovers,' said Derek Parsonage. Stupid name. Stupid man. You've got it all wrong. I'm glad your nose is covered in blackheads, which puzzles me slightly.

'Join me,' said Henry. 'Please. You must. After all, you're my . . .' He'd been going to say 'father'. Well, Uncle Teddy had virtually been his father, for a time. It was difficult to see Uncle Teddy clearly, in the half-light grudgingly conceded by the Chinese lanterns, through eyes blurred by drink, but he didn't look quite as big as Henry had remembered. Was this due to the scale of childhood vision, the distortion of memory, or the effects of age and imprisonment? Of course! Imprisonment!

They joined him.

'Henry is my . . .' explained Uncle Teddy to Derek Parsonage.

Henry wished Uncle Teddy hadn't found it so impossible to define their relationship.

'Uncle Teddy took me in as his son,' he said. 'His house, Cap Ferrat, became my home. Not his fault he went to . . .'

'Henry!' said Uncle Teddy.

'. . . Rangoon,' said Henry.

'Ah!' said Uncle Teddy. When Uncle Teddy had gone to prison Auntie Doris had pretended that she and Uncle Teddy had gone to Rangoon. She ran a hotel now, with her lover, the slimy Geoffrey Porringer, who had blackheads. Of course! That was why Derek Parsonage's blackheads had puzzled him. They were a historical echo.

'Rangoon?' said Derek Parsonage.

'Have some tea,' said Henry. 'It's whisky.'

'I lived in Rangoon for a while with . . . er . . . before we split up,' said Uncle Teddy.

'I never knew that,' said Derek Parsonage.

'Not a lot of people do,' said Henry.

'Are you drunk?' said Uncle Teddy.

'Yes,' said Henry. 'This tea's whisky, you see.'

Uncle Teddy and Derek Parsonage ordered chicken chop suey and another pot of Chinese tea.

Henry wished he'd gone to see Uncle Teddy in prison. It was odd. Martin Hammond was his best friend and he didn't like him. Uncle Teddy was a crook and a liar and had sent him to boarding schools to get him out of the way, and now Henry found that he loved him almost as a father and craved his respect.

'Helen asked me to go to bed with her,' he said, 'but I refused. I'm meeting my lover at the weekend, you see.'

'What a life you lead,' said Uncle Teddy. Derek Parsonage gave a little grin of disbelief, and Uncle Teddy looked worried, as if he thought Henry's fantasizing was the result of the bad upbringing to whose shortcomings Uncle Teddy had contributed more than his share.

'It's true,' said Henry indignantly.

'Of course it is,' said Uncle Teddy.

Henry poured himself some more whisky. The pot was inexhaustible. Uncle Teddy sniffed it. 'It *is* whisky,' he said.

'Course it is,' said Henry. 'I'm not a liar.' He felt that Uncle Teddy looked at him with fresh eyes, perhaps even with respect. He felt another wave of guilt. He could have been brave enough to visit Uncle Teddy *once*. They'd said that Uncle Teddy would feel ashamed of being seen by him, but that was nonsense, which he'd leapt at with relief. 'Uncle Teddy?' he said, desperately trying to sound sober, 'I really am very sorry I never visited you.'

'What?' said Uncle Teddy anxiously.

'In Rangoon.'

'My dear boy, how could you?'

'I know. I know. But still . . . you know . . . I wish I had.'

Uncle Teddy's eyes held Henry's for a moment. Henry felt that there was almost a feeling of father and son between them. Then the effort of fighting the drink began to tell. His head swam and he hiccuped.

'I'm working on the *Argus*,' he said. 'I'm a journalist. I did my national service. I was a soldier in that.' He wanted to say how sorry he was that Auntie Doris had gone off to live with Geoffrey Porringer, but it wasn't a subject he could safely broach, especially while hiccuping. He wasn't sure if he should mention Auntie Doris and he felt that he definitely shouldn't mention Geoffrey Porringer. It had all gone so dark. The lighting was so drunk, and he was so dim. Blast those hiccups. Dignity. Derek Parsonage found the hiccups amusing. God, he hated Uncle Teddy's choice of friends.

43

'Fancy you two running into each other here,' said Derek Parsonage.

'Not really,' said Henry. 'Where else is there at this time of night to run into anybody at anywhere anyway? There isn't.'

'Exactly,' said Uncle Teddy.

'Precisely,' said Derek Parsonage.

'What are you talking about?' said Henry.

'Night life,' said Uncle Teddy. 'There isn't any.'

'In twenty years' time,' said Derek Parsonage, 'this town will be awash with clubs.'

'We're getting in first,' said Uncle Teddy.

'We're bringing sophistication to this dump,' said Derek Parsonage.

'Lightening the grey skies with a touch of mediterranean colour,' said Uncle Teddy.

'Bringing continental elegance to the Rundle Valley,' said Derek Parsonage.

'The Cap Ferrat opens next month,' said Uncle Teddy.

Their food arrived. So did their tea which, to their disappointment, was tea.

'This tea's tea,' said Derek Parsonage.

'You need contacts,' said Henry. 'I have contacts.' He tried to pat the side of his nose knowingly, but missed and poked his finger into his eye. 'Ouch!' he cried, and hiccuped. 'I have contacts with boot-lickers. No, arse-leggers. No.' He poured himself some more whisky.

'You've had enough,' said Uncle Teddy, and he grabbed Henry's cup. Henry grabbed it back.

'You can't start playing my father just when it suits you,' he said. 'And as for your friend, with his bloody blackheads. You know what he is, don't you? A Geoffrey Porringer substitute.'

He was on the verge of being told, in a few blindingly simple words, all the secrets of life, its purpose and its conduct. His head ached from the effort of listening and concentrating, as at last the words came.

Then he woke up. His head still ached, but the words, the secrets, were tantalizingly out of reach, unremembered, dissolved.

44

And he was a young man with a bad hangover, lying in a lumpy bed converted from a lumpy sofa.

Last night! Oh no! He sat up abruptly and wished he hadn't. But he hadn't run into Cousin Hilda. She hadn't seen how drunk he was. There was hope.

Then he heard her voice. Flat. Too upset for anger. 'He's been sick on the stairs.'

He crawled out of bed, staggered across the room, opened the window, breathed in the icy morning air and heard her say, 'He's been sick on the lawn!'

He vaguely remembered going round the back, not going inside, because he'd felt ill.

She turned, and he moved away from the window.

'Oh no!' This time there *was* anger. Icy anger. 'He's been sick on the coal!'

She was hunched with hurt as she banged his breakfast down. Liam's smile froze like condensed breath. Barry Frost stopped humming. A cardboard egg refused to go past the brick in Henry's throat. Only Norman Pettifer seemed oblivious.

'It's going to be a Camembert day today,' he said. 'I just know it.'

As the tram clanked along Doncaster Road towards the Alderman Chandler Memorial Park that evening, Henry held his copy of the *Argus* with pride. Other men were merely reading it. He'd helped to produce it.

He read his story again.

Arthur Bollard, aged 27, of Snowdon Grove, Thurmarsh, was struck in the throat by a pair of tongs at work today, and was detained at Thurmarsh Royal Infirmary.

When he fell from a ladder at Johnson and Johnson Rolling Mills, 34 year-old Benjamin Whateley, of Smith Street, Rawlaston, received injuries to legs, back and hand. He was treated at Thurmarsh Royal Infirmary.

Also treated there was Samuel Willis, aged 15, of Derwentwater Crescent, Splutt, who trapped three fingers in a haulage chain at Drobwell Main Colliery.

Not spectacular, perhaps, but even Martin would have to agree that it was good socialist stuff. To anyone with an ability to read between the lines it must be significant that no bosses were injured that day when struck by falling agendas, choking on fillet steaks or burning fingers on cups of scalding coffee. That was the way to turn the paper leftwards – by stealth.

In Cousin Hilda's basement room the blue stove with the cracked panes roared and crackled. 'Bring me some men, some stout-hearted men,' commanded Barry Frost under his breath. Norman Pettifer confirmed that it had indeed been a Camembert day. Cousin Hilda remained silent, stiff with disappointment and accusation. The pork was stringy, the roast potatoes were like bullets, the cabbage was overcooked. Cousin Hilda gave Henry two halves of tinned pears, while everyone else had three. He hurried out before she could get him on his own, and was in the Pigeon and Two Cushions ten minutes before Tony Preece.

While he waited he read that morning's national papers. Would he ever be working for them?

The big story was the controversy over the government's sale of tanks and arms to Israel and Egypt. The government had pointed out that the tanks 'had been so old that they would have no military value'. They were 'obsolete, ineffective and unreliable for war'. The British government had tried – and would continue to try, as far as lay within its power – to prevent an arms race in the Middle East. By selling obsolete tanks to both sides, presumably. 'Our tanks don't work.' 'Nor do ours.' 'Oh let's give up.' But wouldn't they be angry about being sold useless weapons? thought Henry.

The sniffing waiter – 'It's gone to me sinuses now' – brought them two pints of Hammonds' best bitter.

'So, what's this business matter?' said Tony Preece.

'Well . . . are you still doing your act round the clubs?'

'Oh yes. I couldn't give that up. I'm addicted. You wouldn't recognize the act now, though. I've changed it completely.'

'Oh good,' said Henry. 'Sorry,' he added. 'Are you still . . . er . . . ?'

'Still with Stella, yes.'

'How is she?'

'Older,' said Tony Preece gallantly. 'So come on. Am I about to earn some extra money?'

'Well, I can't actually offer you any money, as such,' said Henry, 'but maybe I could give you some publicity, write a feature about your Jekyll and Hyde existence – by day, ordinary drab insurance man – at night, laughter-maker extraordinaire. If you'd . . . er . . . be my contact from the world of showbiz.'

He was rather hurt when Tony Preece laughed. Somehow he was getting the feeling that nothing very useful was going to come to him out of his contacts from the worlds of sport, industry and show business. In this he was wrong, but then he was to be wrong about so many things, during his career with the *Thurmarsh Evening Argus*.

3   A Sexy Weekend

Sexuality laid her sweet tongue on everything that Henry did next morning. The weather was suitably bright and crisp. He felt a surge of joy as he converted his bed into a sofa. He hummed the 'Ballad of Davy Crockett' while he shaved. As he packed with unsuppressed excitement, Eve Boswell was picking a chicken on his wireless. Podgy Sex Bomb Henry picked a chicken with her.

In eleven hours he'd be alone with Lorna, in the Midland Hotel. He must remember that he'd booked the room in the names of Mr and Mrs Wedderburn.

He had no hangover. He could enjoy his breakfast. The egg was rich and runny. He ate it slowly, relishing it. The fried bread was a stern test of teeth. They all ate that slowly. Barry Frost even stopped humming while he tackled it.

Henry tried, for Cousin Hilda's sake, not to look too delighted about going away, but his body thrilled with anticipation, and he caught her looking at him suspiciously.

Liam hurried off, then Norman. Not wishing to be left alone with Cousin Hilda, Henry hurried through his third piece of toast – two would have seemed too mean, four excessively generous, and Cousin Hilda treated him exactly like her 'businessmen', to prevent embarrassment. A great deal of Cousin Hilda's life was devoted to preventing embarrassment, which might have been why everything turned out to be so embarrassing.

Henry lost his race with Barry Frost, who finished his breakfast *con brio*.

Cousin Hilda closed the door behind Barry Frost, and faced her responsibility resolutely.

'Four days in journalism, and look at you. It can't go on,' she said.

No. It can't. Say, 'No. I agree. For both our sakes, dear Cousin Hilda, whom I love, I'd better move out.' But he couldn't. All he said was, 'I'm sorry.'

'I should think so too. When I think what Mrs Wedderburn says about you.'

He closed his eyes, as if he hoped that existence would go away, if he couldn't see it. What had possessed him to choose Mr and Mrs Wedderburn?

'She says you're such a lovely, polite young man. I must be so proud of you. Proud! What would she think if she knew that the polite young man whom she once lent her camp-bed out of the goodness of her heart had been sick on the coal?'

'I'm sorry about the coal.'

'It's not the coal. It's you. A drunk. Yes, Henry. A common drunk.'

'No, Cousin Hilda. Well, the first time I *was* drunk, yes. It was meeting all the journalists. It was the first time I've ever been drunk.' He didn't want to lie, but felt that he had to, for her sake. 'And the last. The second time it was food. Honestly.'

'I didn't think you'd ever lie to me, Henry.'

'I'm not lying,' he lied. For her sake.

'Do you think Mr Pettifer'll stay if there's always piles of sick on the stairs? Is that any way for the manager of the cheese counter at Cullen's to live?'

'No.' Just say, 'I'm sorry, Cousin Hilda. I'll find a flat.' But he couldn't. 'I'll never do it again, Cousin Hilda,' he said. 'I promise.'

'I know you mean to be a good lad,' said Cousin Hilda. 'I know it's difficult without your parents. I do my best.'

He gave her a quick kiss.

'Give him my best regards,' said Cousin Hilda, sniffing furiously.

'Him?' said Henry. 'Who?'

'Well, Paul, of course,' said Cousin Hilda. 'And you behave yourself with his family!'

At first, Henry thought it a great piece of luck when Terry Skipton said, 'I want you to interview a Mr Gunnar Fridriksen, from Iceland. I want you to find out his impressions of Thurmarsh. I've arranged for you to meet him in the Midland Hotel at three. If you've time, come back and do some book reviews.' Because

Henry knew that he wouldn't have time. He'd sit in the foyer, writing up his notes, until it was time to collect his beloved from the station. National service had taught him the art of making a little work go a long way. It was a lesson, forced upon them by the state, that a whole generation of the nation's manhood would diligently apply to their lives in industry and commerce.

At two minutes to three, he entered the hotel's huge foyer. What an unlikely venue it was for love. Vast armchairs sagged wearily. Huge, ugly chandeliers hung threateningly. Photographs from the halcyon days of steam trains abounded. The thick carpet, rich dark red like old port, seemed to grab his feet at each step. The male receptionist smiled with smarmy superiority.

'Can I help you, sir?'

'Yes. Could you let me know when Mr Fridriksen arrives?' His voice sounded small and self-conscious.

'He's already here, sir. Mr Fridriksen?'

A tall, thin man, so fair as to be almost albino, disentangled himself from an armchair and approached, smiling.

'I have Mr Pratt for you, Mr Fridriksen,' said the smarmy monstrosity. Oh lord, thought Henry, I hope this man isn't still on duty when I book in as Mr Wedderburn.

They sat in a quiet corner, beneath a photograph of 46231 *Duchess of Argyll* steaming through Crewe station past knots of train-spotting schoolboys in baggy, knee-length trousers. Henry's armchair sagged more than Mr Fridriksen's, making command of the interview difficult. He ordered tea with insufficient aplomb.

'I want to ask you your impressions of life here and in Iceland, and how it's different,' said Henry.

'Good. Fire away. I am, as you say, all ears,' said Mr Fridriksen.

Henry thought about Lorna, sticking her tongue in his ear in four hours' time. No! Concentrate!

'You speak very good English, Mr Fridriksen,' he said.

'I fear not,' said Mr Fridriksen. 'I have only the bare rudiments.'

In four hours' time I'll be kissing Lorna's bare rudiments. No! 'Er . . . what's impressed you most about life in Thurmarsh, Mr Fridriksen?' Oh, Lorna. Lorna. I want to taste your Lorna-osity. I want to drink from the fountain of your Arrowness. 'Er . . . sorry, I . . . er . . . I didn't catch all of that, I . . . er . . . I don't do

50

shorthand yet. Could you . . . er . . . could you start again, please?'

Mr Gunnar Fridriksen looked at Henry in some surprise, but with infinite politeness. Their tea arrived, and somehow Henry forced himself to concentrate on the interview.

She seemed smaller, here in Thurmarsh, thin rather than slim, as if she were shrinking from the bustle of town life. Her smile was broad, but so nervous that it looked forlorn. They kissed. He was so excited that, the moment the kiss had ended, he had no memory of how it had felt.

They approached the crumbling, turreted bulk of the great stone-fronted railway hotel and, oh god, the smarmy monstrosity was still on duty.

'I've got a double room booked,' he croaked. 'Mr and Mrs Wedderburn.'

The smarmy monstrosity raised an eyebrow a quarter of a millimetre, and hunted through the list of bookings.

Henry glanced at Lorna. She was blushing. She'd never looked like a country bumpkin before.

'Ah yes,' smarmed the monstrosity. 'Room 412, Mr Wedderburn.' He invested the name with just the faintest hint of irony. 'If you'd just sign the register, Mr Wedderburn.'

Henry signed with shaking hand.

'Mrs Wedderburn?'

Lorna bowed her head as she signed.

'Will you be taking dinner, Mr Wedderburn?'

'Yes,' said Henry defiantly, as if it had been insinuated that he couldn't afford it.

'Would you like an early morning call, Mr Wedderburn?' said the genius of understated insinuation.

'Yes, please.' He glanced at Lorna. 'Er . . . eight-thirty.'

'Very good, sir. A morning paper, Mr Wedderburn?'

'Yes, please. *The Times*.'

'Very good, sir. Mrs Wedderburn?'

'The *Mirror*, please.'

'*The Times* and the *Mirror*.' Just the faintest suggestion that this might be the first time in the history of the hotel that this particular combination had been ordered. Smarmingtons clicked his fingers with astonishing volume. A page boy, dressed like a cross between a Morris Dancer and a colonel in the New Zealand army, appeared from nowhere. 'Take Mr and Mrs Wedderburn's "things" to room 412, Tremlett.'

'I'll carry them myself,' said Henry hurriedly, anxious to avoid the embarrassment and expense of tipping.

'As you wish, Mr Wedderburn.'

They walked towards the gilt-edged lifts, past the very chairs where Henry 'I was the first British journalist to witness the searing horror that is Dien Bien Phu' Pratt had interviewed Mr Fridriksen several centuries ago.

And there, walking towards them, was Colin Edgeley.

'Hey up, our kid,' he said. 'So you're the famous Lorna. Welcome to Thurmarsh, kid.' He gave Lorna a kiss. 'Smashing,' he said. 'You're a belter. We're all in the bar.'

'What?' Oh god, why did I tell him?

'We thought we'd give you a surprise. It's made a change to get out of the Lord Nelson.' He kissed Lorna again. 'Smashing.' And he padded off across the carpet which, unlike the port it resembled, had not improved with age.

'Oh God,' said Henry.

'What?'

'I don't want to go in there and drink with them.'

'Are you ashamed of me?'

'Course I'm not! Lorna! I don't want to go in there because a) I've been awash with drink all week and b) . . .' He lowered his voice. What he was going to say didn't sound like the sort of thing Mr Wedderburn would say to Mrs Wedderburn. '. . . I want to make love to you in room 412. I want to kiss you all over.'

'We don't have to stay long.'

'True.'

'I *am* a bit thirsty. I'm a bit nervous too about . . . you know . . . here. A drink might help.'

He let out a little sigh of tension. She pounced on it.

'You *are* ashamed of me.'

'No!'

'Going out with a country girl who works as a waitress. You think I'm not good enough for you.'

'Lorna! I've experienced enough snobbery to know how much I loathe it. And anyway, they don't need to know you're a waitress.'

Lorna snorted. Oh not another woman snorting. She didn't understand. It wasn't that he lacked confidence in her. He lacked confidence that his new friends had the eyes to see the loveliness and warmth beneath her undeniably rustic manners.

They entered the bar. It had a plum carpet, faded velvet curtains, brown leather upholstery with gold studs, and two more chandeliers. There they all were, sitting at a round table in a large alcove. Ted and Helen and Colin. Ben. Gordon. Neil. The outrageous Denzil. Only Ginny was missing. They looked like a selection board interviewing Lorna for the position of Henry's girl-friend. He tried to avoid the gravitational pull of Helen Cornish's sparkling eyes. In vain. She gave him one of the cool, challenging looks which had been his lot ever since he'd spurned her in the Shanghai. He was shattered by his desire for her, and hurriedly moved his eyes upward, to a large photograph of a Patriot class engine pulling a mixed freight out of Carlisle Upperby Yard in light snow. As a diversion, it was a failure. Men who are interested in women are rarely fanatical about trains. He answered Ted as in a dream. 'Glass of bitter, please.' Lorna ordered sweet cider! I hate myself, thought Henry. Lorna Arrow, you were a dream. A dream that sustained an unhappy soldier through two years in the Royal Corps of Signals. A pin-up that outshone Petula Clark and Patricia Roc inside a young man's locker, and touched the reality of his life barely more than they did. It isn't fair to turn a person into a dream.

'Nice to meet you, Lorna,' said Neil Mallet, who that morning had echoed the views of Crossbencher in last Sunday's *Express* – that the future for Anthony Eden would be even sunnier than the past. The doubters and moaners would be routed.

'So you're a country girl. Well done,' said Denzil. Henry thought this the most meaningless remark he'd ever heard. 'Passion among the cowpats. I love it.' Henry doubted if Denzil had ever seen a cowpat.

'Where are you from, Lorna?' said Ben Watkinson.

'Rowth Bridge. It's in Upper Mitherdale, near Troutwick.'

'*Lovely* country,' said Helen.

Henry usually preferred the laconic understatement of country people to the hyperbole of city folk, but he'd have welcomed a stronger reply from Lorna than, 'It's not bad.' He hadn't realized how strong her Mitherdale accent was. Not that he was ashamed of it. It was lovely. He just wished it wasn't quite so strong.

'Troutwick are in the Wensleydale League, aren't they?' said Ben.

'I don't know,' said Lorna. 'I know they're in summat.'

'What do you do, Lorna?' said Neil Mallet.

'Yes, what is there to do in the country? I've often wondered,' said Denzil.

'I meant, what job does Lorna do?' said Neil.

'I knew what you meant, old dear,' said Denzil. 'I was trying to save you from your conversational banality. Your question sounded like matron checking items on a laundry list.'

Neil flushed at the reference to laundry, then remembered that Denzil was outrageous, and smiled bravely. Henry was pleased at the diversion. It meant that Lorna wouldn't have to answer Neil's question.

'I'm a waitress at the White Hart in Troutwick. It's a hotel run by Henry's Auntie Doris,' said Lorna.

There was a brief silence.

'So how did you meet our young lady-killer, Lorna?' said Helen, in the extra friendly voice she used to women she didn't like. Ted smiled darkly at Henry. 'I always love hearing how people met.'

'We were at school together when Henry was evacuated to Rowth Bridge.'

'I wasn't evacuated,' said Henry. 'I was staying with relations.'

'That's a good one,' said Ted. 'Next time I'm in hospital, if they ask if I've evacuated my bowels, I'll say "No, they're staying with relations."'

'They don't ask if you've evacuated your bowels,' said Neil. 'They ask if you've moved them.'

'I'll say, "Yes. I used Pickfords. Never again. Terribly expensive,"' said Denzil.

Lorna looked from one to the other in some astonishment at

this conversation, and the slightly hysterical laughter that it produced.

'I gather Henry's a great one for reading,' said Denzil. 'Do you read together in bed, Lorna?'

Henry blushed.

'What books do you like, Lorna?' said Ted.

'I like *Woman, Woman's Own*,' said Lorna.

Henry knew her family referred to magazines as books. Why did it matter so desperately?

'Smashing,' said Colin.

Denzil bought a round. 'You have a sweet tooth, Lorna,' he said. 'I have actually,' she said. 'No wonder you like Henry, then. I think he's awfully sweet,' said Denzil, and Henry said, 'I thought you went to London at weekends,' because it had just occurred to him, but it came out so like an accusation that everybody laughed, and Henry pretended that he'd meant it to be funny, and Denzil said, 'So sorry to burden you with my presence, callow youth.' He lowered his voice. Homosexual acts of love were still illegal. 'My friend is arriving on the 8.15. He wishes to see The North.'

The headwaiter approached, in evening dress, his lips pursed. He carried two enormous menus.

'Mr Wedderburn?' he said.

There was a revealing pause before Henry said, 'Oh. That's me.'

'You're dining, sir?'

'Er . . . oh . . . yes . . . I . . . yes.'

'All of you?' The headwaiter's alarm was ill concealed.

'No,' said Henry. 'Just me and my . . . er . . . wife . . . unless any of you . . . er . . . I mean . . .' He looked round the gathering. Heads were hurriedly shaken. Ted said, 'Not me. Life's too precious.' 'Just me and my . . . wife,' said Henry.

The headwaiter handed Helen a menu.

'No. Not me,' she said, smiling triumphantly. 'The other young lady.'

'Ah!' said the headwaiter. 'Madam?' He handed Lorna a menu, and retired as hastily as decorum permitted.

'Mr and Mrs Wedderburn!' said Denzil. 'You have a delicious gift for ornamentation, Henry.'

'It's all in a foreign language,' said Lorna.

55

'French,' said Helen.

'What a snobbish country this is,' said Neil.

'You can talk,' said Ted.

'I beg your pardon?' said Neil.

'You drink in the back bar of the Lord Nelson. Your brother drinks in the front bar.'

'The snobbery isn't ours,' said Neil. 'It's all the other reporters and compositors who don't mix. I'm not a snob, Ted. I've never hidden my lower middle-class origins.'

'I must get home,' said Colin, looking at his watch. 'Same again, everybody?'

'I've just got time,' said Ben. 'Then I must go and give the wife one.'

'Pink gin. Removed,' said Denzil to the waiter. 'You what, sir?' said the waiter. 'The bitters, man. Removed, not left in.' 'Ah. Yes, sir. Only I'm new here,' said the waiter. 'So am I, I do assure you,' said Denzil.

Lorna's menu was unpriced. Henry's wasn't. Sometimes, when he visited Troutwick, Auntie Doris pressed money into his hand when Geoffrey Porringer wasn't looking. Quite a lot, sometimes. Twenty pounds even. She did it out of guilt, so he had to accept, for her sake. He had saved some of it, but he still couldn't afford this. Why had he said they'd be dining?

'What's "es-car-gotts"?' said Lorna.

'Snails,' said Neil.

'Ugh!' said Lorna, so unselfconsciously that everybody laughed.

'Quite right, kid,' said Colin. 'Thee and me's Yorkshire. We can't eat snails.'

'You two are going to experience the worst French meal you've ever had,' said Denzil.

'Oh, I don't know,' said Neil. 'I've eaten here. I liked the bouillabaisse.'

'I thought they were in the French Second Division,' said Ben.

Helen translated the menu for Lorna with barely a soupçon of condescension. Henry struggled with his schoolboy French, but found himself unable to seek help.

The headwaiter approached. Ted said, 'I'll tell you what to order, Lorna.' He leant across Helen, brushing himself against her

56

chest, and whispered something into the ear of the more flat-chested Lorna.

'What's going on, Ted?' said Helen.

'Trust me,' said Ted.

'Have you decided, madam?' said the headwaiter.

Lorna gave Ted an assessing look. 'Have you got any *merde?*' she said.

'Madam!' said the headwaiter.

'Ted!' said Helen, and she kicked him.

'Ow!' said Ted.

'You bastard,' said Henry.

'Below the belt,' said Gordon. 'Final warning.'

'*Merde* is French for . . . er . . . well . . . shit,' said Neil, blushing.

'Many a true word,' said Gordon.

'I'm sorry,' said Lorna to the headwaiter, 'but he told me to ask for it.'

A faint grin appeared at the edge of the headwaiter's mouth. He wiped it off with the invisible napkin of his professionalism.

Lorna plumped for tomato soup and a well-done fillet steak. Henry wished that she'd been more adventurous. He decided that, if he was paying a fortune, at least he'd have something exciting. *Pamplemousse* sounded exciting. So did steak tartare. The head-waiter had gone before Henry realized that he hadn't asked how he'd like it cooked.

'You sod, Ted,' he said.

'Give over,' said Lorna. 'It were just a joke.'

'It wasn't a bloody joke,' said Henry. 'That was no joke, Lorna.'

'We can take a joke where I come from,' said Lorna. She turned to Ted. 'I thought it might be summat rude,' she said, 'but I thought "Oh. What the 'eck? Waiter looks as if 'e needs a bit of life pumped into 'im."'

'Good for you, kid. Smashing,' said Colin.

Henry was pleased to see that Ted looked somewhat abashed. And he was pleased to see that Helen looked rather glad that Ted looked somewhat abashed.

When he went to the Gents, Colin followed.

'She's a smashing kid, kid,' he said. 'I could give her one meself.

Now you listen to me. You hang onto her. And stop looking at that other bloody one.'

What good judges men can be of other men's women.

Silence hung over the cavernous dining-room, as if the amount that was being spent on indifferent food was a source of shared grief between customers and waiters. The tables were enormous, and Henry and Lorna could hardly have rubbed their legs together, under the table, had anything so friendly been in their thoughts. They were cowed by the atmosphere. Customers were almost outnumbered by waiters, and the youngest of the other diners seemed about forty years older than them.

Behind them, Royal Scot No. 46164 *The Artist's Rifleman* was passing through Bushey troughs with the up *Mid-Day Scot*.

Henry's legs ached. He longed for his food with the hunger of a psychotic obsessed with a displacement activity. All the world was drab, save for the exotic promise of *pamplemousse*.

'She's pretty, isn't she?' said Lorna in a low voice.

Henry fought desperately against blushing, and almost managed it.

'Who?' he croaked.

'Helen, of course. Who else was there who's pretty? Denzil?'

'Well . . . yes . . . yes, I suppose she . . . I hadn't really . . . er . . .'

'Bollocks.'

'Lorna!'

Had the dreadful word stirred the over-starched table-cloths? Certainly, somewhere, as if in shock, a spoon scraped noisily against a plate. Had arthritic necks craned to see the source of this verbal outrage, unparalleled in the history of the restaurant of the Midland Hotel, Thurmarsh, in those days before pop groups?

'What?'

'You don't say things like that in places like this.'

'I do. I'm a country bumpkin. Remember?'

'Lorna!'

The elderly wine waiter limped towards them with a vast tome.

'The wine list, sir?'

'Please.'

Henry peered blankly at a long list of names. 'Which would tha prefer?' he said. 'Château Lafite '36 or a glass of Tizer?'

Lorna gave a leaden smile. The memory of their childhood games echoed desolately round the room like a marble in a Wall of Death. The wine waiter waited, breathing asthmatically, as if he expected Henry to choose from a list of three hundred wines in less than a minute. He chose at random a wine he couldn't afford with a name he couldn't pronounce.

Their food arrived. Henry almost cried when he discovered that *pamplemousse* was half a grapefruit. A waitress gripped stale rolls in silver tongs and dropped them onto their plates. They almost shared a laugh.

'How's your tomato soup?' he asked.

'It's tomato soup. How's your *pamplemousse?*'

'It's bloody grapefruit.'

Henry hoped the waitress would offer them another roll, so that this time they might share a laugh, but such largesse was not to be seriously expected.

'What did you think of them?' he said, drawn to the subject of his new friends as a man with vertigo is drawn towards the path's edge.

'I liked Colin.'

'Yes. He's smashing. He liked you.'

'Great. One down, six to go!'

'Lorna!'

The waiter brought Henry his bottle as if it were a priceless antique. On Henry's salary, it was. He poured a tiny drop into Henry's glass. Henry took an embarrassed sip and nodded. The wine waiter filled their glasses to the brim. Years later Henry would remember this, and realize how ignorant the wine waiter was, and wish that he could have his youth back so that this time he could live it without being overawed.

'Gordon liked you,' he said. 'You have to read between the lines with Gordon.'

'Two out of seven!'

He took a sip of wine. A waiter came over and poured a sipful into his glass. He mumbled his thanks at this tiresome gesture.

'Ben liked you.'

'I liked Ben.'

'Ben's all right.'

'Well . . . three out of seven.'

Their main courses arrived. His steak tartare looked very strange.

They watched numbly while five different vegetables, all over-cooked, were piled onto Lorna's plate. Henry had only salad.

At last they were free to eat. He took a cautious mouthful. 'Bloody hell!' he said, louder than he intended. 'It's raw.'

A man at a neighbouring table gave him a pitying 'The barbarians are at the door' look.

The headwaiter hurried over with swift, absurdly small steps.

'Is anything wrong, sir?' he asked.

'Well . . . I . . .' Henry was bathed in embarrassment. 'My . . . er . . . steak. It's . . . not cooked. Is that . . . er . . . ?'

'Steak tartare is raw fillet steak, sir, blended with garlic, tabasco, raw egg, chopped onion, chopped capers and herbs.'

'Oh, I see.'

'We can change it, sir, if you don't like it.'

'No. No. That's fine. It's very nice. I just didn't . . . thank you.'

He wanted to say to Lorna, 'If you're a country bumpkin, what am I? An ignorant provincial hick. And what does it matter?' He couldn't. Why couldn't he? Because it did matter. He'd been tossed like a cork through a land where it mattered very much, and he was only a human being. He took another sip of wine. A waiter hurried over and poured a sipful into his glass. He mumbled his thanks at this annoying gesture.

'What is all this "three out of seven" business, anyroad?' he said. 'You make it sound like some sort of exam.'

'Wasn't it?'

'Course it wasn't.'

'I felt as if I was on trial. As if you 'ad no faith in me. As if you didn't want me, but somebody to bring glory to you. As if a waitress from a country village isn't good enough for your literary friends.'

'Literary friends? Give over, Lorna. Is your steak nice?'

'It's steak. How about yours?'

60

'It's not bad, actually. Once you get used to the idea. It's pretty fiery. Tell us about Rowth Bridge.'

'You don't want to know about Rowth Bridge. You've changed.'

'Course I've changed. We all change.'

'I 'aven't. That's the trouble.'

'I don't want you to change.'

'Yes, you do. You want me to be interesting and keen on books and paintings and ideas and that and foreign countries and things and I'm not.'

He hesitated. 'I would like you to be interested in those things, yes,' he said. 'I think they're good things, but I don't want a different you to be interested in them. I want the you that you are now to be . . .'

'. . . different.'

'No. Well . . . the same, but different. Look, let's leave it. I *am* interested in Rowth Bridge. How are Simon and Pam?'

Simon Eckington, from the post office, had married Pam Yardley, the evacuee, who had been Henry's childhood sweetheart before Lorna.

'All right. They've got two smashing kids.'

'Smashing.'

'You see, you aren't interested. You haven't even asked if they're boys or girls.'

'What are they?'

'Girls.'

'Smashing. Two little girls. Smashing.'

'I love children. I wanted to 'ave your children.'

'Lorna! You will!'

'I'm just a stop-at-home girl. 'ousewife in Rowth Bridge, three bairns, that's me.'

'Maybe you only think that because that's the role society's put you in.'

'No. I like it. I don't want to be a film critic.'

'Who's talking about film critics?'

There was a sullen silence between them. He took a large gulp of wine. A waiter hurried across and poured a large gulpful into his glass. He mumbled his thanks at this irritating gesture.

'This wine's nice, isn't it?' he said.

61

'I think it's 'orrid,' said Lorna.

'Would you prefer cider?'

'Yes, please.'

He tried to attract the attention of a waiter. Suddenly no eyes were looking their way.

'It doesn't matter.'

'Yes it does.'

'Imagine me ordering sweet cider in Hampstead!'

'What's Hampstead got to do with it?'

'What was 'er name? Paul's sister. Diana? Or is she forgotten now you've met the fabulous Helen?'

'Lorna!' He raised his arm imperiously. Two waiters ignored him. They were laying up for breakfast.

'She's a cow, that one. She'd scratch me eyes out except then folk wouldn't know any more that my eyes aren't as pretty as hers.'

'Lorna! She's not like that.'

'You see!'

'Lorna! I couldn't care less about her.' At last he'd made such strong eye contact with a waiter that the waiter couldn't ignore it. 'About time!' he said. The waiter ignored this. 'Er . . . could I have a pint of sweet cider, please?'

'Certainly, sir.' The waiter moved away and called out unnecessarily loudly, 'Pint of sweet cider for table eight, George.' This time the neighbouring diner's expression said, 'The barbarians aren't *at* the door. They're inside. Civilization's over. It's official.'

'I couldn't,' resumed Henry, 'care less about her. But sheer justice leads me to say that she isn't like you think.' He changed the subject. 'How are you getting on with Auntie Doris?'

'She's all right. She's quite generous when that 'orrible man's not around.'

'Geoffrey Porringer?'

''e's 'orrible.'

'I know. I call him the slimy Geoffrey Porringer.'

''e keeps touching me up. Rubbing against me. Making it look accidental.'

'Oh no. That's horrible.'

''e's disgusting. How do folk get to be so disgusting?'

The wine waiter brought the pint of sweet cider as if it were a Mills bomb. Yet, off duty, he never drank anything except dark mild.

'I met my Uncle Teddy on Wednesday,' said Henry. 'I'm going to come to Troutwick and try to get Auntie Doris to go back to him. And I'm going to warn Geoffrey Porringer off you. Nobody rubs up against my Lorna.'

'I'm not your Lorna.'

'You are. I love you, Lorna.'

'You don't. I've lost you, Henry.'

'Lorna!'

He took a gulp of wine. Three waiters raced to pour a gulpful of wine into his glass. He mumbled his thanks to the winner at this infuriating gesture.

The lift took them slowly to the fourth floor and the room which they had still not entered. The huge wooden block to which the key was attached rubbed Henry's leg, mocking his flaccid organ. He couldn't bring himself to admit that it was over, that he wasn't a caring humanist socialist but an obnoxious intellectual snob.

The lift juddered to a halt all too soon. He picked up their cases and staggered into the corridor. Oh no! He was drunk again. He hadn't meant to be, but Lorna hadn't liked the wine, and it was costing him, so he'd had to drink it, and it was rich, heavy stuff, and he wasn't used to wine, and the key turned in the lock, but the door wouldn't open. He heard somebody inside the room. The door opened, and a sleepy man in a tasselled green dressing-gown was standing there.

'It can't 'appen,' said the night porter. 'There's a foolproof system. It can't 'appen.'

'Well, it has happened,' said Henry.

'I'm not saying it 'asn't 'appened,' said the night porter. ''appen it 'as 'appened. I'm saying it can't 'appen.'

'All right,' said Henry. 'It can't happen. But it has happened. What are you going to do about it?'

'I don't rightly know,' said the night porter. 'It's never 'appened before.'

'Well, do you have any other rooms?'

'Oh aye. 'undreds. It's right quiet. Friday night. No business-men, does tha see?'

'Right. Well, can we have one of those hundreds of rooms?'

'Aye, but I'm not allowed to take bookings, tha knows. I'm not like authorized. I'm night porter, like, not reception.'

'You wouldn't be taking a bloody booking. We've already bloody booked into a room with a man in it with a bloody silly green dressing-gown with tassels.'

'There's no call to swear at me, sir. I fought in t'War when tha were too young. I've only got one lung.'

'I'm sorry I swore at you,' said Henry. 'I'm sorry I was too young to fight in the War. I'm very sorry you've only got one lung. I'm sorry I'm drunk. I'm sorry there's a man with a bloody silly green dressing-gown with tassels in our room, but this is the first night of our honeymoon, and Mr and Mrs Wedderburn and I . . . I mean, Mrs Wedderburn and I . . . are looking forward to a bit of . . . to a . . . and we'd like a room to do it in.'

'Well why didn't you say so, sir?' said the night porter. 'I'll give you the bridal suite.'

The bridal suite was enormous. There was a huge sitting-room, in the Midland Hotel's idea of French elegance – more platform fourteen than Louis Quatorze. The furniture was reproduction seventeenth century. The curtains and upholstery were like a tapestry exhibition. Above the ornamental marble fireplace, the Golden Arrow was steaming through Penge on its way to Paris, city of love. Henry agonized over whether to tip the night porter, and decided that he must, because the confusion wasn't his fault.

'God, it's big,' he said, when the night porter had gone.

'Can you afford it?' said Lorna.

'Yes,' he lied.

They examined the rest of the suite. The bed was a four-poster. The bathroom was vast, overflowing with enormous white towels and covered in huge mirrors.

'I need a bath,' he said. 'I'm caked in sweat.'

'That's all right,' said Lorna, in a little voice that pierced his heart.

In the mirrors in the bathroom, seven podgy Pratts with seven tiny organs stepped gingerly into seven immense hot baths. Henry tried to think himself into desire, reliving those snatched, scratchy moments in Kit Orris's field barn, trying to find the love that until this week he'd never doubted, except perhaps for those weeks in Germany. He tried to arouse himself with thoughts of Diana Hargreaves and Belinda Boyce-Uppingham, who had called him an oik. He tried not to arouse himself with thoughts of Helen Cornish.

He dried himself hurriedly, thankful that the steam on the mirrors was hiding him from view. He was sweating again, from fear and the heat of the bath and the steamy fug of the room. He washed himself in cold water – had he ever really felt clean? – and wrapped himself in a voluminous towel. He entered the bedroom. In the four-poster, Lorna was sailing on a gentle sea of dreams. He crept into the bed. It creaked. He lay beside her, barely dry, shivering now. She stirred to put a thin arm round him. 'You're cold,' she said. She began to nibble his ear. He felt nothing. She began to massage his cold body gently. Desperately he thought of Helen, of pulling off her swirling magenta dress in the dim, dusty midnight news-room, of laying her white, curvaceous body on the news desk. He began, just in time, to be aroused. He entered Helen there, amid piles of rejected stories, on the news desk, and it was all right, and Lorna Arrow would never know.

His legs still ached, his head was thick, he'd been in too deep a sleep, and she wasn't in the bed. He knocked the Gideon Bible onto the floor before he found the switch for the bedside light.

He padded naked across the thick carpet into the sitting-room. He switched on the tactful lighting. The room was huge and semi-elegant and empty. The Golden Arrow was steaming eternally through Penge. On an eight-year-old seventeenth-century table, scrawled on a piece of British Railways lavatory paper, was the last word Lorna Arrow would ever write to her childhood sweetheart. It was 'Good-buy'.

On the first part of the journey, Henry faced north. He had a window seat with his back to the engine. His thoughts faced north, too.

Unable to pay for the bridal suite and their expensive dinner, he'd crammed his washing things and clean underpants into the pockets of his duffel-coat, and shuffled guiltily out of the hotel. There was no point in pursuing Lorna. Not yet, anyway. He could hardly go home, when he was supposed to be visiting Paul. So, the obvious thing to do was to visit Paul. He'd phoned from the station. There'd been good news and bad news. The good news was that they had a spare ticket for the rugby international. The bad news was that Paul had phoned him last night, to invite him, and this had surprised Cousin Hilda quite considerably.

So he sat in that over-heated train, worrying about Lorna and how she was feeling, about Cousin Hilda and how he would explain, and about the Midland Hotel and how he would avoid being arrested.

In the Midland lowlands, as the train approached Loughborough, he began to think about his national service. He'd spent five months in those parts, so now he faced sideways, looking out of the window, searching for landmarks.

There were fewer worries here. True, he had a disturbing sense of unfinished business, of a ghost that still had to be laid, but in the main the traumas of those times had already become amusing stories, told at his own expense.

As the train roared through Barrow-on-Soar, it passed under a bridge over which he had ridden silently, a tiny figure in the stillness of a vast dark night on a girl's bicycle, his face blackened with burnt cork, in February, 1954. He'd been unit runner on night exercises, and had been given SQMS Tompkins' daughter's bike. It had been absurdly small for him, and had had no crossbar. His job had been to deliver vital coded messages from mobile HQ to uninterested groups of skiving, snoring squaddies. He remembered prodding a sleeping sergeant in a barn at first light. 'Three red ferrets knocking on green door, sarge.' 'Fuck off.' 'Yes, sarge.'

At Leicester three people got out and he was able to bag a window seat, facing the engine. Bag! That word belonged to his southern days. He was facing south now and so were his thoughts.

As the train snaked through the hunting shires, the rich farmland dusted with snow, he thought about Diana. Oh no. No more women, Henry. But he liked Diana, and there was no harm in thinking about her. In a purely platonic way. Almost. Down, boy.

He had different worries now. Would his friendship with Paul survive better than that with Martin? Would he make his usual provincial *faux pas*? Would Tosser have a good game? Would he still fancy the elegant Mrs Hargreaves, which was ridiculous? Would he manage to borrow fifty pounds off Dr Hargreaves, eminent brain surgeon, which was essential, if he was to pay his hotel bill?

They met outside the ground as arranged. Paul looked impatient and self-righteous. He was fair-haired and slight. National service seemed to have pared him to the bone. 'The others have gone in,' he said curtly, and Henry saw how he'd been as a second-lieutenant.

Henry had discovered how vulnerable the upper middle classes are to good manners. 'Apologize and win' was almost as sound a principle as 'divide and rule'. So now he apologized. 'Sorry I've cut it a bit fine,' he said. Cut it a bit fine? You wouldn't say that in Thurmarsh, you chameleon. 'You know what trains are.'

It worked. 'Oh, that's all right,' said Paul. 'Sorry if I was a bit . . . er. I was afraid we'd miss the kick-off.' They shook hands with unaccustomed formality. 'Good to see you, old chum. Where's your luggage?'

'In my pockets.'

Paul shook his head in amazement at the latest eccentricity of his funny little northern friend, and they entered Twickenham, known the world over as Twickers. Henry felt that he ought to be watching Thurmarsh play Rochdale at Blonk Lane, known no-where as Blonkers.

The great stands were crowded. They made slow progress up stairs, down gangways. A roar announced the appearance of the teams. Alcohol fumes eddied in the raw wind. They edged along their row, disturbing knees covered in rugs, clambering over hampers, causing hip-flasks to be removed from chapped lips. 'Hello, Diana.' Shapeless and bulky in several layers of clothes, she looked more like a Cossack on guard duty than an attractive girl. He ought to have felt pleased, not disappointed. 'Hello, Dr Hargreaves. Hello, Mrs Hargreaves.' Mrs Hargreaves still looked elegant, in five layers of clothes. Dr and Mrs Hargreaves were looking at him oddly. He must look strange, in his old, stained duffel-coat, with crumpled underpants peeping out of the pockets. Hardly *comme il faut!* A tall, rather stern girl raised cool eyebrows at him. 'Judy, this is Henry, an old friend. Judy Miller, my girl-friend.' 'Hello, Judy.' 'Judy's at Girton. She's reading law.' How incredibly dreary. 'Oh. Smashing.' Oh god, I'm sitting between Diana and Mrs Hargreaves. I'm a small piece of podge entirely surrounded by desirable women. A cool, elegant, perfumed kiss on the cheek from Mrs Hargreaves. Why didn't age touch her like it touched everybody else? A huge, hot, wet kiss from Diana, a tidal wave of affection, red wine and garlic. Stirrings of desire, despite her shapelessness. National anthems. Incredible noise. Fervent Welsh singing, absurd among the trim residential streets of South-West London.

How small Tosser Pilkington-Brick looked. Well, not small. Normal-sized. At school he'd seemed enormous. Here all sixteen forwards were bigger than him, and some of the backs as well. Henry felt absurdly nervous for him. Well, was it that absurd? Tosser had been his hero. He'd fagged for him, and had felt a wet warm feeling when Tosser had spoken nicely to him, and Tosser had spoken nicely to him more than once.

England attacked from the start. Their forwards won plenty of good ball. The first time Tosser got the ball, he dropped it. The second time, he managed to catch it, but sent a wild pass which was intercepted by Brace. Towards half-time, M. J. K. Smith made a half-break, Tosser tried a dummy, slipped, and crashed into Cliff Morgan, amid hoots of derision. Henry couldn't believe it. His hero was nervous. He was having a stinker. Diana fell silent. When Tosser knocked on yet again, just before half-time, she clutched Henry's hand very tightly.

'What is it?' he said.

'He's playing so badly.'

She was identifying with his hero! What a magnificent girl she was! But he *would* like his hand back.

'Er . . . you're hurting my hand,' he said.

'Oh, sorry.' She released his hand, stroked it, looked at him thoughtfully, kissed him, and said, 'It *is* good to see you.' Was it Henry's imagination, or did Paul frown?

Henry tried to tell himself that it didn't matter, it served Tosser right. Lampo Davey, for whom he had also fagged, had been right to scorn all this. Hero-worship belonged to childhood. It belonged to the rejected part of his life, at Dalton College. He shouldn't be here, he belonged with Lorna in Rowth Bridge. It was no use telling himself these things. Every time the ball came to Tosser, Henry's heart raced.

At half-time, Dr Hargreaves poured whisky into real glasses from his hip-flask and Mrs Hargreaves handed round rolls spread with home-made anchovy paste. Nobody mentioned Tosser Pilkington-Brick.

In the second half Tosser played a little better, without covering himself with glory. England won the scrums 18–10, and led in the line-outs 55–18, but the backs squandered chances galore and, as the final whistle approached, they were losing 3–4.

'Henry?' said Mrs Hargreaves suddenly, as England surged into a last assault. 'Do you remember the name of that little restaurant near Concarneau where you tried *langoustine* for the first time?' The impossibility of his predicament! Reluctant to be rude, and being asked to recall a Breton fish restaurant at the climax of a great sporting event. 'It's on the tip of my tongue,' he lied.

The ball was passed to Tosser only three yards from the Welsh line. He was going to score the winning try. Pilkington-Brick atones for early errors. Thrilling late winner from England 'newboy'.

And Tosser dropped it. The great, incompetent, unimaginative oaf couldn't catch a ball and run three yards with it. Fury shook Henry's podgy frame. Diana clutched his left hand sympathetically. Mrs Hargreaves grabbed his right hand triumphantly.

'Au Chêne Vert,' she said.

'What?' said Henry blankly.

'The restaurant where you first tried *langoustine*,' said Mrs Hargreaves, as if speaking to a mental defective. 'That is a weight off my mind. I've been worrying about that for days.'

Lucky you, if that's all you've got to worry about, thought Henry.

Dr Hargreaves nosed the Bentley through the slow-moving traffic, in the deepening night, past rows of snug, smug houses, past lines of trim, prim pollarded trees. Henry tried not to feel superior to the hordes who were streaming on foot towards buses and trains. It wasn't easy. He felt a disturbing flicker of sympathy with the arrogance of the rich. Well, it was rather nice, sensing how much Diana was enjoying being squashed against him, sensing how much Judy wasn't enjoying being squashed against him. He let his body fall against Judy's tubular hardness as Dr Hargreaves swung into the main road with the assumption that Bentleys took precedence over Morrises and Singers.

In the Hargreaveses' narrow, four-storey Georgian town house in Hampstead, everyone went to change. Henry's change, in his little room, with an original Klimt above the bed – just how rich were they? – consisted of putting on his crumpled, clean underpants.

Diana looked mature and almost elegant, if slightly lumpy, in black and gold.

They drank dry sherry. Judy said, 'Thank you very much for inviting me. It was a super game.'

'Yes, thank you,' said Henry hastily, partly so as not to be left at the post in the good manners stakes, but also to establish publicly what had never actually been made clear, that he was invited and wouldn't be expected to pay. It was important that he be at his best that evening so that, when mellowness had set in, he could ask to borrow fifty pounds. He'd have to be particularly careful to hide his hostility to Judy. But really! Calling it a super game, when it would go down in history as the day Pilkington-Brick lost the match for England!

'Poor Tosser,' said Diana, as if she could read his thoughts. Her legs began widening below the knee instead of waiting, as legs should, till they were out of sight. How endearing her slightly fat knees were.

If mellowness never did set in that evening, no blame can be attached to anyone but Henry.

70

The moment he entered the Ristorante Garibaldi, with its pale blue walls, pink table-cloths and scalloped pink napkins – no fishermen's nets, hanging Chianti bottles and empty wine bottles covered with stalactites of candle-grease for Dr and Mrs Hargreaves – he thought: Oh dear. I'm going to behave badly tonight.

Did he fight against it? Oh yes. After his somewhat unfortunate opening remark of 'What poncy serviettes' he remained silent for several minutes. He behaved moderately well while eating his *tagliatelle al pesto*, but its elegant greenness reminded him of the less elegant verdancy of the glutinous curries at the Shanghai Chinese Restaurant and Coffee Bar. He felt ashamed of the gastronomic desert that was Thurmarsh. The shame made him feel defensive. His mood wasn't improved when he thanked Dr Hargreaves for the salt and Paul said, 'Henry? Tiny point. Dad's a fellow of the Royal College of Surgeons. They call themselves Mr, not Dr.' Terrific, thought Henry: Lets me get it wrong for six years, then corrects me in public. Which may have been why, when the conversation turned to national service and Judy assumed that he'd been an officer, he said, 'No. And I'm glad.'

'Really?' said Paul, unable to resist the bait. 'Why's that?'

'Do you remember Tubman-Edwards who blackmailed me at Dalton?'

'God, yes. What a monster.'

'He was a second-lieutenant in the Signals. I was on cookhouse fatigues.' He broke off to thank the waiter for his sea bass with Livornese sauce. 'I was at a huge sink full of vast cooking-tins covered in grease and I had to wash them in cold water. That was the sort of merry jape they used to think up to help build our character. Tubman-Edwards was orderly officer. He said, "It's Pratt, isn't it?" I said, "Yes, sir." Sir! He said, "How are you enjoying the army, Pratt?" I said, "Very much, thank you, sir." He said, "Jolly good." That's why I wouldn't have wanted to be an officer.'

'I fail to see the point,' said Paul.

'That's why you could be an officer,' said Henry. Mr and Mrs Hargreaves frowned at his bad manners but, since he was a guest, they said nothing. 'I couldn't accept a system in which I had to say stupid things like "How are you enjoying the army?" to men washing greasy tins in cold water.'

'Isn't the truth of the matter that it was you who was forced to say something stupid?' said Judy.

I can imagine you in court, thought Henry, with your sallow cheeks, your long, thin nose and your determined mouth, but I cannot imagine you in bed with Paul.

'How come?' he said lamely.

'Well, you replied "Very much, thank you" instead of "Not at all, you stupid twit, can't you see I'm covered in cold grease?"'

'I'd have been on a charge.'

'Precisely. So you took refuge in a cowardly lie.'

'Cowardly lie? What you're suggesting would have been suicidal idiocy,' said Henry. 'All right. I amend what I said. I'd have hated to be an officer and been forced to force people like me to say stupid things like I was forced to say.'

Mr Hargreaves gave Henry a tiny nod, acknowledging a good point scored. Henry didn't want to score points. He wanted to give his deeply felt views. He knew he should stop. He couldn't.

'I'll make you a prediction,' he said. 'In twenty years' time, national service will have been abolished, authority and discipline will be breaking down and Disgusted of Tunbridge Wells will be saying "Bring back national service. Give them some discipline." Well, I believe that one of the reasons why authority and discipline will be breaking down will be because a whole generation will have learnt to say "Thank you very much, sir," while meaning "Oh sod off, you stupid twit." They'll also, incidentally, have become deeply imbued with every four-letter word except work.'

There was a loud silence, then Mrs Hargreaves said, 'There's a very interesting exhibition of Portuguese art at the Royal Academy. One knows so shamefully little about Portuguese art,' and Henry wanted to laugh. Suddenly he felt in a good mood. He would redeem himself. 'This sea bass is delicious,' he said, and then he remembered that talking about food while eating it was not considered good form in the Hargreaveses' circle, as he'd discovered when he'd said, 'This stew's nice,' when it was *boeuf bourgignon* anyway, and the memory of *that* humiliation swept over him, and he no longer felt in a good mood, and Mr Hargreaves said, 'Do you think Wales will beat the French?' and Diana said, 'Northern Fiji is highly populated, I hear,' and everybody stared at her in astonishment; and she said, 'The last four remarks were about sodding twits, Portuguese art, sea bass and rugby, so I assumed this was the new style of witty table talk, with every sentence on an entirely new subject,' and Henry looked at her in astonishment – was it possible that she was on his side? – and he said, 'Oh, I agree. Double glazing's the thing of the future,' and she said, 'Ah, but *are* the Peruvian Indians happy?' and he said, 'Well, let's put it this way, a masochist is a person who likes bashing himself against a wall because it's so nice when it starts,' and Henry and Diana laughed but nobody else did, and what might on another occasion have been an amusing conversational fancy was edged with tension. Mr and Mrs Hargreaves looked as if they were being asked to play a new game but hadn't been told the rules. Paul and Judy knew that it wasn't a game and Henry, knowing that he was being foolish, said, 'Being an officer has changed you, Paul. You look as if you'd like to arrest me for conduct prejudicial to good restaurant order and discipline, filthy and idle while eating a sea bass, *sir*,' and after that, although the zabaglione passed off without incident, it clearly wasn't possible to ask Mr Hargreaves for fifty pounds that night.

His bedroom door was opening. It squeaked slightly. He sat bolt upright.

'It's me,' whispered Diana.

'Good God,' he said.

'S'sh!' she whispered as she closed the door.

She removed her dressing-gown and slipped naked into his bed.

'Move up,' she whispered.

He moved up. He was putty in her hands.

'You're tense,' she whispered. 'Relax.'

Yes, yes. Come on, Henry. Rise to the occasion. As it were. It's what you've always wanted. Yes, but not now. If only it wasn't the night after I'd decided I'm no good at the only thing I'm good at. If only it wasn't at the end of the day on which I decided to give

73

women up for ever, for their sakes as well as mine. If only I hadn't had so much to drink yet again. If only she hadn't had so much garlic. There was something to be said, perhaps, for the gastronomic desert that was Thurmarsh. If only they weren't in the room next to her parents.

'Relax,' she whispered. 'Don't wriggle. What's wrong?'

'They'll hear.'

'Oh, Henry. You sounded so rebellious tonight. Was all that just talk?'

'No, but . . . your family . . . I mean . . .'

'Do you want to be like Paul and Judy, carefully not sleeping together tonight out of good manners?'

'No.'

'Everyone does it these days. This is 1956.'

'I know.'

He pressed himself against her naked body. She put her tongue in his mouth. He ran his hands over her warm, chunkily generous body.

'You're lovely,' he said. 'You're so beautiful.' He found himself responding to his own words. 'I love you,' he said. 'I love you with all my heart, darling. Oh, Diana, Diana, I love you.' Slowly, and entirely forgetting to be quiet, he began to rise to heights of feeling and desire, on a tide of words which he didn't mean.

It was clear, in the olive-green dining-room, over the bacon and kidneys – eggs would have been too obvious – that they all knew. It was also clear, despite their politeness, that they disapproved.

Diana came in late, still kissed by sleep, and said, 'Morning, everybody,' with a determined brightness that verged on defiance.

'Did you sleep well, Diana?' said Paul, meaningfully avoiding sounding meaningful.

'Very well indeed,' said Diana, ditto. 'How did you and Judy sleep?'

'I slept very well,' said Paul. 'Did you sleep well, Judy? Was your room quiet?'

'Very quiet,' said Judy. 'I slept very well. Did you sleep well, Henry?'

'I slept very well, thank you, Judy.'

Mr Hargreaves smiled. 'Well, then,' he said. 'It sounds as though everyone slept as well as could be expected. We shall be able to issue a very satisfactory communiqué.'

Diana still hadn't given Henry a direct look. He wished she would.

'And what are you young people planning to do this morning?' said Mrs Hargreaves.

'I'm going to show Henry round the heath,' said Diana rather shrilly.

Henry felt that he could have been exultant that morning, if he hadn't told Diana that he loved her, if he hadn't got to ask Mr Hargreaves for fifty pounds, if he hadn't got to explain to the Midland Hotel why he'd walked out without paying, and if he hadn't got to explain to Cousin Hilda why Paul had rung to invite him for a weekend for which he had already departed.

The sunshine grew steadily hazier, until the sun was just a vague diffusion of yellow light in a dull and darkening mist. There was a smell of snow. Hampstead Heath that Sunday morning seemed alive with interesting people. In Henry's imagination they were philosophers and painters, socialist intellectuals, Middle European exiles, eccentrics and poets. Probably quite a few of them were actually plumbers and insurance brokers.

The path took them out of the trees, onto a bare grassy knoll. Several people were flying kites in the freshening wind. To the south the great city was dimly visible through the thickening murk. The light was growing faintly purple.

'Henry?'

She was finding it difficult to look at him. He didn't like it.

'What?'

'I wish I hadn't come to your room last night.'

That jolted him. 'Oh. May I ask why?' There was no reply. 'I thought you . . . er . . . enjoyed it.'

'This morning,' she said, 'thinking of what you said . . . I had no idea. That you loved me.' She forced herself to meet his gaze. 'I could never love you, Henry.'

Wonderful. It let him off the hook completely. So why did he feel as if a heavyweight boxer had just hit him in the stomach?

Ego? He tried to look blank. He didn't want her to see him with ego on his face.

'Well,' he said, 'so why, if I may ask, did you come to my room?'

'I like you very much and I find you . . .' Why did she have to search so long for an adjective? '. . . appealing.'

He kissed her. Now why did he do that?

'No!' she said. 'Please!'

He held her tight and pressed his crutch into hers, in the midst of all the kite fliers. He kissed her long and slowly on the mouth. Now why did he do that? And she kissed him back, her lips working diligently, until their faces were slimy with each other's saliva. Now why did she do that?

At last the kiss ended. 'You see,' she said. 'It's very simple. I like sex. I'm probably over-sexed.'

'Ah,' he said.

'What do you mean, "ah"?' she said indignantly. 'Is that an adequate response to such an incredible admission?'

'I wasn't sure whether to say "congratulations" or "bad luck".'

'I know. I mean, I'm not promiscuous. Not really. I'd never do it with somebody I didn't like a lot or know really well. But I do enjoy going to bed with men I like. And once not a man. Does that shock you?'

'No. I . . . er . . . don't think I have any right to be shocked by that.'

'Oh? Really? Interesting. Anyway, when you said you loved me, I felt awful. You could never be that important to me.'

'Well, that's . . . wonderful.'

'What?'

'I . . . er . . . you're so lovely, Diana, so attractive, such a nice person, that I said things I didn't mean. I don't love you.'

'Oh.'

'I like you very much. Perhaps I feel all the feelings of love towards you except love itself.'

'Oh. Well, that's all right, then.'

'Yes.'

And they walked back slowly, under a bruised sky, both let off the hook, both feeling offended when they should have felt relieved. Ah, youth! How very like middle and old age it is.

They realized that everyone was wondering what had taken place on their walk. They decided, without needing to consult each other, to play the situation up. Every now and then, during lunch, they gave each other intense glances.

They had fish soup and medallions of rare beef in red wine sauce. Henry wondered, with shame but also with love, what Paul must have thought of Cousin Hilda's meals.

'Were there any paintings out up Heath Street?' said Mrs Hargreaves.

'Oh yes, quite a few,' quipped Henry sparklingly.

'I think you found them very interesting, didn't you, Henry?' said Diana. 'I mean, you don't get a lot of open-air paintings in Thurmarsh.'

Henry was appalled to hear himself say, in betrayal of his whole heritage, 'You don't get a lot of anything in Thurmarsh.'

'Except spittle,' said Judy.

There was an amazed silence. Paul flushed. Even Judy looked horrified. But she had to enlarge on it now.

'Paul tells me people keep spitting up there. On the pavements,' she said.

Paul glared at her. Clearly this was a breach of confidence.

'They do,' said Henry. 'It's because there's such a lot of pneumoconiosis.'

'I think that's a beautiful word,' said Judy.

'Extremely beautiful,' said Henry. 'It must be a great consolation to people who're dying of it.'

'Henry! For Christ's sake!' said Paul.

'Well I'm sorry, but it isn't funny, you see,' said Henry.

'I thought it was parrots, anyway,' said Diana.

'Sorry? You thought what was parrots?' said Paul.

'Pneumoconiosis.'

'That's psittacosis,' said Mr Hargreaves reluctantly.

'What's psoriasis, then?' said Paul.

'A skin disease,' said Mr Hargreaves reluctantly.

'Please! People!' said Mrs Hargreaves. 'What *has* happened to your idea of table talk?'

'Could parrots have psoriasis as well as psittacosis?' said Diana.

'Diana!' said Mrs Hargreaves.

'I wonder if anybody's ever given a parrot an enema for eczema in Exeter,' said Diana.

'You're in a very silly mood today, Diana,' said Mrs Hargreaves. She gave Henry an involuntary look, and he knew that she blamed him for Diana's silly mood. He exchanged intense looks with Diana.

The conversation continued in more subdued vein. On the surface everybody was very civil, but he knew that, while acceptable as a friend, he was not regarded as suitable for marrying Diana, and the fact that he had no intention of marrying her didn't make this any more palatable. He was finding out how unpleasant it is not to be thought good enough, and that provoked unpleasant reflections on his own behaviour towards Lorna.

And he still had to ask to borrow fifty pounds. He'd thought it would be easy to ask for money from the rich. He was realizing that they are the hardest of all to ask.

At last, the gastronomically exquisite, socially unbearable meal came to an end.

'Er . . .' he began, over coffee, in the faintly Chinese drawing-room on the first floor. 'I . . . er . . . I wonder if I could . . .' Oh god, he was blushing. 'I wonder if I could have a word in private, Mr Hargreaves?'

There was an eloquent silence. Henry realized that everybody except Diana thought that he was going to ask Mr Hargreaves for his daughter's hand in marriage. He could hardly suppress a smile at the thought that he could ever bring himself to do anything as feudal as that.

Mr Hargreaves took him to his study. Over his desk was an enormous diagram of the human brain, which struck Henry as sheer affectation. The man must know his way round the brain by now, unless, ghastly thought, he needed a quick refresher after breakfast.

If Henry was tense and nervous, so was Mr Hargreaves. This made Henry all the more furious that he had to ask to borrow money off the man.

'Er . . . I've got myself in a very small financial jam,' he said.

'What? Oh!' It took Mr Hargreaves two seconds to realize that good manners demanded that he attempt to hide his immense relief. 'What sort of a jam, Henry? And how small?'

'Well . . . er . . . not really a jam exactly. I just have a bill, and no money to pay it.'

'That is, in my estimation, a jam.'

Snow had begun to settle on the little walled town garden. They both noticed it at the same moment. It's hard to say which of them was more appalled at the possibility of Henry being snowed in there.

'How much are we talking about?' asked Mr Hargreaves.

'Well . . . er . . .' It sounded such a lot. 'Fifty pounds, actually.'

Mr Hargreaves relaxed, and Henry realized what a small sum it seemed to him.

'Of course, Henry.'

'I could pay you back at two pounds a week.'

'Do you mind my asking how much you earn?'

'Seven pounds ten a week.'

Mr Hargreaves stared at him in amazement.

'Good Lord! That's not very much,' he said.

'I know a lot of people who earn less,' said Henry. 'People who do unpleasant, essential jobs.' Shut up! Not now! Don't pollute the reservoir of goodwill you've built up by not getting engaged to Diana.

'Yes . . . well . . . I think a pound a week would be more practical, don't you?' said Mr Hargreaves smoothly. 'We don't want you failing to keep up the payments.'

'I'd rather die than fail to keep up the payments, Mr Hargreaves.'

Mr Hargreaves gave Henry a look, then nodded briskly.

His train was seventy-seven minutes late, due to snow. If he'd waited till the last train, he wouldn't have got back that night.

He looked at Thurmarsh as if he were a Londoner arriving for the first time. How cold it was. How bleak the station looked. How small, dreary and ill lit the ticket hall was. He felt ashamed.

The town was muffled by snow and almost deserted. There weren't enough taxis, and a queue was forming. Henry trudged across Station Square through several inches of snow. The Midland Hotel had become an enchanted castle.

Why did he feel so nervous? It didn't matter what they thought of him here. He explained the situation to the duty manager, who produced his bill with minimal politeness. He looked the sort of man who's frightened of catching VD off lavatory seats, and handed Henry his battered case as if fearing that it might be contaminated. Henry wondered what he expected to catch off it. Chronic gaucherie? Terminal podginess? Poverty?

He struggled along York Road and turned right into Commercial Street, which ran behind the Town Hall, across decaying Merrick Street. As he walked east, Commercial Street became Lordship Road and began to go up in the world. By its junction with Park View Road it was thoroughly respectable, though already struggling for survival. Two houses had been turned into private hotels. They were called the Alma and the Gleneagles.

Henry's footsteps violated the smooth whiteness of Cousin Hilda's front garden. Inside the house it was raw and dim and silent.

He put his head round the door of the basement room. The 'businessmen' were just finishing the little supper which Cousin Hilda gave them each evening. It was a shock to see them there, in mid-brawn, as if nothing had happened during the last three days.

'My feet are soaked. I'll be down in a minute,' he announced.

The 'businessmen' had gone by the time he returned. The room smelt of greens' water, warm wool and cold brawn. A warm fire burnt in the blue stove with the cracked panes. Cousin Hilda looked beyond the reach of warm fires.

'Where have you been?' she said.

He looked at her in carefully simulated astonishment.

'The Hargreaveses',' he said. 'I told you. Oh, I suppose you were worried by Paul's phone call on Friday night. I wanted to surprise them, so I didn't tell them I was going. I phoned them when I got to St Pancras, but there was no reply. They'd gone out to dinner.' Cousin Hilda couldn't resist sniffing at this extravagance, even though she didn't entirely believe in it. 'So I stayed in a little hotel near King's Cross, and rang them in the morning. It's called the Caledonian. You can check if you don't believe me.' He knew she wouldn't. How could she, without sounding vaguely disreputable? He resented life for providing so many reasons for turning a young man of honest intent into an accomplished liar. He gave her an edited version of the weekend, and felt indignant because he suspected that she didn't even believe the bits that were true.

'What an exciting life they all lead,' said Cousin Hilda. 'How drab all this must seem.'

He attacked his brawn bravely. What a terrible cue she had given him. He couldn't say, 'Yes, it is drab. Horribly drab. I'm leaving.' He said 'No' again, although each time he said 'No' it made it harder for him to say that he was leaving. And leave he must. 'No!' He meant it. He'd much prefer to live here than with the Hargreaveses. Well, say that. 'I'd much prefer to live here than with the Hargreaveses. But, you see, Cousin Hilda, I . . .' He swallowed. Why did he find it so incredibly difficult to say it? 'I'm going to get a flat.' Her lips were beginning to work, with the distress. 'I've been happy here. I regard it as my home. But I've got to live in my own place and lead my own life and find my own feet if I'm to compete in the hard world of the press.'

'Journalists!' said Cousin Hilda. 'Giving you airs! I don't know!'

4　A Difficult Week

'How was the weekend, kid?' said Colin Edgeley.

Henry shrugged.

'You've got a good kid there. You stick with her.'

Colin raised a questioning eyebrow at the failure of Henry's attempted smile.

Henry stuck a sheet of coarse, cheap paper into his ancient, clattering typewriter. He typed slowly, with two fingers: 'Iceland-1.' This identified the story and the page, and exhausted his inspiration.

He turned, as he'd been hoping not to do, to have a quick peep at Helen. He met Ted's dark, deep, ironic eyes and turned away hurriedly. 'Iceland is a country of beautiful women, according to an Icelandic visitor to Thurmarsh.' Rubbish. He tore the sheet out, replaced it, and typed: 'Iceland-1.' He knew that Ginny'd seen him looking at Helen. He leant across to speak to her.

'Do anything exciting this weekend, Ginny?' he said.

'No.'

Good. 'Oh dear.'

The conversation fizzled out after this misleadingly sparkling exchange. 'Hot geysers have a very different connotation from in Thurmarsh . . .'

Gordon Carstairs struggled in, his eyes set deep in his baggy, insomniac's face. 'What sort of a time do you call this?' said Terry Skipton. 'Twenty past nine,' said Gordon with less than his usual obscurity. But when Henry said, 'Morning, Gordon. Nice weekend?' Gordon exclaimed, 'Penalty!' Henry deduced that it hadn't been a nice weekend.

His disobedient head was swivelling round again, to take a sip of Helen's loveliness. She smiled sweetly and returned to her forecast of a revolution in ladies' undergarments. He switched off her loveliness with a sigh, and stepped back into the dark world of his journalistic inexperience.

He finished the story and handed it to Terry Skipton, who began to read it with a face as long as a Sunday in Didcot.

'"Connotation"!' he said. 'What's the meaning of "connotation"?'

'Meaning,' said Henry.

'This is what I say,' said Terry Skipton. 'What's the meaning?'

'No,' said Henry. 'You've mistaken my meaning. When I said "meaning" I was meaning that the meaning of connotation is meaning.'

'Well, if you mean "meaning", say "meaning". They won't understand "connotation" in Splutt. Anyroad, I must read on. I'm riveted.' Terry Skipton read on, with darkening brow. 'It's all about Iceland,' he said.

'He's *from* Iceland.'

'I told you to find out his views about Thurmarsh. I mean, what are we, the *Thurmarsh Argus* or the *Trondheim Argus?*'

'Trondheim's in Norway.'

'Is it? Well, if you're such a Clever Dick you ought to know better than write rubbish like this. I want stuff about Thurmarsh.'

'But Thurmarsh people know about Thurmarsh.'

'They want to know what *he* thinks about Thurmarsh. They couldn't care less about Iceland. It's thousands of miles away. They've never been there. They're never going to go there.'

'I didn't realize people were so parochial,' said Henry.

'I'm deeply sorry that mankind fails to come up to your high standards, Mr Pratt,' said Terry Skipton. 'You'll rewrite that story this afternoon. In the meantime, get round them hospitals and police stations. There's been snow and ice. There'll be accidents. And, regrettable though our parochialism is, please try not to ask the desk sergeant at Blurton Road police station for his views on tribal dancing in Timbuctoo.'

As he walked away, Henry was already regretting making an enemy of Terry Skipton. His new friends were looking at him aghast. Only Gordon spoke. 'Change ends. More lemons,' he said. He sounded as if he meant it to be encouraging.

Henry trudged along pavements swept and pavements unswept. He phoned through a whole crop of minor accidents. He lunched alone, in the Rundle Café. A quantity surveyor, enjoying a cup of coffee after his braised steak, concealed himself behind the *Sporting Chronicle* to hide the moisture in his eyes as he Listened with Mother to the story of Gerald the Shy Guards Van.

That afternoon, Henry bashed out his story.

> Mr Gunnar Fridriksen, from Iceland, likes Thurmarsh [he wrote]. In particular, he likes our grime!
>
> Grime gives the buildings real atmosphere, he avers: 'We just do not have this grime in Iceland. Iceland is so clean, so new.'
>
> Another aspect of our life which wins praise from Mr Fridriksen, who runs an old people's home in the Icelandic capital, is our draught beer. 'It's an acquired taste,' he jokes. 'I have acquired it!'
>
> Mr Fridriksen, aged 43, also likes our gardens – front and back.
>
> The kindness of the ordinary man – and woman! – in the street is another source of praise from the blond Icelander.
>
> And he enjoys our toast. In fact, when he goes home Mr Fridriksen will take a very practical souvenir for his wife. Yes, a toaster!

The unprepossessing news editor read the story in grim silence. 'We'll make a journalist of you yet,' he said.

That evening, at number 66, Barry Frost bolted his liver and bacon, hummed that his desert was waiting so fiercely that he sprayed rhubarb crumble over his fellow 'businessmen', said, 'Dress rehearsal tonight,' and handed them all tickets for the first night. Liam's shining face reddened with excitement. Norman Pettifer talked about Sibyl Thorndike's St Joan. Cousin Hilda affected disapproval, but Henry sensed that she too was excited.

He looked at two flats that evening, but they were awful. He felt like going to the pub, but hurried home and watched *Come Dancing* with Cousin Hilda. Half of him affected lofty scorn. The other half danced to exotic Latin-American rhythms with Helen Cornish, who had sewn all the sequins herself.

On Tuesday he finished his calls quickly, bought the first edition of the paper and had a quick beer in the Pigeon and Two Cushions. There it was, on page 5, under the headline 'He likes our grime'. Three other customers had early editions. One of them said he'd have fancied Ginger's Delight in the one forty-five at Beverley if racing hadn't been snowed off. Another said, 'We should bomb that bugger Makarios.' None of them said, 'By 'eck, there's an Icelander here likes our grime.'

He lunched in the canteen. He announced that he was looking for a flat. Ginny said, 'There's a flat to rent in my house.' Helen said, 'That'd be cosy.' Gordon stared glumly at his toad-in-the-hole and said, 'He was a well-nourished man of average height.' Henry told Ginny that he couldn't see the flat that night. He was seeing *The Desert Song*. Ginny said she was reviewing *The Desert Song*. Helen said, 'That'll be cosy.'

The foyer of the Temperance Hall, in Haddock Road, was drab, draughty and bare save for admonitions against drink. But they had arranged to meet Barry Frost there after the performance.

Cousin Hilda and Mrs Wedderburn looked flushed by their exposure to the wanton world of show business. Liam O'Reilly looked exalted. Norman Pettifer looked vaguely disgusted, as if disappointed not to have seen Edith Evans.

Ginny approached them. Henry noticed for the first time that her legs were slightly bowed.

Why should he feel ashamed of Cousin Hilda and her 'businessmen' in the presence of this bow-legged future war correspondent? And why should he feel ashamed of this bow-legged future war correspondent in the presence of Cousin Hilda and her 'businessmen'?

'Are you going to the pub?' said Ginny.

'Certainly not,' said Cousin Hilda. 'I'm proud to say I've never been in a pub in my life.'

'Then how do you know you're right to be proud you've never been in one?' said Henry.

His belief that he'd scored a debating point lasted two seconds. Cousin Hilda said grimly, 'Because I've seen what it's done to people who *have* been in them.'

Liam looked back wistfully, towards the hall. He'd found things easier to deal with, in there.

Barry Frost appeared, smiling broadly. Henry introduced him to Ginny. There was silence. Neither Henry nor Ginny could bring themselves to give praise. Nobody else realized that they were expected to.

'Well, come on, what did you think of it?' said Barry Frost.

'Grand,' said Liam. 'It was just grand.'

Good old Liam, thought Henry, and then he realized that Liam meant it.

'Very nice,' said Cousin Hilda. 'Especially the women. They were hardly stiff at all.'

'I see,' said Barry Frost.

'Well, not you,' said Cousin Hilda. 'The others. They didn't seem to know what to do with their hands.'

'The scenery was attractive,' said Norman Pettifer.

'It didn't wobble nearly as much as it did when the Baptist Players put on Noël Coward's *Blythe Fever*,' said Cousin Hilda.

'I'm a bit deaf,' said Mrs Wedderburn, who had become Cousin Hilda's friend since Cousin Hilda's other friend, with whom Henry had shared two Christmasses, had died. She was short and stocky and had a thick bandage round her left leg. 'I heard every word *you* said. I thought you and the prompter were the clearest of all.'

'Thank you,' said Barry Frost.

'I admired your presence of mind when the door fell down,' said Norman Pettifer. 'You just opened the hole in the wall and stepped over the door as if nothing had gone wrong. I don't think Johnny Gielgud could have carried it off better.'

'Thank you, Norman,' said Barry Frost. 'Well, you've all made my evening. Who's coming to the pub?'

'Really, Mr Frost,' said Cousin Hilda. 'In front of the boy.'

'Boy?' said Henry. 'I'm nearly twenty-one. I'll tell you what you'd find in a pub, Cousin Hilda. Human warmth. Friendship. Laughter. Fun. Come on, Ginny, love.'

On Wednesday, January 25th, an inquiry set up to find ways of cutting the spending of the National Health Service reported that more money should be spent. Compulsory road tests were introduced for pre-war cars. Henry woke up thinking warm, erotic thoughts about Ginny Fenwick. She was big, warm and lovely. He'd have gone back with her last night if Norman and Barry hadn't been with them. Tonight he'd take a flat in her house. A new life was beginning. He was getting stories in the paper. He'd drink less, and work harder. Every night he would make love to Ginny Fenwick. Her eyes would shine with happiness.

He wanted to make people happy. He wanted to make Cousin Hilda happy. It was a source of great unhappiness to him that he regularly made her unhappy. He dreaded breakfast.

'I suppose you were drunk again last night,' she said grimly.

'I wasn't. It was Mr Pettifer knocked the milk bottles over.'

'Grown men don't tell tales.'

'He wasn't drunk either. He slipped on the icy step.'

The breakfast porridge could have been used as cement for the bricks of spotted dick in the house that Cousin Hilda's cooking built.

Liam entered the basement room next. A trace of the night's wonderment still hung about him.

'Grand morning,' he said.

Barry Frost grunted his greetings. Last night he'd been a showbiz personality. Today he was a tax inspector.

Over his second cup of tea, Norman Pettifer said, 'It's been a dull week so far. Cheddar, Cheddar, Cheddar. I hope today's different. It's discouraging when you pride yourself on the widest selection in the West Riding, and all you're asked for is Cheddar.'

'Don't you *know* what sort of day it'll be?' said Barry Frost. 'Has your uncanny talent for cheese prediction deserted you?'

'Feeling let down after the first night?' said Norman Pettifer. 'I read in a biography of . . .'

'I'm warning you,' said Barry Frost. 'If you mention Sibyl Thorndike or Johnny Gielgud I'll shove this cup right up your arse.'

'Mr Frost!' said Cousin Hilda.

Do, thought Henry. Give me a story. Tax inspector charged with assault after prominent local cheeseman hurt in Spode backside horror during post-theatre fracas.

No, thought Henry. I'm a kind-hearted humanist. I want people to get on well. I don't want them to be fodder for my career. Oh my god. Perhaps I shouldn't have become a journalist.

'I'm sorry,' said Barry Frost, leaving abruptly and banging the door behind him.

'Show business!' said Cousin Hilda.

'I thought it was grand last night,' said Liam. 'I thought it was the best thing I've ever seen in me life.'

The flat consisted of half the ground floor of a detached 1920s mock-Tudor house in Winstanley Road, which ran north through hills dotted with desirable residences on the edge of the town. Ginny had the half of the first floor which was directly above it.

He was shown round by the man from Bulstrode and Snotley. The flat comprised what had originally been the living-room and kitchen. Half the kitchen had become a cramped bathroom. In the now tiny kitchen there were servants' bells in a glass case. They didn't go with the formica table-top and work surfaces. The living-room had been divided by a plasterboard wall into a compact living-room and tiny bedroom. One half of the French windows stood right in the corner of the living-room, and the other half stood right in the corner of the bedroom. The effect was grotesque. The flat was cramped, ill-proportioned and drearily furnished. He took it.

He invited Ginny out, to celebrate. They walked to the Winstanley, a large, mock-Tudor pub where at lunch-times mock-sophisticated businessmen ate mock-turtle soup. The large lounge bar was awash with varnished tables, brown Windsor chairs, horse brasses, hunting scenes, tartan shields, and maps of the clans. The bleak, tiny public bar had been designed, successfully, to repel trade.

They drank glasses of Mansfield bitter. He ran his right hand briefly up her large left thigh. How lovely she was. It didn't matter that her lips were too thick, her nose too splayed, her complexion too red. She was Ginny Fenwick, warm-hearted lover, fearless war correspondent, enveloping earth-mother. They had three more drinks, and he decided that he didn't want to be enveloped just then. Not yet. Not till he'd moved in.

They caught a trolley-bus into town.

'They're ending the trolley-buses next year,' said Ginny. '"Progress."'

The doomed trolley-bus hissed smoothly through areas increasingly less prosperous as it dropped to the junction with York Road.

'Where shall we eat?' asked Henry. 'The Shanghai?'

'Oh not the Shanghai!'

No. Those awful glutinous curries. And Helen might be there.

The trolley-bus stopped briefly outside Fison and Oldsworthy's— *the* place for screws.

'I don't know anywhere, apart from the Shanghai, except the Midland Hotel, and I can't afford that,' he said.

'There's Donny's Bar,' said Ginny. 'It's upstairs at the Barleycorn. Steak and chops. Nothing inspired.'

'That'll be cosy,' said Henry.

'Join us,' said Helen.

'Please do,' boomed Denzil. 'We'll have some civilized conversation and pretend we're in a civilized world.'

Donny's Bar was a long, narrow room with tables along walls of false stone. Henry and Ginny stood in the middle of the room and talked in low voices.

'We'll have to, won't we?' he said.

'Oh yes!'

'What do you mean by that?'

'What I said,' said Ginny. 'We'll have to join them. That's clear.'

'Well, we will. I mean, it'd be rude not to. Wouldn't it?'

'Oh yes!'

'What do you mean by that?'

'What do you mean, "what do you mean by that?"?' said Ginny. 'I mean what I say. Yes, it'd be rude not to join them. And it'd be even ruder to stand here for half an hour, debating whether to join them. So let's join them, since it's what we all want so much.'

'What's that supposed to mean?' said Henry.

'Oh for God's sake,' said Ginny.

They joined them. Henry throbbed with desire for Helen.

'Henry's just taken a flat in my house,' said Ginny.

Oh my god, so I have, thought Henry. 'Where's Ted?' he said, half hoping she'd say, 'We've broken it off,' half hoping she'd say, 'Sending out invitations to the wedding.' 'On a story,' she said.

Cardboard cocktail was followed by medium-rare cardboard with sautéed cardboard and fresh garden cardboard, garnished with cardboard rings and half a grilled cardboard.

'Even in the gastronomic desert that is Thurmarsh, this could hardly be called an oasis,' said Denzil.

It rankled when a southerner said such things, especially a limping homosexual southerner with a hand-carved Scottish walking-stick, a high-pitched voice, and ageing mottled skin stretched across his cheekbones like old parchment.

'You enjoy being superior and mocking about everything, don't you?' said Henry.

'I'm impossible,' said Denzil. 'Hadn't you heard?'

'Yes,' said Henry. 'Often, from you. You seem to think if you say you're unpleasant it gives you *carte blanche* to *be* unpleasant.'

'I think you're a puritan at heart,' said Denzil.

Henry tried not to look at Helen. He tried to find Ginny attractive. Her face was even redder than usual and her nose was shining as she shovelled grub into her large mouth like an excavator. She was eating like that because she was hurt. His heart went out to her, but his genitals went out to Helen. He didn't want to be a virile, sexual person if this was how it made you behave. He put his hand on Ginny's knee, under the table. She kicked him.

'You're quiet tonight, Helen,' said Denzil.

'I only speak when I have something interesting to say,' said Helen.

'Good God!' said Ginny. 'You must live in perpetual silence.'

'Thank you, Ginny,' said Helen icily.

Ginny went redder still. 'Oh, Lord,' she said. 'I honestly didn't mean that to be bitchy. You shouldn't judge everybody by yourself, Helen.'

'And is that also not bitchy?' said Helen, sweetly this time.

'Yes, that was,' said Ginny. 'Sorry, Helen.' Helen looked sceptical. 'I mean it. I hate bitchiness. Life's too short. When I said you must live in perpetual silence, I meant that most of us would speak very rarely if we waited till we had something worth saying.'

They waited quite a while, for something worth saying.

'How are you getting on, Henry, with the fearsome Mr Skipton?' said Denzil eventually.

'I'm terrified of him,' said Henry.

'Me too,' said Ginny.

'He makes me uneasy,' said Helen. 'I can't look at him.'

'Poor Terry,' said Denzil. 'I don't expect he's got a friend in the world. He's at exactly the wrong level of unattractiveness.'

'What do you mean?' said Ginny.

'He's almost deformed. If he *was* deformed, we'd like him. Almost everybody is kind to the deformed and crippled. Nobody is kind to the unprepossessing. Nobody laughs at the mentally subnormal, but everybody scorns the rather stupid. If one is going to be disadvantaged in life, it's to one's advantage to be very disadvantaged. Do you know what I think about Terry Skipton? I think there's a heart of gold in there, which doesn't know how to reach out.'

Could that possibly be true? Henry felt that he'd caught a glimpse of another Denzil Ackerman. Was that true of Denzil also? Was that why Denzil understood Terry Skipton? He had an uneasy feeling that he was surrounded by people who had hearts of gold and that he'd fallen in love with the only one who hadn't.

The evening passed swiftly. Soon Denzil was saying, 'Well, young things, it's bed-time for clapped-out queers. Are you coming, Helen?'

'I'll stay, if that's all right,' said Helen.

'Of course it's all right. Isn't it, Ginny?' said Henry.

'Of course,' said Ginny.

'Be good,' said Denzil.

Am I going to have to pay for both women? thought Henry.

A hand stroked his thigh. Whose was it? He stroked Ginny's thigh. She kicked him. It must have been Helen's hand. He could hardly breathe.

The waitress hobbled towards them on ruined feet. 'Would you like coffee?' she said.

'Please,' said Helen.

'No, thank you,' said Ginny. 'I must be getting home.'

'I'd like coffee,' said Henry.

'Well you stay and have some.'

'But I'm taking you out.'

'Well, thank you. Good night.'

'But we're celebrating my moving into your house.'

'What a delightful prospect. Look, I'm tired. I need my beauty sleep more than some people.' Ginny blushed. Helen didn't. 'Are you coming or not?'

To do Henry credit, he did try to stand up. In vain.

'I want my coffee,' he said.

'Good night,' said Ginny Fenwick.

Henry and Helen gave each other meaningful looks. Their coffee came.

'This coffee's undrinkable,' said Helen. 'Come home with me and I'll make you some proper coffee.'

He wasn't going to miss his chance this time. He called for the bill.

'Let me pay my share,' said Helen.

'No. I insist.' Let nobody say he was mean.

'I earn as much as you.'

'Oh all right, then.' Let nobody say he was obstinate.

The waitress hobbled over with the bill.

'What's this?' he said. 'Two coffees? What about our meals?'

'Mr Ackerman has paid for all of you.'

'I bet you wish you'd insisted a bit harder now,' said Helen.

In the taxi she turned to him, rather disconcertingly, with her mouth opened wide in readiness, like a fledgling expecting food. They explored each other's lips and mouths. Kissing that superb orifice was everything he'd hoped. He felt as virile as a volcano. He put his left hand on the right cup of her bra. She removed his hand. 'Think of the driver,' she whispered. How unexpectedly considerate she could be.

He tipped the driver generously, because of all the kissing.

Helen marched up the drive, as if she couldn't wait to get into her house. She fumbled with the key, as if she was nervous.

Light flooded a neutral hall. She opened a door on the right,

92

and entered ahead of him. He would be able to remember none of the contents of the room, except for Ted Plunkett.

'Hello, darling,' said Helen brightly. 'I've brought Henry home for a coffee.'

On Thursday, January 26th, 1956, three million workers asked for pay rises, the big freeze was followed by floods, and Henry had his first page lead. He felt that his intro was a masterpiece of concentrated information and human interest. Imagine his chagrin when Terry Skipton read it aloud, scornfully. 'A 76 year-old diabetic retired railway guard was making "a miraculous recovery" in Thurmarsh Royal Infirmary today after lying semi-conscious in a rhubarb patch in near-zero temperatures for 10 hours only 300 yards from the council "pre-fab" where his invalid wife Doris and their Jack Russell terrier "Spot" were waiting anxiously for his return from a Darby and Joan hot-pot supper and whist drive.' When the story appeared, the information was threaded through it with the parsimony of an investment manager hanging onto his bills till he got his second final reminders. Terry Skipton called him over and said gruffly, 'Not a bad story, Mr Pratt. You'll learn our style in time.'

Over his roast pork, roast potatoes and cabbage, with tinned pears to follow, Henry failed to tell Cousin Hilda that he had found a flat.

On Friday, January the 27th, the Queen flew over the Libyan desert on her way to Nigeria. Henry had battered cod and chips, with jam roly poly to follow, and failed to tell Cousin Hilda that he had found a flat.

At half past eight he slipped out, and went to the Devonshire in Commercial Road, three hundred yards up the hill towards Splutt, beyond the *Chronicle* and *Argus* building. Upstairs, on Fridays, there was a jazz club with a resident Dixieland band. There he met Colin, Gordon, Ginny, Ted and Helen. Ben had gone home to give the wife one.

Sid Hallett and the Rundlemen comprised trumpet, clarinet, trombone, piano, bass and drums. As Henry entered, they were playing 'Basin Street Blues'. The room was large, dimly lit and crowded. Most people were standing. A buzz of conversation vied with the music. Sid Hallett jigged continually and smiled a lot. He had huge damp patches under his arms. Although not yet thirty, the trombonist and the bass players were developing paunches. All the band had pints of bitter in strategic places. Henry longed for fresh air.

He'd avoided speaking to Ted and Helen since Wednesday night. Now he tried to be casual, saying, 'Oh! Thanks for the coffee, incidentally.' He must have succeeded, because they looked rather sheepish. He thought longingly of the Upper Mitherdale fells.

He tried to have a quiet word in Ginny's ear. It wasn't easy, during 'South Rampart Street Parade'.

'Nothing happened on Wednesday night, you know,' he said. 'I just had a coffee. Ted was there.'

'Ah! Shame!' said Ginny.

'I'm cured of Helen, Ginny.'

'Congratulations. What has this to do with me?'

'Well, I'm . . . er . . . moving into the house where you live.'

'So?'

He was suddenly overwhelmed with affection for Lorna Arrow. He longed to see her. If only he wasn't working tomorrow, on the football paper, *The Pink 'Un*. (When Denzil had seen everybody reading pink papers last Saturday evening, he'd said 'Good Lord! Why are they all reading the *Financial Times*?') He sighed deeply. Colin asked him what was wrong. He told him. Colin offered to work tomorrow instead of him. Glenda wouldn't mind. She was all right, was Glenda. Henry telephoned Auntie Doris and invited himself to stay. She was thrilled. The band played 'Sweet Georgia Brown'. Henry thought about sweet Lorna Arrow.

He crept into the house at 11.43. Not late. Not really. Not drunk. Not very. Better if he didn't meet Cousin Hilda, though. She might not understand that you could have hiccups without being drunk.

She materialized at the top of the basement stairs.

'Henry!' she said grimly.

He decided to tell her that he'd found a flat, now, when he

wasn't drunk, not really, but while his courage was fortified by alcohol.

'I've got something . . .' He swallowed a hiccup brilliantly. '. . . to tell you,' he said.

'Come downstairs,' commanded Cousin Hilda.

'It won't take . . .' Another hiccup was skilfully stifled. '. . . a moment.'

'I'm not having you waking the whole house with your hiccups.' Damn!

'You're drunk again,' she said, as they entered the basement room. The stove was low. There was a lingering aroma of potted meat.

'You can have hiccups without being drunk,' he said. 'Babies have hiccups.'

'You aren't a baby,' she said, as if that proved that he was drunk. He knew that there was a fault in her logic, but couldn't pin it down.

'I'm . . . er . . . I'm going away for the weekend,' he said.

Cousin Hilda sniffed.

'You went away last weekend,' she said.

'I'm going to see Auntie Doris.' Cousin Hilda sniffed. 'I mean . . . after all, she is my . . . I mean . . . my auntie . . . isn't she? And I . . . er . . . I should have told you before, but I thought you'd be cross.' The tension had cured his hiccups. 'I met Uncle Teddy in the Shanghai Chinese Restaurant and Coffee Bar.'

Cousin Hilda sniffed twice, once for Uncle Teddy and once for Chinese food. 'Why should I be cross?' she said.

'Well, not cross,' he said. 'Upset. I know you don't approve of them.'

'It beats me why *you* do,' she said. 'I've never been one for running people down, especially my own flesh and blood, but what did they ever do for you? The minimum. I gave you a good home and was ready to earlier if asked.'

'I know. And I'm grateful.'

'I didn't do it for you to be grateful.'

'I know. But you've got to let people be grateful if they want to. So I'm going to see Auntie Doris and tell her I saw Uncle Teddy. I'm going to bring them together again.'

'Henry!'

'I'd have thought you'd have thought the marriage tie was sacred.'

'I do. But it's none of your business, is it?'

'They love each other. It's just about the only good thing about them.'

'Well, it's your life,' said Cousin Hilda.

'Yes,' said Henry. 'It is. Cousin Hilda? I've . . . er . . . I've found a flat. I'm moving in next weekend.'

Cousin Hilda sniffed. She said nothing. He felt that any remark would have been better than her silence.

'Cousin Hilda?' he said. 'I love you. I love you very much.'

Cousin Hilda sniffed.

5 Meetings in Mitherdale

As the train clattered through the stolid Airedale towns out towards the high country, Henry's spirits soared. On the southern edges of the dewy fields, banks of snow lay against the dry stone walls.

Few people got off at Troutwick. The air carried promises of spring. The breeze carried memories of winter. The sun scoffed briefly at the breeze's warnings. A few drops of rain, mocking the sun, spattered onto the frost-broken streets of the quaint, narrow, stone and whitewash town.

The White Hart stood, white-painted in a dark, stone square, facing the awnings of the Saturday Market. The AA sign, with its two stars, swung squeakily. Behind it, the eponymous beast was frozen in wary pride.

The lobby was dark and leathery, its old oak table strewn with *Country Life* and *The Field*, its notice-board plastered with news of Conservative coffee mornings. It was steeped in a feudal respectability to which neither Auntie Doris nor the slimy Geoffrey Porringer had any right.

The receptionist had been hired for her snootiness, and gave full value. 'Can I help you, sir?' she said, as if the possibility was remote and the 'sir' apocryphal.

'I 'ope so, luv,' said Henry, rediscovering the full Yorkshire tones that his southern schools had weakened. 'I'm Henry.'

'Do you have a reservation, Mr Henry?'

'No, luv. I'm not a Red Indian.'

She didn't laugh, and it *did* cross Henry's mind that this might be because it wasn't funny.

Auntie Doris emerged from the staff quarters behind the desk. She was in her mid-fifties now. Age wasn't withering her charms. It was just making it more expensive to maintain them.

'Henry!' she cried.

'Auntie Doris!'

They embraced. It was like kissing an oil painting. Her hair was blonder than ever. Henry threw the receptionist a triumphant glance, which would have been more effective if he hadn't been covered in Auntie Doris's lipstick and powder, so that he looked like a clown in a decadent thirties night-club in Berlin.

Geoffrey Porringer, sensing emotion from which he had been excluded, oozed onto the scene, clasped Henry's hands and said, 'Welcome, young sir.' Henry peeped surreptitiously at his blackheads. Still a forest of them. Excellent!

They entered the lounge bar, warm, full of antiques, bustling with measured market-day bonhomie. Auntie Doris served them, while Geoffrey Porringer sat beside him and drank.

'We'll have sandwiches this morning,' he said, 'because we're working.' We? I don't see you doing much. 'Tonight we've got the bar fully staffed, so we'll have dinner.'

Conversation with Geoffrey Porringer wasn't easy. Henry couldn't bring himself to mention Lorna, up against whom the man habitually rubbed. He asked if his old teacher, Miss Candy, still drank there. It was a shock to learn that she was dead. People like Miss Candy didn't die, any more than Matterhorns fell down. Her death made him feel sad. 'Yes, she was a good old stick,' said Geoffrey Porringer. He greeted each new arrival loudly. 'Good to see you, young sir.' 'Trust the better half's flourishing, young George?' 'Morning, Arthur. Can't make up its mind, can it?' It began to dawn on Henry that Geoffrey Porringer didn't find it easy to fill the role of mine host, and had constructed a labyrinth of verbal camouflage to protect himself. It began to dawn on him that Geoffrey Porringer hadn't wanted to be slimy, to have a nose festooned with blackheads, and that it was no more his fault than Auntie Doris's that she hadn't waited for Uncle Teddy. Perhaps his rubbing against Lorna *had* been accidental. These thoughts worried him. He'd feel the loss if he couldn't continue to hate Geoffrey Porringer. Supposing becoming a mature adult meant sympathizing with *everybody*? Henry shuddered.

Geoffrey Porringer didn't make disliking him any easier by leaping into action and doing his bit behind the bar. Conversation grew louder. Sandwiches arrived and were consumed. He must go and see Lorna. It'd be awful if, at their next meeting, she was serving him dinner.

He caught the bus to Rowth Bridge. It growled up the narrowing dale, towards the high fells, crossing and recrossing the laughing little river Mither. There were eight houses now, in the hamlet of Five Houses, where Sidney Mold lived, into whose sticky hand Henry had once dug his fingernails.

He grew nervous. What would he say to her? Did he want to take her to Kit Orris's field barn? Did he want to marry her and open her eyes to a wider world? Did he want to marry her and live in Rowth Bridge?

The bus swung past the school, past the Parish Hall, and dropped him by the hump bridge. He walked briskly towards Lorna's parents' council house.

'She's out.'

The anti-climax was shattering. She couldn't be. She had no right to be.

'Do you know where she is?'

'Could be round the Luggs.'

'Well could you give her a message? I'm staying at the White Hart. Could you ask her if she could meet me tomorrow morning? I could pick her up here round about ten.'

He wandered away. Should he call on the Luggs? He set off down the winding back lane towards their cottage. It was sur-rounded by more old cars, baths and prams than ever. He turned back abruptly, before anyone saw him. There were too many Luggs, and he particularly didn't want to see Jane, built like a rugby forward, who'd been his childhood sweetheart before Pam Yardley, who'd been his childhood sweetheart before Lorna. If Lorna was 'round the Luggs', let her remain there undisturbed.

He heard horse's hooves. Round the corner there came a magnificent creature, a real thoroughbred, perfectly groomed, highly strung, shining with health, a superb physical specimen produced by generations of careful breeding. The horse was nice too.

'It's Henry, isn't it?' The face smiled, a social smile from on high. Henry decided that he'd campaign to remove the Elgin marbles from her mouth and return them to Greece. He wished horses didn't make him uneasy, wished she wasn't so far above him, wished he could think of something better to say than

'Yes. Hello, Belinda.' He wished he wasn't nine years old again.

'Whoa, Marigold. Henry's a friend,' said Belinda Boyce-Uppingham, who had once called him an oik.

He heard a parody of himself say, 'You've become a really beautiful woman, Belinda.' Well, it'd be churlish not to admit it. He wouldn't give her the satisfaction of thinking that he was still an oik.

'What are you doing these days?' she asked.

'I'm working as a reporter on the *Thurmarsh Evening Argus*.'

'Oh. Is that . . . ?' She couldn't think of an adjective.

'Interesting?'

'Well, yes.'

'*I* think so.'

He watched her brain whirring through all the connections, seeking new subject matter.

'Have you seen Diana recently?'

He longed to say, 'Yes. We made love last weekend.' He hadn't the courage. He said, 'Yes. I saw her last week.'

'Careful, Marigold,' said Belinda Boyce-Uppingham. 'Don't frighten Henry. She's all right, Henry.'

'I'm sure she is. I'm not frightened.' Why say that, when he longed to edge away from those towering, steaming, chestnut flanks.

'Listen,' said Belinda Boyce-Uppingham, with every semblance of real friendliness. 'I have a nutty uncle near Thurmarsh. If I visit him and I can get away, will you show me the town? Are we on?'

'Yes. That'd be smashing.'

'Wonderful.'

He was getting an erection. She was so beautiful. Life was so unfair. If he made a move, would she leap off Marigold and lose her individuality with him on the muddy verge of the lane? Could he become the third D. H. Lawrence?

'Well, lovely to see you, Henry,' she said. 'I mean that. So glad you're . . . er . . .' Again, she couldn't find an adjective. What had she been searching for? Still alive? Not unemployable? Not totally physically repulsive? Getting erections at the sight of me?

When she'd gone, it was as if the light began to fade. He told himself that it wasn't her fault that she was as she was. This was awful. Supposing, in one day, he found that he didn't dislike either Geoffrey Porringer or Belinda Boyce-Uppingham? What would there be left to cling to?

He realized, to his relief, that the light really was fading from the steely winter sky. He walked over the hump bridge, past his old school, with its high Gothic windows and triangular gables. A car was approaching. He thumbed it. It sped him to Troutwick. By half past four he was asking the snooty receptionist for tea.

Auntie Doris brought it.

'Auntie Doris?' he said in a low voice. 'I want to speak to you alone.'

'Good Lord!' she said. She thought swiftly. 'Go to the Sun at six. I'll try to slip out.'

The Sun was a dark, gloomy pub near the station. Auntie Doris, wafting in on a tide of scent, seemed totally out of place. She kissed him and bought him a beer.

'Auntie Doris?' he said, when they'd settled in a dim corner near the darts board. 'I met Uncle Teddy.' He fancied that she paled, under all the make-up.

'Where?'

'In Thurmarsh. In the Shanghai Chinese Restaurant and Coffee Bar.'

'Good Lord. I . . . knew he'd come out, of course. How was he?'

'He seemed all right.'

'You talked, did you?'

'Oh yes. I . . . er . . . I was a bit drunk, though.'

'Was he . . . er . . . ?'

'There was a man with him. Derek Parsonage.'

'Never heard of him.'

'He has blackheads.'

'I'd need more to go on.'

He wished he hadn't mentioned the blackheads. Did the subject have a fatal fascination for him?

'Did he . . . er . . . say anything about me?'

'No. It didn't . . . you know . . . crop up.'

'Ah. Did he . . . er . . . say anything about . . . anybody else there might be in his life?'

'No.'

'It didn't crop up?'

'No. But . . . er . . . there is one thing.'

'Yes?'

'He's opening a night-club.'

'Oh? And?'

'Well . . . he's calling it the Cap Ferrat. I mean, he wouldn't
name it after your house and the place where you spent your
holidays if there was somebody else, would he?'

'Perhaps not.'

'Auntie Doris? I suppose none of this is my business, really,
but . . . I do love you, you know.'

'I'm not sure I did know, no.'

'Oh. Well I do.'

'I'm not sure I deserve it.'

'Well there you are. I do, anyway. And . . .' He hoped she
couldn't see his blushes. '. . . obviously I wish you'd waited for
Uncle Teddy and were still with him, because . . . you know . . .
so anyway I thought I'd tell you anyway.'

'You don't like Geoffrey very much, do you?'

'Well . . . you know.'

'I like Geoffrey very much.'

'Yes.'

'I like Teddy very much.'

'Yes.'

'Life's complicated.'

He judged it wise to leave it there. He'd sown the seed.

Auntie Doris slipped him thirty pounds.

'Don't tell Geoffrey,' she said.

They went in to dinner fairly late, after the paying customers had
ordered. The dining-room was small and unpretentious, with
whitewashed walls. There was a fine Welsh dresser covered with
good English plates. Lorna handed Henry the menu as if she'd
never seen him before.

He ordered oxtail soup and grilled lamb cutlets. Geoffrey
Porringer spent a long time choosing the claret. 'You'll like this
one, young sir,' he said, with a smile that was barely slimy at all.

The claret was nice. He thanked Lorna for his soup. He wanted to call her 'Lorna' but found it impossible. He thanked her for the lamb cutlets. He thanked her for the potatoes and the cauliflower and the carrots.

'My word, young sir, you're being very polite to our Lorna,' said Geoffrey Porringer.

'Geoffrey! Don't draw attention to it,' said Auntie Doris, who always made things worse by protesting about them. 'He knows her,' she mouthed.

At the end of the meal, Lorna caught Henry's eye and nodded. She could have saved him a lot of tension if she'd done it earlier, but he didn't blame her.

Over his bacon and fried eggs, Henry read the *Sunday Express*. An exchange of letters between Presidents Bulganin and Eisenhower was published. President Bulganin had tried to establish a 20 year American–Russian pact, which would completely ignore Great Britain. President Eisenhower rebuffed the suggestion and said that they already had such a treaty, if the Russians chose to make it work. It was called the Charter of the United Nations. In Troutwick, these sounded like voices from another world.

Geoffrey Porringer drove him to Rowth Bridge. It had rained in the night but the winter sun was breaking through, touching the great mass of Mickleborough with its faint warmth, shining palely on the glutinous fields. Henry's mind went back to the last time he had travelled this road by car, before his national service, with his three best friends, Martin Hammond, Paul Hargreaves and Stefan Prziborsky. Now he wasn't even sure if he liked Martin or Paul, and Stefan, the only Polish-born batsman ever to play cricket for Thurmarsh, had emigrated to Australia.

'What are you doing in Rowth Bridge?' Geoffrey Porringer's voice plopped dully into his nostalgic melancholy.

'Looking up an old friend.'

'Girl-friend?'

'That kind of thing.'

'Jolly good. Keep at it.'

'Yes.'

That was the kind of fatuous conversation he had with Geoffrey

Porringer. He wondered if Geoffrey Porringer suspected that the girl was Lorna.

When they reached Rowth Bridge, Geoffrey Porringer slipped him thirty pounds. 'Don't tell Doris,' he said. Only later did Henry wonder if it was hush money, because Geoffrey Porringer suspected that Lorna had told him about the rubbing against her.

'Sorry I'm late,' he said. 'I had to wait for Geoffrey Porringer.'

Lorna snorted.

They walked slowly, past the jumbled stone houses and cottages, in the watery sunshine.

He felt a stab of horror as he realized that they were approaching the church. He didn't want to run the gauntlet of the village churchgoers, holding hands with Lorna Arrow.

He tried, gently, to remove his hand. She clasped it firmly. He saw people out of the corner of his eye.

The Boyce-Uppinghams were arriving! Lorna squeezed his hand, so hard that it hurt. He could hardly wrench their hands apart. His cheeks blazed. He hoped neither Lorna nor Belinda would see his blazing cheeks. He squeezed Lorna's hand and carried on up the road. He didn't look round.

They were going towards Kit Orris's field barn. She let go of his hand, now that it no longer mattered.

It had always been wonderful, in Kit Orris's field barn. She walked straight past the gate that would have led them to the barn. Had she engineered the whole walk? Was it her revenge? He couldn't blame her.

Belinda would never contact him in Thurmarsh now. Well, he ought to be grateful to Lorna for that.

He couldn't stand the silence any more. 'I was very surprised in the hotel, when I got your note,' he said.

'Were you?' she said.

'I'm sorry about all that.'

'You were ashamed of me.'

'No. No, Lorna.'

'You were ashamed of me, just now, in front of 'er.'

'Her?'

'Bloody Belinda. You were as twined as me arse. You never could walk past 'er wi'out blushing when we were bairns.'

'Give over, Lorna. It's rubbish, is that.'

'I 'ave to go now, Henry.'

'Go?'

'I'm meeting someone.' She couldn't hide a flash of triumph.

'Oh? Who?'

'Eric Lugg.'

'Eric Lugg? He's got leave from the Cattering Corpse, has he?' He closed his eyes, as if that would wipe out his sentence.

'All right, I know I can't spell,' she said. 'I know I'm a right ignorant pig. Well so's Eric, so it's all right.'

'It isn't all right,' he said. 'Look, I'm sorry I said that. I was . . .' Upset at the thought of your slender, lovely body being pawed by a Lugg. '. . . upset. Jealous, I suppose. I mean . . . do you . . . er . . . know Eric well?'

'Course I do. He lives in t' next lane.'

'No. I mean . . . you know . . . have you been . . . out with him?'

'Sometimes.'

'While I was in the army?'

'Sometimes.'

'I see. So I was being lied to.'

'I suppose you just sat in your barracks and thought about me.'

'I never went out with another woman, Lorna. Not once.'

Lorna shrugged. 'We didn't do owt,' she said. 'Not when there was you. Yesterday was the first time.'

And he'd nearly called on them! A dreadful thought struck him.

'You didn't do it in the barn, did you?'

'Course we bloody did. It's like Piccadilly Circus in our 'ouse.'

'I wish you hadn't done it in the barn.'

'Ruddy 'ell,' said Lorna. 'You're a funny one.'

They turned back, and walked in silence. The sun had disappeared.

'It's just . . . well . . . Eric Lugg!' he said. 'Lorna! You're special. Spelling doesn't matter. Education doesn't matter. What matters is . . . you're special. Eric's a lout.'

'He's norra lout. He's a cookhouse instructor. You 'ardly know 'im, 'ow can you say 'e's a lout? 'e's a bit rough, a bit uncouth, bur . . . 'e's all right, is Eric.'

'Is that enough for you, Lorna – "all right"?'

'Bloody 'ell, Henry. I 'aven't said I'm going to *marry* 'im.'

'I should hope not.'

'I might. It's none of your bloody business anyroad. So belt up about Eric Lugg, will yer?'

She flounced off down the lane. In his mind she was already giving birth to endless Luggs while her oafish husband made coarse jokes as he taught his smelly recruits how to bang thick grey gravy onto stale meat pies.

He trudged forlornly down the lane. He was a prig. He was a snob. In his travels through the steamy jungle of the class system, he had become infected with the disease that he loathed so much.

6   A New Life

Winter returned. Thurmarsh and London recorded their coldest days for sixty years. Cousin Hilda's stove roared and crackled.

The national papers reported the warmth and friendliness of the big cold world. After three days of talks President Eisenhower and Mr Anthony Eden declared their complete agreement over the Middle East. They supported Colonel Nasser – for the immediate future, at any rate. In Cyprus, the Governor had friendly talks with Archbishop Makarios. Britain's offer of self-government was expected to be accepted. Archbishop Makarios favoured the ending of terrorism in exchange for an amnesty.

Life was less cheery in Cousin Hilda's small, hot basement, as Henry worked his way through his last six days. He craved the company of his friends in the Lord Nelson. He longed to track down Uncle Teddy. But no. He would be devoted to Cousin Hilda that week. *Fabian of Scotland Yard, The Grove Family, The Burns and Allen Show, Forces' Requests.* If it was on, they watched it, though Cousin Hilda drew the line at *Travellers Tales – Pygmies of the Congo.* 'What's the use of watching pygmies?' she said. 'I'm never likely to see a pygmy.' Henry bit back his reply of, 'Well, this is your chance, then.'

On Monday evening – liver and bacon and rhubarb crumble – he asked Barry Frost, 'Have the Operatic decided what to devote their talents to next?' Barry Frost replied, gruffly, as if suspecting sarcasm, 'Yes. *No, No, Nanette.*'

On Tuesday evening – roast lamb and his last spotted dick *for ever* – he asked Norman Pettifer, 'Are we getting a run on Danish Blue this week?' Norman Pettifer replied, coolly, as if suspecting sarcasm, 'No. It's an extraordinarily average week this week.' Henry said, 'Good Lord! So average, you mean, as to defy the law of averages? That is extraordinary.'

On Wednesday evening – toad-in-the-hole and sponge pudding with chocolate sauce – Barry Frost was subdued. Henry said, 'Is everything all right, Barry?' 'No, everything is not all right. She's broken it off, because I've accepted the lead in *No, No, Nanette*,' said Barry Frost. After the meal, Henry knocked on Barry's door and said, 'Are you all right? I've got my first shorthand lesson tonight, but we could meet afterwards for a drink.' 'Thanks. You're a pal. But no. I've got to face this thing on my own,' said Barry Frost.

On Thursday evening – roast pork and tinned pears – Norman Pettifer was subdued. 'Is everything all right?' Henry asked. Having found a useful formula, he saw no reason to alter it in the interests of so-called conversational glitter. 'They've removed me from the cheese counter,' said Norman Pettifer. There was a stunned silence, into which Henry's 'Oh dear' plopped pathetically. 'Mr McConnon was very nice about it. He had me into his office. "Norman," he said. "This is no reflection on you, but change is the bedrock from which the seeds of our success flower. Young Adrian is a lucky lad to inherit what you've built up."' 'I'm really sorry, Norman. Where are they moving you to?' said Henry. 'General groceries. You know what that boils down to, don't you? Tins,' said Norman Pettifer, with withering scorn.

On Friday evening – battered cod and jam roly poly – Barry Frost was pensive. 'You're pensive, Barry,' said Henry. 'I've resigned from *No, No, Nanette*. Candice has won,' said Barry Frost.

On Saturday, February 4th, an MP warned of the 200,000 elderly who were falling behind the rising standard of living, Ivy Benson spoke of the problems her women's band faced from marriage – 'In one year, I lost three trombones' – the thaw brought hundreds of burst pipes, and Henry reported on his first football match. It was Rawlaston v Ossett Town in Division One of the Yorkshire League.

Unfortunately he had to phone his report through ten minutes before the end, when there were still no goals. 'It was end-to-end stuff in this tense relegation battle at sodden Scuffley Park,' he enthused. 'The "Grinders" created the better chances, but had nobody to take advantage of Macauley's speed. Ossett's powder-puff attack, sluggishly led by Deakins, rarely threatened a staunch Rawlaston rearguard, ably marshalled by the immaculate Linnet.'

His awards were 'Entertainment 6, Effort 8. Man of the Match –
Linnet.' Later he phoned through the result. 'Rawlaston 0, Ossett
Town 2. Goals: Linnet (own goal), Deakins.'

On Sunday morning, at the end of breakfast, he held out his hand
to Liam. 'Goodbye, Liam. And . . . good luck.'

'The same to you, Mr Henry,' said Liam O'Reilly.

'Goodbye, Norman. Sorry about the . . . er . . .'

'I'll get over it,' said Norman Pettifer.

'Goodbye, Barry. Good luck with the nuptials.'

'Yes, well . . .' said Barry Frost. 'We'll see. Whatever will be,
will be.'

'You could make a song of that,' said Henry, and immediately
wished he hadn't.

He went upstairs, converted his bed into a sofa for the last time,
packed his puny collection of clothes, his photo of Len Hutton,
his one shelf of books by Kafka, Evelyn Waugh, Henry Miller and
Captain W. E. Johns, and went down to say goodbye to Cousin
Hilda. His mouth was dry.

'Well . . . thank you very much for everything, Cousin Hilda,'
he said. 'I've been very happy here.'

Cousin Hilda sniffed.

'No,' he said. 'I have. But I can't live off the family for
ever.'

'What are families for?' said Cousin Hilda.

For getting away from.

'I'm not going to be far away,' said Henry. 'You must come to
tea, and I'll come and see you regularly.'

Cousin Hilda sniffed.

'We'll see,' she said.

Ginny welcomed him with a self-conscious smile, a Lancashire
hot-pot and a bottle of robust red wine. Her flat had the same
layout as his but without the French windows. They ate in the tiny
kitchen. She'd laid a red check cloth over the formica-topped
table. He washed up. She dried and put away. He put his arms
round her. His hands tingled at her soft and ample splendour. He
said, 'What about a bit of hanky-panky? I believe the feller

downstairs is out.' She removed his hands gently but firmly and said, 'I think it might be better if we were strictly platonic, now we're house-mates, don't you?' 'Fair enough,' he said. There was plenty of time. 'Can I take you for a nice, platonic drink this evening?' She said, 'I'm going out this evening.'

At 3.22 he began unpacking. At 3.29 he finished unpacking. He listened to *Take It From Here*, *Melody Hour*, *Hancock's Half Hour*, and *Victor Sylvester*. He fell asleep during *Question Time*, unfortunately missing four celebrities exchanging ideas with young hill farmers from Breconshire. He woke to hear Jack Payne saying it with music. At 7.49 he went to the Winstanley. He had three pints of bitter. Nobody spoke to him. They were all in little cliques. He'd never seen such an absurdly self-satisfied lot. They laughed uproariously at jokes that weren't remotely funny. They were cretins. It was a privilege to go home and leave them.

Home? He hadn't even bought any tea or coffee. He was totally unprepared.

During *Grand Hotel*, with Jean Pougnet and the Palm Court Orchestra, he heard the front door slam. Was it her? Could he cadge some coffee and bread?

He heard a man's voice say, very distinctly, 'Neutral territory. Berlin wall.' She'd brought Gordon Carstairs back!

He listened to *Java, Land of the Moonlight Orchid*, in which Nina Epton described a visit to that magical country.

They were making love! He turned up the volume, till Nina Epton was shouting.

He went to bed. He lay there, wide awake, lonely, hungry, in his cramped room. And they began again! It dawned on him that he wasn't going to get much sleep that night. It dawned on him that Podgy Sex Bomb Henry, who had thought himself so precociously successful with older women, wasn't actually doing very well. He'd been toyed with by Helen Cornish. He'd lost Lorna Arrow and Ginny Fenwick. That only left Diana Hargreaves. He'd better make sure of her before he lost her too.

At last Ginny and Gordon stopped. Gordon went home. Henry fell asleep at 4.17. At 6.38 he woke up. A man who was vaguely familiar had been telling him, in thirty blindingly simple words, the secret of life and how to conduct it. He couldn't remember any of it.

The world grew colder. Ominous headlines poured off the presses. The big freeze returns. After the bursts, the frozen pipes. 'Flick Knife' Teds terrorize teachers. Housewives flee Cypriot rioters. Tear-gas used in Algiers uproar. British military police kill Cypriot youth.

There were headlines on Henry's stories too. Chiropodist breaks foot! Man, 83, falls out of bed. Found cuff-link after 42 years.

The early part of Henry's evenings was spent in the Lord Nelson. The middle of the evenings was spent in the Globe and Artichoke, the Devonshire, the Pigeon and Two Cushions. The last part of the evenings was spent in the Shanghai Chinese Restaurant and Coffee Bar, where he hoped to meet Uncle Teddy again, but didn't. How he longed to sit in peace and warmth and watch television with Cousin Hilda. He even looked forward to his second shorthand lesson.

Every evening, shortly before midnight, a gurgling mass of beer and monosodium glutamate arrived back at a home that was no home, and lay awake, marvelling at the virility of Gordon Carstairs. By Thursday night, even Gordon Carstairs was exhausted.

On Wednesday evening Henry telephoned Paul, who was surprisingly friendly and would love to see him that weekend, as would Diana. Henry got so excited that he forgot to go to his second shorthand lesson.

On Friday lunch-time, dreaming of Diana in the Rundle Café while pretending not to be listening to the cautionary tale of Gertrude the Greedy Guinea-Pig, he heard an enormous crash. After about a minute he remembered that he was a journalist, and rushed out.

A lorry had hurtled, just down Rundle Prospect, into the tiny Old Apothecary's House, whose delicate flint and stone dated back to the early fifteenth century. The lorry was jammed into the gaping mouth of the building like a cuckoo being fed by a wren.

The driver was sitting on the pavement, dazed with shock.

Henry sat beside him diffidently. He felt shy of intruding into the man's trauma with his tactless notebook. But the man seemed to want to get everything off his chest. Must get all the facts. Name, age, address. Dave Nasenby (29), of Rawlaston Road, Splutt. Occupation? 'Lorry driver, of course.' Stupid! He was driving along, he braked hard to avoid a cat, he skidded on a patch of ice, lost control, he was going towards two nuns, it was the nuns or the building, he swerved, he just had time to leap out, he'd left it so late that he scraped himself all along the wall. He showed Henry his abrasions. Henry winced. It was a pity the nuns had disappeared, but with his present luck they'd probably have been Trappists anyway.

He caught the London train in good humour, blissfully unaware that the story which was streaming off the Thurmarsh presses began 'A lorry driver had a miraculous escape today when he crashed into Thurmarsh's oldest historical landmark rather than hit two buns.'

The smells of an elegant dinner were drifting delicately around the hall of the Hargreaveses' home. 'Henry! So good to see you so soon,' said Mrs Hargreaves, and he couldn't detect a trace of sarcasm.

'Henry!' Mr Hargreaves was also extremely pleased to see him. Henry was beginning to get worried. 'Dry sherry?'

'Please.'

'Henry!' Paul was extremely friendly too. What had happened? He soon found out. He was no longer a threat.

She entered with a companion who was preceded by a wall of after-shave – still quite a rarity in the smelly fifties.

'Hello, Henry,' she said. 'Lovely to see you again so soon. I think you know my fiancé.'

Henry found himself staring at the large, smiling, indecently clean-shaven moon-face of Tosser Pilkington-Brick.

7 The Opening of the Cap Ferrat

Almost five years after they had disappeared from the Foreign Office, Guy Burgess and Donald Maclean turned up in Moscow. The blizzards returned. The trade gap widened to £74 million. The Football League, alarmed by falling gates, proposed a major reorganization, with four divisions. Malta voted 3–1 in favour of integration with Britain. There were many attacks on Britons in Cyprus.

Several times on his calls, Henry had made a detour to see if he could find Uncle Teddy on the site of the Cap Ferrat, in Malmesbury Street, between Fish Hill and Canal View. This was an area of small, slowly decaying streets and culs-de-sac, sloping damply from the east of the town centre towards the river and the canal. The Cap Ferrat was being converted out of a once-elegant little Regency terrace, which it shared with the Mandarin Fish Bar and the Thurmarsh Joke Emporium and Magic Shop.

On the afternoon of Wednesday, February 15th, Henry found Uncle Teddy. In daylight, he could see that his experience of prison had left a mask of wariness on Uncle Teddy's big, bluff face. His carefully styled crinkly hair was flecked with grey. His dark suit and sober shirt would have given him the respectability on which he had spent so much money, if they hadn't looked so obviously expensive.

Uncle Teddy ushered him out of the building. 'I don't want anyone seeing it till it's finished,' he said. 'It's tight, but we'll make it for Tuesday. I just hope this snow clears. Snow and night life are contradictions in terms.'

'Can we talk somewhere quiet in private?' said Henry.

They walked through the town centre, between mounds of swept snow, and went for afternoon tea in Davy's. Uncle Teddy was like an estranged father, giving his son an uneasy weekly treat.

'I've been looking for you everywhere,' said Henry.

'I've been in France,' said Uncle Teddy. 'Picking up last-minute items. All genuine stuff.'

Uncle Teddy ordered tea for two, and toasted teacake. The waitress had a bunion. The place was full of women who worked all day cooking and cleaning for husbands who got home tired and didn't want to talk. Afternoon tea, while shopping, was a rare chance to rest over-used feet and exercise under-used vocal chords.

'This isn't quiet,' said Henry.

'It's private,' said Uncle Teddy. 'In quiet places you're overheard.'

Henry wasn't sure how to begin. So he started with something else.

'I'm sorry I was rude about Derek Parsonage,' he said.

'Why did you say he was a Geoffrey Porringer substitute?'

'It was just the blackheads.'

'Blackheads?'

'They both have blackheads.'

'Good Lord. Do they?'

'Uncle Teddy! You can't not have noticed. Their noses are festooned with them.'

'I hadn't.'

Is it just me? thought Henry. Is that my real identity? Henry 'Obsessed by blackheads' Pratt?

'I'm sorry,' he said. 'I shouldn't be rude about your friends.'

'Geoffrey Porringer's hardly my friend, Henry.'

A perfect cue. Too perfect?

The waitress brought their tea. 'Teacakes'll be a minute, but we're that busy and we've one grill out of action for maintenance,' she announced.

'Shall I be mother?' said Henry's surrogate father.

'How have you got the money for the Cap Ferrat?' said Henry. 'It must be costing a packet.'

Uncle Teddy touched the side of his nose. Henry wondered if, in shady businessmen's secret societies, they touched *each other*'s noses. Perhaps that was how blackheads were transmitted. Stop thinking about blackheads!

The tea was very strong.

'They use soda,' said Uncle Teddy. 'To make it go further. They save on tea.'

'But spend on soda,' said Henry.

'It's better than bromide,' said Uncle Teddy.

'Did they put bromide in the tea in . . .' The waitress arrived with their teacake. '. . . Rangoon?'

'Sorry about that,' she said. 'He says they're a bit burnt, it's his first day on his own, he's scraped them, but I can take them back if you want.'

'No, no,' said Uncle Teddy. 'Carbon's good for you.'

'I never have liked my teacakes rare,' said Henry.

Uncle Teddy smiled indulgently. 'Could you get something in the paper about the opening?' he said, when the puzzled waitress had gone.

'Damn! *I* should have asked *you* that,' said Henry. 'But I hate using my friends and relations for my work. I'm just not ruthless enough.'

'Too soft.' Uncle Teddy nodded his agreement sympathetically.

'Exactly. I should have been asking you if you'd be my contact from the shady underworld.'

'Henry!'

'Sorry, Uncle Teddy. I didn't mean . . . I meant . . . from the world of the night. The world that wakes up when the rest of us go to sleep.'

'I like that,' said Uncle Teddy. He lowered his voice un-necessarily, amid all the chatter and rattle of cups. 'I've failed you,' he said. 'I suppose you despise me.'

'Actually, I don't seem to,' said Henry. 'I think maybe I'm fatally fascinated by evil.'

'Thank you, Henry.'

'Oh, sorry, Uncle Teddy. I didn't . . . oh heck.'

'Well come on, then,' said Uncle Teddy. 'What's all this about? As if I couldn't guess. You've seen Doris, haven't you?'

'Well, yes, I . . . I see them occasionally.'

'Them? So she and Geoffrey are still cohabiting.'

'Yes. They're still . . . cohabiting.'

'Still running the hotel, are they?'

'Yes.'

'Doing well?'

'I think so.'

115

'What a relief.'

'Uncle Teddy, I . . . I've talked to Auntie Doris.'

'Very wise. It'd have been rude not to.'

'No. You know. Talked. About you.'

'Would you like fancies?' said the waitress.

'Yes, we'll have a selection,' said Uncle Teddy.

'I don't think . . . you know . . . she's entirely happy with Mr Porringer,' said Henry.

'It's hard to imagine that anybody could be.'

'I know. But I think it's . . . you know . . . more than that.'

The waitress brought a plate of cakes and said, 'Go on! Be sinful!'

'Have the éclair,' said Uncle Teddy.

'I don't want the éclair,' said Henry. 'I want the pink, square one. It looks so boring, like the last evacuee in a church hall. I'll put it out of its misery.'

Uncle Teddy shook his head. It was beyond his comprehension that anyone could be so soft as to have sympathy for under-privileged cakes.

'More than that?' he said.

'She said . . . she liked you very much. She said . . . life's very complicated. I mean, Uncle Teddy, if there . . . you know . . . if there's . . . somebody else, just tell me.'

'There's nobody else,' said Uncle Teddy. 'Not in that way. Not at the moment.'

'Would you think it possible you could ever have her back?'

Uncle Teddy picked up a chocolate truffle and examined it as if seeking an answer to the mysteries of molecular structure. Then he smiled, and gave Henry thirty pounds.

'Don't tell Doris or Geoffrey,' he said. 'Or the sniffer.'

English and French celebrities will toast each other in champagne next Tuesday night, when the glamour and glitter of mediterranean life come to brighten up those cold Thurmarsh nights.

Yes! Thurmarsh's very first night-club – the Cap Ferrat – will be opening its doors in Malmesbury Street.

The Cap Ferrat is the brain-child of Mr Edward 'Teddy'

Braithwaite, handsome 55 year-old Thurmarsh industrialist and entrepreneur, who has recently returned to Yorkshire after a five-year 'stint' in Rangoon.

'My aim is to mix good old down-to-earth Yorkshire warmth and meaty grit with a bit of French sauce, that Gallic oo-ta-ta sophistication,' muses Mr Braithwaite, a former pupil at Doncaster Road Secondary School.

He adds: 'Of course it will be a bit naughty, but all good clean family fun. We aim to create a venue where Mr and Mrs Thurmarsh can relax from the cares of helping to build Britain's post-war revival. Not everyone can go to France, so we're bringing France to Thurmarsh.'

Everything – food, wines, décor, even crockery – will be the genuine article. 'I've scoured the Côte d'Azur, spent weeks there, just to make sure Thurmarsh gets the best,' says Mr Braithwaite.

Among the celebrities invited to join in the 'first night' festivities are Michael Venison, Dulcie Crab, Richard Murdoch, Kenneth Horne, Gwen Catley, Maurice Chevalier, Danielle Darrieux and Mr Frank Carnforth, Mayor of Thurmarsh.

'It should be quite a fight,' opines Mr Braithwaite.

'Mr Skipton?' said Henry. 'Could I have a word?'

'What is it?'

'These misprints in this story. I think they're deliberate.'

'Misprints do happen,' said Terry Skipton, 'even on papers like this.'

'Venison *and* Crab seems unlikely. "Fight" instead of "night" is pretty embarrassing. And "oo-ta-ta" instead of "oo-la-la". French sauce. Ta-ta. Tartare sauce. Somebody's playing clever buggers.'

'You're letting your imagination run away with you,' said Terry Skipton.

The pound rose to 2 dollars 81 cents. The price of bread and milk rose as food subsidies were reduced by £38 million. President Eisenhower played golf for the first time since his heart attack in September.

The icy roads were the worst in living memory. The Thames froze at Windsor. The weather prevented the attendance at the Cap Ferrat of Michael Venison, Dulcie Crab, Richard Murdoch, Kenneth Horne, Gwen Catley, Maurice Chevalier and Danielle Darrieux.

A concern for civic dignity prevented the attendance of Mr Frank Carnforth, Mayor of Thurmarsh.

Mr Andrew Redrobe, editor of the *Thurmarsh Evening Argus*, had also declined to attend. His presence might have offended the churches, and he prided himself on having a good relationship with the churches.

Among those who struggled and slithered into Malmesbury Street on the night of February 21st, 1956, were Henry 'Obsessed by blackheads' Pratt; Derek 'Festooned with blackheads' Parsonage; Ted Plunkett and his attractive fiancée, Helen Cornish; Gordon Carstairs and his companion, lusty future war correspondent Ginny Fenwick; Denzil Ackerman, elegant metropolitan sophisticate; ace sports reporter Ben Watkinson and his shy, petite wife, Cynthia; the second D. H. Lawrence; and the Voice of Common Sense, alias 'Thurmarshian', Neil Mallet.

Also present were Bill Holliday, scrap merchant, used-car dealer, greyhound owner and gambler, who was accompanied by Miss Angela Groyne, a buxom red-haired model; Chief Superintendent Ron Ratchett, who was accompanied by his notebook; and Sergeant Botney, of the Royal Corps of Signals, who had travelled down from Catterick Camp in the company of his grim-faced wife to celebrate their wedding anniversary in a manner more sophisticated than could be managed by the Sergeants' Mess, the Naafi or Toc H. They'd left the girls in the care of Mrs Botney's mother.

The revellers sat at traditional southern French tables in a large, low-ceilinged, smoky room lit by the dim red light of impending sin. On the platform, beyond a dance floor that was slightly too small, Alphonso Boycott and his Northern Serenaders were playing slightly naughty dance tunes slightly naughtily. Meals were served by big-busted French waitresses, dressed in white blouses the size of large pocket handkerchieves, black skirts the size of small pocket handkerchieves, and black stockings.

Sergeant Botney smiled uneasily at Mrs Botney. There was a choice of traditional Provençal steak in a watery, timidly garlicky tomato sauce or traditional Provençal chicken in a watery, timidly garlicky tomato sauce, or plain grilled steak or chicken, served with traditional Provençal chips. The journalists, seated at a large table at the back of the room, ate gratis, courtesy of the management.

The champagne and the medium-sweet white wine flowed. The dim light was dimmed still further, and a disembodied voice announced, 'It's cabaret time. Let's hear it from Monsieur Emile.'

Monsieur Emile told them that he was from Gay Paree, but that Gay Paree would have to look to its laurels because the world would soon be talking about Gay Thurmarsh. 'Under ze bridges of Thurmarsh vith you,' he crooned briefly and, since the laughter was a bit thin, he thickened it with some guffaws of his own.

There was a roll of drums.

'Ladies and gentlemen,' said Monsieur Emile. 'I now introduce, vith great pleasure, ze Cap Ferrat's resident dancing girls, all born vairy close to ze coast of France, and bringing a touch of ze Gallic sun and ze Gallic beaches to your town. Ladies and gentlemen, ze Côte d'Azur Cuties!'

Ze four Côte d'Azur Cuties danced vivaciously, with long-legged athleticism and perfect synchronization, that effective substitute for artistry.

There was a roll of drums.

'Ladies and gentlemen,' said Monsieur Emile. 'I now introduce, vith great pleasure, ze Cap Ferrat's resident singer, ze legendary Martine. Need I say more?' He continued hurriedly before any-body could shout 'yes'. 'Ladies and gentlemen, ze legendary Martine.'

Ze legendary Martine sang in a loud, deep, throbbing, harsh, sexy, passionate, smoky, wine-sodden Gallic growl.

'She's like a cross between Marlene Dietrich and Edith Piaf,' said Ted.

'It's a cross we're just going to have to bear,' said Denzil.

Henry hardly heard any of this. He was aware only of what had to be done.

Monsieur Emile announced an interval. He hoped that everyone would dance. Henry sighed deeply.

'All right, kid?' said Colin.

'Yes,' said Henry, irritated. 'Stop trying to protect me.'

He walked slowly towards Sergeant Botney's table. His old sergeant was another of those who looked smaller than Henry had remembered. In fact, his wife looked more fearsome than he did. Henry hesitated. All the pressures of social convention were against him. His respect for good manners shrieked its disapproval. But they'd all sworn that, if ever any of them came upon the rotten sadistic bastard in civvy street, they'd do him. But, then again, it had all been a long time ago. Why not forget it, tonight of all nights?

Because of Burbage.

Because there is a ghost that has to be laid.

Because the Sergeant Botneys of this world get away with it precisely because we allow social conventions to constrain us. We hide behind them, in our weakness and apathy.

'It's Sergeant Botney, isn't it?'

'Yes.' Sergeant Botney looked surprised, but not alarmed. His skin was leathery. Any expression there might have been in his eyes was carefully hidden.

'I'm Signalman Pratt. You don't remember me, do you? Perhaps you'll remember this better. 22912547.'

'Well . . . hello, Pratt. This is my wife, Mrs Botney.'

'Hello, Mrs Botney.'

'Hello.' Unfriendly. Not surprising, really.

'I . . . er . . . I was in your hut, sergeant.'

'So, what are you doing now, Pratt?'

'I'm a newspaper reporter.'

'Well done, lad!'

'Thanks.'

'Where did you get to in your service, then? Make some good pals, did you? Met some good oppos?'

'Oh yes. Great pals. Smashing oppos.'

'Well done, lad.'

'I've never forgotten that first night, sarge. You showed us how to make bed-packs. We made bed-packs. You said they were terrible. You threw them out of the window. It was raining. They landed on wet flower-beds. We fetched them. You said "Lights out." We made our wet dirty beds in the dark at one o'clock in the morning.'

'Let's dance, Lionel,' said Mrs Botney.

'In a moment, dear. Let's hear the lad out.'

'We used to have to paint the coal white,' said Henry. 'We used to have to paint black lines on the floor with boot polish so as to line our beds up, and then we had to wash every trace of the boot polish off.'

'Yes, I was hard,' said Sergeant Botney. 'Hard but fair. "You play ball with me, I'll play ball with you" was my motto.' He produced the cliché as if it were an epigram that he had been honing for hours.

'We spent hours spooning our great rough boots with hot spoons, Mrs Botney,' said Henry. 'Jenkins was the best. You said you wanted all our boots to shine like that, so you could see your face in them. And, since it wouldn't be fair for Jenkins to be idle while we worked, you scratched two lines on Jenkins's boots and made him start again.'

'Stop him, Lionel,' said Mrs Botney.

'Please, Margery,' said Sergeant Botney. 'Leave the lad to me. I'm not frightened of him.' He turned back to Henry. 'It was our job, laddie, to train you so that in war you'd obey orders automatically, however stupid they were.'

'And you did that,' said Henry, 'by giving us stupid orders, so that in all of us except the very stupid the question constantly arose "Is this a stupid order?" And every stupid order we obeyed, we obeyed with more resentment. Supposing every order we ever got had been sensible and justifiable? Don't you think we might have learnt to obey orders better out of respect for those giving the orders?'

'My job was to make a man of you,' said Sergeant Botney. 'I did a good job. That's why you can stand up to me now. Well done, lad.'

'Oh yes, you're not stupid, sergeant. That's why it's all so inexcusable, you sadistic bastard.'

'Now look here . . .' Sergeant Botney leapt up. Mrs Botney

tried to speak. Sergeant Botney silenced her with a look. 'This is our wedding anniversary, lad. 'Nuff said, I think.'

Yes. Not the time. Social convention. Social convention? There aren't any social conventions for Burbage.

'No. Sorry,' said Henry. 'But I was the one who found him, you see.'

'Found him?'

'You don't even remember, do you? Burbage. The late Signalman Burbage.'

Sergeant Botney went pale.

'He hanged himself in the ablutions in our hut, Mrs Botney,' said Henry.

'Stop him, Lionel. I don't want to hear,' said Mrs Botney.

'You didn't make a man out of Burbage, did you?' said Henry.

'I've had enough of this,' snapped Sergeant Botney. 'I'm going to fetch the management.'

'That's all the authority you ever had,' shouted Henry. 'The authority to fetch a higher authority.'

But Sergeant Botney was already out of hearing, separated from them by the pseudo-Gallic strains of Alphonso Boycott and his Northern Serenaders. He strode furiously across the dance floor, parting the dancers like a Red Sea.

'I'm sorry about your wedding anniversary, Mrs Botney,' said Henry.

'Sorry!' Mrs Botney's face was a limestone crag. Peregrines could have nested on her forehead without looking out of place.

'Burbage's death came at a very inconvenient time, too,' said Henry. 'Right at the beginning of his manhood. You'll get over this upset soon enough. Burbage never really got over his death. It seemed to knock all the stuffing out of him.'

Sergeant Botney returned with Uncle Teddy.

'Henry!' said Uncle Teddy.

'You know this boy?' said Sergeant Botney.

'He's my uncle,' said Henry. 'And he knows how distressing it is to come upon people hanging in lavatories. He found my father. Right. I've said all I have to say. I'm sorry I had to do it, Uncle Teddy.'

He hurried away, on legs that were suddenly weak. He was

shaking with the enormity of what he had done. And also with the puniness of it. What had he achieved? He felt flat, depressed. The music sounded very far away. Ben Watkinson was approaching, with his shy, petite wife Cynthia.

'Are you all right?' said Ben. 'You look as if you've seen a ghost.'

'It's funny you should say that,' said Henry. 'I've been trying to lay one. What did you do in the War, Ben?'

'I was a conscientious objector,' said Ben. 'I worked down the mines.' He blushed scarlet. Cynthia took his hand and pressed it with defiant sympathy.

Henry's mouth fell open. He was astonished to find that Ben, who had never discussed feelings or ideals, or indeed anything except football, could have felt so strongly, could have been so brave, and could now be so embarrassed, as if ashamed. He closed his mouth rapidly, in case Ben realized that he was realizing how much more there was to Ben than he had realized. He felt embarrassed at witnessing Ben's embarrassment. He hoped that, in the red light, Ben would think that Henry hadn't noticed him blushing. He wished Ben were a woman, so that he could kiss him. He wished it wasn't so difficult for an Anglo-Saxon male to express deep platonic affection for another Anglo-Saxon male. He wished this revelation hadn't come when he had dipped so deep into his store of social courage. He moved on towards the journalists' table. He longed to sit down. But Gordon had gone to get drinks, and Ginny hurried over to him.

'I wanted a word,' she said.

They stood with their backs to the table, watching the townsfolk moving, with varying degrees of style, to the strains of Alphonso Boycott and his Northern Serenaders. Colin was being flamboyant with an extremely glamorous young lady.

'I suppose you've heard me . . . er . . . us . . . er . . .' began Ginny.

'. . . throwing yourselves around your bed in orgies of sexual excitement? Yes.'

'Oh Lord. I . . . er . . . I hope it hasn't . . .'

'. . . kept me awake, wallowing in loneliness and frustration, night after agonizing night?'

'Oh Lord. I'm sorry. It can't be a very nice welcome to your new

123

flat. But . . . you see . . . the thing is . . . I've never had anything like this. I can't give it up.'

'Of course not. Sex makes us all totally selfish. Look at me.'

'Quite.'

'What?'

'Sorry. Anyway, his wife'll be back soon.'

'Wife??'

'Didn't you know?'

'No. Mind you, he may have told me without my understanding.'

'He is a bit obscure till you crack the code. She's away for three weeks, with the children. After that it'll all be over except for occasional hurried daytime trysts. Unless he leaves her. He says he will. Anyway, I wanted to talk to you.'

'Well, thanks, Ginny. It'll make me feel a lot better tonight when I . . .'

'. . . hear us going at it like rabbits.'

'Yes.'

'Oh Lord.'

Gordon returned. Ginny moved away from Henry as casually as she could. Again, Henry tried to sit down. But Neil Mallet was approaching, with the air of a man bent on a tête-à-tête.

'I want to mark your card,' said Neil, leading him away from the table.

'Oh?'

'I think you . . . like Ginny, and I think she . . . likes you. So I just wanted to say that I don't think you should give up hope. That's all.'

'Well . . . thank you, but . . .'

'On what do I base my optimism?' Neil was having to shout, to be heard above the music. 'Just my powers of observation. You see, Henry, a) I don't believe Gordon loves her or will ever leave his wife for her and b) I don't think she loves him. She's on the rebound.'

'The rebound?'

'She's been deeply in love. She's been badly hurt. I don't blame Helen. She can't help being fatally attractive.'

Helen? Could he mean . . . ?

'She's seen this man she loves lose interest in her the moment Helen came on the scene.'

He did mean . . . but . . . had Ginny loved him?

'But there was nothing to all that with Helen,' he lied.

'What do you mean? They're engaged.'

Henry tried to pretend that he'd thought Neil had meant Ted all along.

'Well, yes,' he said. 'I know . . . but . . .' He was floundering. And he wasn't fooling Neil.

'You thought I meant you?' he said. He almost laughed, then touched Henry's arm affectionately. 'Ginny and Ted were engaged,' he said.

'I'm out of my depth.'

'Not with me here to guide you.'

'Why should you do that?'

'I don't make friends easily, and I know how difficult it can be when you join a new group,' said Neil.

At last Henry managed to arrive back at the journalists' table. He collapsed in an exhausted heap. He felt awful. He knew nothing about life. How could he have presumed to tell Sergeant Botney anything?

And there *were* Sergeant Botney and his bristling spouse, marching out, and . . . oh god . . . they were in step! Henry examined the traditional southern French table-cloth as if he were a buyer whose career depended on his assessment of it. When he looked up, the Botneys had gone, and Colin Edgeley was sliding into the seat beside him.

'Why do I have this fatal impulse towards self-destruction?' said Colin, with a histrionic sigh.

'What are you talking about, Colin?'

'I've just put my life in danger.'

'Give over, you daft twat.'

'You think I'm exaggerating?'

'I think you always exaggerate.'

'Not this time. I've danced with the voluptuous Angela Groyne.'

'Is that her name? She's quite something.'

'She's Bill Holliday's girl-friend.'

'Bill Holliday?'

'Scrap king of the Rundle Valley. Leader of the Thurmarsh Mafia. Rich. Powerful. Evil.'

'So?'

'I've danced with his girl-friend. He's possessive to the point of mania.'

'How do you know?'

'She told me. He won't even let her see her girl-friends, in case she meets their boy-friends. I'm a dead man, Henry.'

'Don't be stupid, Colin. Thurmarsh isn't Chicago.'

'It isn't Tunbridge Wells either. Still, I can look after myself.' Colin produced a knife from his pocket. 'I'm prepared, and not like a boy scout.'

'Are you serious, Colin?'

'This is a tough old world, Henry.' He flung a painful burst of lifelong friendship across Henry's shoulders. Later, Henry would remember Colin's words.

The floor show resumed. Henry thought he was watching it, but afterwards he could remember nothing except the climax, when the legendary Martine and the Côte d'Azur Cuties joined in an increasingly sexy finale.

There were gasps as it became clear that the girls were going to strip. Was Thurmarsh ready for this? What would the wives of bank managers and managing directors think? This wasn't a sleazy stag night. Had Uncle Teddy gone too far? Henry suffered agonies of shame and fear, as the girls slowly removed their top hats, their white gloves, their black stockings. They whisked off their traditional mediterranean dresses with almost indecent haste. Chief Superintendent Ron Ratchett whistled so loudly that two councillors thought it was a signal for a police raid, and left hurriedly.

Then, when Martine and the Cuties were down to their bras and panties, they turned into five Edith Piafs, and regretted nothing. Thurmarsh didn't know whether it regretted or was relieved, and applauded loudly to hide its confusion. Several balloons descended from the ceiling.

They sat with a bottle of champagne, the three of them, in the deserted, smoky room. Uncle Teddy, Henry and Derek Parsonage.

'I'm sorry about . . . er . . .' mumbled Henry.

'I think we can afford giving their money back to Sergeant and Mrs Botney,' said Uncle Teddy.

'Yes. The omens look good,' said Derek Parsonage.

'I hate that kind of systematic petty sadism under the excuse of authority. You must have come across a lot of that, Uncle Teddy,' said Henry. 'In Rangoon,' he added hurriedly.

'The oriental mind is different to ours,' said Derek Parsonage. 'Well, what did you think of it all, Henry?'

Henry couldn't bring himself to say that he'd liked it. Why did everything Uncle Teddy do have to be to some degree a con?

'Were the Côte d'Azur Cuties really French?' he asked.

'No. Nobody said they were,' said Uncle Teddy.

'Monsieur Emile did.'

'No,' said Derek Parsonage. 'He said they were born close to the French coast. They were. In Folkestone.'

'Their real name is the Kent Hoppers,' said Uncle Teddy.

'Clever,' said Derek Parsonage.

'Is Monsieur Emile French?' said Henry.

'Oh yes,' said Uncle Teddy. 'But he isn't from Gay Paree. He's from Gay Charlesville-Mexières.'

'But it doesn't have the same ring,' said Derek Parsonage.

'What about the legendary Martine?'

'She's French, she's called Martine, but she isn't legendary,' said Uncle Teddy.

Uncle Teddy and Derek Parsonage laughed. Henry didn't.

'Don't sit there with the weight of the world's shortcomings on your shoulders,' said Uncle Teddy. 'It'll destroy you.'

'It's show business,' said Derek Parsonage. 'What is show business but illusion?'

When Derek Parsonage had gone home to bed, Uncle Teddy poured the rest of the bottle.

'Oh dear oh dear,' he said.

'Sorry,' said Henry.

They sat in exhausted silence.

'I'm grateful to national service,' said Henry. He couldn't leave it alone that night. 'It's shown me how cruel people in positions of authority can be if their attitudes get any kind of nod from a higher authority.'

'Yes . . . well . . . I can see that you feel the need to justify your extraordinary behaviour,' said Uncle Teddy.

Henry felt that Uncle Teddy wanted to say something affectionate. He wanted to say something affectionate to Uncle Teddy. He wanted to tell him that he loved him. He'd managed to tell Cousin Hilda and Auntie Doris. It wasn't so easy, with a man. Go on. Try. 'I don't suppose there's much point in you and me discussing anything,' he said. 'We wouldn't agree. I imagine you're pretty right-wing about everything. Villains usually are.' No!! 'Sorry, Uncle Teddy. I'm all churned up. I . . . er . . . I really am sorry. Because I'm really . . . er . . . quite fond of you, you know.'

There was a pause. He was blushing. He hoped Uncle Teddy wouldn't be too embarrassingly fulsome in reply.

'You're right about villains,' said Uncle Teddy. 'I wonder why.'

'Well left-wingers are left-wingers either because they're poor or because they're idealists,' said Henry. 'Not many villains are poor, and none of them are idealists.'

'You can be quite clever sometimes,' said Uncle Teddy.

'I know,' said Henry. 'So why is my life such a mess?'

8 Lost Heads

A thaw brought floods throughout Europe. 6,000 Midland car workers were put on a four-day week. In South Africa, 400 white women, wearing black sashes, stood with bowed heads in protest at a law removing coloured workers from the common roll. Mr Andrew Redrobe summoned Henry to his office.

'I'm going to give you a tremendous opportunity,' he said. 'Do you think you're ready for it?'

He could hardly say 'no', but it seemed presumptuous to say 'yes'.

'I hope so,' he said.

'I plan a major series of features, and I believe you're the ideal man to do it.'

'Thank you very much, sir.' Henry was too busy trying not to show how flattered he was to worry about that 'sir'.

'It's about the total *ineptitude* of *English education*,' said the neatly dressed editor, banging his right hand on his desk three times for emphasis.

'Thank you very much, sir,' said Henry.

When he told Terry Skipton that he would be spending three days down south, visiting his old schools, the news editor accepted the prospect of his absence with equanimity.

'But what about my calls?' said Henry, somewhat nettled.

'We've a seventeen-year-old joining us. You'll move on to general reporting.' Terry Skipton shook his large, bulbous head disbelievingly. 'Your apprenticeship is over, Mr Pratt.'

The next task of Henry 'He probes the facts behind the facts' Pratt was to telephone the headmaster of Thurmarsh Grammar School. He dreaded this. He'd crossed swords with Mr E. F. Crowther before.

'Mr Crowther? My name's Henry Pratt. I'm a recent old Thurmarshian,' he began, self-consciously. He still hadn't got used to telephoning from an open-plan office, with all his colleagues listening. 'Pratt.' He smiled sheepishly at Ginny. 'P-R-A-T-T.'

'Ah! Pratt!' said Mr E. F. Crowther. 'Sorry. It's a bad line. Yes, I remember you. You interrupted me with a fatuous joke when I was giving the school the benefit of twenty years of careful thinking about life.'

'That's me.'

'For a while quite a lot of people referred to you as Guard's Van Pratt.'

Ginny and Colin were surprised to hear Henry say, 'Guard's Van Pratt?'

'I said, "In every part of the army, from the Pioneer Corps to the Guards, there were Thurmarshians in the van",' said Mr E. F. Crowther. 'You said, "The guard's van."'

'No, sir.' Damn! 'Actually you said, "In every walk of life there are Thurmarshians in the van. I said, "The bread van."' He made a face at Ginny and Colin.

'Well, anyway,' said Mr E. F. Crowther, 'what a pleasure it is to renew acquaintanceship with a wag of your calibre.'

'I'm twenty-one in a couple of weeks, Mr Crowther,' said Henry. 'I'm no longer a . . . er . . .'

'. . . foolish youth who thinks his asinine comments are of more value than the accumulated wisdom of his elders.'

'Quite.' Henry was uneasy about this series. He didn't share his editor's obsession that *all* English education was bad. Within a system too rigid, too remote, too class-conscious, too exam-oriented, he'd been taught by some splendid teachers like Miss Candy and Mr Quell. But Mr E. F. Crowther was not among them. He'd make a splendid start to the series. He was a pillock.

'How can I help you, anyway?' said the headmaster.

'I'm a reporter on the *Argus*, Mr Pill . . . Crowther.'

'Good Lord!'

'I'm doing a feature on the total . . . range of English education. And . . . er . . . I wondered if I could a) interview you and b) have *carte blanche* to . . . er . . . talk to people in the school.'

'There are corners of the school on which no female eyes have ever been clapped. Would you plan to cart Blanche everywhere?'

'What?'

130

'It was a joke. I was seeing how you liked being interrupted with juvenile jokes. A pathetic piece of tit for tat which I already regret. Forget my foolishness. Certainly I'll see you. Would two-thirty on Friday be convenient?'

'Fine.'

'Good. I have to go now. I have an appointment.'

The police would later believe that these were the last words that Mr E. F. Crowther ever said to anybody.

On the morning of Friday, March 2nd, 1956, Henry made his rounds of hospitals and police stations for the last time. 'Sorry, nothing for you today,' was the general refrain. 'Damn. Oh well, thanks anyway,' was the reply of caring young humanist Henry Pratt on learning that the great Thurmarsh public had been so selfish as to refuse to lose important limbs in unusual ways for the gory delectation of their fellow citizens.

He lunched in the Rundle Café, on sausages, mash and beans. He sat opposite the assistant manager of the Halifax Building Society, whose eyes became moist during the treacle pudding, perhaps because the mortgage rate had gone up to 5½%, or perhaps because his trousers were too tight, or perhaps because he was overcome with emotion at the tale of Penelope, the Porcupine who hated being prickly.

He walked up Rundle Prospect, turned left into Market Street, then right into Link Lane. He approached the long, sober, brick-built school with its rows of regular, disciplined windows. The sky was the colour of cold, thin gravy. He tried to feel the carefree joy that he'd once imagined to be the permanent condition of all those who'd left school. It was no use. He felt all the cares of adulthood and also, beneath them, a residual echo of all the anxieties of childhood.

He went up the wide stairs to the first floor and along the clean, barren corridor which stretched towards the horizon, its emptiness broken only by fire buckets. His hollow footsteps rang out through the fragile calm of the working school. He knocked on the door of Mr E. F. Crowther's study, and was surprised to find it opened by a bulky man with a square head and splay feet. No policeman had ever been concealed more uselessly in plain clothes.

'Yes?'

'I've got an appointment to see Mr Crowther. What's happened?'

'When did you make this appointment?' said the policeman.

'Wednesday afternoon. On the phone.'

'What time?'

'Oh . . . about three, I suppose.'

'Come inside.' The burly policeman closed the door behind them. 'We're trying to do this discreetly,' he said. 'Our psychiatrist has warned of the danger of mass hysteria in schools.'

'What's happened?' repeated Henry.

The study was light and airy. There were neat piles of books, and the three internal walls were covered with graphs and rosters.

'Mr Crowther walked out of here at three o'clock on Wednesday afternoon, and hasn't been seen since. You may have been the last person to speak to him alive.'

'Good Lord! I mean . . . headmasters don't disappear into thin air.' Henry was dismayed to find that, after the first shock, his thoughts were mainly for himself. This could kill off his series. They could hardly lash into educational incompetence if it turned out to be a tragedy. Henry 'He probes the facts behind the facts' Pratt would be strangled at birth. This gave him another thought. 'I'm a journalist!' he exclaimed. 'Can I use the phone?'

'No. Now then, this phone call to the headmaster . . .'

'I have to ring my paper. I have to warn them to hold the front page.'

'They've held the front page.'

'What?'

'It's in the paper already. The disappearance was reported at 11.02.'

'Where to?'

'Darmley Road.'

'Bloody hell! That must have been five minutes after I'd left.'

'Anyroad up, I'm in charge of the investigation, and I'd like to hear about this phone call. All right?'

Everything went in the notebook. The bread van. Carting Blanche. Two feeble jokes given immortality by events. The police officer became taut with significance on hearing that Mr

Crowther had said, 'I have to go now. I have an appointment.'

'Did he say anything that might have suggested a depressed state of mind?' he asked.

'You mean . . . ?'

'It's a possibility. We're dragging the river and the canal.'

'No. Well . . . there was something odd.'

'Yes?'

'He said his joke had been a pathetic piece of tit for tat. He said he regretted it.'

'I don't see owt odd in that. He should have regretted it and all.'

'You didn't know him.' Henry felt a stab of shock as he realized that he was assuming that Mr Crowther was dead. 'I mean, that was practically an apology. I'd say it could indicate an unusual state of mind. Rather as if the Pope said, "Sorry. I've dropped a clanger. Well, nobody's infallible, are they?"'

Colonel Glubb Pasha, the British commander of Jordan's Arab Legion, was dismissed by King Hussein. The MCC apologized for an incident in which a Pakistani umpire sprained his shoulder while trying to avoid being doused with water by members of the England cricket team after a dinner. Henry travelled to Skipton to meet Auntie Doris.

A sharp shower soaked him as he walked from the station to the Craven Tea-Rooms, in a cobbled yard off the wide main street of the pleasant, stone-built market town.

Inside the tea-rooms, the smell of fresh coffee mingled with the faintly rotten fug of drying clothes. Pots, cups and people steamed.

'I . . . er . . . I saw Uncle Teddy,' said Henry.

'Oh?'

'He . . . there . . . er . . . isn't anybody else.'

'No?'

'No.'

'Oh.'

'Yes.'

'Well!'

'Quite. I . . . er . . . I asked him if he'd ever thought of . . . er . . . I mean it just cropped up, I didn't say you'd said anything, well I couldn't, you hadn't . . . if he'd ever thought of . . . er . . .

133

trying to get you back. He was very encouraging. Very encouraging indeed.'

'What did he say?'

'Nothing. He changed the subject.'

'You call that encouraging?'

'Well, yes. Under the circumstances. Compared with what he could have said. I mean, he could have said, "That bloody bitch! After what she's done to me?"'

'Henry!'

'No! Auntie Doris! I'm not saying that, and nor is he, that's what I'm saying. I mean, under the circumstances, wrong though it'd be, you could imagine somebody saying that. But they haven't. I think that's encouraging.'

The door opened and let in a blast of cold air and a well-bred couple who bred dogs well. They shook the drips off themselves with only marginally more consideration than the dogs they bred might have shown.

'I don't know that there's any point in all this,' said Auntie Doris. 'I don't know that I could ever walk out on a man.' She must have sensed the struggle Henry was having not to raise his eyebrows. 'I never walked out on Teddy. *He* left *me* . . . because he had to. I just . . . couldn't live without a man.'

Henry felt a twinge of his puritan conscience. He knew it to be hypocritical, in view of his own behaviour, but he was powerless to prevent it. Auntie Doris must have sensed it too. She had very acute antennae where her own affairs were concerned.

'Oh, I'm not talking about the physical side,' she said. She lowered her voice, just too late to avoid the interest of nearby customers. 'I'm talking about security. Without a man to hold me together I disintegrate. Oh, I know I've never loved Geoffrey the way I loved Teddy, but . . . but he couldn't run the hotel without me. He can't keep staff. He's been good to me, in his way. He needs me, and I need to be needed.'

The indignation exploded in Henry's head. In his life Auntie Doris was a wall of make-up, a sudden gust of scent, a blaze of dyed hair, a spirit of romance all the more moving because it was never quite real. She deserved better than Geoffrey Porringer. He'd help her get it.

'"Good to you"?' he said. 'The reason he can't keep staff is because he can't keep his wandering hands off them.'

'Henry!'

'Lorna told me. He rubs up against her. Touches her up and makes it look accidental. I'm sorry, Auntie Doris. Don't look like that, Auntie Doris. I'm only telling you because . . . Uncle Teddy's there. Waiting. Calling his club Cap Ferrat. Remembering.'

'Arrange for me to see Teddy, will you, Henry?' said Auntie Doris grimly.

Drunken Everton fans damaged a train taking them home from Manchester. Eoka terrorists blew up an air-liner in Cyprus. The talks between Britain and Archbishop Makarios foundered over the question of rights for Turkish Cypriots. The police found no trace of Mr E. F. Crowther.

Henry met Uncle Teddy in the Cap Ferrat on Tuesday lunch-time. They sat at a table near the bar, with glasses of whisky. The room, which at night had been made to look tawdry by the presence of mild sinfulness, now looked even more tawdry because of its absence. In daylight, when the traditional mediterranean table-cloths hadn't yet come back from the laundry, it was only too obvious that the traditional mediterranean tables had been mass-produced in Retford. Henry felt a sickening lurch of nerves. He'd burnt Auntie Doris's boats. Supposing he'd got it wrong?

He hadn't got it wrong.

'Splendid,' said Uncle Teddy. 'Well, well. I'm going to ring her up, Henry. Strike while the iron's hot. You've done a grand job. Just grand. You can leave it to me now. I'm going to invite her for a champagne dinner. Oh, Henry, Henry! Everything's going to be all right.'

'Yes.' Henry had a terrible feeling that he was going to cry. Desperately he composed himself, so that he could say, without his voice breaking, the words that must be faced. 'I love you both, you see.'

For an awful moment he thought Uncle Teddy was going to ignore this, but he didn't.

'I love you too, son,' he said.

9   The Closing of the Cap Ferrat

He dressed rapidly. This time, if there was a scoop, he was going to be there.

He slammed the front door behind him. A startled cat knocked a dustbin lid off, and he could hear the hollow clanking of goods vans in the distant marshalling yards. Those were the halcyon days of shunting.

He hesitated. If Gordon didn't leave his wife, it wouldn't increase Henry's chances with Ginny if he roared off in search of fame, leaving her asleep. Besides, he was fond of her. He wanted her to share the glory.

He went back inside, and knocked on her door.

'What is it?' she groaned, her voice coated in sleep.

'There've been a tremendous number of fire engines. I think there's a big fire.'

'Thanks.' She was wide awake immediately. She'd scented battle. 'I'll just jump into some clothes.'

He had erotic visions of the ample curves of her naked body as she leapt across the room into a pair of slacks.

She joined him in less than three minutes. What a woman! He glanced at her face in the dim light of the hall. It was drowsy, blotchy, replete. He felt a stab of jealousy.

If only they'd had cars. Not many reporters did, in those days. They struggled through the misty, sulphurous night towards that distant glow. Down Winstanley Road, down York Road, round the back of the Town Hall, past the brooding court house with its absurdly large Doric pillars, across the deserted High Street into Market Street, two panting, unfit, overweight journalists, one sated with sex, the other weakened by the torments of frustration.

The fire sent a shiver down Henry's spine. Fire was primitive. It raised echoes of atavistic superstition. He wondered, afterwards, if he'd already known that it was the Cap Ferrat that was burning.

Doors were open in the old, condemned, rat-infested houses in Canal View. In their curiosity, people were letting the world see them in their curlers and face creams, their thick corded pyjamas and dog-worn slippers.

They turned the corner of Malmesbury Street and gasped. The flames were shooting thirty feet into the air from the stricken club. Showers of sparks were leaping into the night and drifting slowly onto the vulnerable roofs of neighbouring buildings.

The street was jammed with fire engines and the police had erected cordons to keep the disaster-watchers at bay.

Henry and Ginny hurried forward. Henry showed his press card for the first time and croaked, 'Press.' A policeman gave them a hard look, then nodded them through.

Huge hoses were arcing impotently onto the crackling inferno. On the roof of the Thurmarsh Joke Emporium and Magic Shop, four firemen with breathing apparatus were trying to find a way into the burning night-club. Oh god! Uncle Teddy might be in there. Henry ran towards the blaze, ran into a wall of shimmering, impossible heat. A fireman grabbed him.

'It's my uncle's club,' he shouted.

'You can't go in,' said the fireman. 'We're doing our best. Keep out of our road, for Christ's sake.'

'Yes. Yes. Sorry,' said Henry.

Ginny was busy without looking busy, asking firemen questions so casually that they were able to continue their work and didn't think not to answer. Henry caught sight of a familiar face. Monsieur Emile, from Gay Charlesville-Mexières, small, dapper, moustachioed, staring fixedly at the ruins. Henry hurried over to him.

'My uncle,' he said. 'Mr Braithwaite. The owner. Is he in there?'

'No, no. I think no one is there. We all leaved. I seed Mr Braithwaite lock up. He leaved with Mr Vicarage.'

Henry's knees trembled. He hadn't known how worried he was until he realized how relieved he was. As the release swept over him, he heard a tiny, stubbornly pedantic corner of his brain say, 'Parsonage. His name is Parsonage.' He hardly listened to Monsieur Emile, rabbiting on among the flames. 'I go home. I have a friend in Nice. Maybe we open a club there. For Thurmarsh, is bad. For Mr Braithwaite, is bad. For me, maybe I shouldn't say so, is not so bad.' Even as he spoke, there was a small explosion. A great bundle of flaming newspapers shot out of the Mandarin Fish Bar and landed among the firemen, scattering them briefly.

'Come on,' yelled Ginny, above the roar of the flames, her face shining in their glow. 'I've got the basic facts. Let's ring the nationals. We might just catch the late editions.' Getting paid 'lineage' was an acceptable perk for local journalists. Ginny gave him a few phone numbers and the basic facts as they hurried to the phone booths in Tannery Road. They passed Ted and Helen, hurrying down Fish Hill towards the scene. Ted looked as if he'd been interrupted in coitus. Helen looked immaculate, not a hair out of place, as if she were rushing to a fire in an American film.

'How many appliances are there?' he asked, as they reached the phone boxes.

'Seventeen. Twenty-two. Twenty. Eighteen.'

'What?'

'Vary it. Make it look as if the stories are coming from different sources.'

'What about the truth?'

Ginny snorted and rang the *Daily Herald*.

Henry enjoyed phoning the nationals. John Carpenter, who worked for the *Thurmarsh Chronicle*, banged on the door with all the authority of his thirty years as a journalist and asked how long he'd be. He shrugged, and made a gesture which might have indicated that he'd be two minutes. Three calls later, when John Carpenter was angrily pointing to his watch, he sang out, 'Only one more.' He didn't care. Uncle Teddy was safe. He was playing his part in the telling of a big story. John Carpenter had concentrated on him because he thought he'd be softer than Ginny. He was wrong. Henry was a hard man now. 'All yours,' he said generously as he left. John Carpenter, who had once been sent packing from Cousin Hilda's because of his drinking habits, scowled. Henry grinned.

He hurried back to the scene of the fire. The hoses were still gushing mightily, but the flames continued to roar their defiance. Henry found himself wondering what would happen to Alphonso Boycott and his Northern Serenaders, the legendary Martine and the Côte d'Azur Cuties.

'Oh my God!' moaned a pale man at his side.

'I know,' said Henry. 'And it only opened two weeks ago.'

'I'm not insured,' said the pale man. 'I forgot to renew the insurance.'

'You what?'

'On Timpley's. That's mine, the tobacconist's. Next to the magic shop. That's my livelihood there. That's thirty-three years. They say the whole block may go.'

A shower of sparks landed on the roof of Timpley and Nephews. George Timpley shuddered and said, 'Oh my God' again. Henry flinched too as the sparks danced on the roof like ducks on a hot plate.

Then he realized that he was standing next to a story. Never mind Ginny and Ted and Helen charging around. He had a human interest story all to himself. One man's night of fear. I shared the agonizing vigil of Thurmarsh tobacconist George Timpley, aged ?, as he watched the sparks landing on the roof of his tobacconist's.

It would be a good story if the building were saved, but it would be a better story if it burnt down. Don't even think like that! But I have to. I'm paid to. I'm a journalist. Good news is no news.

A tobacconist watched as his life's work went up in smoke. No! Stop it! Oh god, if you exist, which I doubt, let Timpley and Nephews survive this night. The man didn't even have any sons. That 'and Nephews' pierces my heart. This may be just a little back street tobacconist's to me, but to him it's his dream. Tobacconist's pipe-dream goes up in smoke. No!

George Timpley gave Henry his life story. It poured out compulsively. Henry scribbled surreptitiously, hoping some of what he wrote would be legible. George Timpley never even noticed. He was staring fixedly at his little shop. He was every fireman, every hose, every jet of water, every spark of fire. He seemed puzzled when Henry asked how old he was.

'Fifty-seven,' he said. 'Why?'

An explosion ripped out part of the wall of the Thurmarsh Joke Emporium and Magic Shop. Glass tinkled into the street. Fake cakes, bottomless tumblers, diminishing Woodbines and impossible spoons were hurled high into the sky. The air was full of

139

sneezing powder, itching powder and electric snuff. Whoopie cushions, goofy teeth, joke spiders and pop-up ties rained down on the bewildered firemen. A large cardboard box of Naughty Fido dog turds, ordered but not yet collected by the Winstanley Young Conservatives, soared into the air, hovered, burst, and showered its unsavoury contents all over Malmesbury Street. Brightly coloured snakes burst from posies of flying flowers.

Then the smells came. The burning of rubber. Rubber doves, rubber eggs, rubber coat-hangers, rubber ears. The burning of plastic billiard balls and wobbly cheese. And, over and above it all, the stench of the stink bombs.

The roof slowly caved in. The chimney crumbled. The vanishing cigars vanished. The vanishing ink vanished. For its last and greatest trick, the shop itself vanished. There was a gaping hole, beside Timpley and Nephews where, a minute before, the Thurmarsh Joke Emporium and Magic Shop had stood.

The hard-pressed firemen donned breathing apparatus, to protect them from the stench of blocked drains and rotting greens unleashed by the stink bombs. They trod on farting cushions as they fought to quell the blaze. Hoses shook, sending water zig-zagging through the sky, as men sneezed violently, scratched desperately, or ducked to avoid being hit by false noses.

Henry ducked to avoid a flying, melting dog turd, which struck George Timpley full in the face. Helen approached him, still immaculate. Suddenly her dignity was assailed from all sides. She was racked by a fit of violent sneezing. She slipped on a plastic fried egg which her watery eyes couldn't see. She fell over, backwards. She subsided, still sneezing, her superb legs swinging in the air, her tempting thighs visible to a world that wasn't interested, onto a pile of top hats, seamless sacks and whoopie cushions, which gave off a gentle volley of soft, mournful farts. And Henry laughed. He laughed and laughed and laughed. He laughed for a dozen Young Conservatives. Hysteria had him in its grip.

Derek Parsonage approached. His face was white. He said 'Oh my God' so often and so fervently that Henry almost didn't believe he meant it. He tried desperately not to laugh. It was incredibly childish, but each sneeze, each fart set him off again. His cheeks ran with tears.

'Where's Uncle Teddy?' he managed to say. 'Didn't he go off with you?'

Can water freeze in a furnace? It felt to Henry that his tears of laughter froze on his face, there in front of the burning Cap Ferrat, as Derek Parsonage said, 'No. He went back in. He said he'd forgotten some papers.'

All fires stop somewhere, and this fire stopped at the Thurmarsh Joke Emporium and Magic Shop. Even in his sorrow at the probable death of Uncle Teddy, Henry felt happy for George Timpley, who was led away, crying helplessly from relief.

The Mandarin Fish Bar had also gone, and the wreck of the Cap Ferrat still smouldered sullenly. The sensation-seekers dispersed reluctantly.

Henry walked slowly home, through the early morning streets, with Ginny Fenwick. The first buses and trams and doomed trolley-buses were running, with a few grey-faced passengers. Milkmen were about, and a yellow municipal lorry was washing a cobbled street. The tension and the grief had made Henry feel extremely sexy. He placed his right hand on Ginny's large left buttock, and cradled its slow, rhythmic movements as she trudged wearily homewards. She smiled at him, rather sadly. At the door of his room his eyes asked an optimistic question and she said, 'No. Sorry.' They snatched a couple of hours of restless sleep in their separate flats.

10 Hard Man Henry

It was a sunny Monday morning in spring. In the gardens of the substantial houses on Winstanley Road, the daffodils were in bloom and the tulips were budding up nicely. The bleak country-side between the towns and pit villages was briefly touched by beauty. Hedges became an astonishing pale green. Trees grew brown and furry with buds. Song-thrushes sent messages of joy across the rusting cars and vans in Bill Holliday's dump.

The sap was rising all over the northern hemisphere. On the lake, in the Alderman Chandler Memorial Park, the mallard and teal were frisky, performing their elaborate displays with relish, entering into their absurdly brief copulations with spirit. In the gloomy animal cages, a moth-eaten marmot looked vaguely puzzled at the absence of moth-eaten marmot mates.

Upstairs, Gordon Carstairs's sap was rising with a stamina to make mallards green with envy. His family were away for a week, and he was making the most of it.

And what of Henry, alone in the flat below, with no outlet for his rising sap? Was *he* green with envy? No. He had no more time for negative emotions. He was an ambitious young journalist. He was Hard Man Henry.

He had first felt that new strength of his on the night of the fire. It had been severely tested in the days that followed.

Hard Man Henry it had been who'd telephoned Auntie Doris, after the body of Uncle Teddy had been found in the Cap Ferrat, burnt beyond recognition. Analysis had shown that he'd been clutching a fire extinguisher at the moment of death. Henry had said, directly and simply, 'I'm afraid I have very bad news. Uncle Teddy is dead.' Auntie Doris had cried. So had Henry. Hard men don't need to feel ashamed of tears.

Hard Man Henry it had been who'd trudged across the gravel to the front door of number 66, Park View Road, who'd refused to be baited when Cousin Hilda had said, 'Ah! A stranger!', who'd told her, 'I'm afraid I have bad news. Uncle Teddy is dead.' Cousin

Hilda had sniffed. 'As they live, so shall they perish,' her mordant sniff had said.

Hard Man Henry it had been who'd written up the death of his uncle. 'Don't do it if it distresses you,' Terry Skipton had said. 'It's my job,' Henry had replied.

Hard Man Henry it had been who'd cancelled his twenty-first birthday party, made the funeral arrangements and given the vicar the salient facts for his oration.

Hard Man Henry it had been who'd sat, calmly, between two sniffing women, one sniffing with sorrow, the other with disbelief, as the vicar's tributes had rolled round the magnificent, sparsely filled, Perpendicular parish church of St Peter's. 'Ill health prevented him serving his country during the War, but he was tireless and active "on the home front" . . . After the War, his import-export business contributed vastly to the revival of his nation . . . In recent years he worked in Rangoon in, it can now be told, a secret capacity, but he never lost his love of Thurmarsh.'

Hard Man Henry it had been who, after the service, had said, 'Cousin Hilda. I don't think you've met Geoffrey Porringer' and had left them to it, while he took the opportunity of a brief chat with Auntie Doris, in the tiny churchyard, surrounded by the clothes shops and shoe shops of central Thurmarsh. 'I spoke to him a couple of days before he died,' he'd said. 'He said he was going to invite you for a champagne dinner. He said everything was going to be all right. I think he died in peace, looking forward to better things.' Auntie Doris, a stricken ship yawing in a sea of emotion, had clutched him and gulped helplessly. Henry had held her firmly. 'Geoffrey's all I have now,' she had said. 'I'm really sorry now that I said what I said,' he had said. 'I'm not,' Auntie Doris had said. 'I know where I stand now. I know how to deal with him.' She'd kissed him, covering him in mascara and salt tears. 'Thank you, son,' she had said. Henry had remained dry-eyed. If he hadn't, Auntie Doris might have drowned in her own tears.

The United States had sent 1,700 marines to the Mediterranean, to try to prevent hostilities between Egypt and Israel. Britain had deported Archbishop Makarios to the Seychelles. French troops had killed 61 Algerian rebels after a mutiny. Mr

Krushchev had denounced Stalin, throwing Russia into ferment. A bomb had been found in the bed of the Governor of Cyprus.

Henry's career had continued to be dogged by misprints – 'She lives alone. Her hubby is underwater fishing,' in an interview with a local athlete; 'The repeated flooding is a source of continual irrigation to him,' in a story about an angry farmer; 'The compensation is dripping down the walls,' in a story about bad housing. But hard men rise above such things. And it was a keen, jaunty Henry Pratt who strode to the tram stop, hungry for a new week's work, that sunny Monday morning in spring.

On the tram, he glanced through the morning's *Thurmarsh Chronicle*. Colonel Nasser was accepting aid from Russia, and was no longer seen as the West's great hope in the Middle East. In the Grand National, the Queen Mother's horse, Devon Loch, ridden by Dick Francis, had inexplicably slipped 55 yards from the finishing post, when leading comfortably. The Thurmarsh trams were to be scrapped. A council official scoffed at warnings of a possible fuel crisis.

The tram rattled perkily along Winstanley Road, unaware of its impending doom. Henry smiled warmly at Gordon and Ginny. Hard men are above self-pity.

That morning, sitting beside the representatives of the *Rawlaston Gazette* and the *Splutt Advertiser*, in Thurmarsh Juvenile Court, Hard Man Henry gave a hard look at two would-be hard youths who had burnt pet rabbits with candles. He fought desperately against feeling embarrassed as a ten-year-old girl told how her father had put his Peter in her Mary. She was taken into care. His fellow reporters didn't take this story down. In the 1950s, the problems of incest and sexual abuse of children were rarely reported.

'We can't print mucky stories about incest,' said Terry Skipton, when Henry complained about the omission of his story. 'What do you think we are?'

'Presenters of the truth about the society we live in,' said Henry. Hard men don't mind sounding naïve.

Robert Newton died of a heart attack. The government agreed to the integration of Malta, with three Maltese MPs sitting at Westminster. Henry attended number two magistrates' court, and listened, in that sombre panelled room, to a case in which a 34 year-old builder, of no fixed abode, was accused of stealing lead off a church roof. The reporters predicted, on the basis of his sartorial inadequacy, that he'd get six months. As they dress, so shall they reap. The chairman was elderly, with yellowing skin, sunken cheeks and a deaf-aid. As the police described how they chased the accused's lorry, stopped it in Hortensia Road, Rawlaston, and found it to contain the lead missing from the roof of St Michael's Church, Crambolton-on-Rundle, Henry sensed that the chairman was having difficulty in hearing, and this surmise proved correct for, in sentencing the man to six months' imprisonment, he commented sternly, 'If you are going to continue to be a road user, you are going to have to drive much more carefully in future.'

Two things about the story that appeared in the paper upset Henry. The gremlins had struck again. His intro began: 'A Thurmarsh builder who was caught red-handed with a sorry load of dead taken from a Rundle Valley church . . .' And the comment of the chairman of the magistrates had been omitted.

He approached the news desk fearlessly. Behind him, in the sunlit afternoon news-room, elderly typewriters clacked at varying speeds. In front of him, sore-eyed sub-editors in shirt-sleeves were thinking up pithy headlines and crossing out offensive copy. Henry had eyes only for Terry Skipton, hunched and staring, like a wounded eagle.

'Two complaints, Mr Skipton. There's another deliberate misprint. "A sorry load of dead." It sounds as if somebody's been desecrating the graveyard.'

'If somebody was deliberately desecrating your stories, Mr Pratt, they'd hardly do it in a way that made them sound more interesting.'

'Mr Skipton? Are you saying all my misprints are natural mistakes?'

'No, I'm not, Mr Pratt. It's all a bit rum. I'm keeping my eyes skinned, actually.'

This took Henry aback. It had crossed his mind that the culprit might be Terry Skipton. Though he didn't think so. He thought he knew who it was. He glanced round, and saw his suspect watching him. The suspect looked away, hurriedly. Suspicion began to harden into certainty.

'And the second complaint?' said Terry Skipton.

'The magistrate's comment has been left out.'

'Complain to the editor if you're not satisfied.'

'I just might,' said Henry. 'I just might.' He didn't want to complain. It'd be much easier to give up. But hard men don't do what's easy.

'It appeared to belong to a different case, a traffic incident,' said Mr Andrew Redrobe.

'That was the whole point,' said Henry. 'The magistrate's as deaf as a post. He thought it *was* a traffic case. But we can't have our authorities looking ridiculous, can we, or the whole system might collapse?'

Sunlight was falling onto the editor's green-topped desk. Specks of dust churned lazily in its rays.

'I think I ought to tell you that he's a personal friend of mine,' said the editor.

Hard Man Henry gulped. But he wouldn't back down.

'I'm sure he is, sir,' he said. He didn't mind that 'sir'. He was prepared to make tactical withdrawals in order to take the main ground. 'Deafness is no bar to friendship. But surely it is to being a magistrate?'

'I agree. Perhaps I should drop a word in the relevant ear.'

'Not a deaf one, I hope.'

Mr Andrew Redrobe gave Henry a long, hard look. Henry just managed to force himself to return it.

'We pride ourselves on having a good relationship with the courts,' said the editor.

'You seem to pride yourselves on having a good relationship with everybody,' said Henry.

'We do. A local paper has to work in the community. If the community clams up against it, how could it ever get good stories?'

'Are you saying that if you ever got a chance to expose something rotten in the community you wouldn't do so because that could kill your chances of getting the stories you need to expose something rotten in the community?'

There was a long silence. The editor tapped on his desk with a silver pencil. Henry knew that he'd gone too far.

'Your exaggerated comments do reflect a real dilemma,' said Mr Andrew Redrobe. 'It's a question of degree. Find me a major scandal, which I think it my duty to print, and I'll print it fearlessly. But not stories about deaf magistrates. Good. I'm glad we've had this little chat. I'm grateful for your invaluable advice on how to run my newspaper. Let's hope you stay here long enough to be able to continue to give me the benefit of it. Goodbye, Henry.'

Little did Henry dream that one day he would be in a position to put the editor's sincerity on this question to the test. Indeed, if he'd had a more suspicious nature and a more highly developed news sense, he'd have been on the trail of that major scandal already.

'Name all the winners of the FA Cup between the wars,' said Ben Watkinson, at their corner table in the back bar of the Lord Nelson.

'Life's too short,' said Henry. The pub's familiar smell of intrigue and carbolic didn't charm him that evening.

'Hard Man Henry,' said Gordon Carstairs, who was sitting beside Ginny in shared satiety.

My god, thought Henry. Can he see into my head?

'Windows,' said Gordon.

'Windows?' said Henry.

'Windows in your head,' said Gordon.

Colin Edgeley returned from the toilets, looking grim.

'Mick Tunstall's back,' he said. 'He's in the other bar.'

'He didn't do anything last time,' said Henry.

'I hadn't danced with Angela Groyne then.'

'What's that got to do with it?' asked Henry.

'Mick Tunstall works for Bill Holliday.'

All this irritated Henry. Real hard men don't advertise their hardness.

He bought a round, and looked back to see Ted and Helen laughing over a page of the *Argus*. He didn't need to ask what they were laughing at. A sorry load of dead. All doubt was removed. They'd be sorry. They'd wish they were dead.

He handed the drinks round, banging Ted's glass on the table.

'Are we permitted to share the joke?' he said.

Ted looked at him in astonishment.

'It's you, isn't it?' said Henry.

'What's me?' said Ted.

'Putting misprints in my stories. Trying to ruin my career. Come outside.'

'What?'

'A fair fight. Or are you scared?'

'I don't want to fight you,' said Ted wearily.

'Stop it, Henry,' implored Ginny.

'Other way, ref!' said Gordon.

'Give over, kid,' said Colin.

'Stop calling me kid,' said Henry. 'Are you coming, Ted, or not?'

'No.'

Henry poured Ted's glass of bitter over his head. Ted sat there in astonishment, dripping with beer. Helen's eyes flashed.

'All right,' said Ted. 'No little pipsqueak pours beer over me and tells me I'm destroying his career.'

Well, you've got what you wanted, Henry Pratt. A fight, with Ted Plunkett, outside a town centre pub. 'Brawling journalists were a disgrace,' says barrister. 'If you are going to continue to be a road user, you will have to drive better than this,' says deaf magistrate. 'Goodbye, Henry,' says Mr Andrew Redrobe.

'This is stupid,' said Ginny.

Yes.

The seven journalists went outside, into the fading light. In Leatherbottlers' Row it was already almost dark. Ted took off his beer-soaked coat. Henry removed his curry-spattered jacket. Denzil Ackerman turned the corner into the alley at a brisk limp. He stopped, his mouth open in exaggerated astonishment, until he realized how inelegant it looked.

'Come on, you two. Call it off,' said Ben, the pacifist.

There was a pause.

'No,' said Ted.

There was another pause.

'No,' said Henry.

The two reporters circled round each other, warily. Then Henry attempted a blow, which missed easily. Ted retaliated with a punch that missed almost as easily. Henry hit Ted on the side of the head. Ted launched a rain of blows, some of which found the target. Henry hung onto Ted and managed to punch him in the stomach. Ted gasped and almost collapsed on him, pushing him back into the wall. Henry pushed the gasping Ted off him, stumbled forward wearily, landed a punch on Ted's face and moved in to finish the job. He aimed a huge punch. When it missed, he fell over. Ted leapt at him, and pummelled his ribs, then grabbed him by the hair and yanked him agonizingly to his feet. Henry kicked Ted's shins and butted him. Their heads clashed, and they both reeled away. Ted recovered first, and into that inept and inelegant struggle he managed to inject one good punch. It sent Henry crashing into the wall. He subsided in a crumpled heap, blood gushing from his nose. He passed out.

When he came round, Ted was kneeling beside him anxiously and Ginny was holding a blood-soaked handkerchief to his nose. He was glad to see that Ted's face also showed signs of damage. One eye was closing up.

'You'll be all right, kid,' said Colin.

Ben looked at his watch anxiously. 'Time I was giving the wife one,' he said.

'Wife!' said Gordon. 'In the mouse house!' He kissed Ginny, and hurried off to his returning wife. Ginny looked inconsolable. Henry, lying with his head on the cold stone, looked up at Ginny's legs and dress and longed to put this to the test.

'Sorry,' said Ted. 'I've messed you up a bit.'

'I asked for it,' said Henry. 'It was the wrong way to deal with it. I'm sorry.'

'You don't still think Ted arranged those misprints, do you?' said Helen.

'Didn't you, Ted?' said Henry.

'Of course I didn't, you stupid prick.'

'Ted's wicked,' said Helen. 'He's horrid. He's a tease. But he wouldn't hurt a fly.'

'If he found a spider in the bath he'd be sarcastic to it till it went away,' said Ginny, and blushed at memories of Ted and baths.

'Oh God!' said Henry. 'Oh God, I'm sorry, Ted.'

A taller, sharper, younger, less benevolent version of Neil Mallet emerged from the front bar of the Lord Nelson. His brother, the compositor. Henry's eyes met Ted's. He looked away. The sudden revelation of Neil Mallet's guilt set his spine tingling and filled him with a curious sense of shame, which he didn't wish to share with another human being. He hoped Ted would make no comment, but Ted said, 'He's envious', forcing Henry to say, 'Envious? Of me?'

'I think he saw you as a natural ally,' said Ted. 'A natural friend. Another lonely, hopeless case, unable to strike up human relationships.'

'Thank you very much,' said Henry.

'Ah, but you aren't, are you?' said Ted. 'You have the ability to inspire affection. When he realized that, he couldn't resist his campaign of mischief-making.'

'But he seemed as friendly as ever,' said Henry.

'Ah well,' said Ted. 'Ah well.'

He wished Denzil hadn't come too. As the taxi made its way to Winstanley Road, his face and body stung, his head throbbed, his blood explored painful places, his sensuality leapt and he felt a deep desire for Ginny. He felt that, if they had been alone, his predicament would have awakened her sexuality. The need to avoid pain from his bruises would have added salt to the stew of their love-making. Her soft, warm kisses on his swollen eyes would have been as nectar on a bee's tongue. But Denzil had come too.

His legs were still wobbly. They supported him, one on each arm, to the front door, across the hall, into his impersonal little flat.

'I'll make him some tea and hot food.' Heart-warming words, but not from Denzil. Speak out, Ginny.

'Oh. Right. Thanks,' said Ginny. And off she went!

He felt so tired.

'Scrambled eggs do you?' said Denzil.

'I'm not hungry.'

'You must eat.'

'OK, then.'

'Best I can do, with your measly stores.'

So tired. Denzil clattered away, finding crockery. Upstairs, Ginny clumped about. Spring-cleaning? Barricading herself against bruised sex maniacs?

Henry sat at the little formica-topped kitchen table and ate scrambled eggs on toast, with weak tea. He found it difficult to swallow.

'Come on holiday with me.'

The words drifted around inside his painful head, bumped meaninglessly against his bruised eyes, and finally impinged upon his consciousness.

'What?'

'Come on holiday with me. I see we've put down for the same fortnight. I want to show you Italy.'

What? Why? Oh!

'Well . . . er . . .'

'Have you anything arranged?'

'Yes, I . . . yes. Something arranged. Yes.'

'What?'

'What?'

'What have you arranged?'

'Oh . . . er . . . with my aunt. I'm going to Filey, with my aunt.'

'You can't turn down Italy with me for Filey with your aunt.'

'I can. I have to.'

'I have the offer of a villa in Amalfi.'

'I have the booking of a boarding house in Filey.'

So tired. Go, Denzil, please.

'I thought you were going with your friend,' said Henry.

'Yes . . . well . . .' said Denzil. 'That's over. We split up over a lost tie-pin.'

'So tired.' He realized that he'd said the words out loud by mistake. 'Sorry, Denzil,' he said. 'I'm sorry about your friend. Very sorry. And thanks for everything. But . . . er . . . I'd quite like to be on my own now.'

'Are you sure you'll be all right?'

'Yes. Denzil? Thanks.'

'Pleasure.'

Suddenly the man's speckled brown parchment skin was looming towards the limited field of vision left by his puffy eyes. The man was kissing him full on the lips.

'Denzil?' he said, in a quavering voice which seemed to come from a very long way away. 'I really would prefer it very much if you never did that again.'

Hundreds of miles away, almost as far away as Amalfi is from Filey, the door of his flat closed gently behind Denzil Ackerman.

Henry limped into the office. Terry Skipton gawped at his black eyes and swollen nose.

'Mr Pratt!' he said. 'What does the other feller look like?'

'You'll see in a minute.'

'What?'

Terry Skipton was not overjoyed to learn that two of his reporters had been brawling.

Denzil had given Henry the films to review. 'Review' meant 'Regurgitate the publicity material.' He tried to bury himself in them. 'Pairing sultry Italian siren Anna Magnani with craggy Burt Lancaster was a . . .'

Denzil limped in. Henry blushed invisibly beneath his bruises. The surging blood explored new areas of pain around his cheekbones. He avoided Denzil's eyes. '. . . risky idea, perhaps, but it's a risk that comes off triumphantly. Set in a semi-tropical Gulf Coast town, *The Rose Tattoo* is . . .'

Ted entered, arm in infuriating arm with Helen. Ted's face was puffy, and he had one black eye. Henry approached him immediately.

'I'm really sorry about what I did,' he said. 'I think you've been fairly amazing about it.'

Ted looked embarrassed and grunted. Henry realized that he disliked having his basic good nature discovered. Helen blew Henry an ambiguous little kiss.

'The tragic death of James Dean would make *Rebel Without A Cause* worth seeing even if it was a bad film. It isn't. This study of American juvenile delin . . .'

Ginny looked bleary, as if she'd been catching up on lost sleep. She rebuked Henry for not waiting for her. 'I didn't want people to see you with me. They might have thought you'd been beating me up,' he explained. He realized immediately that she might take this as a comment on her size. He was glad she couldn't see his blushes beneath the bruises.

'. . . quency is a brilliant exploration of a transatlantic middle-class mal . . .'

Henry tried not to look at Neil. He knew that Ted and Helen and Ginny were all trying not to look at Neil. Neil seemed to sense that something was up. He turned and looked at them all not looking at him. Henry's spine tingled. 'Your faces!' said Neil. 'What's happened?'

'We had a fight,' said Henry, in a shaky voice. 'I accused Ted of sabotaging my stories with misprints. I had the wrong man, didn't I? Ted doesn't have a brother in the print room, does he?'

The blood drained from Neil Mallet's face. His mask of geniality faded. A gleam of hatred lit up his eyes. A snarl played cruelly round the edges of his mouth. Too late, the mask returned. Henry couldn't look at him any more. '. . . aise. Dean plays a crazy, mixed up . . .'

Colin entered dramatically. He had two black eyes and a puffed-up face criss-crossed with Elastoplast. His right hand was heavily bandaged. Neil Mallet slipped past, out of their lives, a tormented ghost, with a pile of books tucked underneath his arm instead of his head. Colin hardly noticed him. He looked across the news-room and smiled triumphantly, as if to say, 'You see. I wasn't making it up.' The gap in his mouth had widened by a tooth.

'You should see the other feller,' he said.

'Nasty one, I'm afraid, Mr Pratt,' said Terry Skipton. 'Motor cyclist killed in a collision with a lorry. Twenty years old. Name of Smailes. Lived with his family in Matterhorn Drive.'

His nose had returned to normal, but there was still a little yellowy greenness round the eyes. He took a deep breath as he walked up the garden path, past two tiny landscaped ponds cluttered with gnomes, storks, windmills and tiny bridges. He rang the doorbell. The cheerful chimes sounded indecent in that house of grief.

He found himself facing a comfortable woman in her late forties. She showed no outward signs of grief. His throat was dry. His stomach was churning.

'I'm sorry to disturb you at a time like this, Mrs Smailes,' he said. 'I'm . . . er . . . I'm from the *Argus*. I . . . er . . . I've been asked to ask you one or two questions about your son. It won't take a minute. Er . . . I understand he was quite a promising all-round sportsman.'

Mrs Smailes had gone deathly pale.

'Was?' she said. 'Was?' she repeated on a higher note. 'What's happened to him?'

There was a pained silence. Hard Man Henry joined Henry 'Ee by gum I am daft' Pratt, Podgy Sex Bomb Henry and all the other dead Pratts whose ghostly forms would stalk two paces behind him for the rest of his life.

11   A Run on Confetti

Grace Kelly married Prince Rainier III of Monaco. After fierce border battles, Egypt and Israel agreed an unconditional cease-fire. The Archbishop of Canterbury accused Mr Harold Macmillan of debasing the spiritual currency of the nation by introducing premium bonds. Stanley Matthews, recalled at the age of 42, made all four goals as England beat Brazil 4–2. A dry spring gave way to a cold, wet summer.

Seated at an outdoor table in the magnificent Piazza del Campo in Siena, on a golden September afternoon, Henry would wryly tell his homosexual companion, 'I spent as much on confetti in the summer of '56 as I did on French letters in the autumn of '52.'

So many modern works were included in the Royal Academy's summer exhibition that Sir Alfred Munnings refused to go to the annual banquet. A frogman, Commander Lionel Crabb, was found drowned near Soviet ships while engaged on secret work during a visit to Britain by Messrs Bulganin and Krushchev. Mr and Mrs James Hargreaves requested the pleasure of the company of Henry·Pratt at the wedding of their daughter Diana Jennifer to Nigel Timothy Anthony Pilkington-Brick, on Saturday, June 9th.

Britain offered independence to the Gold Coast. It was revealed, a year after the event, that in May, 1955, 251 men had taken turns to go into a forbidden area to avert a crisis at Windscale Plutonium Factory at Sellafield. It was revealed, after eleven days of soul-searching, that Henry Pratt would attend the wedding of Diana Jennifer Hargreaves and Nigel Timothy Anthony Pilkington-Brick.

A teacher who spoke on ITV about unruly conditions in secondary schools was sacked by the London County Council. In Cyprus there were reprisals against Britain after the hanging of two terrorists. Talks on the independence of Singapore broke down after the chief minister described Britain's offer as 'Like a Christmas pudding with arsenic sauce'. Len Hutton was knighted.

The day before he left for the Diana-Tosser wedding, Henry received the heart-warming news that Mr and Mrs Basil Cornish requested the pleasure of his company at the wedding of their daughter Helen Marigold (Marigold!) to Edward Sampson (Sampson!) Plunkett, on Saturday, July 14th.

At the tram stop that morning, Ginny looked dreadful. Her face was blotchy. Her eyes were red and runny. She gave her red nose a blow so gargantuan that he wanted to pretend he wasn't with her.

'I think I'm getting a cold,' she said.

He touched her muscular right arm. 'Why've you been crying?' he said.

'It's so stupid,' she said.

'They've invited you,' he said.

She nodded. Tears ran down her cheeks. She looked far too vulnerable to be a war correspondent.

What a couple they'd make at Ted and Helen's wedding: Henry still obsessed with the bride, Ginny still in love with the groom.

Only one thing marred the perfection of the wedding of Diana Hargreaves and Tosser Pilkington-Brick, which took place not in Hampstead, but at Holy Trinity Church, Brompton, because that was where Diana's parents had been married. Diana looked splendid in a picture gown of white satin, embroidered with diamante and drop pearls, with her tulle veil held in place by a high coronet of pearls. Tosser looked like a Michelangelo sculpture dressed by Savile Row. The three pages, scaled down editions of Tosser, looked charming in knee-breeches of Parma-violet satin and coats of cyclamen satin trimmed with silver braid. The hats and dresses of the female guests were wonderful to behold.

Tease us no more, you cry. What was this one thing that marred the perfection?

It was Henry. He felt absurd in his hired morning suit. The assistant had said, 'You're lucky, sir. You're right on the edge of our range.' 'On the edge of your range?' he'd said, determined not to be overawed. 'So what happens to the gigantic, the obese, the minute?' 'People who . . . er . . . diverge from the norm to an abnormal degree cannot hire, sir. They have to have clothes made to measure,' the attendant had said. 'It's the law of the market place, I'm afraid,' he'd added, seeming not in the least afraid. 'It's one more example of the cruelty of an inequitable world,' Henry had said: '"Oh, you're rather handicapped. We'll handicap you some more."' 'Anyway, sir,' the attendant had hurriedly repeated, 'you're lucky, as I say. You're . . .'' . . . on the edge of your range. Hanging on to the rim of normality. Not grotesque by a hair's breadth. Terrific. Thank you!' Henry had said.

And so, although dressed in a morning suit at a gathering full of men in morning suits, Henry felt distressingly conspicuous as he approached the church, on foot. The rain had held off. There was a great crowd of bobbing hats. He caught a glimpse of a radiant Belinda Boyce-Uppingham. He saw many men whose large frames and moon-faces proclaimed them to be Pilkington-Bricks. And, with a surge of joy that astounded him, he saw Lampo Davey, Tosser's study-mate at Dalton. Elegant, fastidious Lampo, for whom Henry had fagged. He'd had to rebuff Lampo's advances. Lampo turned, and saw him and, to Henry's surprise, Lampo's face lit up also. There was a moment when they almost, instinctively, kissed. Two young Englishmen kissing each other in morning suits at a society wedding in 1956! Henry went cold all over, at the enormity of the escape. 'Henry, good to see you!' 'You too, Lampo!' 'What are you doing now?' 'I'm a reporter on the *Thurmarsh Evening Argus.*' 'Delicious! Priceless! You're too absurd.' 'What about you? Not still in Crete?' 'Oh, that. No. That was a mistake. The Cretans are absolute sweeties, but dreadfully basic. Opportunities for mime artists are minimal. No, I'm at Cambridge. Terribly banal.'

The vicar's voice rolled round the church like well-bred thunder. The congregation sang with suspicious fervour. Henry felt deeply irritated. Diana Hargreaves, whom he adored, was throwing herself away on the oaf who'd lost the match for England.

He also felt worried. He was getting nowhere with women, yet he was having to resist the advances of Denzil, and Lampo had almost kissed him. Was he attractive only to men?

Not quite. As the bells pealed out their joy over a grey London, and the guests slowly filed past Diana, kissing and praising her, she whispered to him, 'Are you jealous?' 'Of course not,' he said,

157

smiling. 'Oh dear,' she said. 'I'd like you to be a little jealous. There'll always be a corner of my heart that's just for you,' and he walked off, weak at the knees.

At the reception, in the flower-bedecked Sisley Suite of the Gore Towers Hotel, he wandered among the flowers, gazed at the Sisleys, nibbled salmon in aspic, marinated carp, jellied lamb cutlets, cold pigeon pie. He sipped the champagne with the restraint its quality deserved. He talked to Paul. The gap between them was widening remorselessly. He talked to Judy, who clearly would marry Paul. Their conversation was a miniature gem of non-communication.

Mrs Hargreaves approached him, elegant in a cream and gold brocade suit. His loins stirred irrelevantly.

'I love Sisley, don't you?' she said.

'Er . . . yes . . .' he said. Why could he not admit that he'd never seen a Sisley painting in his life until today, and that it was only because the subjects were French and the style impressionist that he had the impression that Sisley was a French impressionist? Why be ashamed, when he knew that nothing is less sophisticated than believing that sophistication matters?

He glanced at the pictures, seeking an intelligent comment. 'Snow at Louveciennes 1874'. 'Snow at Louveciennes 1878'. 'Near Marly – Snow on the road to Saint-Germain 1874–5'. 'Floods at Port Marly'. He couldn't say 'Rotten luck Sisley had with his weather.' He said, 'They're pretty.'

'Yes!' said Mrs Hargreaves, as if she thought he'd said something really clever. 'Not a fashionable word today, and I wouldn't want you to think I'm with Munnings – he's so dull he has no right to criticize anybody – but if we can't enjoy prettiness what hope is there for us?'

They examined 'Early Snow at Louveciennes 1870' in silence. He'd have to say something. 'I find them elegiac,' he said.

'An excellent word,' said Mrs Hargreaves. 'Everybody knows roughly what it means. Nobody knows quite what it means. Dear Henry!' She ran one finger down his cheek and moved elegantly away. Henry turned and came face to face with Mr Hargreaves.

'Good, aren't they?' said Mr Hargreaves. 'Jamot said Sisley had no ambition except to be the delightful minor poet of the country

158

and the seasons. I find that rather difficult to reconcile with some of his late haystacks, don't you?'

Courage.

'I have to say I don't know much about Sisley's late haystacks.'

'Ah.'

'I don't know much about his early haystacks either.'

'Ah.'

Belinda Boyce-Uppingham approached, oozing, if not sexuality, an aura of healthy vigour and cleanliness that would do almost as well. 'Henry!' she said. 'How you do keep popping up in my life.'

Mr Hargreaves was able to escape from Henry while pretending that he was tactfully leaving him with Belinda.

To his horror Henry heard himself say, 'I know. We've got to stop meeting like this.'

'I hope not,' she said, fervently.

Did she mean it? He felt an erection trying to find room to express itself, just below the marinated carp, in a suit into which he'd only just been able to squeeze himself in flaccid sexlessness after a modest breakfast. Journalist in society wedding fly-button horror. Down down. Probably she didn't even remember that she'd once called him a 'bloody oik'. Social indignation strangled his erection.

'Still scribbling away on your paper, are you?' she said. Well, at least she'd remembered, but 'scribbling'!

'Yes,' he said. 'Scribble scribble!'

'Jolly good,' she said. 'Henry? Will you let me say how sorry I am for something awful I called you many years ago when I knew no better?'

The bell rang for round two of the fight between Henry's erection and his hired suit.

'Ah! Robin. There you are. Meet Henry Pratt,' said Belinda. Henry found himself looking at a tall man with thighs like oak trees and skin like sandpaper, who was looking down on him like a member of the Royal Family admiring a pumping station whose workings bored him to distraction. The fight was stopped. The hired suit was declared the winner.

'Hello, Henry Pratt,' said Robin. Henry asked Robin about his views on Sisley's late haystacks. Robin's eyes glazed over, and they made a hurried escape from him, which freed him from the necessity of making a hurried escape from them.

He approached Tosser and congratulated him.

'Thanks, Henry,' said Tosser loftily, as if Henry were still his fag. This irked Henry, and he couldn't resist saying, 'I saw the Wales match.' Tosser made a cheerfully wry face and said, 'Oh Lord. Did you? I had a bit of a stinker.'

The man didn't even seem mortified! How insensitive could you get?

Lampo joined them, smiled his slightly twisted, sardonic smile and said, 'Hands off, Tosser. You're married now,' and Henry thought he was going to blush.

'Careful of La Lampo, Henry,' said Tosser. 'Her spell in the WRACS has made her more sexually devious than ever.'

'Did you do national service, Lampo?' said Henry, with such surprise that Lampo laughed.

'Yes. I couldn't think of a decent excuse,' said Lampo. 'I became a sergeant in the education corps. Priceless.'

Tosser drifted off at last.

'What a bore he is!' said Lampo affectionately. 'I wonder whether he'll bore her to death or crush her to death.'

'Oh I hope they're happy,' said Henry, with a depth of feeling that surprised him. 'I like Diana.'

'Randy little bugger, aren't you?' said Lampo. 'Henry? Come to Italy with me.'

'What?'

'I assume you *are* given holidays from your sordid tasks. I'm going to Italy for several weeks. Pop over and see me. I want to show you Italy.'

'Well, I . . . er . . .'

'No strings attached. I know how horrified you are by the homosexual side of your nature.'

'Lampo!'

'Sorry. I can't help teasing. I'm so pleased to see you.'

'Why?'

'God knows. Absurd, isn't it? Henry, it is true that, absurd though you look in those clothes . . .'

'Thank you.'

'. . . perhaps *because* you look so absurd in those clothes, I would, were your views on the matter different, enjoy . . . a relationship. But not in Italy. Italy's too beautiful for sex. Nobody in Venice or Siena could possibly have eyes left for you. In Runcorn or Barnsley I might try to seduce you, to take my mind off the surroundings. In Italy you'd be safe. Please come.'

'Have you ever been to Barnsley?' said Henry, glowering.

'Of course not!' said Lampo. 'Oh dear. I've offended the Yorkshireman in you. I notice you don't bother to defend Runcorn. Henry, on your holidays, if you can tear yourself away from the delightful towns of South Yorkshire, with their fine public buildings, spacious libraries, ample toilet facilities and charming citizenry, will you let me show you the most beautiful cities in the world?'

'Why does everybody want to show me Italy?'

'Everybody?'

'Our arts editor. An ageing queer with parchment skin and a limp.'

'A limp what?'

'Oh God. Why did I describe him like that? How ungenerous. But why do you all want to show me things? As if I didn't know.'

'Oh. So you know. Why do we?'

'Because I'm a blank page. I have no personality. You all want to create me in your image.'

'What mawkish rubbish. Henry, I can't speak for your arts editor with his limp parchment, but I want you to come to Italy because you're not blasé. With you I can live each day as if it's my last and look at Italy as if I've never seen it before. Will you come?'

'Yes.'

Henry was as surprised by his answer as Lampo.

The last British troops left Suez 'quietly and with dignity', in accordance with the 1954 Anglo-Egyptian agreement. Charges for school meals, passports, driving tests and higher education classes were increased. Martial law was declared in Poznan after 38 people including communist officials had been killed in riots. In the Wimbledon finals, Lew Hoad beat Ken Rosewall and our very own Angela Buxton lost to Shirley Fry. On the day before the wedding of Helen and Ted, Henry received a letter from Auntie Doris.

Dear dear Henry [she wrote]

My Geoffrey and I are to be married on Saturday, August 18th, in Skipton. A lot of people are going to say we should have waited, but I'd been parted from Teddy for a long time so 'the damage had been done'. Geoffrey's all I have now and I hope you'll come and give us your 'blessing'. Who knows what would have happened if I'd met my Teddy again but that's all 'past history', as they say. I think I should tell you I told Geoffrey what you told me. He admitted it. He just couldn't help himself, and he hates himself for it. You'll find, Henry, unless you're very lucky, that 'the physical side of things' brings as many problems as joys and those without 'skeletons in the cupboard' are lucky. Geoffrey's promised not to do it again, and I'll be watching him. So what you told me's put me in a position of strength. I expect that seems shocking to you but, remember, we're quite elderly business people marrying as much for convenience and security as for love. Don't despise things like convenience and security, Henry. You'll come to value them as the body starts to disintegrate. Oh dear! I am cheering you up, aren't I?

Anyway, Geoffrey wants to be good friends with you and wants you to come to the wedding. He says if ever things don't work out in 'the world of journalism' there'll always be a job for you in the catering industry. We also want the sniffer to come. Oh Lord, I shouldn't call her that, should I? Hilda and I are chalk and cheese but blood is thicker than water, as they say. We're sending her an invite but suspect she might refuse. We know how close you are to her, so would you be an angel and use your famous charm?

Henry, my darling, your silly old auntie has realized over the years that she loves you very much.

XXXXXXXXXXXXXXXXXXXXXXX (One for each year of your life and one for luck) Doris

'How close you are to her'! He hadn't been to see her for weeks. 'Your famous charm'!

He felt touched by this letter, and less upset than he'd have expected at the thought of Auntie Doris marrying Geoffrey Porringer. But he did also feel a little depressed.

Would he ever be done with other people's weddings?

On Saturday, July 14th, 1956, Cypriot terrorists warned that, for every Greek child killed by the security forces, Eoka would kill a British child. Marilyn Monroe, arriving in Britain for the first time, was asked who she wanted to meet, and said, 'Sean O'Casey and Dame Edith Sitwell.' Sir Anthony Eden said, 'We are in mortal peril, not of immediate unemployment, but of poverty by stages.' Ex-King Farouk of Egypt offered to remarry his first wife, Farida. She refused. Ted Plunkett did marry Helen Cornish. Henry pocketed three handkerchieves, in case Ginny needed them.

Ben Watkinson was picking them up and driving them to Buxton. Ginny knocked on Henry's door five minutes before Ben was due to arrive.

She was wearing green and looked at her largest, but he knew that he wouldn't need the handkerchieves. She was a war correspondent, going to the front line.

'Will you do something for me?' she said shyly, very embarrassed.

'If I can.' Her embarrassment made him cautious.

'Will you make it look as if you and I are . . . you know? Gordon's wife'll be there.'

The reception was held in the ballroom of the Palace Hotel, a large stone hydro, standing above Buxton like a lesser château which had somehow become separated from the Loire. The ballroom was a high-ceilinged, elegant room, with huge windows overlooking gardens which sloped to a domed hospital and the dignified, classical, dark grey spa town.

Henry stuck to Ginny like a parking ticket. Helen was so radiant that Henry wondered if she was regretting the marriage already. She had looked achingly lovely as she'd walked up the aisle in what she would have described, in one of her fashion articles, which Ginny despised, as a beautiful wedding gown of lace and pleated tulle, with a short train, a full-length veil with a crown of orange flowers, and a bouquet of white orchids, stepha-notis and lilies. She kissed Henry warmly, as if finding him attractive for the first time in months. And then Denzil was approaching. It was happening again. He was only attractive to queers and brides.

'When are you off to Filey?' said Denzil. 'Filey?' said Henry, awkward in his dark suit. 'Filey. With your aunt,' said Denzil. 'Oh. Yes. Filey. I'd forgotten. Because I'm not,' said Henry. 'Not going to Filey? I invited Henry to Italy, Ginny. He said he was going to Filey,' said Denzil. 'Well, I'm not. I'm actually going to Italy, funnily enough. Change of plan,' said Henry. 'But not with me,' said Denzil grumpily. 'Well, I can't. I'm going with my uncle,' said Henry. 'Ah, your uncle! Not your aunt,' said Denzil. 'No. I was telling Ginny only yesterday, funnily enough. Wasn't I, Ginny?' said Henry. 'Telling you what, Ginny?' said Denzil. 'About his uncle and his aunt,' improvised Ginny. 'They were very good to him as a child. They've split up. He goes on holiday with them in alternate years. He thought this was an aunt year, but it's an uncle year. This is a different uncle from the one who was killed, of course, otherwise Henry wouldn't be going on holiday with him.' 'Right,' said Henry. What a wonderful woman she was. If only he loved her.

Denzil wasn't sure whether to believe them, and in any case he was grumpy and jealous. Henry felt that Denzil was diminishing as he got to know him better. He wanted Denzil to be stylish and outrageous, not grumpy. And yet, as Denzil diminished, Henry found that he liked him more.

Denzil introduced them to Helen's younger sister, Jill. She was a little shorter than Helen, fractionally fat, somewhat flat-chested, with a tiny mouth. She was shy, gawky and, Henry suspected, sensual. He desired her very much indeed. Ginny tucked her arm into his and led him through the throng, out of danger.

They spoke, briefly, to several of Helen's relatives and to Ted's mother, who seemed to be his only relative. The champagne flowed. Henry could see Ted, over by the cake, glowering at the champagne as if blaming it for not being Mansfield bitter. Colin Edgeley called it a ponce's drink. 'Glenda likes it,' he said. 'Pity she couldn't come.' Henry didn't want to feel guilty about liking champagne. He wanted to be a man of the people, drinking pints out of straight glasses. He also wanted to be a connoisseur of fine wines. He wanted to be all things to all men. Was he in fact nothing to anybody?

Ginny clasped his arm even more firmly as they found themselves talking to Gordon and Hazel Carstairs, who were also firmly indivisible. Hazel was fair-haired, blue-eyed and slightly plump. She looked tired. Henry thought her attractive, in a very middle-class, trim way, which didn't seem to go with Gordon. 'Hello, young lovers,' said Gordon without a hint of shame. 'Not a bad wedding, is it? Pity it's such a grey day, though.' Henry was amazed. He'd never known Gordon deliver such a comprehensible message. It was so banal that he felt ashamed for Gordon. 'It's a shame we couldn't have had a bit of sun,' Gordon continued, 'but at least the rain's held off.' Didn't he speak in code when accompanied by his wife? Was it all an act? Or was this the act? He looked Gordon straight in the face and received a totally blank look in return.

'How are you, Ginny?' said Hazel. 'I'm almost surprised to find you're still on the paper. Gordon never speaks of you any more.' Henry was afraid that Ginny would blush, but she was made of sterner stuff than that. Then he was afraid that *he* would blush. Luckily, Ginny replied, 'Doesn't he? Well, I don't see much of him. I'm otherwise engaged these days, aren't I, love?' 'He's blushing. You're embarrassing the young man, Ginny,' said Gordon. Henry felt obliged to take part in this repellent charade. 'I've got a flat in the same house as Ginny,' he said. 'Say no more!' said Gordon, and Henry was happy to obey. Hazel smiled throughout this exchange, and Henry had an uneasy feeling that her smile hid bottomless pain and that she saw through the charade completely and despised them all utterly. But he might be wrong about this, because he also had an uneasy feeling that, for a journalist with an international future, he knew very little about people.

He was glad to move on to Ben Watkinson and his shy, petite wife Cynthia. Another couple who didn't trust each other to go their separate ways, but steered side by side round the crowded ballroom as if on a slow, invisible dodgem car. 'I hope the light's better in Leeds,' he said. 'Why?' said Cynthia, astonished. 'The cricket,' said Henry. 'Silly me. I might have guessed. Bloody sport again,' said Cynthia. Ben glared at Henry. Henry thought this unfair. It was hardly his fault if he never talked to Ben about anything except sport. He'd tried to shift the relationship onto a more personal level, now that he knew about Ben being a conscientious objector. It hadn't worked. He didn't think Cynthia looked the sort of person to whom you went home to give one, in mid-evening, on the rug, before supper. Was all that another lie? Colin passed by, his plate piled high. For a man who professed to have no interest in food, he couldn't half shovel it in when it was free, thought Henry uncharitably.

And every moment of every conversation, even as Helen kissed him bubblingly on the cheek, as if there were champagne in her veins instead of blood, he was aware of the exact spot in the room occupied by her sister. 'Dear Henry,' said Helen. 'You won't desert us when we're knee-deep in nappies, will you?' 'Excuse me,' he said, and he strolled over towards Jill, leaving Ginny and Helen alone together, united in their displeasure at his abrupt departure, but with nothing whatever to say to each other.

He caught up with Jill just as she was leaving the buffet. His heart was pumping.

'Hello, Jill,' he said. 'What's it like being Helen's sister?' Oh no. The world's most stupid question. Quite rightly, she ignored it. His next question was no more sparkling, but infinitely more answerable. 'What do you do?'

She blushed. Shy! Warm, too.

'I'm still at school till July.'

'Good Lord! You look too old. Mature. Grown-up.'

'Excuse me. I must . . . er . . . move on.'

'Yes. Yes, of course.' Be bold, Henry. 'Jill? Will you come out some time?'

'No, sorry, I . . . sorry.'

'Why not?'

'I don't know you.'

'You would know me if you came out with me.'

'No.'

'Give me one good reason why not.'

'I don't find you remotely attractive.'

She walked on past him, her face grim and blazing. His face was blazing too. He had an uncomfortable feeling that everyone at the reception was looking at him. He hurried to the buffet, and began piling a plate with things that he didn't even see. Never in the whole of his life would he ever again risk humiliation by having anything whatsoever to do with a woman. He felt an arm on his arm. It was Ginny's. She'd seen his humiliation and suffering and, even though he'd deserted her, she had come to his rescue. What a magnificent woman she was. He loved her.

Sir Bernard Docker, sacked by the Birmingham Small Arms Company for extravagances including having five Daimlers with special bodywork built for the exclusive use of himself and Lady Docker, sent out 10,500 telegrams declaring that he wasn't extravagant. The pay of farm workers went up 6s. to £7 1s. for a 47 hour week. Hungary's hated boss, Matyas Rakosi, resigned amid open jubilation in Budapest. Britain and the United States withdrew their offer to loan Egypt £7,500,000 to start work on the Aswan Dam. Colonel Nasser retaliated by nationalizing the Suez Canal Company. It was the wettest July for 100 years.

The rain battered on the rotting window frames at the back of number 66, Park View Road. A bowl of dying chrysanthemums stood on the unlit blue-tiled stove. A faint aroma of toad-in-the-hole lingered. Cousin Hilda switched the television off.

'You needn't switch it off,' said Henry.

'It's a poor night,' said Cousin Hilda. 'We've had Alma Cogan. All we've got now is some play by some Russian, some people looking at paintings and talking, and a lot of Austrians yodelling on their zithers. I ask you! Who plans these things?' ITV hadn't come to Thurmarsh and, even when it did, Cousin Hilda would die of boredom rather than watch it. 'Anyroad,' she continued. 'It's common to keep the television on when strangers call.'

'I'm not a stranger,' said Henry.

'Mrs Wedderburn said to me the other day: "I haven't seen that nice young Henry recently. Does he visit you regularly?" She can be right nosy, when she's a mind to it, can Mrs Wedderburn. Well, I couldn't lie. I said, "He comes as regularly as you'd expect a busy young man to visit an elderly relative."'

'I'm sorry. I keep meaning to.'

'Intentions are cheap.'

'I know. But I am busy. I will come more often. I promise. I think of you a lot.'

'Thoughts don't cost.'

'I know.'

Cousin Hilda didn't offer him so much as a cup of tea, for fear it would pollute the purity of his motives in visiting her.

'So what have you come about?' she said.

'I haven't come about anything,' he said. 'Can't I just have come to see you, because I want to?' Oh god. How do I raise the subject of the wedding now? 'How's Liam?'

'The same as always.'

'And Mr Pettifer? Having a run on Stilton, is he?'

'You seem to have forgotten that he's been moved to general groceries. But I suppose it's natural for young people to be self-centred these days.'

He ignored this. 'How's he bearing up?' he asked.

'He puts a brave face on it, but he's a shadow of his former self.'

'And Mr Frost?'

'He has peace of mind. He's made the right decision. He's abandoned the lure of the bright lights and is looking forward to buckling down to the responsibilities of marriage.'

Bless you, Cousin Hilda. A cue!

'Talking of marriage, I suppose you got Auntie Doris's invitation.'

Cousin Hilda sniffed. 'It went where it belonged. In the dustbin.'

'Cousin Hilda!'

'You expect me to accept? Marrying a man who runs a pub, with your Uncle Teddy barely cold.'

'It's a hotel, actually.'

'That makes it all right, I suppose. I thought you didn't like him, anyroad. Slimy, I seem to recall, was your description.'

'I wish I hadn't said that now.'

'Why? Isn't he slimy?'

'Well . . . yes . . . I suppose he is . . . but it doesn't seem generous.'

'Generous! If he's slimy, he's slimy. You can't avoid facts.'

'No, but . . . I think sliminess is in the eye of the beholder. And I beheld it. And I wish I hadn't.'

'So you regard my conduct in throwing Doris's invitation to her wedding with this slimy person while the husband she abandoned is still practically warm into the dustbin as unjustified?' Cousin Hilda just managed to hang onto her syntax, but the effort had exhausted her.

'No, but . . . she'd like you to be there.'

'I hardly think that's likely.'

'I know she would. She asked me to ask you.'

'So that's why you came round!'

'No. I'd forgotten about that. Then you mentioned Barry Frost's wedding, and it all came back.' Cousin Hilda sniffed. 'I *had* forgotten it.'

'I didn't say owt.'

'No, but you sniffed.'

'What?'

'Sometimes, when you disapprove of something, you sniff. You probably don't realize you're doing it.'

'I see.' Cousin Hilda sniffed. 'I'll try to stop it if it upsets you.'

'It doesn't. I just . . . look, I know Auntie Doris would like you there because . . . well, I don't think there'll be many family, and blood is thicker than water, as they . . . I mean, I don't approve, but . . . I forgive. Can't you forgive?'

Cousin Hilda sniffed.

'Something puzzles me, Cousin Hilda,' said Henry. 'I'm not a Christian any more, but I can forgive. You are, and you can't. I thought forgiveness was a big bit of the . . . er . . . the whole caboosh, but . . . it worried me a bit when I was a Christian. It seemed to me that some Christians didn't have any forgiveness in their hearts at all.'

Cousin Hilda's new cuckoo clock, a reminder of Mrs Wedderburn's holiday in Lucerne, a reminder that Cousin Hilda had never been abroad, ticked remorselessly.

'I'll come,' she said.

He didn't want her to. It would be embarrassing. It would have been so much easier without her.

Why had he gone to such lengths to persuade her?

'Oh good,' he said. 'That's grand.'

He kissed her.

She sniffed.

Jim Laker bowled England to the Ashes at Old Trafford, taking 9 for 37 and 10 for 53. There were several feet of hailstones in Tunbridge Wells on August Bank Holiday Monday. Aly Khan sought a new divorce from Rita Hayworth. Egypt refused an invitation to a conference in London to establish an international system for operating the Suez Canal. An air lift of British troops to the Mediterranean began. The Foreign Secretary, Mr Selwyn Lloyd, said, 'We are not bellicose. With Britain force is always the last resort.' Eoka called for a truce in Cyprus. And on Saturday, August 18th, Auntie Doris married Geoffrey Porringer.

As he walked towards the low, crenellated, blackened stone church of Holy Trinity, Skipton, with its squat, solid tower and huge black clock with gold numbers, showing that it was 11.22, Henry's mind went back to the War years, when his mother had brought him to the town for a treat. They'd seen *The Wizard of Oz*, and a display of blitz cookery by a team of girl guide advisors. He wished it was that day now, and the wedding wasn't taking place, and Cousin Hilda wasn't walking with pursed lips at his side.

In the church there were memories of childhood too. There was Auntie Kate, five foot one, white-haired, beaming. In the War Henry had lived with her and Uncle Frank at Low Farm, outside Rowth Bridge. Uncle Frank had been dead for eleven years. Henry was filled with shame and horror as he realized how long it was since he'd seen or even thought about her. She lived in Skipton now, in a house with lurid patterned carpets, with her daughter Fiona and Fiona's husband, Horace Brassingthwaite, the assistant bank manager with the artificial leg. In the War Fiona had been a princess who'd read Henry stories from comics when he'd had measles. Now she was a wife, a mother of three, a sweeper of lurid carpets. She and Horace were in the church, too.

The remaining guests were Ollie Renishaw, barman at the White Hart, and Geoffrey's son Stephen and daughter Geraldine. Eight guests, occupying just two of the numbered pews, each with its own door, beneath the great beamed roof. Henry recalled the splendours of Diana's marriage to Tosser, and felt sad. 'We wanted it small,' Auntie Doris said later. 'We could have invited lots of customers but, once you've started, where do you stop?'

Henry felt that Geoffrey Porringer made a surprisingly impressive figure. Now that he'd settled in the country, he was slowly, imperceptibly becoming less slimy. Of course nothing could be done about his blackheads. Nobody, in secret laboratories in Cumbria and Suffolk, was giving hamsters blackheads in order to find a cure for the condition in humans. Henry felt that he might even become quite fond of the man, for Auntie Doris's sake, now that the die was cast, provided he could desist from rubbing against waitresses and calling him 'young sir'.

The little group trooped through the cold August rain, down the wide high street and into the Black Horse, where they had booked a private room.

They took sherry before the meal. Cousin Hilda sniffed.

'Come on, Cousin Hilda,' implored Henry. 'Just the one.'

'Certainly not,' said Cousin Hilda.

Geoffrey Porringer told Geraldine that she could have 'just the one'. Geraldine Porringer was sixteen years old. She looked like her father, except that she had no blackheads.

'Don't order me around, Dad,' she said. 'I've come here to enjoy myself because I'm happy to see you happy.' After that, Geoffrey Porringer made no comments about Geraldine and drink.

Ollie Renishaw, a tall, dour man with bags under his eyes, had a drip on the end of his nose. Cousin Hilda sniffed meaningfully but, since he had already realized that she sniffed at regular intervals, he took no heed. Geraldine, onto her second sherry, whispered to him. He blew his nose hurriedly. Within minutes the drip was there again. It was as if a washer in his nostril was on the blink.

'I was right happy at Low Farm,' Henry told Auntie Kate. 'The happiest time of my life.'

'Oh, I hope not,' she said, but he could tell she was pleased.

'I wish I'd come to see you more often,' he said.

'Why haven't you?' said Horace, and Henry tried not to look at his artificial leg.

'Because young men are self-centred,' said Henry.

Horace opened his mouth, but could think of no reply so, wisely under the circumstances, he closed it again.

'I hope Graham'll manage on his own,' said Ollie Renishaw.

'Relax,' said Auntie Doris. 'Forget the bar. You aren't indispensable. Nobody is.'

'Oh aye. I know that,' said Ollie Renishaw. 'But it's the price rises. He hasn't got the hang of them at all.'

'So we'll lose a bit of money,' said Auntie Doris. 'Never mind. It's our wedding day. Enjoy yourself.'

'Right,' said Ollie Renishaw grimly. 'Right.'

Geoffrey Porringer was very fussy about where everybody sat, at the big table, in the beamed, low-ceilinged room. 'You look after Geraldine, young sir,' he told Henry.

On Henry's other side was Auntie Kate. Cousin Hilda was put next to Ollie Renishaw.

There was good red roast beef and claret. Cousin Hilda asked for a well-done slice off the edge and complained that she'd been given too much. She glanced at Henry every time he took a sip of wine, so he said, 'This is a very nice wine,' and her lips moved painfully, and he wished he hadn't said it.

'It's a thoughtful little number,' said Stephen Porringer, who was twenty-one and a trainee manager at Timothy Whites. 'It combines the strength of a Burgundy with the finesse of a claret.' Henry detected no trace of self-mockery.

Geraldine whispered in his ear, 'Don't you think my brother's a prick?' Henry felt overcome with sorrow that she wasn't attractive. She deserved the best of men, and wouldn't get him because the world is a cattle market. He whispered back, 'A total prick.'

'Whispering?' said Stephen. 'A state secret, or may we share it?'

'Certainly,' said Henry. 'I was telling your sister she combines the purity of a good Chablis with the sweetness of a vintage hock.'

Geraldine chortled. Stephen didn't.

'I'm awfully happy for Dad,' said Geraldine. 'He was so sad when our mother died.'

Henry realized with a shock that he'd never dreamt that

Daphne Porringer had died. He'd assumed that Geoffrey had left her, or that she'd left Geoffrey.

'So where do you live?' he asked Geraldine.

'With my mother's childless married sister,' said Geraldine Porringer. 'It wasn't thought right that I should live with Daddy, partly because he wasn't married to your auntie, and partly because he runs a pub.'

'So they objected on two premises, one moral, the other licensed,' said Henry, and to his shame he found himself wishing that he could have said it to somebody prettier. Geraldine Porringer would be liked by everybody and loved by nobody.

With Auntie Kate he reminisced about the village school, Miss Candy, Billy the half-wit, Jackie the land girl and other ghosts.

'There's a wedding reception at the Crown this afternoon,' said Ollie Renishaw sadly.

Geoffrey Porringer made a tiny grimace. Auntie Doris leant over towards Cousin Hilda and said, 'The Crown's a pub on the opposite side of the square from us, Hilda.'

'The relative position of public houses in Troutwick is of no conceivable interest to me, Doris,' said Cousin Hilda. Henry had to admire her. He decided that, for Cousin Hilda's sake, he wouldn't have any more wine.

'It's a Rowth Bridge wedding,' Auntie Doris told Auntie Kate. 'They couldn't have the reception there. The groom's banned from the Parish Hall and his dad's banned from the Three Horseshoes.'

'That sounds like the Luggs,' said Auntie Kate.

'It is. Eric Lugg,' said Auntie Doris.

Henry felt himself going cold.

'Who's he marrying?' he asked, trying to sound casual.

'One of our ex-waitresses,' said Ollie Renishaw. 'Lorna Arrow. She . . .'

'Careful what you say, Ollie,' said Auntie Doris, who always made things worse by protesting about them. 'Lorna used to be a great friend of Henry's.'

'I was only going to say she left us very suddenly,' said Ollie Renishaw.

'Thank you, Ollie, but I think we'd best draw a veil over that,' said Auntie Doris, who sometimes made things even worse by protesting about them twice. She smiled at Geoffrey Porringer, a warm smile, a forgiving smile. Henry saw Geoffrey Porringer relax, and realized how little the man felt able to want from life now. To be able to relax, to be let off the hook, these were his ambitions.

The waiter offered Henry more wine. After the startling news about Lorna Arrow, he hadn't the strength to refuse. He compromised. 'Just half a glass,' he said. 'I don't want to drink too much.' Cousin Hilda's lips twitched. 'You already have,' said her twitch.

'We'll get drunks from the wedding tonight,' said Ollie Renishaw. 'I hope we'll be able to handle them. We don't want trouble with you away on your honeymoon.'

'Stop worrying,' said Auntie Doris. 'Oh, he is a worry-guts.'

'Where are you going?' said Fiona.

'Interlaken,' said Geoffrey Porringer.

'Very nice,' said Horace Brassingthwaite. 'A lovely spot.'

'You know it?' said Geoffrey Porringer.

'No,' said Horace.

'We will,' said Ollie Renishaw.

'Will what?' said Auntie Doris.

'Get drunks in.'

'Luggs,' said Auntie Kate.

'Drunk Luggs,' said Fiona.

'Is that serious, drunk Luggs?' said Geoffrey Porringer.

'Geoffrey!' said Auntie Doris. 'We're going on our honeymoon.'

'I'm not saying we aren't,' said Geoffrey Porringer. 'I'm only saying, not being acquainted with drunk Luggs, is it serious? Should we recruit extra staff?'

'It *is* serious,' said Henry. 'You *should* recruit extra staff. I'll come.'

There was silence. It seemed that the prospect of the availability of Henry to deal with hordes of drunk Luggs didn't remove entirely the worries of Geoffrey Porringer and Ollie Renishaw.

'The more hands, the better,' said Henry. 'I'd like to help you, Geoffrey.'

Geoffrey Porringer looked surprised. But pleased. 'Thank you very much,' he said. 'I accept, young sir.'

Cousin Hilda sniffed loudly.

'What's that supposed to mean, Hilda?' said Auntie Doris.

'What's what supposed to mean,' said Cousin Hilda.

'That sniff. One of your loudest.'

Cousin Hilda sniffed. '"One of my loudest"?' she said. 'I'm sure I don't know what you mean, Doris.'

'At moments of disapproval you sniff, Hilda. Probably you don't realize you're doing it. I wondered to what particular disapproval we owed that snorter?'

'To me working behind a bar,' said Henry. 'But I won't be working, Cousin Hilda, because I won't be paid. I'll be helping Auntie Doris, who helped bring me up – as you did, of course, and thank you – by letting her go on her honeymoon with an untroubled mind.'

'I thought you were coming home with me,' said Cousin Hilda. 'We were going to have supper with Mrs Wedderburn. I've left cold for my businessmen.'

'I'll just have to forgo Mrs Wedderburn for the greater good,' said Henry.

Cousin Hilda sniffed.

'Promise you won't refuse to serve me because I'm under age,' said Geraldine Porringer.

'I'm afraid I'd have to,' said Henry. 'Even though in your case it'd be unnecessary, because you're so mature.'

'Geraldine's squiffy,' said Stephen.

'Am not, prick,' said Geraldine.

There was non-vintage port, with the cheese.

'What's the time?' said Cousin Hilda, as soon as she decently could. 'I'm thinking about my trains.'

'Twenty-two minutes past two,' said Henry.

'I hope Graham won't forget to ring the bell for last orders,' said Ollie Renishaw.

Ollie Renishaw drove back, in his rusting blue van, as if convinced that Graham would have missed a smouldering fag end, which would reduce the White Hart to rubble. Brief beams of sunlight were breaking through the dark canopy of the clouds, lighting up the occasional sycamore, a distant stone barn, the corner of a field on the far hills. It was as if lace curtains were briefly parted, to allow a vision of a beautiful woman.

The van screamed to a frenzied halt, beside the unburnt hotel. It had started to rain again.

Henry's motives in offering to help man the bar were not entirely unselfish. He didn't really expect trouble. He believed that the Luggs became involved in frequent fights because, since they had a reputation for becoming involved in frequent fights, people frequently picked fights with them, accusing them of frequently picking fights with people. Tonight, in the comparative gentility of the White Hart, nobody would pick on them.

His real motive was to visit the reception of Mr and Mrs Eric Lugg.

He walked slowly across the square, between the stalls, in his only suit, still wearing the buttonhole from the other wedding. He had bemoaned the frequency of weddings that summer, and now here he was on his way to yet another one, to which he hadn't even been invited.

He approached the Crown with increasing reluctance. There was a great roar of talk and laughter. But he must go on, now that he had come this far.

He entered the pub, and said, 'Hello' to Edna, the landlady. She remembered him, and escorted him to the function room.

The room was awash with rustic good humour. There were the remains of a sit-down ham tea, but the lads in their bursting suits were congregating once more at the bar, cradling pints in their great outdoor hands.

Lorna looked at him in astonishment and turned as white as her virginal dress. 'Henry?' she said. 'What are you doing here?'

He was unwelcome. Well he would be. Why hadn't he thought of that?

'Auntie Doris and Mr Porringer got married today.'

'My God!'

'I know. And I thought, as I'm here, well, I couldn't miss the chance of wishing you every happiness.'

'Thanks.'

In her relief, she kissed him warmly. He wondered what she had thought he'd come for. How thin she was.

Eric Lugg hurried up. How huge he was.

'You remember Henry?' squeaked Lorna.

'Oh aye. I remember Henry,' said Eric Lugg. 'I called him the evacuee squirt.'

'Lorna and I were good friends once,' said Henry. 'Before your time, of course.'

'"Before my time"?' said Eric Lugg. 'What does tha mean "Before my time"? There never was a time before my time.'

'No. No,' said Henry. 'Oh no. No. No, I just meant, I liked Lorna. She liked me. We liked each other. And I thought, Well, I know what those Luggs are like. Friendly. If Eric Lugg ever found out that an old friend of Lorna and of his sister Jane had been in Troutwick and hadn't come in to drink to their happiness, he'd be one angry insulted Eric Lugg.'

Eric Lugg digested this speech slowly. 'Have a pint,' he said at last.

'Right,' said Henry, deeply relieved. 'Thanks.'

He couldn't talk to Lorna on her own. He felt a million miles away from her. He was deeply upset that she was marrying Eric Lugg, an instructor in the catering corps. He was deeply upset that he was deeply upset that she was marrying Eric Lugg, an instructor in the catering corps. He grinned at Eric Lugg and allowed himself to be embraced almost to the point of strangulation by a very drunk Jane Lugg, whom he had once courted, till she had nits. It crossed his mind that she might have been a better choice for England than Tosser Pilkington-Brick. He nodded and chatted with his old friend Simon Eckington, with his old tormentor Patrick Eckington, with Simon's wife Pam, whom he had once courted, till she had nits. He chatted with Lorna's parents, with Luggs known and Luggs unknown. He chatted and laughed with everybody except Lorna, his first consummated love. He insisted on buying a large round of pints, which he couldn't afford, in lieu of a wedding present. He clinked glasses with Eric Lugg.

Eric Lugg clasped him in a hugely affectionate embrace. 'You're one of us,' he said.

Oh no, thought Henry, as he grinned his sheepishly pleased apparent agreement. Oh no, Eric. One of somebody I may be, although I haven't found out who yet. One of you, that I most definitely am not.

12 A Day in the Life of 22912547 Signalman Pratt

'There's been a mistake, sergeant,' said Henry desperately, peering out from under the slightly damp sheets and gently festering blankets, and looking up at the hard, threatening face of Sergeant Botney. 'I've done my national service.'

'Well now you're doing it again, laddie,' said Sergeant Botney. 'And it's three years this time.'

'You can't do national service twice, sergeant.'

'You can if the authorities say so, son. And they say so. They've decided they need you. Gawd knows why.'

'But I have a budding career as a reporter, sergeant.'

'Well now you're going to have a budding career as a soldier, sunshine. Who are *you*??'

This question was barked at Signalman Brian Furnace, who had just popped up from under the sheets.

'Signalman Furnace, sarge,' said Signalman Furnace.

'Two soldiers in one pit!' thundered Sergeant Botney. He pulled back the bedclothes and stared down at the naked intertwined bodies of Henry and Signalman Furnace. 'Two naked signalmen in one pit! I've never seen anything like it. What's going on?'

'We love each other,' said Signalman Furnace.

'You what?? You love each other?? This is the British army. You're on a charge. Filthy and idle and stark bollock naked on parade. Get down to the charge room.'

'As we are, sarge?'

'As you are. No! As you were. Get dressed, you dirty little buggers.'

'Aaaaaaaaaaaaaaaaaaaaaaaaaaaaaaaaaaaghhhhh!' shrieked Henry. He pointed towards the ceiling. The inert body of Signalman Burbage was swinging gently in the draught.

'Come down from there, Burbage!' shouted Sergeant Botney. 'Committing suicide on duty. I'll have you for this.'

'Sorry, sarge,' said the dead signalman. He whipped a knife from his pocket and cut the rope that was holding him. His inert body dropped across Henry's. Henry screamed. And woke up.

He was drenched in sweat. Oh, thank goodness, oh sweet and wonderful life, it had been a dream.

Where was he?

He was lying on a palliasse, on a groundsheet, in a large tent. Rain was drumming on the canvas. There was a smell of wet grass, and damp rubber, and male feet, and male sweat, a vaguely disgusting goulash of damp and perspiration. Men were snoring, breathing congestedly, farting in their sleep. The charm of mankind. As opposed to womankind. He couldn't believe that a tent full of women could have been so repulsive.

He was in the army! It hadn't been a dream! He hardly dared look up.

No inert body was swinging there. No naked signalman's body was intertwined with his.

Of course. He was back in the army, for a fortnight, for the first of his three annual territorial reserve camps. He was on the Pennine moors, not more than thirty miles from Rowth Bridge.

They'd be waking up soon, this rag-bag of strangers. Strangers! He'd hoped to meet Michael Collinghurst. He'd hoped and feared that he'd meet Brian Furnace. He'd hoped to see at least some of his old muckers – Taffy Bevin, Lanky Lasenby, Geordie Stubbs. Even Fishy Fisk, who smelt of herrings.

Reveille reverberated over the sodden moors. A curlew trilled defiant rivalry. Men stirred, groaned, swore, farted, belched. The charm of mankind, shamed by a curlew's trill. Nobody hurried. Discipline was lax. The old fears had died down. It was a shambles. It was raining. Nothing to hurry for.

At Richmond Station, in September 1953, at the beginning of it all, Henry had said, 'I'm a man.' Sweat streamed off him at the thought of that grotesquely premature boast.

If he'd been a man, he wouldn't have joined in the destruction of Burbage. Burbage was clumsy. Timid. Shy. Not intellectually brilliant. A little odiferous. There's no point in idealizing him because he's dead. He was a clumsy, smelly, hopeless case. Hopeless. Dead. Hanged himself.

179

Sergeant Botney had made them laugh at him by numbers. 'Squad will laugh at Signalman Burbage, squad . . . wait for it . . . squad . . . at Signalman Burbage . . . laugh!' And all together they had shouted, 'Signalman Burbage smells two three ha two three ha two three ha ha ha.' Man's natural inhumanity to those weaker than himself had been tempered by unease, by a sense of their own weakness, by the knowledge that they weren't being beastly to Burbage of their own free will but because they were under orders, they were only one rung above him on the ladder of humiliation. Afterwards they'd told Burbage that they hated doing it, didn't mean it, only did it because they had to.

They'd still done it. Henry too. He'd not said, 'I refuse to laugh at Signalman Burbage, sergeant. It's cruel and humiliating and I'd rather go to military prison in Colchester.' He'd said, 'Ha two three ha two three ha ha ha.' And Burbage was dead. Hanged himself.

People were getting up. Armpits of tangled hair were appearing and being wearily scratched. The charm of mankind.

Henry went through the deepening mud to the ablutions. He thought about Flanders, and didn't complain. He endured breakfast. He thought about Eric Lugg, and *did* complain. Back to the tent, waiting. A shambles. There were no wireless sets here, so he couldn't employ the only craft the army had taught him. Some days they were shown things. Today, somebody was supposed to show them flame-throwers. Nothing happened. They mooched in a damp tent. Gus Norris approached him.

'Pratt? You're an educated sort of geezer, ain't yer?'

'I can't demur.'

'What?'

'Nothing.'

'No, I mean, you are, ain't yer? Educated. Well, more than me, like.'

'I suppose so.'

'They can't keep us 'ere, can they? Only it's me dad's shop, see.'

'What?'

'. . . 'e's goin' into 'orspital, i'n' 'e? Next munf. I'n' 'e? Bleeding backside's bleeding bleeding. Got to 'ave a hoperation, 'asn' 'e?'

'I'm sorry.'

'I gotta run the shop 'cos it's me mum's nerves with me nan ill an' all. 'aven' I?'

'Well, yes, Gus, I suppose you have.'

'They can't make us do anuvver two years, can they? I mean, because of the crisis and all that and everything. In the Middle East and that. Can they?'

'Of course they can't.'

'Only some of the lads said they can. I mean, with the canal and the oil and everything and that. Only it's me dad's shop, innit?'

'We're here for a fortnight, Gus. They *are* calling up a few special reservists. They don't just call you in for a fortnight and then keep you. If there's ever a general mobilization, it'll be done later. And you'll probably get exemption on compassionate grounds, because of your dad's arse.'

'Honestly?'

'Honestly, Gus.'

'I wish I knew fings. I wish I was an educated geezer like you.'

An educated geezer. He'd never thought of himself as that. Thought of himself as uneducated, because he hadn't gone to university. Could probably have just about squeezed in, if he'd tried. Hadn't ever really thought about it. Why not? Because nobody in the family ever had? Because he was frightened of not squeezing in? Because he was frightened of squeezing in and being so much worse than everybody else? Because he was in love with the romantic concept of 'real life'? Too late to think about it all now, anyway. *Je ne regrette rien.* The Edith Piaf of the *Thurmarsh Evening Argus.*

They were told to get fell in. They got fell in. The late August rain continued. They marched four miles up sodden tracks. They were told to get fell out. They got fell out. They stood, in their capes, watching nothing. The rain eased off. A mobile canteen provided them with hot food. It was cold curry. 'They said we'd 'ave 'ot food,' said Gus Norris. 'It is hot,' said Henry. 'Mine's stone cold,' said Gus Norris. 'So's mine,' said Henry. 'I fought you said it was 'ot,' said Gus Norris. 'It is,' said Henry. 'What are you on about?' said Gus Norris. 'The curry is a hot curry, even though it's stone cold. We can't get them on that one, the sods,' said Henry. 'I wish *I* was an educated geezer,' said Gus Norris.

An officer addressed them through a megaphone. 'Erm . . . hello, men,' he said. 'Erm . . . we were going to have a demonstration of . . . erm . . . flame-throwers, which I think you'd all have found very . . . erm . . . I know I would, but there you are, apparently there's been a . . . erm . . . through no fault of ours, we're rather in the hands of the flame-thrower chappies, so I'm afraid we'll rather have to scrub round that one for the moment, which is jolly bad luck. However, never fear, we are hoping to arrange a . . . erm . . . and it *is* at short notice, so you'll have to bear with us, a . . . erm . . . display of . . . erm . . . camouflage techniques, which should be jolly interesting. So . . . erm . . . for the moment . . . stand easy.'

Since they were all standing easy already, there was no response to this instruction. And at that moment Henry caught sight of Brian Furnace and understood immediately that the ghost which still had to be laid wasn't Burbage, but Brian Furnace. The whole thing was such a shambles that there seemed to be no objection to walking about, so he wandered over towards Brian. A pair of grouse flew low over the moors towards them. Catching sight of several hundred soldiers, and knowing that it was after the glorious twelfth, they veered away, in understandable panic, and disappeared over the mist-drenched horizon. Henry walked up to Brian with a heart that was beating like a grouse's wings.

'Hello, Brian.'

Brian swung round and looked quietly astonished.

'Henry!'

Brian looked so placid. Always so placid. His face still boyish, but his arms strong and muscular. He worked for his father, who was a builder in Fareham. Brian liked working with his hands. It was hard to believe that Brian's heart had ever beaten like a grouse's wings.

'Yes.'

'My God!'

'Yes. We'll go for a few drinks tonight, eh?'

A rendezvous arranged, Henry wandered back to his unit. The officer spoke again through the megaphone.

'Erm . . .' he said. 'I'm afraid, men, I have bad news for you.'

'They've found the flame-throwers,' shouted a wag.

A volley of cries from NCOs rang out over the wet moors. More grouse flew off. Their cries of 'Go back' mingled with shouts of 'Shurrup' and 'Belt up, that man' and 'Hold your tongue, the officer's talking.'

At last order was restored sufficiently for the officer to continue talking.

'Erm . . .' he said. 'Efforts to locate the camouflage team at short notice have unfortunately failed. Perhaps they . . . erm . . .' His voice took on an exaggeratedly jocular tone, signalling and destroying the joke. '. . . perhaps they were too jolly well camouflaged, what?' The sergeants laughed uproariously. The corporals smiled. They only laughed uproariously at the sergeants' jokes. The men didn't laugh at all. 'So . . . erm . . . let's all get fell in and see if we can have a jolly good march back to base.'

They had a jolly shambolic march back to base. Once, in Germany, that creep Tubman-Edwards had said, 'Any complaints?' and Lanky Lasenby had said, 'Yes, sir. There's an awful smell of shambolic in the bogs' and Tubman-Edwards had said, 'Don't you mean carbolic?' and Lanky Lasenby had said, 'Have you been in the bogs recently, sir?' and everybody had laughed and the great lump of blackmailing yak turd had decided to find it amusing too so as not to lose face and Lanky Lasenby had got away with it as usual.

After their jolly shambolic march, they had a jolly disgusting tea – what *did* Eric Lugg teach them? – and then Henry and Brian walked five miles, on a bitterly cold and grey but no longer wet summer evening, to the Red Lion at Scunnock Head, an old copper miners' pub, the third highest in Britain. There, in the flagged bar, at a bare wooden table, in front of a fire that was roaring even in August, Henry and Brian drank good, strong Stones's bitter and talked of everything except what mattered.

They laughed about the method of marching that Lanky Lasenby had invented. The front ranks took huge steps, the back ranks took tiny steps, the squad elongated like a concertina, and they could never find anybody to blame.

They laughed about the language of Corporal Pride. Cousin Hilda, whose look could strangle swear words at birth, approved of national service as character-building. Henry wished she could have met Corporal Pride. He hadn't been a man of many words, but a man of one word said many times. He used it as adjective, noun and verb. They laughed as they recalled him saying, 'Wot you done to this rifle, Pratt? The fucking fucker's fucked.'

What they didn't talk about was their night-time embraces in German haystacks, their nights in a back street hotel in Aachen, with the church bells ingrained upon their guilt.

Henry had decided what he'd say. He'd say, 'Brian. I'm sorry I didn't write. But . . . it's over, you see. It was just because the sergeant warned us of the dangers of the *Fräuleins*, and Lorna was so far away, and there I was, awash with youthful sexuality, in that strange, masculine, military world. And I liked you. But I've found out now that I'm completely heterosexual. Sorry, Brian.'

He'd say it on the long, dark walk back, when Brian couldn't see his face.

They set off, briskly, through the raw night.

'I'm sorry I didn't write,' said Brian, just as Henry was going to say 'I'm sorry I didn't write.' Which left Henry saying the infinitely less impressive: 'Yes. So am I.'

'I'm engaged,' said Brian.

'What?' said Henry.

'To this nurse from Truro.'

'Ah. Great.'

'It was just . . . you know . . . the sergeant warning us about the *Fräuleins* and everything.'

'Yes.'

'Sorry, Henry.'

'What?'

'You're upset, aren't you?'

'No. It's just that . . . I was going to say the same thing to you.'

'What?'

'About us. And the sergeant and . . . er . . .'

'Oh. Well, that's all right, then, isn't it?'

'Yes. I'm engaged too. She's called Jill Cornish. She's an air hostess.'

They would avoid each other for the rest of the fortnight and, when they'd gone home – Gus Norris's fears were unfounded – Henry would never hear again from his national service lover.

He crawled onto his palliasse, utterly exhausted, and was soon asleep.

Sergeant Botney was waiting.

'Right, you 'orrible little man,' he said. 'I've got you where I want you now. You're going to be sorry you ruined my wedding anniversary, Signalman Henry Pratt. You've signed on while pissed, sunshine. I'm going to ruin your next fifteen years.'

13   In the Land of Romance

The famous landmarks of Florence floated like islands above a sea of red roofs. Around those great domes and bold elegant towers, those soaring triumphs of individual inspiration, lay the unified dignity of the city, the classical lines of the stark palaces, the genius of communal restraint. It was as if the eternal clash between the freedom of the individual and the discipline of the state had been frozen, in stone and marble, here on the banks of the Arno.

It was impossible, walking in that great city, set among hills dotted with crumbling golden villas, silvery olive trees and lines of dark cypresses, to believe that at that very moment, in Thurmarsh, under a lowering sky, in a dusty news-room, Terry Skipton was assigning reporters to magistrates' and juvenile courts.

'Podger!'

A Pavlovian *frisson* ran down Henry's spine. Only in the army had they called him Podger.

Michael Collinghurst, tall, hook-nosed, with blue eyes and light brown hair, was crossing the dark, elegant Via Tornabuoni towards them, smiling from stick-out ear to stick-out ear.

Henry's face lit up at the sight of his old friend. Lampo Davey's face darkened at the sight of Henry's face lighting up. A dark-haired, older young man in fawn open-neck shirt, blue shorts, red socks and sandals crossed the road reluctantly to join them.

'This is Father Ellis,' said Michael Collinghurst.

Father Ellis smiled austerely, carefully. He had very hairy legs and had shaved carelessly. Why should I be surprised when priests are hairy? thought Henry.

They went to an open-air café in the Piazza della Signoria, studded with statues, dominated by the crenellated, machicolated Palazzo Vecchio, with its high, slim, boldly off-centre tower.

Michael and Henry ordered extravagant ice creams with delight. Father Ellis ordered an extravagant ice cream with shame. Lampo ordered an espresso coffee.

'Well, Henry,' said Michael. 'You are how?'

'Bad not too, oh. Grumble mustn't,' said Henry.

'To you again see, very it's good,' said Michael.

'Too you,' said Henry.

Father Ellis and Lampo Davey looked puzzled.

'It's a little had we habit,' explained Henry. 'Words our orders unusual in putting.'

'Hours military boring slight the easement of for,' said Michael.

Father Ellis and Lampo seemed pained at these juvenilia.

'I've decided to become a Catholic priest,' said Michael, with that sudden simplicity which Henry remembered so well.

Henry realized that his dismay was discourteous to Father Ellis. He tried to smile. It was a failure. Lampo relaxed when he saw Henry's dismay. The ice creams arrived. Lampo frowned.

'I'm twenty-one years old,' said Henry. 'I like ice cream.'

'Some Anglo-Saxons lose all restraint when they go south,' said Lampo. 'I like self-discipline and austerity. I think I'd make a good monk if I believed in God.'

'If you can say that,' said Father Ellis, through a mouthful of ice cream, 'I think you're very close to coming to God.'

'Yes, I've had a narrow escape,' said Lampo.

Michael laughed. Father Ellis flushed and tried to look as if he wasn't enjoying his ice cream.

'How's your religious state, Henry?' said Michael. 'I remember hearing all about your discovery and loss of faith in Thurmarsh.'

'It's lost for good, I think,' said Henry.

'Never say that,' said Father Ellis.

'I believe in good and evil,' said Henry. 'I don't believe that there's an actual being, shaping our destinies. I've never seen why there's any difficulty in believing in good and evil without believing that they're imposed from above. And even if God did exist, I don't see why people should take his authority upon themselves in his name. The last thing we need, in our spiritual life, is a system that's as authoritarian and hierarchical as the system we're saddled with in our temporal life.'

Henry felt exhilarated. This was European café life, and he was part of it! He attacked his ice cream with renewed relish.

'Lunch together have we shall?' said Michael.

'Idea splendid a what,' said Henry, before Lampo could make

their excuses. He felt happy. In putting his words in the wrong order, Michael wasn't simply fooling. He was telling Henry that their friendship could survive his entry into the priesthood.

'Put don't more any order wrong in words, Michael,' said Henry.

'Right quite,' said Michael. 'Sorry oh. Done I've again it!'

Father Ellis frowned at his protégé.

'You have a very frivolous side to your nature, Michael,' he said.

'Because he's deeply confident about his basic seriousness,' said Henry. 'I think you aren't confident enough about your seriousness to be remotely frivolous.'

Father Ellis's unevenly shaven face flushed. Henry realized that, if you were going to be rude to people, you had to be careful not to hit upon the truth. He'd have to fight against the dangerous intellectual confidence which this beautiful city was imparting to him.

They strolled along dark streets that smelt of heat and cats and peppers and distant drains. They wandered through noisy markets, full of people with caustic yet gentle faces. In the church of San Lorenzo, they gazed in awe at sculptures by Michelangelo. They were massive, yet delicate. They were vibrant with individual life, yet steeped in universal meaning. How Henry hoped that, in the face of this most supreme art, which couldn't be described in words because otherwise it wouldn't have needed to be created in marble, nobody would say anything.

'Amazing,' said Father Ellis. 'Truly incredible. What an artist.'

They ate in a restaurant in a tiny, dark square called the Piazza dei Maccheroni. They ate outside, under an unnecessary awning. The wine flowed. Michael drank with all his old gusto. Father Ellis drank with less gusto, but even greater capacity. Lampo drank sparingly. Henry was glad to be in the presence of people who were greedier than Lampo. Four days of Lampo's company had made him feel almost bestial.

'I wonder if people ever thought all these buildings were too new,' said Lampo. 'All this dreadful modern development. Appalling.'

'I think there was a much clearer consensus about what was beautiful in those days,' said Michael. 'But I think when we gaze at them now we're much too romantic and forget why they were built. No doubt there were boards in front of them announcing, "Another Prestige Development for the Medici Family".'

Father Ellis gave Michael a look, as if realizing that he was going to be a troublesome priest.

Henry and Michael ate pasta and *saltimbocca.* Father Ellis plumped for *minestrone* and steak florentine. Lampo ate only one course – Parma ham and fresh figs, lightly spattered with black pepper.

'We're going to Siena tomorrow,' said Michael. 'Why don't you come too?'

Lampo was planning to take him to Siena the next day. He knew that Lampo wanted them to be alone together, in Siena. This casual lunch in the Piazza dei Maccheroni had been a revelation. Childhood friendships had failed him. New friendships had puzzled him. Close friendships with homosexuals filled him with tension. But here, in Michael Collinghurst, with whom he hadn't communicated since his army days, he knew that he'd found true friendship, beyond all sexuality, friendship cemented by humour, friendship for life. He didn't need to prove it by going to Siena with Michael. He could afford to be generous to Lampo. 'Sorry,' he lied. 'We can't tomorrow.'

If they hadn't gone to Siena later than planned, Henry might never have met the young woman who would become his wife.

An old woman with black clothes and a sunny heart showed them to a large, rather bare back room with a double bed. Henry threw back the creaking shutters and gazed out. Swifts shrieked over the jumbled tiled roofs of Siena. The stern, narrow, shady medieval streets plunged into a deep valley and marched up the other side towards the cathedral. The great brick building, with its marble bell-tower, seemed huge against the darkening sky. Henry sighed. He sighed because you can't hold beauty in your hands and feel it. He sighed because of the double bed.

That night he lay so close to the right-hand edge of the bed that there was a danger of his falling out.

Lampo laughed. 'I'm not intending to ravish you, you know,' he said.

Lampo slept as delicately as a cat, on that still, hot night, naked under a single sheet, in that lumpy, twanging Italian bed. Henry lay still, stiff as a board, listening to the lone mosquito. At first light Lampo woke, padded across the room and opened the shutters, which didn't creak for him. Henry pretended to be asleep. It seemed eternal, that night, and Henry thought about people who are imprisoned for thirty years.

In the morning, Henry had five inelegant bites. Lampo had none. Perhaps the lone mosquito liked the taste of tension.

It was a surprise to find that the city was alive, and not frozen in time. They climbed through streets that were seething with humanity. Tiny vans were delivering trays of bread and figs. The cries of vendors mingled with the ecstatic greetings of people who were meeting for the first time since the previous evening.

Henry gazed in awe at the rich, decorated façade of the cathedral, a Gothic fantasy resting on three Romanesque portals. The interior, with its forest of striped black and white marble pillars, was stunning. The floor of the huge, bare nave was marble also, and covered in decorated paving showing Bible stories. An Englishman was reading a guidebook in a loud hiss. 'The interior may seem over-elaborate to many with more spare northern tastes.' No! Not to this northerner. Henry tried to close his mind to all words, to see only shapes and colours and patterns. A baby doesn't wonder at the world any the less because it hasn't yet got any words with which to describe it.

He was filled with joy. He could flower under this southern sun. There was more to life than he'd ever dreamt. There was more to himself than he'd ever believed. In that great religious building Henry, who had no religion, felt in a state of grace. He felt good. He felt strong. He felt pure.

After two hours of feeling good and strong and pure, he felt extremely hungry.

They wandered, through curving shaded streets, past pinky-red Gothic palaces, towards the Piazza del Campo, the great central square of that most female of cities. In front of them were two bare-legged young women in cotton dresses. The one in the white dress had thin, vulnerable legs. The one with the yellow and white horizontal stripes had slightly fleshy legs.

Gently curving, gently sloping, shaped like a scallop, vast in scale, surrounded by pink palaces with curving façades, dominated by the vast Palazzo Publico and its pencil-thin tower, the Piazza del Campo could turn even an itching, sweating, frustration-soaked, mosquito-ravaged, immature, repressed English podge-clot from thoughts of slightly fleshy legs.

But not for long. The moment he looked round, he saw that yellow and white striped dress being helped into a chair by a suspiciously attentive waiter in the nearest of several restaurants with outdoor terraces.

'Let's eat there,' said Henry. He hurried across to the restaurant and, before Lampo could stop him, sat at the table next to the two girls.

Lampo frowned.

The moment he heard the girls speak, Henry leant across and said, 'Ah! You're English.'

The gaunt one frowned, as if to say, 'If we'd wanted to meet English people we'd have gone to Southwold.' Fleshy legs smiled. Her mouth was crowded with big, strong, white teeth, which protruded slightly. She had sandy hair.

Henry introduced himself and Lampo, who smiled with suspiciously immaculate politeness. The one with sandy hair was called Anna Matheson. The gaunt one was Hilary Lewthwaite.

'Lewthwaite,' said Henry. 'The only Lewthwaite I know is a clapped-out draper's in Thurmarsh.'

'That's our shop,' said Hilary Lewthwaite.

'When I say clapped-out,' said Henry, 'I mean I really like it. I love old-fashioned shops. When I was a kid, Lampo . . .' He dragged Lampo into these reminiscences as if he were a recalcitrant mule. '. . . I used to be absolutely fascinated by the thing they had that whizzed the change around on wires.'

'The Lamson Overhead Cash System,' said Hilary.

A waiter brought menus to both their tables.

'Where are you from, Anna?' said Henry, leaning across towards her.

'Ullapool Grove,' said Anna Matheson.

'In Thurmarsh?'

'Yes.'

'Look . . . why don't we share a table?'

'Great idea,' said Anna Matheson.

She explained to the waiter.

'He won't understand you just because you speak louder,' said Hilary.

Lampo explained, icily, in impeccable Italian.

'Ah! You share table. Is good,' said the waiter. He seemed pleased for the girls, and held their chairs out for them with a pleasant smile. Lampo had a pleasant smile too, but Henry knew that beneath it he was seething. Hilary had flashed a quick look at Anna, beseeching her not to move. Now she smiled thinly, grimly. She was as pale as a barn owl, while Anna was golden brown.

'Ullapool Grove!' said Henry. 'I can't get over it.'

'Do try,' said Lampo.

'No, but . . . I mean . . . it's a coincidence, isn't it?'

'Yes,' said Lampo. 'Oh yes.'

'Where do you live, Hilary?' said Henry.

'Perkin Warbeck Drive,' said Hilary.

'Where's that?' asked Henry.

'It runs from Lambert Simnel Avenue through to Wat Tyler Crescent,' said Hilary reluctantly.

'Has anybody got a street map of Thurmarsh?' said Lampo. 'No? What a shame. It would have eased the monotony of looking at Siena.'

'Siena's lovely,' said Henry hastily. 'It's like a beautiful, gentle, passionate woman.' He looked into Anna Matheson's eyes. They were blue and, he fancied, hungry. He liked what he saw in Anna Matheson's eyes. He was trying not to tremble. He'd always known that, when love came, it would come like this, as quick and joyous as a swift on the wing.

In the square, beyond the awning, toddlers chased pigeons and a soldier gazed into the fountain with his sweetheart. The waiter took their orders.

'This is a bit different from the Rundle Café,' said Henry.

'You don't eat in the Rundle Café?' said Anna.

'Sometimes,' admitted Henry. 'The Rundle Café's a café in Thurmarsh, Lampo.'

'No!' said Lampo. 'You amaze me. It has such a Parisian ring.'

'I had a holiday job there once,' said Anna. 'You wouldn't eat there if you could see their kitchens.'

'You wouldn't eat there if you could see their food,' said Henry.

'For goodness sake,' said Lampo. 'Here we are in the most beautiful square in Europe, and you're talking about a bloody awful café in Thurmarsh.'

'You've eaten there, Lampo?' said Henry. 'It *is* bad, isn't it?'

Lampo stared at Henry coldly. Hilary snapped a bread stick in half as if it reminded her of a man she'd hated.

'You're very quiet, Hilary,' said Henry.

'I've got nothing to say,' said Hilary.

Anna gave Hilary a beseeching look. The waiter brought their starters – melon for Lampo, soup for the girls, *antipasto alla senese* for Henry. Henry put his left hand on Anna's right knee, under the table. She slid his hand up under her dress, laying it gently on her warm, bare thigh. Their eyes met.

'When you say a holiday job,' he said, 'where were you on holiday from?'

'Thurmarsh Grammar.'

'I don't believe this.'

'Oh, I do,' said Lampo. 'What more natural if one lives in Thurmarsh?'

'You too, Hilary?' said Henry.

Hilary nodded, as if finding it disagreeable to remember Thurmarsh Grammar School for Girls.

'I was at Thurmarsh Grammar School for Boys,' said Henry. 'I founded the Thurmarsh Grammar School Bisexual Humanist Society. Did you know Karen Porter or Maureen Abberley?'

Each ringing Thurmarsh name thudded into Lampo like a harpoon into a whale. He thrashed around in disbelief. 'Do let's forget the beauty of Tuscany,' he said. 'Thank goodness there's no danger of our discussing the art gallery and its treasure chest of Siennese painting. Come on. Let's talk some more about Karen Porter and Maureen Abberley.'

'They're very beautiful,' said Hilary.

'Karen Porter and Maureen Abberley?' said Anna.

'The paintings,' said Hilary grimly.

'My God, they're doing a double act now,' said Lampo. 'The Elsie and Doris Waters of Siena.'

'They're just a couple of prick teasers,' said Henry.

'Elsie and Doris Waters?' said Anna.

'Karen Porter and Maureen Abberley,' said Henry.

Lampo groaned. The waiter brought their main courses. Anna removed Henry's hand from her thigh, stroking it gently with one nail before she gave it back to him. Anna and Henry attacked their food with gusto. Lampo and Hilary picked at theirs. If Lampo had been heterosexual, there would have been two perfect pairings. But how was he to arrange an assignation with Anna without upsetting Hilary and, more important, upsetting Lampo, his friend and host?

'What are you doing this afternoon?' he asked.

'The cathedral,' said Hilary hastily.

'The cathedral, it seems,' said Anna.

'Well, I mean, we decided that,' said Hilary.

'What would you rather do, Anna?' said Henry.

'I don't know. Do you have any suggestions?' said Anna.

'We're going to the art gallery,' said Lampo hurriedly.

'We're going to the art gallery,' said Henry.

'Well, I mean, we decided that,' said Lampo.

'I just *said* we're going there,' said Henry. 'So what are we arguing about?'

'I wouldn't mind going to the art gallery again,' said Anna.

'*Again?*' said Hilary, and Henry couldn't decide whether she was being dim or awkward. 'You said you found religious paintings depressing.'

'I do,' said Anna, 'but, as you said, they're very beautiful, very spiritual. You kept telling me what an important stage in the development of perspective they illustrated. I'd quite like to have a look at that aspect of them again.'

'Well, I'm sorry,' said Hilary. 'I'm not going there again. They *are* beautiful, but too male-oriented for me.'

'Look, if it's any problem,' suggested Henry, '*we* could go to the cathedral again.'

'I'm not going to the cathedral again,' said Lampo.

'You said it was one of the loveliest buildings in Europe,' said Henry.

'It is,' said Lampo. 'I saw it this morning. I remember it distinctly. Big thing with pillars. I don't want to see it again.'

The waiter looked puzzled as he took away their plates. Puzzled by the atmosphere. Puzzled at the food left on Lampo's and Hilary's plates.

'You go and see the pictures, then,' said Henry. 'I'll go to the cathedral.'

'I want to see the pictures with you,' said Lampo.

'Oh God.'

The waiter brought a large bowl of fruit.

'There's no problem,' said Lampo. 'You go to the cathedral. I'll go back to the room and read, and tomorrow we'll look at the pictures.'

'We'd better get the bill and get on, whatever's happening,' said Hilary. 'Our bus leaves at five.'

'Bus?' said Henry. 'You aren't staying in Siena?'

'No.'

He had second thoughts about going to the cathedral. There was hardly going to be an opportunity for ardent love-making in the North Transept, or even for declarations of love, especially with Hilary tagging on. His first meeting with Anna would end in anti-climax. And he knew where she lived. He could meet her in Thurmarsh. Their life stretched before them.

'Look,' he said. 'I don't want to upset you, Lampo. Or Hilary.' He smiled at Hilary. Her answering smile was as thin as the ham in a railway sandwich. 'Why don't the girls go to the cathedral, and we'll go to the art gallery, and I'll arrange to see the girls later in Thurmarsh.' He put his hand on Anna's thigh. She put her hand on his, sealing the pact.

The waiter brought one bill. Lampo worked out what everyone owed. Henry didn't think that was stylish. He longed to pay for Anna's meal, but didn't see why he should pay for Hilary's, especially as she hadn't finished it.

'Quite reasonable, really,' said Anna. 'We had a drink in a café out here last night, and it was terribly expensive.'

'It would be,' said Lampo. 'You pay extra to sit outside. You're expected to sit as long as you like. You paid a reasonable price for a front seat in the stalls at the theatre of life.'

'In Thurmarsh you'd pay less because you had to look at the view,' said Henry.

'We're back in Thurmarsh,' said Lampo. 'Goodie goodie. How I've longed for a reference to it this last dreary hour.'

The waiter took their money. Henry felt disagreeably mean.

'Come on, Anna,' said Hilary. 'Time to go to the cathedral.'

'Yes, *sir*. Coming, *sir*,' said Anna.

They stood up. Henry waved away the waiter with the change. They walked out, into the fierce sun. They walked up a narrow alley, into the Via di Citta, past the imposing Chigi Saracini Palace, round the corner and up the hill. Henry wished he had the courage to take Anna's hand. They came to the parting of the ways.

'Well,' said Anna, 'this is *arrivederci* time.' She kissed Henry. He hugged her briefly. She kissed Lampo. Politeness demanded that Henry kiss Hilary. Their cheeks touched lifelessly. She didn't kiss Lampo.

The girls set off towards the cathedral. Henry stood and watched them, although Lampo set off impatiently towards the art gallery. Anna turned and waved. Henry waved back. He was trembling with love, as a great ship trembles on the ocean.

Great indeed were the masterpieces hung in the red-brick, late-Gothic Palazzo Buonsignori. Delicate indeed were the works of Guido di Siena, Taddio di Bartoli, Pietro Lorenzetti, Ambrogio Lorenzetti, Duccio di Boninsigni and many more. Names little known outside Siena, men long dead, but immortalized in these gentle works.

Henry found that a little religious painting went a long way. He couldn't feel the excitement, in these cool, silent rooms, that he'd felt in the cathedral. He wished there weren't quite so many madonnas with quite so many *bambini*. He wished that so many of the madonnas didn't look constipated. He wished that so many of the *bambini* didn't look as if they were heroically suppressing wind in the service of art. He wished that the men didn't look quite so disapproving of such fripperies as women and children, as if they found even a virgin birth too vulgar for their refined sensitivities. Was this the subtly subversive intention of the artists, or was it the product of Henry's imagination?

He was in love. He was lonely. He was in the wrong mood. In several of the pictures there was a priest holding a red book. 'Is that the Michelin guide, do you think, Lampo?' he said. 'Is that some medieval Father Ellis wondering where to eat after the adoration is over? "Little place round the corner does the best veal in Bethlehem. And the carafe myrrh is very reasonable."'

'For God's sake, Henry,' said Lampo.

'I'm sorry, Lampo,' said Henry. 'But I can't help thinking how much more interesting all this would be if they hadn't had to paint religious subjects all the time.'

Lampo didn't reply. Henry had spoilt his afternoon.

When they left the gallery, Lampo was still sulking. They walked slowly, past pink and gold palaces, through a hot city that was slowly crumbling, as it had always slowly crumbled. In the doorways of small dark shops and bars, men with faces that were cynical but not cruel talked the day away.

Cautiously, Henry touched Lampo's arm.

'It's a lovely city, Lampo,' he said. 'I promise I won't mention Thurmarsh again the whole holiday. Oh my God!!'

Denzil Ackerman's limp seemed even worse than usual, and his right eye had been comprehensively blackened.

'I thought you were in Amalfi,' said Henry.

'How touching that you're so pleased to see me,' said Denzil. 'Aren't you going to introduce me to your uncle?'

They stood stock-still in the middle of the Via di Citta. Businessmen and fat mothers swirled around them. Elegant young men drifted past them. Three American girls in unwise shorts, licking peach and pistachio cornets, bumped into them.

'Ah! Yes!' said Henry. 'Denzil, this is my Uncle Lampo. Uncle Lampo, this is Denzil Ackerman.'

Lampo shook hands with Denzil like an automaton. He seemed stunned by his sudden elevation to uncledom.

'You're much younger than I thought you'd be,' said Denzil.

'What?' said Lampo.

'I always imagine uncles as rather grizzled,' said Denzil. 'Pipe-smokers. Wearers of carpet slippers.'

'I smoke nothing, and I'm glad to say I own no slippers of any kind,' said Lampo. 'I must be . . .' He raised a sardonic and inquiring eyebrow at Henry. '. . . a rather unusual uncle.'

The tide of humanity swept them back into the sunlight of the Piazza del Campo, as if it were a whirlpool and they were three dead eels.

'Uncle Lampo isn't a bit grizzled,' said Henry. 'You'd never guess he was thirty-seven.' He turned to Lampo. 'Denzil asked me to come to Italy with him,' he said. 'I said I couldn't because I was going with you.'

'Ah!' said Lampo.

'I . . . er . . . I explained that, you being my uncle, naturally I had to come with you.'

'Ah!' said Lampo.

'I mean, not that I didn't want to. I did. I wanted to go with you both.'

'Henry and I are colleagues,' said Denzil. 'In Thurmarsh.'

'Where else?' groaned Lampo.

'How's your wife?' said Denzil.

'My wife?' said Lampo.

'My aunt,' said Henry. 'Since it's several years since you split up, I expect you've almost forgotten you ever had a wife.'

'Almost,' said Lampo.

'I told Denzil how I got in a bit of muddle,' said Henry. 'I thought it was my year to go to Filey with auntie. But of course it wasn't.'

'Shall we stop for a drink?' said Denzil.

'Not me,' said Lampo. 'I'm finding it quite a strain pretending to be so much younger than my thirty-seven years. I'm for a lie-down.'

'Shall we meet up for dinner later?' said Denzil.

'An excellent idea,' said Lampo. 'It's always interesting meeting my nephew's friends.'

They dined in a little back street trattoria, at a table next to six exuberant Finns. Henry was uneasy. He was worried that Denzil and Lampo, his two friends from different parts of his life, wouldn't like each other. He knew that he was feeling rather ashamed of his friend, but he didn't know which friend he was feeling ashamed of. At first, he assumed it must be Denzil. He flinched at the artificiality of his voice, the affected outrageousness, as he gave his views on the merits of the Siennese School of Painting. But Lampo adopted an infuriating air of self-satisfied superiority. Henry felt that Lampo must see through Denzil's affectations, and Denzil must dislike Lampo's priggishness. And the Finns, who clearly understood English, were probably artists and laughing at them both. Oh, hot and uncomfortable young Yorkshireman, damp and inelegant between your two queer friends.

Denzil asked for the wine list and insisted on ordering a very expensive bottle of Chianti, although everyone else was drinking the house wine. It took them ten minutes to find the bottle. It arrived encrusted in dust and dirt. The waiter showed Denzil the completely illegible label. Denzil nodded. Lampo smirked. The Finns grinned. Henry sweated.

He tried to remain cool and detached, but heard himself say, 'You two ought to get on well. You've a lot in common.'

They immediately revealed one thing that they had in common. They both disliked the idea that they had a lot in common.

'Really?' said Lampo. 'What have we in common?'

'Well . . . I mean . . . you know . . . you're both . . .'

'. . . as queer as coots,' said Denzil, unnecessarily loudly. He roared with laughter.

'No! Well . . . I mean . . . yes, but . . . that wasn't what I meant.' Why did he mind that the Finns were listening? The likelihood of his meeting them again was remote. 'I mean . . . you both . . . hate sport, love art, admire style and dislike vulgarity. You're both outrageous. You're both contemptuous of the second-rate.'

'We sound insufferable,' said Lampo.

'Two insufferable people,' said Denzil. 'Is that a sound basis for friendship?'

'Either we'd find each other insufferable or the fact that the rest of the world found us insufferable would bind us together,' said Lampo.

'Contemptuous?' said Denzil. 'What am I ever contemptuous of?'

'Thurmarsh.'

'Ah well. It's impossible not to be contemptuous about Thurmarsh, dear boy. Do you know, Lampo, there's nothing in the town . . . nothing! . . . that could credibly be described as a delicatessen.'

'My God!' said Lampo. 'What do you do for peppered salami?'

'You see!' said Henry. 'You're both such snobs.' But he was pleased. They were getting on well. It was going to be all right.

'Not snobs,' said Denzil. 'Preservers of standards.'

'When have you seen me snobbish?' demanded Lampo.

'At school,' said Henry.

'At school?' said Denzil. 'Surely you weren't at school together?'

'Oh no. No. No,' said Henry. 'No. Of course not. He's sixteen years older than me. No, I . . . er . . . I *heard* you were snobbish at school, Lampo. Living off egg mayonnaise with anchovies. Doing mimes. Your snobbery's a legend in the old alma mater.' At the end of term concert, Lampo had done a mime representing 'Sir Stafford Cripps in the Underworld'. It had died a death. What a death it had died. Henry found himself smiling at the memory. Lampo and Denzil stared at his smile with curiosity. He wiped it from his face and tried to eat his spaghetti elegantly. He failed. He wiped that from his face too.

'This wine's undrinkable,' said Denzil. 'Sorry. Mario!' he sang out. '*Vino horribile. Vino repulsivo.* We'll try some of your plonk. *Il plonko rosso, per favore.*'

Henry cringed at Denzil's arrogance and insensitivity, in front of the Finns, in front of Lampo, who spoke impeccable Italian and had such immaculate courtesy towards those whom he thought inferior to him, which was practically everybody. Yet the waiter, who'd have hated Henry, if Henry had behaved like that, smiled indulgently, as if Denzil were a child. Lampo smiled and frowned at the same time, as if wanting to despise Denzil but finding it impossible.

'Did you not discover . . .' Suddenly Denzil seemed to become extremely arch. '. . . your . . . er . . . your tastes till you were married, Lampo?' he said.

'What?' said Lampo. 'Ah. Yes. Precisely. That's what did for the marriage, of course.'

The house wine arrived. Lampo poured it. He gave Henry half a glass. 'Henry's parents entrusted his moral well-being to me,' he told Denzil. 'They were particularly anxious that I should save him from the perils of drink.'

For their main course they had *piccato di vitello*, with various sauces. Henry's was *pizzaiola*, thick with tomato, garlic and capers. Denzil's was *marsala*, mature with wine. Lampo's was *al limone*, as tart as an old cat's gaze.

'I can no longer ignore that eye,' said Lampo. 'Painful though it may be for you to discuss it, Denzil, I have to ask you how you came by it.'

Henry had been appalled by Denzil's black eye. Was every journalist on the *Argus* destined to have one before the year was out?

'You know perfectly well I'm longing to tell you,' said Denzil.

'I know,' said Lampo. 'That's why I didn't ask you.'

'Bitch,' said Denzil indulgently. 'It's a very sordid story.'

'What a relief,' said Lampo. 'I was frightened it might not be.'

'I had a brief affair in Amalfi,' said Denzil. 'He cut up rough when I wouldn't give him money. He struck me with a piece of lead piping. End of sordid story. Pity. He was a dear boy, too.'

'I'm not sure you should talk about this sort of thing in front of my nephew,' said Lampo. 'He's very innocent. He's led a sheltered life.' Henry reached for the wine bottle. 'Not yet, Henry. When uncle says.'

'Oh for God's sake,' said Henry. 'Lampo isn't my uncle, Denzil.'

'Oh my God!' said Denzil. 'How this revelation has shattered my illusions!'

'You knew!' said Henry. 'You knew all the time.'

'You made it up so as not to come to Italy with me. You prefer the company of young queers to old queers,' said Denzil.

'There's nothing between me and Lampo,' said Henry.

'Oh good,' said Denzil. 'I was a bit worried about that.'

He smiled at Lampo. Lampo smiled back. Henry's blood ran cold. He fought hard against believing the unbelievable. He heard, vaguely, their chit-chat.

'Were you happy at school, Lampo?'

'No. I should have been a naval rating.'

'I don't follow you.'

'I'm very good at repelling boarders. Henry was one of the many boarders I repelled.'

Denzil laughed. What could Lampo see in this ageing and affected journalist, with his limp, his parchment skin, his hand-carved Scottish walking-stick and his black eye?

'Did you have an unhappy youth?' Lampo asked.

'Yes,' Denzil replied. 'I think I cheered him up quite a bit.'

Lampo giggled! Giggled! Lampo . . . giggled.

'Mario?' called Denzil.

The waiter, whose name was Angelo, approached indulgently.

'Bring us a bottle of champagne,' said Denzil.

Lampo frowned. He thought champagne too obvious. But he said nothing.

They had arranged to meet at eleven, in a café in the great square. Lampo came alone, elegant in fawn, scattering the pigeons.

'Well,' he said, 'I imagine you enjoyed having the bed to yourself.' He ordered an espresso. Henry ordered a cappuccino. 'You could dream of Anna to your heart's content.'

'Dreams! They're all I ever get.'

'Well, I've got my dream.'

'Denzil??'

'It shocks you, doesn't it?'

'Not shocks. Astounds.'

'We're lonely, Henry.'

'Lonely! You! I've always envied you your sophistication.'

Lampo gave his slightly twisted, slightly weary smile. A Belgian tour party filed into the square.

'I'd have thought sophistication was quite a recipe for loneliness,' said Lampo. 'Don't you think I felt lonely as I saw bloody Tosser leading Diana to the altar? Don't you think I was bitterly envious?'

'But you don't want that, Lampo.'

'That doesn't stop me feeling envious.'

'Of Tosser??' said Henry, so loudly that a passing pharmacist turned to see what passion was stirring this young Englishman. 'You're worth ten thousand Tossers.'

'Another recipe for loneliness,' said Lampo. 'Henry? We have the use of a villa in a place called Marina di Pietrasanta, on the Versilian Riviera.'

'I might not want to go to the seaside.'

'You might not be being invited to go to the seaside,' said Lampo gently.

'What?'

'Homosexuality is illegal. Every time my feelings are stirred I become a criminal. Would you begrudge Denzil and me four days alone together, safe from prying eyes?'

'Bloody hell, Lampo,' said Henry. 'The only reason I didn't go off with Anna was because I was too considerate to you.'

'One of life's little lessons,' said Lampo, smiling his twisted smile. 'Never be considerate to your social superiors unless it suits you. We'll never be considerate to you unless it suits us.'

Lampo paid for the coffee. Denzil was limping towards them. They went to meet him. They stood in the very middle of the great square, in the hot sunshine. Henry knew that his grumpiness was a lost cause.

'I wish I'd recorded it. It would have saved a lot of bother,' he said. 'I've said it in London. I've said it in Buxton. I said it in Skipton and Troutwick on the same day. I may as well say it in Siena. "I hope you'll both be very happy."'

14 In Love

Droplets of dew hung on every leaf and every blade of grass. Thin grey clouds scudded across a leaden sky.

Ginny looked dreadful. Her face was blotchy. Her eyes were red and runny. She gave her nose a blow so gargantuan that he wanted to pretend he wasn't with her.

He put an affectionate hand on her muscular right arm.

'What's happened?' he said. 'Why have you been crying?'

'I haven't been crying,' she said. 'I've got a cold.'

'How's Gordon?'

'He's got a cold.'

The doomed tram groaned as it descended into the dim, sulphorous valley. How mean the streets looked. The traffic came to a complete halt outside Fison and Oldsworthy's – *the* place for screws. Ginny sneezed like a Bofors gun. They crawled past the Popular Café, whose emptiness daily belied its name. On the right was a large bomb-site. Why did English towns never look finished?

The news-room was yellow, brown and grey. Yellow light on a grey morning. Yellow-brown fingers of chain-smokers putting yellowing paper into grey typewriters. Grey hair, yellow teeth and a brown jacket as Terry Skipton ordered him laryngitically to number three magistrates' court. He had a cold. Ted and Helen asked him, nasally, about his holiday. They had matching colds. Everyone had colds, in this disgusting northern land.

And yet . . . it was a magic land. For did it not contain Anna Matheson?

The statue of Sir Herbert Rustwick in Town Hall Square was coated in pigeon droppings. The absurdly large Doric pillars of the court house were black with grime.

A milkman had sold watered milk. A motorist had struck a police car after failing to look left. A displaced Pole had stolen back the seventy pounds he'd lost at poker. It was a morning of small defeats and petty betrayals.

He'd lost touch with world events while he'd been at camp and in Italy. After lunch he went to the newspaper's library, on the ground floor, behind the huge small-ads department, and read the back numbers.

Egypt had expelled Britons. Britain had expelled Egyptians. A mission to Cairo, led by the Australian Prime Minister, Mr Menzies, had ended in deadlock. The plans of Mr Dulles, US Secretary of State, for an Anna users association – no, concentrate. A canal users association – had been described by the leader of the Labour Party, Mr Gaitskell, as so weak that a better name would be the Cape Users Association. In Cyprus, Eoka terrorists had resumed their activities. There'd been violence in Tennessee, Kentucky and Texas as black pupils were escorted to schools that had previously been all-white. Anna had broken the world water speed record at Lake Mead, Nevada. Not Anna! Donald Campbell. Russia had withdrawn from an athletics match against Britain after Anna Ponomareva – *Nina* Ponomareva – a discus thrower, had been charged with stealing five hats, worth £1 12s. 11d., from C & A Modes. Sir William Penney, director of the Anna Bomb Tests – Atom Bomb Tests – at Maralinga, had announced that, due to bad weather, Britain's sixth atomic weapon might have to be exploded on a Sunday. In the end it had been exploded on a Friday. 'Was there pressure?' the *Sunday Express* had asked.

That afternoon, Henry had a phone call.

'It's your friend from the world of industry.'

'Good Lord.'

'I've got a story for you. A scoop.'

'Good Lord.'

'There's no need to be sarcastic.'

'No. Sorry.' Impossible to be excited about scoops, just now. Anna would be home from work in two hours' time.

They arranged to meet in the Pigeon and Two Annas.

After work, trembling with excitement, Henry went to a phone box. Matheson T. J., Tudor Lodge, 17, Ullapool Drive. Thurmarsh 6782. He couldn't ring it. Phones were so impersonal. Much better to call on her later, pretending that he was passing on his way home from his interview.

'Cracking goal of Tommy's Saturday week,' said Martin Hammond. 'Literally rocketed into the net.'

The bar smelt of furniture polish. They sat below the picture of the great flood, and drank glasses of bitter.

'I missed it,' said Henry. 'I was in Italy,' he added, trying to sound blasé and much-travelled. 'Good game, was it?'

'Oh I didn't go,' said Martin. 'But I always read the report. Because of Tommy. Because of the old days.' Henry felt that Martin clung to memories of childhood because he needed to convince himself that he had once been a child. 'Paradise Lane Gang! Those were the days.'

'You hated them,' said Henry.

Martin ignored this. 'What's the minimum wage in Italy?' he asked.

'I've no idea! Well, come on, then. What's the story?'

Martin leant forward and spoke in such a conspiratorial whisper that the scattered early evening drinkers all tried to listen.

'A councillor is in cahoots with a council official to buy up property in the town centre.'

'Which councillor?'

'I don't know.'

'Which official?'

'I don't know.'

'What property?'

'I don't know.'

'Well, thank you, Martin. This is riveting news,' said Henry. 'Actually that wouldn't make a bad title for the trade magazine of the riveting industry. *Riveting News*.'

'There's no need to be sarcastic,' said Martin.

'Sorry,' said Henry. 'It's just that it is the teeniest bit on the vague side.'

'I thought you could burrow. I mean . . . you're the journalist.'

'That's true.'

'It could take the lid off a steaming cauldron of corruption and incompetence. It could reveal the cancer in the municipal body politic.'

'You're right. Thanks, Martin. I'll burrow. How did you come across the story, anyroad?'

'I have my channels.'

'It's hard for me to burrow if you don't give me any idea where I should burrow.'

Martin sighed, then shed a layer of his self-importance.

'I heard it on a crossed line,' he said. 'We've been getting crossed lines. I rang to complain and got this crossed line.'

Henry laughed. Martin looked at him in surprise.

'What did this man say on this crossed line?' said Henry.

'Summat about . . . er . . . the official could use his powers to get certain properties empty or summat. To tell you the truth I was that excited at what I was hearing that I didn't listen that carefully. I got frightened they'd sense me there, listening. I think they may have done. One of them said they shouldn't talk about it on the phone and could they meet in some pub after the council meeting.'

'Would it be too much to hope that you've remembered which pub?'

'I can as it happens. Summat to do with Dr Livingstone.'

'The Livingstone?'

'Could have been.'

Henry ordered two more beers from the waiter, whose name, he had discovered, was Oscar.

'What's the status of shop stewards in Italy?' asked Martin.

Henry looked at him in astonishment. 'I don't know,' he said. 'I was looking at the most beautiful cities in the world. I wasn't asking people about shop stewards.' It was a shock to realize that he hadn't had a single conversation about anything with an Italian. It was a shock to realize that he wasn't confident that his attitude of amused superiority to Martin was remotely justified.

'How are you today?' inquired Henry, when Oscar brought the drinks.

'Very well, thank you, sir,' said Oscar. 'It's right ironical. I'm a shocker for colds, me, and now everybody's got one and I haven't!' He walked away, sensed their disappointment, and returned. 'I'll tell you what I have got,' he said, like a parent offering a child a consolation treat. 'And it's summat I never ever have. I'm usually the other way, if anything, if you take my meaning.' He lowered his voice and produced his nugget. 'I haven't been for five days. Five days.' He nodded twice and moved off.

'How's work?' said Henry.

'Ruddy awful today,' said Martin. 'Mr Templeton's canary escaped and got into the mechanism. Charlie Fancutt risked his life to rescue it.' Henry's face must have revealed his astonishment. 'Well, he's managing director, is Mr Templeton. And he's very attached to that canary. It's a descendant of the canary that his grandfather sent down the pit so if the air was poisoned they'd find out when it died. Which it didn't, presumably, or it wouldn't have had descendants. Unless it died after it had had its descendants, of course.'

'Now that *is* a story,' said Henry.

Tudor Lodge was a large, detached house with a pretentious curved gable, set back from the road up a steep drive. One curtained window was lit.

If only he wouldn't shake. What was wrong with him? And his legs weren't steady. He'd drunk more than he'd intended.

He rang the bell. It sounded harsh and obtrusive.

He found himself facing a fairly tall, slightly overweight, rather good-looking, even potentially charming man. Should he wish to charm. Which, just then, he didn't.

'Yes?' said Mr Matheson cautiously. 'Can I help you?'

'Is . . . er . . .' His voice was trembling, and he was panting after the steep drive. 'I . . . er . . . can I speak to Anna, please?'

'Anna doesn't live here any more.' He made it sound like the title of a tragedy.

'Oh . . . er . . . I see. Well . . . er . . . could you tell me where she does live?'

'I could, yes,' said Mr Matheson. 'The question is, should I?'

Oh no. A headmaster.

'I want to see her. I'm a friend. Could you please tell me where she lives?' he panted.

'Well now,' said Mr Matheson. 'I have to ask myself whether it's safe to give my daughter's address to a trembling, panting, remorselessly monosyllabic young man who arrives at my door after ten o'clock at night, dressed like a bad journalist and considerably the worse for drink.'

Anger gave Henry pride. He drew himself up to his full height, a gesture which would have been more impressive if he hadn't still been three inches shorter than Mr Matheson. 'Mr Matheson,' he said. 'I met your daughter in Italy. I like her very much. I had the depressed instinction that she liked me. I know she'd like to see me.'

Mr Matheson switched on his charm. His voice relented. 'I dare say she would,' he said. 'I'll tell her you called and ask her to get in touch with you. All right?'

'Well . . . yes. Thank you,' said Henry. 'Thank you.'

He turned away. Mr Matheson coughed discreetly.

'Er . . . don't you think you ought to give me your name and address?' he said. 'Anna isn't a mind-reader.'

'Oh. Yes. Sorry.' Henry emitted a strangulated laugh. He longed to say that he was Jasper Phipps-Ockington, but it would defeat the object of the exercise. 'I'm Henry Pratt. I live at 239, Winstanley Road. I'm not on the phone.'

'No.' Meaning, 'You wouldn't be.'

'Or she could phone me at . . . er . . . the *Argus*.'

'Ah.'

As he slithered down the drive, Henry felt that it had not been a wildly propitious first meeting with his future father-in-law. Would they laugh about it, over the port, at family Christmasses to come?

Next day, Anna didn't ring. Terry Skipton liked the canary story.

On Wednesday, Anna didn't ring. Nor did Mr Gaitskell, the Queen, Cousin Hilda, Auntie Doris, Sir Leonard Hutton or any of the population of the West Riding.

On Thursday, October 4th, 1956, at 3.27 p.m., Henry's phone burst into heart-stopping life. He let it ring five times, so as not to seem too eager, then grabbed it in panic, in case she should ring off.

The male voice disconcerted him totally.

'Sorry,' he said. 'I missed that.'

'It's your contact from the world of sport. I've got a story for you.'

She was never going to ring. He'd been a brief Italian fantasy, a good idea on a hot day, long forgotten.

He arranged to meet Tommy in the Winstanley at seven.

Ginny approached his desk rather tentatively.

'Are you in tonight?' she croaked.

'Yes and no,' he said cautiously.

'I'm really fed up with this cold. I felt like popping over to the Winstanley for a few drinks.'

'I'm meeting one of my contacts there at seven,' said Henry grandly. 'I'm sure we'll be through by . . . oh . . . shall we say eight-thirty?'

Tommy didn't turn up until twenty to eight. He didn't apologize.

His scoop was hardly earth-shattering. The whole team was going to autograph the plaster of a seventeen-year-old girl who'd broken her leg when she'd fallen down a flight of steps at the match against Mansfield Town. But Henry rewarded him by buying another round.

''ey oop, our Tommy,' said a passing customer. 'If tha doesn't score Saturday we'll know why, won't we? 'cos tha's been supping.'

Tommy sighed. 'It's no use me coming in places like this,' he said.

'He was only joking,' said Henry.

'He was joking if we win,' said Tommy. 'He wasn't if we lose.'

'Would you like another drink?' said Henry.

At the bar, Henry found himself standing beside Mr Matheson. This was his chance to redeem himself.

'Good evening, Mr Matheson,' he quipped wittily.

Anna's father stared at him politely but blankly.

'Henry Pratt,' he said. 'I called on Monday night.'

'Oh yes. Yes.'

'Did you give Anna my message?'

'Oh blast. I forgot. I'm so sorry. My memory!' said Mr Matheson. 'I'll ring her tomorrow.' He smiled. It was a charming smile. Henry wanted to glare. The man's lack of consideration had caused him three days of mental anguish. But he didn't feel like glaring, because this news meant that Anna hadn't been neglecting him, so he smiled back.

'I'm buying a drink for Tommy Marsden,' he said. 'He's giving me a story.'

'Jolly good,' said Mr Matheson. 'Well . . . keep at it. Nose to the grindstone.' Mr Matheson's nose didn't look as if it had ever been anywhere near a grindstone.

Tommy waxed ungenerous about his team-mates. Muir was yellow. Ayers was as thick as two short planks. Gravel was shagging himself to death.

The sparkling level of the conversation didn't survive the arrival of Ginny.

'I'm a colleague of Henry's,' she said. 'On the paper,' she added, as if not trusting Tommy's intelligence, and perhaps she was justified in view of Tommy's next remark. 'What, writing and that?' he said.

'Yes. What do you do, Tommy?' inquired Ginny.

Henry kicked her under the table. She glared at him.

'Tommy's the star of Thurmarsh United,' hissed Henry.

'Oh yes! I remember now,' said Ginny. 'I read about you. You saved a penalty, didn't you?'

'Tommy's the centre forward,' said Henry.

Ginny sneezed. It was like the eruption of a human Etna. She turned towards Tommy, who recoiled. 'I'm one of those people who're never ill,' she said. 'So when I am, I get it really badly.'

Tommy searched vainly for a reply.

Ginny sneezed again.

Henry glared. 'Ginny lives in the flat above me,' he said.

Tommy looked at his wrist. He wasn't wearing his watch, but he didn't allow this to put him off. 'Time I was off,' he said.

'There's no need to go on my account,' said Ginny.

'Nothing personal,' said Tommy. 'But Mr Mackintosh says it's unprofessional to expose ourselves to germs unnecessarily.'

'Well, thank *you*,' said Ginny, when Tommy had gone.

'What for?' said Henry.

'Disowning me. "Ginny lives in the flat above me." Meaning, "This monstrosity isn't my girl-friend."'

211

Henry said, 'Ginny! I wasn't disowning you.' After a pause he added, 'And you aren't a monstrosity.' If he could have started the conversation again, he'd have put these two comments in the opposite order.

Ginny began to cry, silently.

'Ginny, love! What is it?' he said.

'Gordon's never going to leave his wife.'

Henry felt an immense tenderness towards her. He grasped her hand. He wanted to say something really nice. 'I think you're a smashing journalist,' he said. 'Thanks. What every woman wants to hear,' she said. He leant forward and licked the salt tears off her cheek. 'I've got to blow my nose,' she warned. 'I don't mind,' he said bravely. And then he saw Mr Matheson staring straight at him. He shrank from her. 'My nose-blowing revolts you,' she said. He said nothing. What could he say? 'No. I like it.'? 'Well, you are a pretty horrific performer on the old hooter.'? 'It's nothing to do with your nose. The father of my future fiancée is staring at me, and I'm embarrassed.'?

When Mr Matheson went to the Gents, Henry tried not to follow him. But he had to explain himself.

He stood next to Mr Matheson, at the urinals.

'The young lady I'm with is not a girl-friend, Mr Matheson,' he said. 'She lives in the flat above me. She has a bad cold, and she's depressed, and she believes that the man she loves, who also has a cold, incidentally, will never leave his wife. I'm trying to cheer her up.'

Mr Matheson stared at him in astonishment. 'What an angel of mercy you are,' he said.

As he walked out of the Gents, Henry felt that it had not been a wildly propitious second meeting with his future father-in-law. Would they laugh about it, over the port, at family Christmasses to come?

The weather was cold, with snow as far south as Leek, in Staffordshire. The Middle East crisis was debated in the United Nations, amid rumours that Mr Dulles was 'de-toughening'. 21 soldiers were arrested in Cyprus after demanding an assurance that they'd be home by Christmas. 15 guardsmen in Malta protested about a rumoured kit inspection. 250 reservists complained about bad food and army 'bull' at an RAMC Depot in Cookham.

Gradually it dawned on Henry that Anna would never phone, because her father would never tell her that her company was sought by a short, podgy, trembling young drunk who dressed like a bad journalist because he was a bad journalist and followed him into pub lavatories while having dates with women with bad colds. It also dawned on him that if he wrote her a letter her father could hardly refuse to forward it, because he couldn't know who it was from.

On Wednesday, October 10th, Seretse Khama, chief-designate of the Bamangwata tribe, returned to Bechuanaland for the first time since his exile for marrying Ruth Williams, a white London typist. When she'd married him, Cousin Hilda had said, 'It's her mother I'm sorry for.' Henry had said, 'If I was a typist and married a tribal chief, I'd expect you to be thrilled.'

Anna must have got his letter but still she didn't ring. He wondered if Cousin Hilda would be thrilled when he married her.

He had a permanent pain in his testicles as he thought about her, and was finding it difficult to walk without doubling up. He went for his lunch at the Rundle Café, because she'd worked there. A hosiery salesman listened with bated breath to the tale of Sammy, the Squirrel who'd lost his nuts. Henry envied Sammy the Squirrel. That afternoon, he busied himself with his film reviews. His phone didn't ring.

On the next day, when he returned from number two magistrates' court – he made dog noises, she mewed like cat, court told – Colin Edgeley said, 'A girl rang for you. Very sexy. She'll ring at nine-fifteen tomorrow morning.' Henry tried not to blush, and failed.

Most of the usual crowd drifted to the Lord Nelson, drawn by no greater impulse than habit. Ben bet Henry that he couldn't name the four league teams whose names ended with the same letter as they began. He tried, to please Ben, but his heart wasn't in it. He got Liverpool and Charlton Athletic, but missed Northampton Town and York City. Helen pressed her thigh against him and quizzed him about the phone call from the sexy lady.

It struck him with a shock of shame that he hadn't been to see

Cousin Hilda since he'd got back from Italy. He'd go tonight. If he didn't, Anna wouldn't ring. No. That was juvenile. But he'd go anyway.

Gordon and Ginny left early, after an elaborate debate about which film to see, although everybody knew they weren't going to the pictures. Ben announced that he was going home to give the wife one. Henry asked if anybody had peppermints. Ben and Colin, the married men, both had peppermints.

The fog was returning, after a fine day. Henry's peppermint breath made clouds of steam as he crunched the gravel outside number 66.

The fire crackled economically in the blue-tiled stove. The smell of pork and cabbage lingered. Cousin Hilda switched Frankie Howerd off.

'Don't switch him off for me,' he said.

'He's nearly finished,' said Cousin Hilda, 'and then we've only got some documentary or something about violence against witnesses in Liverpool and then some woman and Edgar Lustgarten, who isn't even English, having the cheek to think they can solve people's personal problems. Though I like the *Horse of the Year Show* at nine-fifty. I'm not struck on the horses, but Dorian Williams speaks beautifully.'

'How's Liam?' he inquired.

'He's Liam.'

'And Mr Pettifer?'

'Mr Pettifer is a disappointed man. He has a jaundiced view of life.'

'And Mr Frost?'

'Married. Living in Rawlaston.' Cousin Hilda sniffed. 'I have a Mr Peters in his room and a Mr Brentwood in your old room. Mr Peters is used to fine things, and Mr Brentwood has a hygiene problem. Things aren't what they were, Henry. We've seen the halcyon days of paying guests. We won't see them again in our lifetimes.'

'I suppose not.'

'So how was Italy? I got your card.'

'Oh. Good. It was very nice. It's a very beautiful country.'

Cousin Hilda sniffed. 'Well, I suppose it would be, if you like that sort of thing,' she said. 'Wensleydale's good enough for me. I see no cause to gad off abroad. But I expect it's all different now. Mrs Wedderburn's nephew's just been to Germany. I shouldn't fancy that, after the War. But she says it looks very picturesque, to judge from his three postcards, though too many conifers for her liking. She said, "And have you had some nice cards from Henry?" "Just the one," I said. She said, "The Italian post is very slow. I expect the others'll arrive after he's been to see you, which he'll do as soon as he gets back. He's such a thoughtful boy." I said, "He is, and he knows my views about extravagance, and he wouldn't want to worry me by inundating me with needless postcards." That told her. There's a nosy side to Mrs Wedderburn.'

Henry told her about Florence and Siena. He told her about meeting Michael and Denzil. He didn't tell her about Anna or about Denzil going off with Lampo while he trudged round Lucca and Pisa on his own. She said she didn't see anything clever in building things that leant. Thurmarsh church could have been built leaning, but where would have been the sense of it?

When Cousin Hilda began laying up for the little supper that she gave her 'businessmen', Henry made his excuses. He couldn't face seeing Liam, who was Liam, or Norman Pettifer, with his jaundiced view of life, or Mr Peters, who was used to fine things, or Mr Brentwood, who had a hygiene problem.

It was 9.17 before his phone screamed into life. Those two minutes seemed endless.

Tactful typewriters clacked all round him.

'Henry Pratt, *Evening Argus*.'

'Hello!'

'Anna!'

'Hello, Henry. How super of you to write. I was thrilled to get your letter.' In her voice there was still the warm sun of Siena.

'Were you? Oh good. Super.' Super? That's not one of my words.

'I hoped you'd get in touch.'

'Did you? Oh good. Super. Look, Anna . . . er . . .' He hardly dared ask her out, which was ridiculous, when she'd phoned him. '. . . how about coming out one evening?'

'Lovely. When?'

'How about . . . ?' He wanted to say 'tonight' but knew better than to insult her by suggesting that she might be free at such short notice. '. . . next Tuesday?'

'Wednesday would suit me better.'

'I'll just have a look in my diary.' He stared into space and counted to twenty. 'Yes. I can work round things and manage Wednesday.'

'Super.' Her voice sounded posher than he'd remembered. 'There's a little pub near where I live called the Cross Keys.'

'I know it.'

'Seven-thirty?'

'Right.'

'Super. Next Wednesday, then. Save yourself for me.'

What did it matter that he'd been insufficiently masterful? Who cared that he'd let her name the day, the place and the time? She'd said, 'Save yourself for me.'

He did.

Britain and France agreed with Egypt on the main principles for international control of the canal. President Eisenhower described the talks as 'most gratifying'. It looked as though 'a very great crisis' was 'behind us'. Nina Ponomareva was given an absolute discharge at Marlborough Street. The Bolshoi Ballet decided to stay in Britain for three extra days. Russians were good people. The world was a nice place. Henry Pratt was in love.

The Prime Minister was enthusiastically received at the Conservative Party Conference in Llandudno when he said that Britain reserved the right to use force. His speech was less well received in Cairo, where they didn't appear to understand that it had been aimed at the Tory faithful. There was a gun-fight in a Hungarian airliner between security police and 'bandits' trying to flee to the West. But these were small clouds.

At 7.17, on the evening of Wednesday, October 17th, Henry entered the Cross Keys, in Brunswick Road. It was a little Victorian pub in a low stone terrace, dwarfed by the primary school. That steep-roofed fortress, with its green institutional guttering and Dutch-style gables, filled Henry with memories of humiliation and of phenomenal farting, which were inappropriate to this important evening in his life. Why had he agreed to meet her here?

The bar had a grey-green patterned carpet with one hole and two bad stains. There were 9 low tables, with maroon bench seating round the walls, and 22 ugly wooden chairs. There were 39 bottles of drink behind the bar. There were 17 cracks in the ceiling. Behind the bar, pinned to a board, were 7 postcards. In the lurid sky above a Swiss funicular railway on one of the postcards, there were 7 puffy white clouds. Henry counted all these things, between 7.17 and 8.04, which was when he decided that she wasn't coming, which was when she came.

'I'm sorry I'm late,' she said casually, as if she didn't know that he'd been enduring torment. 'You know how it is.' He wanted to say, 'No, I don't. How is it?' Did she mean she tried to be on time and failed? Or had she kept him waiting deliberately? He didn't know her. Well, of course he didn't. He'd only met her once. They'd never been alone together. Yet he felt that he knew her. He felt resentful of her for not being in the image in which he had recreated her. She was a little smaller than he'd expected. A little fleshier, too. Her eyes were greener. Her mouth, with those faintly protruding teeth, was smaller. He felt jealous of her independent existence. He hardly understood these feelings. He only knew that she'd caught him on the hop by coming in just as he was getting up to leave. She'd ruined the most important moment of his life.

She kissed him on the cheek and said, 'This is nice,' as if their meeting were a glass of wine, and then she stood back and looked at him and said, 'You're just as I remembered!' which must have been because she hadn't thought enough about him to distort him in her mind. She smelt of expensive perfume, and he wanted her to smell overwhelmingly of herself. He was dismayed by her casual self-assurance, while he was rigid with tension. It was all going wrong already. He didn't like her. It was a nightmare.

Somehow he got through the motions of offering her a drink. She asked for a Pernod. A Pernod, in Brunswick Road! They hadn't got any. He hated her. She settled for a gin and It. She lit a cigarette. She wasn't a goddess.

'You're trembling,' she said.

'I feel terribly cold,' he lied.

'I hope you aren't getting flu,' she said. 'I can't stand sickly people.'

Thurmarsh woman condemns the sick. Her remark was so patently absurd that he began to feel better. Anna Matheson had been a dream, and he was coming out of it already.

They sat side by side, under the curtained window, on the maroon seating, facing the bar.

'This is a bit different from Siena,' he said, and groaned silently at the most fatuously self-evident remark ever made.

'Italy was a big mistake,' she said. 'Well, not Italy itself.' Big of you. Your peninsula is not an error, says Englishwoman. 'Going with Hilary. I just have this thing about illness.'

'Is Hilary ill?'

'In her mind. I mean, don't get me wrong, I like old Hillers. But it would have been a big mistake going away with her even if she hadn't been so depressed. I like lying on beaches and meeting young men. She likes looking at old buildings. The only young men we met were you and your queer friend. He is queer, isn't he?'

'Lampo? Yes. But I thought you seemed quite interested in Siena.'

'We had a bargain. Half the time on the beach, half the time looking at old stones. Hillers ruined the beach for me. Wouldn't sit in the sun. Wouldn't inflict her horrible body on the Italians. Absolute pain in the un-sunburnt backside. Poor old Hillers. She finds life so difficult. Do you find life difficult, Henry?'

'Incredibly.'

'Oh God! What is wrong with people? I mean if you're really poor or something frightful like that, fair enough, you should be miserable. But not people like us. Tell me about your holiday? Did you have a good time?'

He told her about Lampo and Denzil. She laughed at the misfortunes of Henry 'A gooseberry in Tuscany' Pratt, proving that she was a good listener and had very white teeth, despite her smoking. When he offered her another drink, she insisted on paying. 'Daddy says local journalists are pretty miserably paid,' she said. 'I think he's trying to put me off you.' He asked her what she did. 'Oh, I help run a sort of beauty parlour thing,' she said. 'It's the new thing.' During their third drink, she held his hand and he was surprised to feel a stirring in his loins. When he said he was a socialist, she said, 'How could you?' as if he'd betrayed the natural order of things and democracy had never existed. She disagreed with him so cheerfully that he decided that she simply didn't realize that he might find it distressing to discover how much they disagreed. During their fourth drink she ran her tongue quickly round the inside of his right ear and gave him a very meaningful look. He put his right hand in the fold of her dress. She felt extremely soft. He was finding that it didn't matter as much as he'd thought that they disagreed about almost everything. He hardly dared suggest a change of scene, so well were things going, but he must offer her a meal and it was almost a quarter to ten.

'Where would you like to eat?' he said. 'I only know three places. The Midland, which is pretty awful and probably closed. The Shanghai, which is very awful and definitely open. And Donny's Bar, upstairs at the Barleycorn, which is competent and may be closed. Thurmarsh is a bit of a gastronomic desert.'

'Why don't you come back to the flat and I'll knock you up an omelette? Much more fun,' she said.

He couldn't speak. He nodded. She smiled, patted his knee and said, 'Good. We'll have fun. Let's pick up some wine and go.'

The Cross Keys had two bottles of wine. Henry bought the white one. It was yellow.

They walked along Brunswick Road, holding hands. They turned right into Cardington Road, which ran down the hill, parallel to the main road, back towards the town centre.

Her flat was in a basement. On the doorstep, she kissed him full on the mouth.

The living-room was tiny, with a folding table, two armchairs, two upright chairs, a hissing gas fire which had been on all evening and a reproduction of 'Greylag Geese Rising' by Peter Scott. On the mantelpiece there were invitations to three parties and a clock that had stopped.

'I'll show you the flat,' she said. She opened the door of a tiny, pink bedroom. 'This is Sally's room. She's away.' She showed him her bedroom. On the credit side, it was larger. On the debit side, it was even pinker. He felt that he was a helpless piece of cork, bobbing through the evening on the tide of Anna's wishes.

The omelettes were fluffy and runny. The unchilled white wine was a tease, constantly promising to be undrinkable and then withdrawing from the brink.

Anna raised her glass and said, 'To our friendship. I'm so glad you got in touch.'

'To you, Anna,' he said. 'God, I want you.'

'That's nice,' she said. She apologized for her father's disapproval of him.

'Is he a headmaster?' he asked.

'God, no!' she said. 'He looks down on teachers. He's a solicitor. Why did you think he's a headmaster?'

'The pedantic way he used words.'

'That goes with all the speeches he makes.'

'Speeches?'

'He's on the council. He's leader of the Tories.' She stood up. 'Right,' she said. 'That's that. I think it would be rather nice if we went to bed together now, don't you?'

He could hardly breathe. 'Er . . . yes . . . that would be very rather nice. Yes,' he said. 'I've just got to go to the lavatory first.'

She snorted a laugh. 'God, you're romantic,' she said. 'I'm not a great reader but I can't remember that happening in any of the great love affairs of literature. "Romeo, Romeo, wherefore art thou, Romeo?" "Can't you guess? Won't be a sec, Juliet."'

'They're fiction,' he said. 'This is real life.' But he wasn't convinced. He couldn't really believe it was happening.

When he returned she was sitting stark-naked, Rubenesque, smiling, absurd in a cheap brown armchair.

He was appalled. How could he explain that he'd wanted them to undress together, slowly, shyly, gently? How could he say that he found her behaviour grotesquely insensitive and unsubtle? How could he say that she'd ruined a moment that should have been of shared tenderness?

'Don't you want me?' she said. 'Do you find me too fat? I am a bit fat.'

'Anna! Oh, Anna! Course I want you.'

She began to undress him. He dreaded the moment when she

would see how unaroused he was. He looked at the greylag geese and felt that he would never emulate them.

He stood white and podgy and sweating and unaroused before her. She pulled him to the floor and began very solemnly to kiss him all over. He remained tense.

'What on earth's wrong?' she said.

'I'm very much afraid this isn't going to work,' he said.

'Oh God!'

Years later he would still break out in a sweat of embarrassment when he remembered the next few minutes, as he clumsily got dressed in that tiny basement room, while the naked solicitor's daughter sat and watched, beside the hissing fire, beneath the rising geese.

15   Dark Days

Dark days. Rain, drizzle and fog. Suez, Hungary and Henry. Lost illusions. How small was Henry's humiliation compared to the humiliation of Great Britain. How puny his loneliness compared to the rape of Budapest. But it was his own humiliation and loneliness that flooded him each morning when his alarm clock summoned him to the responsibilities of consciousness. How could it be otherwise? He wasn't Budapest. He wasn't the Suez Canal. He was Henry Ezra Pratt, locked in that little body of his.

He couldn't tell anybody about Anna, couldn't turn her into one of his funny stories, couldn't become Henry 'Ee by gum she 'ad nowt on' Pratt.

The Queen released the first nuclear power into the national grid. An increase in prescription charges to 1s. per item was criticized by the British Medical Association. President Eisenhower suffered a bloodshot eye when two pieces of confetti got into it during a ticker tape election rally. Henry spent the weekend writing letters to Anna and tearing them up.

Hazel Carstairs had taken the children to their granny's for the weekend. Henry kept his wireless on very loud, to protect him from the sounds of satisfactions that he would never know. Anne Shelton kept telling him to lay down his arms. Frankie Laine had a woman to love. Henry didn't. Doris Day informed him that whatever would be, would be. Stupid tautologous female. Bill Haley rocked complacently through the rye. Selfish bastard. The Ying Tong Song drove him mad. 'When Mexico gave up the Rumba,' sang Mitchell Torok. 'When Henry Pratt gave up women,' said Henry grimly.

At last he'd completed a letter that didn't make him cringe with embarrassment.

Dear Anna [he'd written]
Thank you very much for coming out with me, and for giving me the omelette. It was delicious. I'm afraid I failed to

round the evening off in the way you'd hoped. It's not something that's ever happened to me before. I think it may have been partly the drink, but that isn't the whole story. I certainly wouldn't want you to think it was because, when I saw you with nothing on, I didn't fancy you. I think you're extremely beautiful.

The truth is, Anna, that in Siena I believed that love had come to me like a swift on the wing. What mindless twaddle! What romantic nonsense! Love isn't like that. I don't believe in love at first sight. It's an insult to one's partner, an insult to love and an insult to oneself.

I believe that love must come gradually, as you get to know people really well, and probably I only function really well as a sexual being when I'm in love. Can we meet again, get to know each other better, and try again? I'd like that.

Please write.

Thank you once again for the omelette. It was delicious.

All best wishes

Henry

The moment he'd posted the letter, it made him cringe with embarrassment.

Poland was on the verge of war. The headlines rolled off the presses. Soviet leaders fly to Warsaw. Poles 'Going too far to independence'. Gomulka returns to power in Warsaw. Poland rebuffs Russian Navy.

The headlines rolled off the presses in Thurmarsh too, onto Henry's stories. Splutt WI enjoyed potato lecture. Cyclist drank too much. Barmaid (27) hit customer (42) after remark about bust (38).

War in Poland was narrowly averted. It was reported, almost as an afterthought, that Hungary might be the next East European country to demand genuine independence from Moscow. The discovery of arms on a ship in Alexandria Harbour lent substance to French claims that Egypt was supplying the Algerian rebels.

Thousands marched to demand freedom in Budapest. The Russian tanks rolled in. Unarmed civilians were mown down in the streets. The world was shocked. Britain, France and the United States asked the United Nations to condemn the Russian use of force. Henry received no reply from Anna. He hadn't expected that he would.

Israeli troops swept 100 miles into Egypt, on a two-pronged drive towards Suez. Britain and France gave the Israelis and the Egyptians 12 hours to withdraw their forces to a distance 10 miles from the canal. Israel agreed. Egypt didn't. The Anglo-French invasion of Egypt began. Only later would it emerge that these moves had been agreed by Britain, France and Israel, in a secret meeting at Sèvres. Still Anna didn't reply. It would be several months before her secret emerged.

The back bar of the Lord Nelson was in ferment. The police and criminals were mostly for the invasion. The lawyers were divided. Ted, who'd become 'Thurmarshian' after the departure of Neil Mallet, was taking the newspaper's official line. He was solidly behind Eden. It was a regrettable but necessary action to protect our interests. Helen agreed. Gordon was scornfully against it. Ginny was wracked by visible conflict. The eyes of the war correspondent lit up. The warm-hearted private self thought it a tragic mistake. Pacifist Ben was quietly, doggedly angry. Colin, a socialist who verged on communism, found himself in terrible confusion. His pugilism welcomed the chance of a scrap for our lads. His chauvinism thought Nasser deserved a bloody nose. His communism couldn't forgive the Russians for betraying his ideals, and couldn't forgive the Suez adventure for diverting world pressure off the Russians. Denzil saw it all as a tragi-comic opera. The world was a cynical place and he couldn't understand why everybody was so surprised and shocked.

And Henry? He was appalled, but he was also appalled at how difficult he was finding it to feel as appalled as he felt he should. He knew, with a part of himself, that he didn't love Anna, that she didn't love him, that she wouldn't reply to his letter. But another part of him was still obsessed with her, still expected that letter every day. And that part of him knew that Anna would be in favour of the Suez operation. And that part of him wondered if it was possible for people who disagreed so fundamentally about something so fundamental to ever truly love each other. And that part of him prevented the parts of him becoming the whole of him.

Occasionally he felt a trickle of returning happiness, of relief that Anna hadn't replied, of freedom. These feelings didn't last long, because it depressed him to feel happy at a time like this.

A large British fleet sailed east through the Mediterranean towards Egypt. In the United Nations there was an American resolution asking members to refrain from the use of force and a Russian resolution asking Israel to withdraw its forces from behind the armistice line. Britain and France vetoed both resolutions. Henry felt the sharpest stab of anger that he'd yet managed.

Denzil asked Henry to spend the weekend with him and Lampo, in his town house. They wanted to thank him for bringing them together. He couldn't refuse. He didn't want to refuse. It would get him away from Thurmarsh, where Anna's ghost stalked every street. It would get him to London, where every journalist wanted to be, at this time of historical significance.

It was Friday, November 2nd, 1956. There was uproar in the Commons. The Egyptian air force was systematically crippled by bombing raids. The English and French navies were closing on Suez. Henry was closing on Denzil's town house, in a little mews in Chelsea. And feeling, as he moved away from Anna's orbit, more and more angry about world events.

A little jewel, Denzil's town house. Clearly his private means were on a fair old scale. Small, slightly over-full of good Georgian and Victorian furniture. Many vases. Numerous miniatures. Little and pretty, making limping Denzil seem elephantine and clumsy.

Something different about Lampo. What?

'The news is awful,' said Henry.

'Never mind,' said Denzil. 'None of that need touch us here.'

Do we have any right to say that? The words formed themselves, but Henry didn't say them. It wasn't the time.

'Show Henry some of my biscuit tins. He'll find them amusing,' said Denzil. It was suspiciously like an order. We have ways of making you find our biscuit tins amusing. Careful, Henry.

'Biscuit tins?'

'Denzil collects biscuit tins. He has a rather amusing collection.'

Let's tell the Hungarian rebels. It'll be a great consolation to them as they're crushed under tanks. Careful, Henry. Unfair. What harm are Denzil's biscuit tins doing? And this isn't the time. Lampo showed him a Peak, Frean tin, with a buxom black woman carrying an earthenware pot on her head. 'Very nice,' he said, the pitifully inadequate praise of a confused Anglo-Saxon.

He realized what was different about Lampo. He was contented. At the height of his discontent he had consented to spend a weekend with two contented and consenting adults. And they were putting him through this ordeal to thank him! It really took the biscuit. And, to put the tin lid on it, at a time of international crisis they kept showing him biscuit tins. 'Very nice,' he said, as Lampo showed him the Pied Piper of Hamelin, on a limited edition produced by McFarlane, Lang & Co.

Denzil in a blue apron! They had *coq au vin*. Denzil called it 'my famous *coq au vin*'. Velvet wine. And then Armagnac. He'd never drunk Armagnac before. Not the time to ask to see the news.

Bed-time. What a test. Was he capable of truly unselfish emotion? Could he feel free from envy, lying there, separated only by a wall from his two friends? Because . . . it had to be asked . . . had he really failed with Anna because he was, after all, a latent homosexual? A trying night. Not a lot of room for worry about Hungary and Suez.

Fitful sleep. A little self-pity. A few noises from hearty drunks outside. Not much envy, really. The answers to the questions that he'd set himself were cautiously encouraging. Cautiously encouraged, he fell into a deeper sleep.

A man who was vaguely familiar was approaching. The man began to talk. In a few blindingly simple words, he revealed all the secrets of life, its purpose and its conduct. Henry woke feeling utterly exhilarated. All his problems had been solved. The three great crises – Suez, Hungary and his sex life – were crises no more. And then the words faded, dissolved, forgotten, as if they had never been.

Never mind. What a day Denzil and Lampo laid on for him. They went to the Tate Gallery and saw the Braque exhibition. How had he managed to live without cubism? They went to the Paris-Pullman Cinema and saw Fernandel in *Don Camillo's Last*

Round and Jacques Tati in *Monsieur Hulot's Holiday*. How had he managed to live without Jacques Tati? They dined in a little French restaurant where Denzil was known. Oh sophistication! Oh classic, clichéd yearning of an unsophisticated Thurmarsh youth. How had he managed to live without being known in little French restaurants?

He felt no envy, no jealousy. He felt no embarrassment, when Lampo and Denzil touched each other, briefly, illegally, under the table. He no longer felt it strange that Lampo should have fallen for this ageing, limping journalist with the blotched parchment skin.

And on that Sunday morning, the November sunshine streamed into the little house, straight onto a striking picture of several native boats which adorned a Huntley and Palmers biscuit tin. Henry began to feel uneasy about the distance between himself and world events. Lampo and Denzil laughed at him. They felt he was exaggerating his importance in the scale of things.

It was Lampo's turn to cook lunch. They had sole with wine sauce, and flinty white Burgundy. Henry assuaged his conscience by talking about Suez and Hungary. Lampo and Denzil had a phrase for every subject. On Empire: 'The colonists found people who were like children, looked after them and educated them, and then were hurt when they turned into adults.' On politics: 'Politicians always do in a crisis what they should have done in the previous crisis.' On American politics: 'How politicians love peace when other nations are at war.' On Suez: 'The Englishman's traditional love of the underdog is strictly for peacetime only.'

On the train back to reality, the Sunday papers rolled over Henry's pleasure like Russian tanks over Hungarian fingers.

In Budapest, the tanks completed the obliteration of freedom. Radio Budapest was silenced. Its last words were, 'Help Hungary . . . Help . . . Help . . . Help.'

Sterling plunged. The government asked the Americans for help. The Americans wouldn't give it unless we stopped fighting. The Anglo-French invasion stopped, too late to avoid political defeat, too early to bring military victory. Diana Dors denied she was dating Rod Steiger.

In Parliament Square and Whitehall, while Henry had been

admiring biscuit tins, huge crowds had been chanting, 'Eden must go' and, 'Law, not War.' Henry was filled with shame that he hadn't been among them.

Dark days. Rain, drizzle and fog. Suez, Hungary and Henry. Lost illusions. The illusion that Britain could still be a great world power in military terms, could act in isolation from the United States, could alter the geography of the world. The illusion that, in communist Eastern Europe, there could be democracy, freedom or equality. The illusion that Henry Ezra Pratt could love, or be loved.

16   A Sleuth Wakes Slowly

At 9.28 on the evening of Thursday, November 8th, 1956, Henry Pratt entered the large lounge bar of the Winstanley. He was alone and listless.

At 9.29 his spine tingled. Martin Hammond had said that a councillor had arranged to meet a council official in a pub that was something to do with Dr Livingstone. Livingstone had met Stanley. Could he have meant the Winstanley?

He asked Martin from the public phone opposite. 'That's it,' Martin said. 'I knew it was summat to do with Livingstone. Why? Interested at last, are you?' 'I'm beginning to get a gut feeling about it,' said Henry. 'We journalists work on gut feelings. This could end up even bigger than the canary.'

As he returned to the bar, Henry saw Mr Matheson ordering a drink. His spine tingled again, and both the hairs on his chest stood on end. His brain was working at last.

Mr Matheson was a councillor, and he drank in the Winstanley! Henry knew, with that gut feeling of his, that Mr Matheson was *the* councillor. He was looking at Henry strangely. Why was he looking at Henry strangely?

Because Henry was looking at *him* strangely. He tried not to look strange, and approached Mr Matheson.

'Are you all right?' said Mr Matheson.

'I had a terrible pain,' said Henry. 'Indigestion. I'm all right now.'

Mr Matheson didn't look convinced. 'I thought you looked happy,' he said. 'Almost triumphant.'

'I like pain,' said Henry. 'I love indigestion. I went to a public school and became a masochist. I belonged to the indigestion society.' Oh god. Would he never behave normally in the presence of this man?

Mr Matheson looked a little alarmed, then switched his full charm on Henry, who found himself smiling as he accepted a drink. He felt absurdly grateful. This worried him. Perhaps, if Mr

Matheson bought him enough drinks, he'd lose the will to expose his corruption.

'I understand you met Anna and didn't quite hit it off,' said Mr Matheson. 'What a shame. She needs careful handling, Henry. We've probably sheltered her too much. Cheers!'

Henry Pratt, investigative journalist, was in a determined mood. Nothing would stand in the way of his investigations. Never again would he allow himself to become entangled with, or humiliated by, a woman.

His determination lasted until 6.37 on the following evening, when Helen's sister Jill entered the back bar of the Lord Nelson, blushing shyly. Her youthful confusion and sexuality overwhelmed him. Her physical vulnerability, her air of barely controlled emotion, aroused him deeply. He felt as if he'd gone over a hump bridge too fast.

It had been, until Jill's arrival, a rather listless Friday evening. Gordon had said '*Ennui*' and Henry didn't think he'd been referring to a French playwright, though with Gordon you couldn't be sure. Colin had announced he must get home to Glenda. Ben had said it was time to give the wife one. But now they all accepted a drink off Ted. 'Oh, we're staying, are we?' said Ginny, and Gordon said, 'Frail craft. Tidal waves.' Henry tried to go home, but found himself buying a round. He tried to hide his feelings for Jill. He knew he'd failed when Helen pressed her thighs against him.

Another drink came. He was powerless to leave. When Ted said they were going to show Jill the jazz club, he said he'd go for half an hour.

And all the others went too.

The smoky upstairs room at the Devonshire was packed and noisy. Ginny was sullen. She didn't look attractive when sullen. Henry tried to concentrate on the music of Sid Hallett and the Rundlemen. They were playing 'Basin Street Blues'.

Helen said 'Don't you still fancy me at all?' during a particularly loud burst of trumpet. 'You're married,' he said. 'I'm disappointed in you. You're getting boring,' she said. 'I know. Utterly boring.

So, please, Helen, be bored by me, and leave me alone,' he said. She didn't hear him.

He stood close to Jill, almost touching her. After all, it was possible that her remark that she didn't find him attractive had been a subconscious reaction to her fear of the deep feelings he was stirring up in her.

At last he spoke. 'Do you like jazz?' was his sparkling opening remark. She didn't hear him, because 'When the Saints Go Marching In' cannot be played softly. 'They're loud, aren't they?' he said. 'What?' she said. 'They're loud, aren't they?' he said. 'Sorry?' she said. 'It isn't worth repeating,' he said. 'What?' she said. 'I said it isn't worth repeating,' he said. 'What isn't worth repeating?' she said. 'What I said,' he said. 'What did you say?' she said. 'They're loud, aren't they?' he said. 'I can't hear you. They're too loud,' she said.

Ben interrupted. 'Guess the first thing the wife will say to me tomorrow,' he said. 'Oh, shut up, Ben,' said Henry. 'Correct,' said Ben.

When Jill left the room, Henry followed her. He hovered by the top of the stairs, between the bar and the toilets, among the people arriving and departing. When she returned, he said, 'Jill? You remember I asked you out at the wedding?' She blushed and said, 'Yes. I'm sorry. I was a bit rude.' He said, 'Please! I asked for it. Er . . . Jill? You're so incredibly lovely. *Will* you come out some time?' 'You're asking for it again,' she said. 'I don't want to. I think you're horrible. Leave me alone.' Helen walked past and heard! Jill returned to the crowded bar. Helen gave him an angry look. His cheeks blazed.

All he had to do was walk down the stairs and go home. But he couldn't run away. Pride demanded that he went in and finished his drink. Then he'd make his escape.

'We're going to the Shanghai for a curry afterwards,' said Ted. 'Are you coming?'

'Count me in,' he said.

They met in the Labour Club, of which Tommy was an honorary member. Henry bought two halves of bitter. They sat in a discreet corner, beneath a portrait of Ramsay MacDonald. They could hear the clunk of snooker balls from the back room. The carpet was red.

Tommy unveiled his second scoop. The team was going to make a record, to play to a small boy who was in a coma.

'Terrific,' said Henry. 'Who says footballers have no heart?'

Tommy Marsden looked at him suspiciously.

'I may have another scoop an' all soon,' he said.

'What sort of a scoop?'

'I'm not at liberty to say anything yet.'

'Give over, Tommy,' said Henry. 'We're friends. Former members of the Paradise Lane Gang. You can trust me.'

Tommy looked at him doubtfully.

'Have a drink,' said Henry.

He bought two glasses of bitter.

'I may be going on t'transfer list,' said Tommy. 'You'll be t'first to know if I do.'

'Leave Thurmarsh?' said Henry.

'Can Muir and Ayers give me the through balls I need if I'm to utilize my speed? Can they buggery? I've got the scoring instincts of a predatory panther, and I'm being sacrificed on the altar of mid-table mediocrity.'

'You've been reading too many press reports.'

'You what?'

'Nothing.'

'I've got a lethal left foot.'

'Your right arm's not too bad either.'

'You what?'

'Nothing. Have a drink.'

Henry bought two glasses of bitter.

'What about loyalty to the team that made you?' said Henry. 'What about loyalty to the town that took an urchin off the streets and turned him into a star?'

'You've been reading too many press reports,' said Tommy. 'Listen. Only last night I heard about one of t'directors, who's buying up half t'town centre dirt cheap so he can redevelop it at vast profits. Loyalty to Thurmarsh? Don't make me laugh.'

'Which director?' said Henry.

'I've told you too much already,' said Tommy.

Henry bought two glasses of bitter. This time it didn't work.

It didn't matter. His spine had tingled again. He had his gut feeling again. This tied up with Mr Matheson and the corrupt council official, or he wasn't Henry 'The man nobody muzzles' Pratt.

In Hungary there were acute food shortages. Ten million people refused to go to work. The future of the Soviet puppet régime of Mr Kadar hung in the balance.

It would take months to clear the ships that were blocking the Suez Canal. The Anglo-French forces and the Israelis refused to retreat until a United Nations peace-keeping force was installed. Colonel Nasser refused to behave as if he'd been defeated.

On the evening of Thursday, November 16th, Henry 'The man nobody muzzles' Pratt installed himself in a corner of the large, over-furnished, over-decorated, surprisingly Caledonian lounge bar of the Winstanley, in the hope that Mr Matheson was a creature of habit, and would again meet the corrupt council official after the council meeting.

He sipped his beer slowly, and read Anna's letter for the fifth time. It belonged to the 'anyway' school of letter-writing.

> Dear Henry [she'd written]
>
> Thank you for your letter, and I'm sorry I've taken so long to reply. You know how things are. Anyway, I'm writing at last.
>
> Frankly, I think I must have had a bit too much to drink that night. Anyway, I'm sorry I did what I did and I certainly don't blame you for what happened. Or didn't happen! Thank you for taking me out and for asking me out again.
>
> Anyway, I'm afraid I'll have to say no, because something has cropped up. A man I've known for some time has asked me to live with him. He's quite a bit older than me, but very kind, and I like him. Anyway, after much soul-searching I've decided to go. Who knows if it'll work, but then I'm not sure if I'm ready for marriage and babies and all that just yet. If ever! Squealing brats I call them. Anyway, we'll see.
>
> Anyway, Henry, there's one thing I'd seriously like to say. It's none of my business, of course, but I honestly think you

233

went for the wrong one that day in Siena. Old Hillers is pretty desperate for a man, though unfortunately she doesn't realize it. She's very serious and high-minded but I think you are too. You're both fairly screwed up (in the nicest possible way!) and I think your repressions might be made for each other. I hope you don't mind me saying this.

Anyway, all the very best for the future, and I'm still glad I met you and that you asked me out.

Lots of love

Anna

PS If you run into my parents, please don't tell them all this. They think I'm staying with my pen-friend, a dreary girl who wants to become a nun! Ugh!

The thought of pale, repressed, mentally ill Hilary, with her horrible body, appalled him. Anyway – oh god, Anna's style must be catching – he resented being described as screwed up and regarded as a last resort for lost girls who were desperate for a man.

The bar was filling up steadily, with the pipe-smoking, dog-owning populace of the neighbourhood. Ginny Fenwick and Gordon Carstairs entered. They joined him, which was awkward, but he could hardly object. Besides, he was always happy to be in close proximity to Ginny. She might yet become his lover when she finally accepted that Gordon would never leave his wife.

'May I tell Henry?' she asked.

'Burgess and Maclean,' replied Gordon.

Ginny interpreted this as meaning 'yes'. 'Gordon's wife has left him,' she said.

Henry felt absurdly depressed by this news. And he didn't know what to say. 'Congratulations,' seemed unfair to Hazel. 'Oh, I am sorry,' was clearly inappropriate. He settled on 'Ah!' There was a pause, as if they expected more. They weren't going to get it. After all, he didn't even know if he was supposed to know that Gordon had been intending to leave her. And already his mind was whirring with the possible implications on his domestic peace. Would there be more or less amorous couplings above his head?

'Er . . .' he said. 'Will you . . . er . . . er . . . live in your house, then, Gordon?'

'No,' said Gordon. 'Kippered walls.'

'He means it's dripping with evidence of marital bitterness,' said Ginny. 'The walls are stained with smoked fish thrown in anger.'

'Ginny's got it!' said Gordon.

'So, you'll . . . er . . . live in the flat, then?'

'Tick tock,' said Gordon. 'Tick tock.'

'My flat is a place of clock-watching, of snatched moments, soured by tension and insecurity,' explained Ginny.

'Ginny's got it!' said Gordon.

Henry was forced to say, yet again, 'I hope you'll both be very happy.' He added a mordant rider: 'I always thought Ginny'd make somebody a very good interpreter.'

Gordon laughed, said, 'Fifteen, love!' and chalked up a score on an invisible blackboard.

'So you'll find somewhere else to live?' Henry asked.

'Somewhere that's totally ours,' said Gordon with surprising clarity.

Ginny smiled proudly. Suddenly Henry no longer felt crabby and jealous. He kissed her warmly and said, 'I hope you'll be very happy, love,' in a voice that only just avoided cracking.

He bought them a drink.

It was almost closing time when Mr Matheson entered with a thick-set, grey-haired man with a long nose and a heavily lined face. Could he be the council official? Henry's heart was pumping. He offered Ginny and Gordon another drink. 'I buy the drinks tonight,' he said. 'To show how happy I am for you.'

'Game, set and match to Pratt H.,' said Gordon.

Henry almost blushed. How he wished that were his real reason, rather than the only way he could think of for meeting Mr Matheson's contact without arousing the curiosity of his two colleagues.

'Hello, Mr Matheson,' he said. 'We're going to have to stop meeting like this.'

Mr Matheson looked as if nothing would please him more. Then his good manners took over. 'Henry Pratt!' he said. 'Hello!'

'I'm a reporter on the *Argus*,' said Henry to the grey-haired man, in a tone which he hoped would sound a little threatening if he was corrupt, but not too rude if he wasn't.

'Howard Lewthwaite,' said the grey-haired man.

Hilary's father! Good lord!

'*Councillor* Lewthwaite,' said Mr Matheson.

Councillor Lewthwaite smiled at Henry as if to suggest that he would never dream of pulling rank.

Henry felt disappointed. The man was a councillor, so he couldn't be the corrupt official.

'Hilary's father?' he said.

'Yes.'

'Good Lord. What a coincidence.'

'Not really,' said Mr Matheson. 'It's through our friendship that our daughters met.'

'I met Hilary and Anna in Siena,' explained Henry to Mr Lewthwaite.

'Yes. Hilary mentioned it,' said Mr Lewthwaite. 'I think she liked you.'

'Good Lord,' said Henry and Mr Matheson.

Henry felt insulted that Mr Matheson had also said, 'Good Lord!' But Mr Lewthwaite explained.

'Yes,' he said. 'She doesn't have a good word for many men.' He sighed. 'She's a problem.'

As Henry bought his round, he had to fight against his desire to accept that, because Mr Lewthwaite was not a corrupt council official, Mr Matheson was innocent. And this because the man had smiled at him twice! Pull yourself together, he told himself. Fight his charm. Never trust a man who smiles too much. Otherwise, you won't be worthy of being called Henry 'The man nobody muzzles' Pratt.

Henry began to realize how difficult it is to conduct an investigation when your employer, your colleagues, and – most difficult of all – the objects of your investigations mustn't know about it.

A minor inspiration attended his next move, however. He met Ben Watkinson in the Blonk, after the match, in which Thurmarsh beat Workington 3–1 with goals from MUIR, AYERS and GRAVEL, who didn't look, respectively, yellow, thick and knackered. Indeed, they all had better games than Tommy. The embers of hero-worship were cooling, as surely, if more slowly, than they had cooled for Tosser Pilkington-Brick.

The Blonk was a large, brick-built road house at the junction of Blonk Lane and Doncaster Road. It was a cold, bare cathedral of booze. Yet sometimes, before matches, when it was thick with smoke and laughter and the good humour of the visiting supporters, it was possible to sense, in that badly heated barn, a throbbing vitality, a good-natured tolerance, a sharpness of cheerfully cynical humour which still made Britain, at times, to Henry, in 1956, an exhilarating place in which to live.

There was a hint, in the air, of the cruel power of a northern winter, but the memory of victory kept the supporters warm as they attacked the smooth, silky Mansfield bitter.

'Name all the Club's directors and their occupations,' said Henry.

Ben's eyes lit up. 'Clive Woodriffe, solicitor,' he said. 'Ted Teague, funeral director.'

'Correct,' said Henry, who had no idea whether it was.

'Laurie Joyce, road haulage contractor. Colin Gee, property developer.'

Ah! 'Correct.'

'Sid Kettlewell, steel baron. Roland Padgett, cutlery magnate. One more.' Ben stared at his beer, brow furrowed in concentration. 'Sorry. It's gone. Put me out of my misery.'

This was awkward. 'I can't.'

'You mean you don't know?'

'No. No! What I mean is . . . I don't want to see you defeated. I'll give you five minutes.'

For four minutes they both suffered. 'It begins with G,' moaned Ben. 'I know it begins with G.' Then his eyes shone with triumph. 'Fred Hathersage, property developer.'

Oh no! There were two property developers.

They met in the Liberal Club, of which Tommy was an honorary member. Henry bought two glasses of bitter. They sat in a quiet recess, below a portrait of Asquith. They could hear the clunk of snooker balls from the back room. The carpet couldn't decide whether to be orange or green.

237

Henry said he thought Muir, Ayers and Gravel had played well.

'One swallow doesn't make a summer,' said Tommy.

No, thought Henry, but three swallows make an empty glass. 'Same again?' he said.

'No, *I'll* get *you* a drink,' said Tommy.

'Oh. Thanks.' Henry tried not to sound surprised.

Tommy didn't move.

'About that business you were telling me about,' said Henry. 'Which bit of Thurmarsh is Colin Gee getting his hot little hands on?'

'It isn't Colin Gee,' said Tommy. 'He's all right, Colin.'

So it was Fred Hathersage. Henry felt ashamed of his ruse, now that it had succeeded so easily. Magnanimous in victory, he said, 'Same again, is it?'

'I've said . . . I'll get you a drink,' said Tommy.

'So which bit of Thurmarsh is Fred Hathersage getting his hot little hands on?' said Henry.

'I've told you too much already,' said Tommy Marsden.

Henry couldn't bear their empty glasses any more.

'Look, let me get the drinks,' he said.

'I've told you. I'm getting you a drink,' said Tommy.

A middle-aged man emerged from the snooker room, with two empty glasses. His eyes lit up as he saw Tommy.

'Tommy Marsden!' he said. 'By 'eck, that were a cracker you scored against Oldham. What are you having?'

'Oh. Ta very much, Mr Grout,' said Tommy. 'I'll have a pint of bitter. And so will my friend Henry.'

Tommy Marsden smiled.

'Told you I'd get you a drink,' he said.

There were at least 49 obstacles blocking the Suez Canal, and almost as many obstacles blocking a political solution of the crisis. The Prime Minister cancelled all engagements, due to overstrain. In Hungary, the régime was having great difficulty in persuading a hostile populace to go back to work.

Henry telephoned Fred Hathersage from a telephone box in Market Street, opposite Howard Lewthwaite's drapery shop. Not that he had any interest in Hilary, having no great yen for screwed up, repressed, high-minded, mentally ill problem girls with horrible bodies.

'I'll see if Mr Hathersage can speak to you,' said his secretary. 'He *is* in conference.'

Henry noticed two gaping holes on the eastern side of Market Street, both quite close to Lewthwaite's. You don't go up to somebody with several teeth missing and say, 'My word! Your remaining teeth are magnificent!' The gaps discredit the whole mouth. So it was with the eastern side of Market Street.

'Mr Hathersage could see you next week,' said his secretary.

A young woman of about Hilary's height emerged from Lewthwaite's and crossed the road. But it wasn't her.

'Would that be all right?' said Mr Hathersage's secretary.

'Fine. I'll see him then, then,' he said.

He had to ring back to find out that his appointment was for 3 p.m. next Wednesday. Could the sight of a girl who might have been Hilary throw him into such confusion? That was ridiculous.

The first Hungarian refugees arrived in Britain. Petrol was to be rationed to 200 miles a month from December 17th. The Prime Minister left for three weeks' complete rest in Jamaica, on doctor's orders.

It was not without trepidation that Henry 'The man nobody muzzles' Pratt approached Construction House, an unprepossessing raw concrete block set back off Doncaster Road, and fronted by an area of dead, sodden grass, pitted with worm casts. He was faced again with the recurring problem that he couldn't ask the questions he wanted to ask without revealing that those were the questions that he wanted to ask.

Fred Hathersage's office was on the third floor. 'Mr Hathersage is in conference,' said his secretary, who had scarlet nails. She flashed him his ration of smile – three-quarters of a second.

After seven minutes, during which nobody emerged, Henry was ushered into a large room from which there was no other exit. Fred Hathersage was alone, seated behind a huge, heart-shaped desk. It seemed that, after their conference, his colleagues must have been lowered to the ground by window-cleaner's cradle.

Fred Hathersage was bulky and bald. When he stood up, Henry

couldn't quite hide his surprise at finding that he was only five foot two. Fred Hathersage couldn't quite hide his displeasure at the surprise that Henry hadn't quite hidden. But he said, 'Mr Pratt!' as if Henry's appearance in his office was the culmination of a lifetime's ambition. The handshake was vicious, though.

Henry sat in a chair which dwarfed him.

'I'm . . . er . . . planning a series of articles called "Proud Sons of Thurmarsh",' he said. 'I wanted to produce a dummy article first.'

'And you thought I'd be a suitable dummy.'

'Yes. No! I mean . . . I thought you'd make a good guinea-pig. I mean, an article on you would help sell the series to the editor.'

Fred Hathersage was flattered. He talked freely. He'd begun life on a building site. (Childhood was discounted entirely, since it had earned him nothing.) He'd worked his way up, founded his own company, gone into armaments. Regretfully, he'd decided that his skill in making armaments would be more use to his country in war than his less proven ambition as a fighting man. After the War he'd made it his mission to help repair the damage caused by the Luftwaffe. A new Thurmarsh. A better Thurmarsh, rising from the ashes like a phoenix, he said, waving his arms excitedly in the direction of a photograph of the south elevation of the controversial new Splutt ambulance station, which had risen from the ashes like a controversial new ambulance station. If he could die feeling that he'd embellished Thurmarsh and its environs, he'd die a happy man.

When he stopped – he was panting considerably, and probably *had* to stop, for medical reasons – Henry took a deep breath, stared at a photograph of the north elevation of the controversial new headquarters of the Thurmarsh and Rawlaston Building Society, which couldn't possibly embellish any environs, and said, 'Do you have any large-scale plans with regard to Thurmarsh town centre, Mr Hathersage?'

'Nothing concrete,' said Fred Hathersage.

'Oh good,' said Henry. 'I don't like concrete.'

Fred Hathersage glared at him.

'It was a joke,' said Henry.

Fred Hathersage exploded into a condemnation of youthful cynicism, of lack of respect for authority, of louts who defaced controversial ambulance stations. When he stopped – he was panting considerably, and probably *had* to stop, for medical reasons – Henry apologized and asked again if he had plans for the town centre.

'Nothing definite,' said Fred Hathersage. 'But, should urban renewal become desirable in certain areas, I'd like to hope that local people, who understand Thurmarsh, would be entrusted with it. What would outsiders be interested in? Profits. Money. LSD. Pounds, shillings and pence. Lolly. Ackers. Lucre. Shekels. The old spondulicks.' Fred Hathersage realized that he was getting quite excited at discovering how many words there were for money. He changed the subject. 'I'd like to see a city of the future rise up on the banks of the Rundle. A city of magic. A city of glass.'

'What about our old buildings, our heritage?' said Henry.

'I like old buildings,' said Fred Hathersage. 'But they're old. Does the future lie in the past? Does it?'

'No.'

'Precisely! Listen. My ambition is to provide work so that there'll never be another depression. Lasting, decently paid work. The working people of Thurmarsh are very close to my heart.' Fred Hathersage thumped himself inaccurately, to illustrate this. It seemed to Henry that the working people of Thurmarsh were actually very close to Fred Hathersage's wallet.

'But do you not have a Rolls-Royce, and a huge pseudo-Gothic mansion above Thurmarsh Lane Bottom?' said Henry, who'd done his research.

'I have to,' said Fred Hathersage. 'Regrettably, we live in a world where appearances matter. I'm a plain man, Mr Pratt. I'm proud to say I prefer tinned salmon to the real thing. Why not? It's nature improved by technology. But could I drive up to the Midland Hotel in an old Austin Seven and order tinned salmon with bottled mayonnaise? It'd be, "Hey up, old Hathersage must be on t'rocks." Such comments in the business jungle can be self-fulfilling. So, it's fresh salmon and lobster thermidor, when I long for fish and chips. It's a sacrifice I have to make. I'm a prisoner of my success.'

Henry had a dreadful thought. Fred Hathersage didn't mean a

word of it. Then he had an even more dreadful thought. He meant every word.

As he walked down Doncaster Road, Henry had an uneasy feeling that his article, if ever printed, would make him a laughing stock. He also had an uneasy feeling that he hadn't got very far with his inquiries.

He wanted fresh air, and took a roundabout route back to the news-room. It took him, as it chanced, past Lewthwaite's. He'd proved that he couldn't cope with healthy, unrepressed women with beautiful bodies. Perhaps Hilary represented the only kind of girl with whom he could cope. Maybe she worked in the shop, if her condition was stable enough to permit her to work anywhere.

At the last moment he didn't dare go in. He walked along Market Street, past Fish Hill, turned left into Rundle Prospect and went for a cup of tea in the Rundle Café. It was a grey, raw November evening, fading almost imperceptibly into night. The café was hot and bright and steamy.

He had seen, in Siena, that Hilary was interested in the arts. She'd been brought up in the narrow world of English provincial drapery. Her friends were philistines. Her father was a Tory politician. She thirsted for culture, for art, for wide horizons. Could not her mental problems be because of this? Mentally sick she might be, but perhaps not irremediably so, if given the patient love of a gentle, caring young man. Shy and repressed, but not irremediably so, if warmed in the love of an amusing and witty young man about town, even if the town he was about was only Thurmarsh. But he had friends in Hampstead and Chelsea. He had an aunt who'd been to Cap Ferrat. Who better to introduce this unsophisticated girl to the great world outside, to art, literature, theatre, gastronomy?

Henry 'Sisley's late haystacks are amazing' Pratt stepped out from his glittering mind into the cold blackness of a Thurmarsh evening. He hurried up Rundle Prospect, and turned right into Market Street.

Henry 'Don't have the *pamplemousse*, darling, it's only grapefruit' Pratt boldly entered the dingy interior of Lewthwaite's. On all sides there were vast rolls of pink and brown material. He approached Mr Lewthwaite.

'I . . . er . . . I happened to be passing,' he said, in a voice whose nervousness would have revealed to somebody a great deal less shrewd than Howard Lewthwaite that there was nothing remotely casual about this encounter. 'I . . . er . . . I wondered if Hilary was around . . . at all. I've some photos of Siena I'd like to show her.'

'I'm afraid she's away,' said Howard Lewthwaite. 'We aren't expecting her back for some time.'

Away! Not expected back for some time! Henry had visions of high walls topped by broken glass, of a huge dark building with rows of depressingly small windows, and an air of deadly calm.

'Away?' he managed to croak.

'At Durham University. She's in her final year there.'

17 Proud Sons of Thurmarsh

On Monday, December 3rd, Selwyn Lloyd told gloomy Tories and contemptuous socialists that it was safe for the British and French forces to withdraw from Egypt, though the French pointed out that there were no guarantees that the United Nations force would remain. In the middle of typing the sentence 'There's a double dose of delight for connoisseurs of the creepy at the Roxy next week when sci-fi shocker *X The Unknown* is paired with gruesome French frightener *The Fiends*,' Henry was summoned to the editor's office.

Mr Andrew Redrobe liked his article on Fred Hathersage! Asked to suggest follow-ups, he could only think of Tommy Marsden. The editor suggested Peter Matheson. 'He *is* the Thurmarsh Conservatives. He also happens to be a close personal friend of mine, but that's irrelevant.' He left the editor's office dazed, thrilled and horrified in equal proportions.

On Tuesday, December 4th, thousands of Budapest housewives forced their way past Russian soldiers and heaped flowers on the tomb of Hungary's unknown warrior. Britain's roads were littered with cars that had run out of fuel. The *Daily Telegraph* said that the whole Suez affair had been bungled by the government to an incredible degree.

Henry interviewed Tommy Marsden for his series 'Proud Sons of Thurmarsh'. Tommy said that he'd thought of moving to a bigger club, but had decided that his future lay with the town that had taken an urchin off the streets, and turned him into a star.

On Wednesday, December 5th, women spat and jeered at tanks in Budapest, Judy Grinham won a sixth gold medal for Britain in the Melbourne Olympics, and Henry's portrait of Fred Hathersage was unleashed upon an unsuspecting Thurmarsh.

On Thursday, December 6th, 50 workers' leaders were arrested in Hungary, and Fred Hathersage complained about Henry's article. Henry was summoned again.

'I never made this attack on young people. I like young people,' said Fred Hathersage.

'Do you have your shorthand notes, Henry?' said Mr Andrew Redrobe.

Henry, who hadn't kept up his shorthand lessons, went to his desk, produced a notebook full of somebody else's old shorthand notes, reserved for just such a purpose, and handed it to Fred Hathersage. Fred Hathersage stared at the meaningless scrawls blankly, while the editor examined the shiny wet roofs of the town.

'Oh, well, I may have done,' admitted the diminutive property developer grudgingly.

On Friday, December 7th, the Anglo-French forces withdrew 20 miles from the Suez front line. To add to the fury of retired majors everywhere, they were replaced by Indians. The entire parish council of Puddletown decided to resign unless Dorset County Council rescinded its decision to change the name to Piddletown.

Henry wrote a letter to Hilary.

> Dear Hilary [he wrote]
> This grey Thurmarsh December day makes me think of Siena in September. What a pleasant lunch that was. I found out from your father that you're at Durham University. I expect you'll be back for Christmas. It'd give me great pleasure if I could take you out some time. Perhaps you'd get in touch when you get back. You can phone me at the *Argus* or write to 239, Winstanley Road.
> I do hope we can meet.
> With all best wishes
> Henry (Pratt)

Henry was pleased that he'd written. His one regret was that it was possibly the dullest letter in the history of the universe.

On Saturday, December 8th, Russian 'storm units' poured into Budapest. Scores of Hungarians were killed in clashes with police and Russian troops. Henry received a letter from Auntie Doris. It was in the 'inverted commas' school of letter-writing, which seemed to be taking stronger and stronger hold of Auntie Doris as she grew older.

> Dear Henry [she'd written]
> Geoffrey and I'd love it if you could come for Christmas, but of course we'll understand if you have to spend it with 'the sniffer'. (I shouldn't call her that. Smack smack, naughty Doris.) Poor dear, I don't expect she's got anybody, and you've got to sympathize even though it's her own fault. We can't have her here, we've advertised a festive Christmas and people might demand their money back. We're 'full to the rafters' but one of our customers could put you up, all very nice, no 'slumming it'! I do hope you'll come. I'll never forget what you did regarding poor Teddy and like to think that if he'd lived we'd have 'worked something out'. Not that I'm unhappy. Geoffrey is good to me, but two waitresses have left recently, so I suspect he's 'up to his old games'. So you see I'm a bit of a lonely old bird. It's my big regret I never had children. It was 'not for want of trying', as they say. So you see you are my son to me, and I hope you'll come.
> With lots of love from your soft old auntie.
> XXXXXXXXXXXXXXXXXXXXXXXX (One for each year, one for luck and one for Christmas)

On Sunday, December 9th, martial law was declared in Hungary, there was the first feeble sign of United Nations interest in clearing the Suez Canal and, at the end of a mild, wet afternoon, Henry walked through the Alderman Chandler Memorial Park towards Cousin Hilda's. Three barn owls sat miserably on a rail in the tiny aviary, beside the sad animal cages. On the pond a mandarin duck looked absurdly ornate in the gloom. The park keeper was waiting, with the over-emphasized patience of the congenitally impatient, to lock up.

A faint aura of expiring sprouts drifted through the silent house. The stove was glowing.

'I wondered what's happening about Christmas?' he said, after the preliminaries.

'What do you mean . . . "what's happening?"?' said Cousin Hilda.

'Well, I've been invited by Auntie Doris.'

Cousin Hilda sniffed. 'I could say summat about guilty consciences,' she said, 'but I won't.'

'She says I'm like a son to her.'

'I suppose you aren't to me!'

'She never said that.'

'Some folks don't need to. Some folks are very good at hinting.'

'So I wondered . . . er . . . what you were planning?'

'I'm giving the Canaries a miss this year.'

He managed a laugh.

'And I've sent my regrets to Sandringham.'

He managed another laugh.

'I just wondered,' he said, 'whether you'd be . . . er . . . alone. Or whether you'll spend it with Mrs Wedderburn.'

'Mrs Wedderburn's three sons are very good to her and have her in turn on a strict rota system.'

Henry found it hard to imagine that Mrs Wedderburn had ever made love three times.

'Are they triplets?' he asked.

'Whatever makes you say that?'

'Nothing. I wondered if . . . er . . . any of your "businessmen" will be with you.'

Cousin Hilda opened the cracked glass doors of the stove, and poked around unnecessarily.

'Mr O'Reilly will be here,' she said. 'He has nobody. It's sad.'

'And Mr Pettifer?'

'Yes. He seems to have washed his hands of his whole family.'

'And Mr Whatsisname, who's used to fine things?'

'Peters. I understand there's a sister in Morecambe.' Cousin Hilda sniffed. 'I dare say her house is chock-a-block with fine things.'

'And Mr Chelmsford, with his hygiene problem?'

'Brentwood.' Cousin Hilda went pink. 'I'll make some tea,' she said, and went into the scullery, where she banged about.

He went to the door of the scullery and got a welcome breath of air. The last of the light was fading over the mercilessly pruned rose bushes and tiny, sodden lawn.

'Mr Brentwood's left,' she said. 'It was right embarrassing. Oh, I *was* embarrassed. Norman Pettifer and Mr Peters gave me an ultimatum. Either him or them. I said, "Give him a chance. I'll give him a fortnight's grace. If he still smells at the end of it, he's out."'

'What did you say to him?'

'I said, "May I have a word on a personal matter, Mr Brentwood?" "Personal matter?" he said. "I've had complaints," I said. "Complaints?" he said. "That you smell," I said. "Smell? Smell where?" he said, going very white. "In my basement," I said. "No. I mean where on me do I smell?" he said. I haven't been so embarrassed since I asked Mr O'Reilly's advice when you had your little problem when you were little with your little . . .'

'Backside.'

'Precisely. "Nowhere in particular, Mr Brentwood. All over," I said. "I believe the technical term is BO." He said something very unnecessary. He said "I suppose you're telling me that BO stands for . . ." I can't say it.'

'Bugger off.'

'Precisely. I said "Mr Brentwood! Only one person has ever spoken to me like that in my life, and that was a parrot!" I said, "You've a fortnight's grace to get things right. All bath charges are suspended for the duration." He left next morning. I found a note. "Thank you for telling me what you told me. It must have required courage and I'm sorry I was rude but I was mortified. I know what has to be done and I'll do it, but I can't face that lot downstairs."'

'I'll spend Christmas with you, and go to Troutwick afterwards,' said Henry.

Cousin Hilda sniffed.

'As you wish,' she said.

On Monday, December 10th, Henry interviewed Mr Matheson for 'Proud Sons of Thurmarsh', in Tudor Lodge. Mr Matheson took him into his study, and gave him twelve-year-old malt whisky from a cut-glass decanter. He had a paperweight in the form of Sir Winston Churchill, complete with cigar.

Henry was hoping that on Thursday, after the council meeting, he would catch Mr Matheson with the council official, thus completing the link. Until then he was lying low.

Mr Matheson talked about his vision of a universally prosperous Thurmarsh, and believed it could be achieved if the people on the shop floor weren't greedy. He went pale when Henry asked whether it would matter if the managerial and professional classes were greedy, but the moment passed and his self-command returned. He was a lounge iguana, basking on the rock of his certainty, in the sun of his self-esteem. The power and smoothness of his charm, and of his whisky, made disliking him hard work, but Henry wasn't frightened of hard work, and kept thinking, 'You wait. I'll get you.'

On Tuesday, December 11th, the IRA blew up a BBC relay system in Londonderry, the Postmaster-General, Dr Hill, announced that the BBC and ITV would be allowed to fill the 6–7 p.m. gap, hitherto sacrosanct so that children could be put to bed, Henry's interview with Tommy Marsden appeared as the second in his series 'Proud Sons of Thurmarsh', and Tommy Marsden was transferred to Manchester United for £18,000, without telling Henry.

On Wednesday, December 12th, more Soviet troops moved into Hungary, where there was still a general strike 'unique in the whole history of the labour movement', and Henry reviewed the Splutt Vale Iron and Steel Company's pantomime. Martin Hammond was Widow Twankey. He was terrible. Henry praised everybody. Truth was too precious to be wasted on such trivia.

On Thursday, December 13th, two Ulster barracks were bombed, 52 terrorists were held in Cyprus, there were angry demonstrations and arrests in Poland, double white lines were introduced on British roads, and Mr Matheson entered the lounge bar of the Winstanley with a paunchy, careworn, balding, middle-aged man who was threatening to burst out of a shiny suit in several places.

Henry approached them and said, 'Hello, Mr Matheson. Can I get you and your friend a drink?'

'No, thank you,' said Mr Matheson, putting an affectionate arm on Henry's shoulder. 'We have a personal matter to discuss.'

'Oh. Right,' said Henry.

'Let me get you one, though.'

'No, thank you. Not if you've . . .'

'. . . a personal matter to discuss,' said the balding man in the disastrous suit.

'I'm Henry Pratt, incidentally. I'm a reporter on the *Argus*.'

'Nice to meet you, Henry.' The balding man held out a limp, fat hand. It was like shaking an exhausted flounder.

There were several things Henry might have said. 'What's your name, you secretive swine?' 'Personal matter? That's a laugh.' 'You think you needn't worry about me, don't you? Well, you're wrong. Nobody muzzles Henry "The man nobody muzzles" Pratt.'

What he actually said was, 'Well, I mustn't keep you from your personal matter.'

On Friday, December 14th, the Queen Mary arrived in New York 17 hours late after making a detour because the Greek captain of a Panamanian cargo ship had a persistent nosebleed. Henry arrived at the Rundle Café more than two hours late after hanging around outside the Town Hall, in the cold of the gathering winter, hoping to see the balding official return from lunch, hoping to stalk him through the corridors of local power and identify him as he entered his office. In vain. At five past three, freezing and starving, he attacked his dried-up meat and potato pie with relish. He recognized the man having a cup of tea at the next table.

'George Timpley, of Timpley and Nephews!' he said. 'I interviewed you on the night of the fire.'

'By 'eck,' said George Timpley. 'I thought I knew you.'

'How are you?' said Henry, thickly, through overcooked pastry.

'I've been condemned.'

'You what?'

'My shop. Condemned. By the council.'

Henry moved over to join him.

'I say condemned,' said George Timpley. 'They haven't actually condemned it as such. They've offered to buy it. If I don't sell, they'll make a demolition order on the grounds that it's unsafe. That's tantamount to condemnation, i'n't it?'

'It's blackmail. What are you going to do?'

'I'm going to sell. What else can I do, next to a blackened hole? An empty site rubs off on neighbouring properties. Her in corner house on end's selling an' all.'

'Corner house? What corner house?'

'Next to me on me right, on t' corner wi' Rundle Prospect. They say she's unsafe an' all.'

Henry began to think seriously about the area around the Cap Ferrat. But still not seriously enough.

On Saturday, December 15th, the Japanese actor Sessue Hayakawa got carried away by his role and punched Alec Guinness on the nose during the filming of *The Bridge on the River Kwai*. Alec Guinness accepted his apology and said, 'I'm bleeding for my art.' On the eve of petrol rationing, almost all petrol stations were closed. Henry bought Christmas presents, including a tea-cosy and tartan bedsocks for Cousin Hilda, a box of exotic honeys for Auntie Doris and cigars for Geoffrey Porringer. His other purchases were less inspired and need not detain us.

On Sunday, December 16th, the AA gave hundreds of stranded motorists enough petrol to get home. Henry, on foot, explored the area between Market Street and the river. The weather was cold, with a thin wind across the Rundle. Exhausted Siberian snow clouds dropped listless sleet over the silent Sunday town.

Three small streets, Canal View, Fish Hill and Rundle Prospect, ran eastwards down the gentle slope from Market Street to the river. Three small streets, Tannery Road, Malmesbury Street and Glasshouse Lane, ran at right angles to them. The whole area had an air of blight. Right at the centre of it was the great hole where the Cap Ferrat had been. There were other, smaller gaps in this neglected, stained mouth. Several teeth needed filling badly. Others were ripe only for extraction. The Old Apothecary's House still had a gaping cavity, where old rubbish gathered. The Roxy Cinema, that yellowing old molar, no longer bothered to replace

posters which wags had altered to Poxy. There were four empty
cottages in Canal View. Several warehouses in Glasshouse Lane
were boarded up, their trade gone when the Rundle silted. The
Elite Guest House was elite no longer. The Old Gas Showrooms
were used by Snugkoat Ltd as a store. Several tiles had slipped on
the roof of the Paragon Surplus Stores. Outside number 11,
Tannery Road, the board that announced 'Tarpaulins Made,
Hired and Repaired' had come loose at one end and was hanging
towards the uneven pavement. On the peeling shop front of
number 6, Fish Hill, the sign announced ' ontinental patisserie'.
Nothing was quite right in these streets. In the Artisan's Rest, the
bitter tasted like liquid hair. The landlord said, 'We don't see
strangers of a Sunday' so accusingly that Henry almost said, 'I'm
sorry. I'll go.'

And yet, in those modest streets, there were good simple
buildings, Georgian, Victorian, Edwardian. If they were improved, if the warehouses were restored, if the gaps were sensi-
tively filled, it could become a delightful area. Henry Pratt,
investigative journalist, would fight to discover the truth. Henry
Pratt, proud son of Thurmarsh, would fight to preserve what
remained of the heritage of his town.

On Monday, December 17th, Hilary rang him at the office. Canal
View, Fish Hill, Rundle Prospect, Tannery Road, Malmesbury
Street and Glasshouse Lane were forgotten.

18   A Festive Season

He entered the gleaming back bar of the Pigeon and Two Cushions three minutes late. The Christmas decorations were rather sparse. She was already there, dressed in a black jumper and a rather demure check dress in two shades of green. He was no more nervous than any young man would be who was taking out a screwed up, repressed, depressed, high-minded, mentally ill problem girl with a horrible body.

She kissed him lightly on the cheek. He took off his duffel-coat and bought drinks. He glanced at her body. Its repulsiveness didn't appear to be due to abnormality of shape. She was less thin than he'd remembered, and taller. As tall as him. She had a long, serious nose and a wide, really rather beautiful mouth. Her eyes were a deep brown. He sensed a wariness in them. She was extremely pale.

'You're very pale,' he said. 'Have you been ill?'

'People are always asking me that,' she said. 'No. I'm as fit as a fiddle. I just am very pale.'

He asked if she'd eaten. She'd had enough not to starve if they didn't eat, but not so much that she couldn't shovel in a bit more if they did. This surprised him. He remembered her as a poor eater. He wondered if her mental illness consisted of bouts of starving herself and gorging herself. He went to the phone, with a decisiveness that surprised him, and rang Donny's Bar. They had one table left. He booked it.

She asked him about his work. He spoke briefly about it, then changed the subject to her studies. She was reading English. He asked about her course. He was so busy sieving her replies for evidence of mental illness that their sense escaped him entirely. He hoped she hadn't noticed, and tuned back in hurriedly. 'But don't let's talk about me,' she said. 'I'm boring.' It was a statement of fact, not a coquettish attempt to elicit a protesting 'No, you aren't!'

Oscar came on duty and smiled at them. Henry told Hilary

about him, his colds and constipation. Strangely, considering how serious and high-minded she was, she laughed.

He ordered drinks, introduced Hilary, and asked Oscar how he was.

'I've had a touch of flu. Otherwise, mustn't grumble,' he said. 'Except for my little trouble.'

'Your little trouble?'

'Summat I wouldn't like to discuss in front of a lady.'

Hilary ordered the next round and even offered Oscar a drink. He beamed his approval of her. Henry felt puzzled. No sign of mental illness so far. 'I'm boring,' was the only slightly odd thing she'd said.

She paid for the drinks. Oscar moved away, and then turned round, just as she said, 'I need the Ladies. Where is it?'

'It's round the back,' said Oscar, in a near-whisper, as if finding it indelicate to talk about the Ladies in front of a lady.

'Thanks,' she said, and hurried off. She was wearing flat shoes, which made her legs look thin.

'"Thanks"?' said Oscar, puzzled.

'For telling her where the Ladies is.'

'What?'

'She asked where the Ladies is. You said, "round the back."'

'Oh! No! No! My little problem that I couldn't mention in front of a lady. I knew you'd be worrying about it and I thought, if I said "round the back," that might take away uncertainty without causing offence.'

Hilary returned.

'I can't find it,' she said.

'It's in t' corridor on t' right,' said Oscar.

Hilary stared at him.

'It's his problem that's round the back,' said Henry.

Hilary gave them a rather wild look, then hurried off.

They found it hard to avoid bursting into giggles every time they thought of Oscar. He asked her about Durham and she told him how beautiful it was. Of course her nose was too long, but when her face shone with pride, Henry felt that she was beautiful. He said, 'I'd like to see Durham,' and there was silence where her reply of, 'You must come and see me' might have been.

With every second of normality, his anxiety grew. Would she suddenly throw a fit or reveal that she thought she was Florence Nightingale? What would he do if she suddenly rolled around, frothing at the mouth, or shouted, 'Put that light out! Don't you know there's a war on? And get me some lint.'

She did neither of these things.

They walked the short distance to Donny's Bar. It was raining hard. As soon as they were out of earshot of the pub, they burst into laughter over Oscar's piles. He hugged her and tried to kiss her. She struggled free. 'No,' she said.

Was it starting? Would she start screaming?

Nothing happened, except that she strode so fast, through the pinging rain, that he could hardly keep up.

'Don't go so fast,' he said.

'Sorry,' she said.

She touched his hand.

'Sorry,' she said.

They entered by the side door and went up the stairs to Donny's Bar.

'You're soaking,' he said.

'I won't melt.'

She couldn't meet his eyes. Was she sinking into a private world of madness? Would she sit motionless at the table, in a catatonic trance, to the embarrassment of the Christmas revellers?

Donny's Bar was heavily festooned with paper chains, and there was a large party, wearing paper hats, seated at five tables that had been pulled together. The waiter apologized for them.

'It's nice,' said Hilary.

Henry felt almost weak with relief at her normality.

'It's nothing special here,' he warned, when they'd got their menus.

'It's fine.'

They ordered rump steaks, with onion rings extra, and a bottle of red wine. Hilary clasped his hand and gave it a quick squeeze, but she wasn't fully relaxed. Twice she looked round rather anxiously. Paranoia? Did she believe she was being followed, by little green men or the CIA?

She asked again about his work, and he abandoned his attempt

255

not to be self-centred, in the interest of keeping her happy. Their steaks arrived. She ate heartily, and laughed at his disasters. How few fillings she had. How he wished, despite her laughter, that his career so far had been more of a triumph. Well, soon it would be. Then he remembered that her father was a great friend of Councillor Matheson. There could be problems ahead, if . . . if what?

She examined the list of desserts at greater length and with more intensity than it deserved. He had another sharp stab of fear. Perhaps it was schizophrenia. Would she say, '*I'll* have the strawberry ice, and *I'll* have the apple pie.'?

She said, 'Nothing for me, thanks. I'm full.' He almost loved her for her normality.

They nursed the remainder of the wine and chatted pleasantly, though they sometimes had to shout to make themselves heard above the shrieking of the festive party.

'I'm sorry about them,' he said.

'For goodness sake,' she said. 'They're enjoying themselves. They're briefly unhierarchical. It's intoxicating.'

'What?'

'The rigid class system in their office is suspended for the duration of the festivities. They're hysterical. They're free, after twelve long months in a straight-jacket. I know how they feel.'

Oh no. Did she mean she'd been in a straight-jacket? He had to find out, without arousing her suspicion. It would need subtlety.

'I . . . er . . . I should think it's . . . er . . . pretty awful in a straight-jacket,' he said.

She looked at him in astonishment.

'What?' she said.

'Being in a straight-jacket. I shouldn't think it's very nice.'

'I heard what you said. It was just that it sounded as if you thought I had first-hand experience of it.'

'What?' he said. 'No. No! Why on earth should I think you'd been in a straight-jacket?'

'I don't know.' She laughed. 'Can we change the subject? It's becoming a bit of a straight-jacket.'

He searched for a change of subject.

'You must have arguments with your father about the class system,' he said.

She looked puzzled. 'Why?' she said.

'Well, you obviously hate it, and he's a Tory councillor.'

'He is not. He's a lifelong socialist. Why did you think he's a Conservative?'

'Well . . . he's a draper.'

'I don't think it's compulsory for drapers to be Conservative.' There was a dryness in her tone. She smiled, to take the sting out of it.

'He's a friend of Councillor Matheson.'

'Outside the council chamber. Conservatives *are* human beings, you know. Fellow citizens of the British Isles. It's a kind of love-hate relationship with Uncle Peter anyway.'

Uncle Peter! It *was* going to be difficult to tell her about his investigations.

And what about his evening with Anna? Should he mention that?

'I . . . er . . . I took Anna out,' he said.

'Yes. She told me. I wondered if you'd mention it.'

Thank goodness he had. He wondered how much Anna had told her about it. Could he ever tell her the whole story?

'I thought she was the one I fancied,' he said. 'I can be remarkably stupid sometimes.'

He was astounded to hear himself say this. She said nothing. He thought she might have responded to his implied compliment to her, or argued against his harsh assessment of himself, but she did neither.

He asked her if she'd heard from Anna.

'Yes,' she said. 'I had a dreary letter from Toulouse. She's staying with a pen-friend who's going to become a nun.'

'Yes,' he said. No. He mustn't have secrets from Hilary. 'That's the official story. She's actually living with an older man.'

'I knew she was lying,' said Hilary. 'Oh, I do find that depressing.' Ah. A clue? 'I find it all so depressing.' Ah. 'Going to Italy with her was depressing.' Ah.

'Why?'

257

'We just drifted apart, inch by inch.' Ah. 'I'm not blaming her. It was mainly my fault.' Ah.

'What do you mean, your fault?'

'Do we have to talk about that? Do I have to endure cross-examination?'

'No. Of course not.'

The office party shrieked at something the accounts manager had said. Henry and Hilary looked at each other rather forlornly, as the waves of laughter crashed around them.

She wanted to pay her share. He refused.

As they left, the Christmas party apologized insincerely for the noise. 'It's been fun,' said Hilary. 'Go home and have one for me,' said an intoxicated head cashier. 'It's the only one you'll get tonight,' responded a tipsy typist. Everybody shrieked. Henry and Hilary hurried out, embarrassed that the subject had been raised.

It had stopped raining. There were queues for the buses and trams, and no taxis to be seen. Buses and taxis had been reduced, due to the petrol crisis. The doomed trams seemed to say, 'I told you so,' as they clattered towards extinction.

'I'd much rather walk really,' said Hilary.

Claustrophobia? Cabophobia? Busophobia?

'I love walking,' she said. 'I love fresh air.'

Agoraphilia?

They walked along York Road, past the junction with Winstanley Road, up out of the grime into the desirable suburbs. They turned left into Lambert Simnel Avenue, and right into Perkin Warbeck Drive. It seemed a very Conservative area for a Labour councillor.

He dreaded arriving at her house. He had no idea whether to kiss her or not.

'This is it,' she said, outside a pleasant brick house. One light still shone, as if they were waiting up for her to see if she was all right.

She kissed him and was gone, without even saying good night. She didn't turn to wave. They'd made no plans to meet again.

In Eastbourne, Dr John Bodkin Adams was accused of murdering a rich widow. Lord Radcliffe's proposals for Cyprus were published.

There would be a period of self-government under British sovereignty, with 6 of the 36 members of the legislative assembly nominated by the Governor. Later, when self-determination came, partition between Greek and Turkish Cyprus was a possibility. Nobody seemed to regard these proposals as a Christmas present.

Henry couldn't bear even to look at his article on Peter Matheson. The glory which he hoped to win from his exposure of municipal corruption would be considerably reduced if every rogue whom he exposed had been praised to the skies by him as a 'Proud Son of Thurmarsh'.

When he drew back the curtains from his absurdly positioned French windows on Christmas morning, he was surprised to see a covering of snow, turning the shared front garden into a Christmas card.

He didn't feel Christmassy. His head ached unpleasantly. His eight cards sat sadly on the mantelpiece. They were from the Hargreaveses, Auntie Doris and Geoffrey, Cousin Hilda, Mrs Wedderburn(!), Martin Hammond and family, Lampo Davey, Ginny, and Ted and Helen, with seven kisses naughtily added beneath Helen's name. Ginny had put one kiss.

The house was silent. Ginny had gone to her family. Gordon and Hazel were spending Christmas together, for the sake of the children, though in separate beds. Ginny was terrified that there'd be a reconciliation. She was terrified of this insight into her own heart – terrified that she wished that those young children, who needed love and stability, should be denied them so that she could have her man. She'd told Henry this, beneath tartan shields draped with holly, in the thronged, frenzied lounge bar of the Winstanley, awash all around them with goodwill for all men, including, Henry hoped, those sorts of men who were never seen in the Winstanley, such as blacks, gypsies, queers, communists, Jews and foreigners. She had cried, and blown her nose while others blew squeakers.

He went into the cold, bleak hall, the no-man's-land of the rented sector, and found it. His ninth card. Underneath the printed message there were no easy kisses, no biro love, no postal coquettishness, but a single, simple sentence, written in an

259

elegant but perhaps too careful hand. 'Thank you for a really enjoyable evening. Hilary.'

The silence of the house became peaceful. It was extraordinarily pleasant to telephone the Lewthwaites, from a really rather delightfully proportioned telephone box, and ask for Hilary. It was delightful to listen to her warm, semi-northern voice, to wish her a happy Christmas, and arrange to meet her in the Pigeon and Two Cushions on the 28th. It was singularly stimulating to crunch the snow in the Alderman Chandler Memorial Park, to say 'Happy Christmas' to the ocelot and the marmot and the three mangy barn owls, to sit in Cousin Hilda's stifling basement and drink Camp Coffee and *two* glasses of sweet sherry, what a momentous concession to the season, delivered with just two mild sniffs, one for each glass. What could be nicer than dry turkey, black gravy, undercooked streaky bacon and burnt chipolatas, with bullet-like roast potatoes, watery sprouts, soft red carrots, and stuffing from two different packets? What did it matter if Liam O'Reilly didn't have the conversational sparkle of a Wilde or Shaw? His pleasure at this feast was Henry's pleasure. Cousin Hilda's pleasure at Henry's pleasure was Henry's additional pleasure. What did it matter if Norman Pettifer's heroic efforts to conquer his jaundiced view of life for the sake of the party were only intermittently successful? Liam had a green hat with two crowns, in his cracker. Norman Pettifer had a clockwork frog. He watched it, with his bemused, disappointed grocer's face, as it hopped across the table. Liam got the threepenny bit in the pudding. Cousin Hilda smiled at Henry because he wasn't disappointed.

It would be untrue to suggest that the day was entirely free from tedium. The most lively game of Snap loses some of its sparkle after the first two hours. A purist might complain that the switch to Happy Families came too late. But this was a small price to pay for seeing Cousin Hilda happy.

And then he went to Troutwick and saw Auntie Doris happy. The train was an hour late, due to snow. The great hills shone white all around. They ate roast pheasant with game chips, and not even Geoffrey Porringer's blackheads could spoil the perfection of the day. Henry was staying in a cottage owned by a Mr Cadge, a man of few words and fewer blankets.

When the last exhausted resident had staggered to bed, Henry sat between Auntie Doris and Geoffrey Porringer on stools at the empty bar. Auntie Doris leant across Henry's back and whispered something. Geoffrey Porringer said 'Yes' and turned to Henry. He smiled with a not totally successful attempt at avuncularity. It was unsuccessful, partly because he was drunk and partly because he had no feel for the avuncular even when sober. 'Son,' he said, 'you're a little belter. Where are my children this Yuletide? Eh? But you. You're a horse of a very different kettle.' He breathed whisky over Henry. 'Doris, your auntie, my beloved, my little . . . chickadee . . .' He tried to resemble W. C. Fields. Only the nose succeeded. 'My little angel wishes you to come on holiday with us. We've hired a villa. They *call* it a villa. Bungalow, I expect. View of the sea. In February. And Doris said, "I want Henry to come. He's the son I never had." Those were her very thingummies. "Ask him yourself," she said. "Otherwise he may think you don't want him." I mean, it's not a honeymoon or anything. You won't be *in the way*.' Geoffrey Porringer winked. 'February. Can you make it?'

'Where?' said Henry.

'Cap Ferrat,' said Geoffrey Porringer. 'Very attached to Cap Ferrat, my little chickadee. Been there a lot. Knows it well.'

'Shut up about all that, Geoffrey. You don't want to remind Henry of all the good times he and I had with Teddy, do you?' said Auntie Doris, who always made things worse by protesting about them. She kissed Henry, enveloping him in scent and powder and lipstick and brandy. 'Please come, darling,' she said.

'For you, Auntie Doris, I'll even tolerate the rigours of the Côte d'Azur,' said Henry.

He wriggled free, wished them good night and went across the cobbled square to sleep, in his duffel-coat, in Mr Cadge's cottage.

She kissed him as before. No more. No less. Again, she was wearing flat shoes. She had a tiny blood blemish on her chin. They discussed their Christmasses. Oscar arrived, smiled, pointed at his backside and gave a thumbs-up. A table of strangers stared at him in astonishment. Henry felt very close to Hilary, as they fought together against hysteria.

Snow and ice covered 80% of main roads. In Hungary there was a wary truce as the nation awaited reforms. There were as many stories about the Suez Canal as there were spokesmen. It would be open in seven weeks/ten weeks/fourteen weeks. British salvage ships would/would not be allowed to work with British crews. The clearance was going well/badly/not at all.

On December 29th, Henry and Hilary sat in the Pigeon and Two Cushions and talked about life. On the 30th, they sat in the Pigeon and Two Cushions and talked about life. Talk. Desire. Kisses. A few seconds longer each night. On the 30th, in Perkin Warbeck Drive, her tongue was briefly, luxuriantly, inside his mouth. Like a snake. Then she was gone. Like a snake.

On New Year's Eve, in Paris, a Bolivian tourist wrote a postscript to the year. He threw a stone at the Mona Lisa. He explained, 'I had a stone in my pocket and was seized with a desire to throw it.' He didn't explain why he had a stone in his pocket.

The rain and the petrol rationing made it the quietest New Year's Eve in London for many years.

In Thurmarsh there was rain also, and Henry was invited to two parties. A bottle party at Ted and Helen's. A small gathering of family and friends at the Lewthwaites'.

Ted and Helen's party would be fun. Three women for whom he had felt great stirrings would be there. Helen, playful with him whenever she felt she had a rival. Ginny, relieved and ashamed because Gordon had come back to her. Jill, scornful. Ben would sit beside his shy, petite Cynthia all evening. Colin was said to be bringing Glenda. That would be an event. There'd be lots of drinking and lots of laughter.

The Lewthwaites' party would be quite dull, Hilary said, and fairly embarrassing. The only other person under forty would be her obnoxious fifteen-year-old brother, Sam.

It was no contest.

'Are you my sister's new lover?' said Sam.

There was uneasy laughter.

'Shut up, pest,' said Hilary.

Peter Matheson was there, with his tall, rather stiff wife Olivia. Well, that was to be expected. Less expected was the balding man with the catastrophic suit, who'd been discussing 'a personal matter' in the Winstanley with Mr Matheson.

Four middle-aged people were crammed into a large floral sofa. There were also three large floral armchairs, six Windsor chairs from the dining-room and a wheelchair. In the wheelchair was a pale woman whose face shone with the serenity of suffering accepted with dignity.

'Meet my mother,' said Hilary. 'Mummy, this is Henry.'

Mrs Lewthwaite smiled gravely.

'Hello, Henry,' she said.

'Hello, Mrs Lewthwaite,' he said.

'My name's Nadežda,' she said. 'I'm Yugoslavian. Everyone in England ignores my beautiful name, and calls me Naddy.'

'Then I'll call you Nadežda,' he said.

Hilary gave him a look as if to say, 'Come on. There's no need to put on too perfect an act.' She didn't explain why her mother was in a wheelchair.

Everybody praised his article on Peter Matheson, although Olivia seemed a little dry, saying, 'I don't know anybody whose opinion of himself needs bolstering less than Peter.' She was trying to look relaxed, but maintained something of the air, among all these socialists, of a Victorian missionary looking for good qualities among cannibals.

'Have you heard from Anna, Hilary?' said Mr Matheson.

'Yes,' said Hilary. 'She's . . . er . . . in Toulouse, with this pen-friend.'

Henry was terrified that he was going to blush.

'That's what she told me,' he said. 'Apparently she's going to become a nun. The pen-friend, not Anna. I can't see Anna becoming a nun!' He remembered that the Mathesons thought Anna led a sheltered life, and did blush.

'We had a letter. Not very informative,' said Olivia.

'Eloquent with evasion,' said Peter Matheson. He seemed as pleased with his phrase as he was worried about Anna.

'And now you're going out with Hilary,' said Olivia drily.

'Yes! I seem to be going through them in alphabetical order!' Henry went scarlet as he realized the possible implications of his phrase. 'I don't mean . . . er . . .'

'We didn't think you did,' said Olivia Matheson coolly. 'I think we know Anna better than that.'

'And Hilary too,' said Peter Matheson, slightly too hastily, after slightly too long a pause.

'Excuse us,' said Hilary. 'I must introduce Henry to everybody.' She led him away.

'For God's sake,' she said. 'What made you say that?'

'Embarrassment,' he said. 'I find embarrassment incredibly embarrassing.' He remembered Diana Pilkington-Brick, née Hargreaves, saying that, years ago, on another embarrassing occasion.

She introduced him to the balding man in the disastrous suit, who on this occasion was wearing a disastrous sports jacket. He was Herbert Wilkinson, Chief Planning Officer. Henry's spine tingled.

'We met before,' he said. 'You were busy with a personal matter.'

'No mystery about it,' said Herbert Wilkinson. 'Peter Matheson's nephew is marrying our daughter.'

Henry felt a lurch of doubt at discovering that the two men really had been discussing a personal matter. Then he encouraged himself with the realization that he had uncovered opportunities for nepotism.

There were too many people to constitute a group, but not enough to make a successful party. It was all slightly dull, and Henry was so glad that he was there. Little pieces of party food were handed round. There was too much food for snacks, and not enough for a meal, and the food was rather uninspired, and Henry was so glad that he was there. The drink flowed just fast enough to make him wish that it was flowing faster. At midnight they listened to the chimes of Big Ben. They all stood up, except for Nadežda. They linked hands, and formed a large circle among the chairs. Hilary and Howard Lewthwaite were at the side of Nadežda's chair, leaning down to bring her into the circle. They sang 'Auld Lang Syne' without quite enough conviction, as if they thought it absurd, when life is so short, to welcome the end of an old year and naïve, when life is so brutish, to welcome the beginning of a new one. Not all of them knew the words, and it was all vaguely embarrassing, and Henry was so glad that he was there. Then, rather absurdly, they clapped, and stopped clapping too soon, as if they realized that it was absurd. There were no silly hats, no squeakers. They moved around, in slow rotation, and kissed each other, rather formally, wishing each other a happy 1957. Olivia Matheson presented her cheek as if it were a rare privilege. Henry said, 'Happy New Year, Mrs Matheson,' and added, silently, 'in which your husband will be ruined.' Henry and Hilary hugged each other, and he said, 'Happy New Year, my love.' My love! It was the first time he'd used the word 'love'. He gasped at the revelation. He bent down and kissed crippled Yugoslavian Mrs Lewthwaite. How cold her cheek was. She said, 'Be careful with Hilary.' His eyes filled with tears and oh no here was Sam approaching. If Sam saw his tears! He fought the flood back and said, 'Hello, pest.' Sam nodded his approval curtly and said, 'You're better than any of the last eight. Maybe you'll last.' Howard Lewthwaite clasped Henry's hands in his, and said nothing. Henry told Hilary that he must talk to her.

'That sounds ominous,' she said. 'I know the perfect place. But it'll be cold.'

'I don't mind,' he said.

They put their coats on and wandered out, away from that anti-climactic gathering of middle-aged people who didn't quite know what to do now that it was 1957. The rain had almost stopped. They walked off, away from the faint light filtering through the cosy, curtained windows, into the vast black universe beyond. Hilary guided him across the squelching lawn to a rustic wooden summer house. It was milder than of late, but still cold. And there, sitting on a circular bench that ran round the inside of the summer house, on that winter night, they talked.

At first it was difficult. He wanted to ask her about those remarks that people kept making, about her mental illness, about her being a problem. But he didn't know how to begin.

She shivered.

'You're cold,' he said, putting his arm round her.

'Not really. More frightened,' she said.

'Frightened? Of me?'

'Of me. Of me and you and the world.'

265

'Are you having sexual intercourse in there?' called out Sam.

'Shove off, object,' said Hilary.

'You'll get splinters,' warned Sam.

'Belt up, monster,' said Hilary.

Sam belted up and shoved off.

'He likes me to be rude to him,' said Hilary. 'It's the only kind of affection he can deal with at the moment.'

'I know.'

'You know a lot.'

'Not enough. Not nearly enough.'

'You want to, don't you? Make love.'

'Very much.'

She told him why she was frightened. She told him of the man she had loved, who had left her for another. She told him how she had fought her despair, and sought consolation, after a few drinks, after a party, with a man she hardly knew. And how the man had gone too fast, and she had tried to draw back. She couldn't look at Henry as she told him how the man had raped her. She told him how the man had got away with it, because if a woman had a few drinks, was pleasant to a man, flirted a bit with him, the world said she was asking for it. She told him what it was like to wake up in a hospital ward, among total strangers, not knowing where you were, and to realize, gradually, that this was the same old you, the same old earth, the fight had to go on, you hadn't taken a large enough dose, you'd been found too soon, by people who would always wonder whether you'd meant to be found, when you'd yearned for the peace of eternal blackness. She told him what it was like to face the distress of those you loved and realize that you had almost killed your crippled mother. She told him what it was like to realize that you had no alternative but to try not to do it again. 'I'm permanently diminished by the disgust I feel,' she said. 'I think you ought to go.'

'I'll never go,' he whispered.

She kissed him gently, on the lips.

'I don't know if it can work,' she said.

'Of course it can,' he said. 'You know it can. You've known these last few days.'

266

'I've known I hope it can,' she said. 'You're the first man I've felt even remotely safe with since it happened.'

'I'm not sure if that's a compliment,' he said.

'It's meant to be the greatest compliment I've ever paid to anyone.'

They clutched each other, and sat motionless and silent.

'Anna said . . .' he said at last.

'Anna said what?'

Could he? Should he? 'Anna said . . . you were mentally ill.'

'I've had a lot of depression,' she said. 'And I tried to kill myself. And I went very inward. If that's mental illness, I'm mentally ill.'

He clasped her left hand. It was icy. He had to fight the temptation to tell her that her tiny hand was frozen.

'Every day I hear the screams of the world,' she said.

'What?'

'My parents taught me how to care, and now I can't stop. I hear the agony of people imprisoned without trial. I hear the repression of minorities. I hear the knock on the door in the middle of the night. I hear the screams of the wounded in obscure border wars between countries whose names I can't pronounce. Not all the time. But every day . . . somewhere . . . some time . . . If that's mental illness, I'm mentally ill.'

He laid his cheek upon her cold cheek. Mother Nature, that old softie, sent a shaft of moonlight across the trim suburban lawn. Hilary shuddered.

'I love you,' she said.

He couldn't speak.

'I never thought I'd hear myself say that again,' she said.

He couldn't speak.

'What a responsibility,' he sobbed at last. His tears streamed. She massaged his hands gently. 'I'm so happy,' he moaned absurdly.

She lent him a small white handkerchief. He felt brutish, violating it.

'You're a complete fool, you know,' he said. 'I'm clumsy, insensitive, thoughtless, hopeless. I'm a case.'

How they talked, as the clouds drifted back across the moon, as if to say that they shouldn't expect too much from 1957. He told her about his childhood, all his schools, all his humiliations. He told her about Denzil and Lampo, in Siena. She laughed.

Suddenly she gave a screech of laughter. 'You *did* think I'd been in a straight-jacket,' she said. 'Poor Henry. How brave you've been, waiting for the eruption of madness every second of every day.' She laughed till the tears ran. He joined in sheepishly. She talked again about what a mistake her holiday with Anna had been. And yet something had been achieved, something of the spirit of Italy had entered her soul. She'd begun, slowly, to enjoy life again, in Durham. She'd begun to hope, to her surprise, that she would see, in Thurmarsh, the funny little journalist she'd met in Siena. She talked about her girl-friends in Durham. She talked about going to London, with Clare and Siobhan, to protest about Suez. Oh god, he wished he'd been there. What did you do in the Great War, Daddy? I admired biscuit tins, son.

She talked about the dreadful days of her mother's polio attack, two years after Sam was born. She talked about the bronchial days, towards the end of winter, when each year grew more dangerous for her mother. Then they put their tongues in each other's mouths and kissed and kissed and kissed. The saliva grew cold on their slurpy faces, and their tongues grew slow and gentle, slower and gentler, and more sensitive, and then they removed their tongues and hugged each other.

Her father banged on the door.

'Are you coming in?' he said.

'We're coming,' she said.

In they went, through the French windows, creeping, whispering, so as not to wake her mother or the object.

'We were talking,' she whispered. 'Talking and kissing.'

Howard Lewthwaite touched Henry gently on the shoulder.

'Would you like to stay?' he said. 'On the sofa?'

'It'd be lovely to know you're there,' said Hilary. 'It'd be lovely to start 1957 by waking up in the same house as you.'

Howard Lewthwaite touched Henry gently on the shoulder.

Oh, the bitter-sweet evenings of talk and beer and desire and frustration and the continuing steady improvement of Oscar's haemorrhoids. Oh, the lingering good night kisses in Perkin Warbeck Drive.

Oh, the difficulty of having to investigate Hilary's so-called Uncle Peter, who was her father's friend, not to mention Herbert Wilkinson, who was also her father's friend. Howard Lewthwaite would hardly relish being told, by a twenty-one-year-old, that his choice of friends was unwise, that he was naïve. If only he had more courage. If only Hard Man Henry hadn't become a ghost.

Stanley Matthews and Donald Campbell were given CBEs. C. P. Snow was knighted. A left-wing government under a military dictator was formed in Syria. Egypt abrogated the Anglo-Egyptian treaty of 1954, denying the basis on which Britain could use the Suez Canal in time of war. John Foster Dulles, who had done so much to turn a disastrous Anglo-French victory into an even more disastrous defeat, said that the US had a major responsibility to help prevent the spread of Soviet imperialism in the Middle East. The pleas of road hauliers for more fuel were rejected.

Henry summoned up his courage. On Thursday, January 3rd, he told Hilary of his investigations. She said they must tell her father. He'd know what to do.

Gertie Gitana, who'd become synonymous with 'Nellie Dean', died at the age of 68. The Egyptians refused to let United Nations troops move ships out of the canal. They wouldn't negotiate with Britain and France until new governments came into power, and then only if they apologized for the deeds of their predecessors.

Howard Lewthwaite walked to the Midland Hotel on the following Tuesday, and gave Henry and Hilary lunch. None of them had the *pamplemousse*. They talked of Suez. 'What have we got,' asked Hilary, 'in exchange for splitting the nation, weakening the Commonwealth, the Atlantic alliance and the United Nations, diverting the world's attention from the Russian atrocities in Hungary, and harming for ever our capacity to take a credible position of moral leadership in the world?' 'Nothing,' said Henry. 'As much as that!' said Howard Lewthwaite. They laughed. Lowering his voice, even though the nearest customer was twenty feet away, Henry told Hilary's father about his suspicions. Howard Lewthwaite went quite white, and shook his head several times. He waved a waiter away, brusquely. 'Thank you,' he said, 'but I'm perfectly capable of pouring wine.' He promised to look into the matter immediately.

Sir Anthony Eden resigned, due to ill health. Harold Macmillan became Prime Minister. Oil promised by America still hadn't materialized.

He met Hilary in the Winstanley at noon. It was the last Sunday before her return to Durham. The proximity of the Winstanley to his flat was not accidental. She arrived with her father, on foot. Howard Lewthwaite was keen to be seen not wasting petrol by as many voters as possible.

He bought the youngsters a drink. They sat in a quiet corner.

'I've had one meself,' said Howard Lewthwaite.

'One what?' said Hilary.

'An offer from the council. For Lewthwaite's. I haven't told Naddy yet. I daren't tell her till the spring. She's so frail in winter these days.'

'You'll refuse the offer, of course,' said Hilary.

Her father stared at his glass of beer. 'I don't know as I can,' he said. 'Drapery as we know it is finished. The east side of Market Street as we know it is finished. I'm in trouble. The offer is strictly fair, if mean. Doesn't cheat me or the ratepayers. I don't know if I *can* refuse it, Hilary.'

'But Lewthwaite's!'

'All things come to an end, Hilary.'

'But this is wicked manipulation,' said Henry.

'Is it?' said Howard Lewthwaite. 'I'm at liberty to refuse. I choose not to. What's wicked about that?'

'But you're a councillor.'

'Exactly. And I still only get a very basic price. Doesn't sound like corruption, does it?'

'Well, what about the tobacconist?' said Henry. 'Did you ask the planning officer about that?'

'I did. He said the house is no longer safe, now it's next to a gaping black hole.'

'It looks safe to me,' said Henry.

'Herbert says the foundations are undermined. Would you guarantee its safety?'

'No, but what about the woman on the end. Her house isn't next to a gaping black hole.'

'It will be, when the tobacconist's is gone.'

'That's ridiculous.'

'Is it? The woman doesn't want to stay there, a little house beside a gaping black hole. She wants to be rehoused. Nobody is suffering, Henry.'

'Thurmarsh is. Those streets are full of good old buildings. What'll we get in their place?'

'A brave new world, perhaps,' said Howard Lewthwaite. 'How conservative with a small c you are.'

'Are you saying there are no secret plans for redevelopment?' said Henry.

'Not that I know of.'

'But what about Fred Hathersage? He's buying stuff up all over the area.'

'Have you proof of that?'

'I've been told.'

'Maybe he thinks the area is ripe for development. He has eyes. We can't stop him seeing. Properties become available. We can't stop him buying.'

'I don't understand this,' said Henry. 'You've got deadly political ammunition against the Tories, and you pooh-pooh it.'

Hilary and her father gave Henry long, rather sad looks.

'It's a Labour council, darling,' said Hilary.

Of course it was. He'd been concentrating on Peter Matheson so much that he'd quite overlooked the fact.

'Peter Matheson's leader of a minority,' said Howard Lewthwaite. 'Unless there's corruption on our side, too, he won't get anywhere, even if he is corrupt.'

'Could there be corruption on your side?' said Henry.

'I hope not. It wouldn't say much for me as deputy leader.' Howard Lewthwaite looked at his watch. 'I must be getting off,' he said. 'Got to put the veg on for Naddy's dinner. Look, I'll keep digging. I promise. Be good.'

The weight of their discussion faded slowly, like a shadow on a recovering lung. By the time they left the Winstanley, all that was forgotten.

It was a mild, spring-like afternoon. There was very little traffic in Winstanley Road. The petrol shortage was giving the town back to pedestrians.

'My . . . er . . . flat's close by here,' he said.

'Is it really?' said Hilary drily.

He intended to be oblique, ask her if she'd like to see it, offer her a sandwich. She wasn't a person to whom it was easy to be oblique. 'Come on, eh?' he said.

She nodded bravely.

He didn't dare speak, for fear she would change her mind.

'It's usually me goes too fast,' she said. 'Slow down. I'm not going to back out. I've gritted me teeth.'

They crossed the road, hand in hand, he in an ecstatically ambiguous state between excitement and fear, and she with gritted teeth. A robin scolded them for their immorality. Henry had never felt less immoral.

He hurried her through the sterile entrance hall, and lit the gas fire in the living-room. She laughed at the French windows.

'The other half of them's through here, in the . . . er . . . bedroom,' he said.

'I bet you say that to all the girls,' she said. 'You must come and see my French windows.'

He led the way into the bedroom. He lit the gas fire in there, too. She began to undress and he remembered, with a thud of fear, what he'd completely forgotten in the excitement of their growing love. She had a horrible body. Never mind, he told himself, as she undressed tensely, determinedly, as if for a medical, with her back to him. Never mind. Men are far too influenced by physical appearance. I love you, Hilary, the person, the woman. The body is unimportant.

She hopped into the narrow, single bed and covered herself with the bedclothes. But he had seen, in that brief moment, when he hadn't dared to be seen to be looking, that her body was not horrible at all, but more beautiful than he could have dared to hope. He climbed in beside her, feeling hot and cold and awkward and ardent.

And so, in the cramped atmosphere of his tiny, unattractive bedroom, on a mild Sunday afternoon in January, in a flat in a converted mock-Tudor house in respectable Winstanley Road, Henry Ezra Pratt and Hilary Nadežda Lewthwaite embarked upon a journey that might, with luck, take them from gritted teeth to ecstasy.

'There's no hurry whatsoever,' he said. 'It doesn't matter if nothing happens. Cuddling is enough.' But it wasn't. It wasn't nearly enough.

His patience and gentleness surprised him. Slowly, Hilary ungritted her teeth. Eventually he took her, rather swiftly, unsatisfactorily, messily. She was too tense to have an orgasm. That was what it was, a taking. Bad. Bad. Taking wasn't loving.

The daylight faded. The gas fire produced a low, red glow. She began to stroke him. Slowly, together, they sailed away from the land of gritted teeth. In the cave of his room, in the cave of his bed, in the cave of his arms, in a cave within a cave within a cave, Hilary found a place that was safe enough for her. This time, they gave instead of taking. Hilary uttered one single gasp. A gasp of incredulous joy. Outside, people were walking to evening service, down Winstanley Road.

'Hilary Lewthwaite?' Henry whispered into her left ear. 'Do you think that, when your exams are over, you could bear to become Mrs Henry Pratt?' And then he had an awful worry, a terrible fear that he'd dreamt it all. Because he could have sworn that Hilary Lewthwaite replied, 'I don't think I could bear not to,' and people didn't say things like that, in real life, on Sunday evenings, in one-bedroom flats in Winstanley Road, to people like Henry Pratt.

After ecstasy, tea. He padded carefully across discarded clothes and shoes. He closed the curtains and switched on the light. She blinked, and smiled, and he realized that, when she was happy, she had the most beautiful face that he had ever seen and that his inability to recognize this possibility in Siena made him irredeemably unworthy of her.

He went through into the living-room, and closed those curtains too. She joined him. The gas fire threw a dim red glow over her lovely body. She put her bare feet on his bare feet. She was taller than him now. She kissed him.

He switched the light on, and went into the kitchen.

The front door slammed. Heavy footsteps trudged across the hall. There was a loud knock on his door.

'Can I come in?' It was Ginny. Her voice sounded urgent.

He raised a questioning eyebrow. Hilary nodded. He almost wished that he didn't love her, so that he could fall in love with her at this moment.

'Just a minute,' he said. 'I'm not dressed. Come down in a few minutes.'

They tried to dress quickly, but he wanted to kiss her again and again before she disappeared into the commonplace world of the clothed. 'Thanks for agreeing,' he whispered. 'She sounded desperate,' she whispered. They weren't quite sure why they were whispering.

Ginny's eyes and nose were red. She gave a gasp when she saw Hilary. What a day it was, for the gasps of women.

'This is Hilary,' said Henry.

'Gordon has gone off with Jill,' said Ginny.

'Oh, Ginny!' said Henry. 'Oh, I'm sorry, Ginny.' Often he'd failed to find emotions to go with his expressions of sorrow. Now it was the word that was pitifully inadequate for what he felt.

'I was good enough to be his bit on the side when he was married. I'm not pretty enough for him to spend the whole of his life with,' said Ginny. 'There she is, practically straight out of school, ripe to be astounded at his virility, ripe to be impressed by his knowledge of life. No wonder he couldn't resist her.'

Henry tried to put a comforting arm round her, but she shook it off.

'Men are such bastards,' she said. 'I should regard myself as lucky to get away. What an escape I've had.'

The last thing Henry wanted, now that he'd won Hilary's delicate confidence, was an eloquent tirade against the shortcomings of men. He could think of no other way of shutting Ginny up, except to say, 'Hilary and I are engaged.'

Ginny burst into tears. Hilary rushed to her, put her arm round her and held her. Henry felt absurdly redundant.

'I'm sorry,' said Ginny. She sniffed, searched for a handkerchief, couldn't find one. Hilary lent her one quite inadequate for her purposes. She blew her nose as prodigiously as she
could.

Henry had said it so often. Now, at last, but not in the
circumstances that he would have chosen, it was said to him.

Ginny kissed Hilary. Then she kissed Henry.

'I hope you'll both be very happy,' she said.

The next morning Ginny was at her desk as usual, looking
indestructible, larger than life. Gordon slunk to his desk, looking
smaller than life. Ginny made no mention of Henry's engagement. Nor did he. He didn't yet feel sufficiently sure that it had
happened.

It was Hilary's last day before her return to Durham. They met
in the Pigeon and Two Cushions. They were both nervous,
wondering whether they could ever live up to yesterday.

Oscar came straight over to them, and handed them a note.
Could he be congratulating them? Was he psychic? No. The note
read, 'Acute laryngitis.' They met his gaze, and he nodded
solemnly. They fought to maintain control of themselves. They
looked deep into each other's secretly laughing eyes and were
enveloped once again in the certainty of their love. Good old
Oscar. When he bought the next drink, Henry offered him one.
Oscar mimed that he'd have sixpennorth with them, he'd pour it
later, and would gargle with it.

'Shall we go home and tell my family?' she said.

They went home and told her family. Henry bent down to kiss
her mother's cold cheek. Naděžda's eyes were filled with tears, and
he didn't know whether they were tears of joy or sorrow. Was she
overjoyed at Hilary's capture of a young man of such warmth,
kindness and character, or had she hoped for something better
than a short, fat, provincial journalist? Howard Lewthwaite
seemed caught in the grip of contradictory emotions – half
pleased, half worried. Henry was disappointed at his reaction.
Sam said, 'Have you had it off yet, and if so where have you put it?'
Henry said, 'Belt up, horror.' Sam smiled, well content. Howard
Lewthwaite produced the bottle of champagne they'd have drunk

if Labour had won the last election. Yet he still didn't seem as pleased as Henry had expected.

Hilary walked with him to the end of Perkin Warbeck Drive. There, at the junction with Lambert Simnel Avenue, under a street lamp dimmed to save fuel, their faces clung briefly to each other, and then she was gone. She didn't say goodbye. She didn't look back.

19 Startling Information

Next morning, he told his friends that he had an announcement to make and would like to see them in the Lord Nelson that night, after work. Only by celebrating could he fill the grey emptiness of a January without Hilary.

That afternoon his phone rang, an event rare enough to be worth recording.

'It's your contact from the world of entertainment.'

'Tony! Hello! How are you?'

'Very well. I've got a story for you,' said Tony Preece.

'Oh!' He just managed not to say, 'At last.' 'What is it?'

'I can't talk on the phone, but I'm on tonight at that Mecca of Hysteria, Splutt Working-Men's Club. How would you like to see the new act?'

'I'd love to. But I can't tonight. Can't you tell me what your story's about?'

'Arson and murder.'

'I'll be there at half eight.'

Everyone came to the Lord Nelson except Ginny. She'd said, 'I can't face it. He'll be there. Perhaps she'll be there.' Even Terry Skipton came.

Henry blushed becomingly, and said, 'I've got some news for you. I'm engaged.'

There was a murmur of false astonishment and genuine delight, especially from the married men. It gave them an excuse for not going home which their wives could hardly not accept.

Terry Skipton had one glass of champagne-type sparkling wine, wrinkling his face as if it were medicine. He was a better judge than he knew. Colin thumped Henry's back so vehemently that he was bruised for a week. Denzil gave him a quick kiss. Chief Superintendent Ron Ratchett had a discreet word in Denzil's ear, but not too close to Denzil's ear. 'Please, sir,' he said. 'We all have to live side by side, unfortunately. I can turn a blind eye so far and no further. It's still illegal, and long may it remain so.' Colin borrowed a fiver off Gordon and bought two bottles of champagne-type sparkling wine. Ben said the wife would understand if she was given one later than usual, under the circumstances. Gordon borrowed a fiver off Ted and bought two bottles of champagne-type sparkling wine. Henry thanked him in such surly fashion that Gordon said, 'Come on, Henry. Come *on*. If you were free as air, would you marry Ginny?' 'That's a bit different. I haven't been using her to fulfil my animal needs,' retorted Henry. 'We'll sup some lotion tonight, kid,' said Colin. 'I have to go. Family celebration,' said Henry. They were upset, as if they'd discovered that their expensive theatre tickets were valid for the first act only. Gordon was particularly angry, because he'd cancelled an evening with Jill. Henry slipped away as soon as he could.

Splutt Working-Men's Club was a long, low, uncontroversial brick building with many windows, situated opposite the con-troversial new ambulance station. It looked as if a large army hut had strayed among the small shops and low terraces of Splutt High Street, set low in a heavily industrialized valley, three and a half miles north-west of Thurmarsh.

He met Tony and Stella, his brassy blonde companion, by the long, bleak bar counter. Tony was attacking a pint of bitter with whisky chaser. It was more than three years since Henry had seen Stella, when for the second time he'd sat through Tony's appalling comedy spot as Talwyn Jones, the Celtic Droll.

'So what's this story?' said Henry.

'Not now,' hissed Tony, as a large, loud, florid man approached. He was wearing a large, loud, florid suit and was accompanied by a tall, buxom young red-head. The man was smoking a large cigar. The red-head wore large gold earrings and an engagement ring. Henry had seen them somewhere before.

'Hello, Tony,' said loud suit. 'Are you performing or just visiting?'

'Performing,' said Tony.

'Oh 'eck,' said loud suit. 'Shall we go 'ome?' He roared with laughter. Gold earrings smiled mechanically. 'Only joking,' said loud suit. 'I hear tha's gorra new act. Let's hope it's better than t' owd 'un. Eh, Angie?' He roared with laughter again.

Of course! Bill Holliday, used-car salesman, scrap tycoon, gambler, leader of the Thurmarsh Mafia, and Angela Groyne, model, with whom Colin had once, unwisely, danced.

'You're wearing your engagement ring, Angela,' said Stella.

'Aye. It's on again, i'n't it, Bill?' said Angela.

'This time it's for good,' said Bill Holliday. He slapped his fiancée's bottom.

'I can't wait for your new act,' said Henry, when Bill Holliday and his future wife had moved off with their brandies. 'I never thought that Welsh act was really you. You've got a perfectly good personality of your own. All you need to do is build on that, exaggerate it slightly, not seek refuge in heavy regional disguises.' Stella was glaring at him. 'I'm not criticizing him, Stella,' he said. 'I'm praising him. I'm telling him to have more confidence in the real Tony Preece. He was a dead duck in that act the moment he came on in a bright red suit, with a giant leek in his buttonhole, wearing a pith-helmet and one roller-skate, and nobody laughed. However good he was, there was no way back. That's all I'm saying. So, come on, what's this story?'

'Sod the story,' said Tony Preece, and he stormed off backstage.

'What have I done?' said Henry.

'You'll see,' said Stella.

The room was filling up. They hurried to a table. Stella sighed deeply. Those three years hadn't been kind. She looked thin and gaunt. There were dark bags under her eyes, and her artificially bright hair only served to highlight the haggard look of her hard, brassy face. Her legs were like matchsticks. Henry knew how much she loved Tony. He knew what a false signal that hard face gave to the world. He liked her very much, so he said, 'You're looking grand, Stella.'

She ignored this remark contemptuously. 'He'll be throwing up now,' she said. 'He's worse than ever these days.'

'Why does he do it?'

'He says there's got to be more to life than selling insurance.' She sighed deeply. 'We're engaged now, you know.'

'I didn't. Oh, Stella! I'm so glad.'

He hugged her with an impulsive warmth that surprised them both. She smelt of cheap perfume, anxious sweat, cigarettes and sweet Martini.

'I'm engaged too,' he said.

'Henry!' There was an element of surprise in her voice, which irritated him faintly. She gave him a more formal, strangely shy little kiss.

He bought her a sweet Martini.

'Don't forget the cherry,' she called after him.

He didn't forget the cherry.

'When's the great day, then?' he said, raising his glass.

'We haven't fixed a date yet. It's taken us six years to get engaged. It'll take a few more to get married. You?'

'No. No date yet.'

The harsh lighting, so unflattering to thin, haggard, artificial blondes whose real gold is locked deep in their hearts, was dimmed, not without a few jerks and delays, which aroused jeers from the thronged tables in the long, beery, smoky room.

'Now then! Now then!' said the concert secretary, whose teeth almost fitted. 'Letth have no repetithion of the behaviour of latht week.' He glared at them with all the ferocity at his command. Henry's mind went back to his headmaster at Dalton College, who also lisped, though his was a lishp, not a lithp. Sometimes it seemed as though there was a theme to Henry's life, with recurring motifs of failure and absurdity. He might have welcomed this thought once, even exploited it. Not any longer, because he wouldn't be able to bear it if any failure or absurdity attended his relationship with Hilary.

'It wath,' continued the concert secretary, 'and I won't minthe my wordth, a blot on the good name of Thplutt. All right, nobody'th pretending that Enrico and Ernethto, mind-readerth with a differenthe, were a good act. Letth fathe it, they were crap. But they came from acroth the thea. What thort of an imprethion of Yorkthire hothpitality have they taken back to the Ibernian peninthula? Our firtht act tonight ith a muthical trio, altho from acroth the thea, who are dethcribed ath three thtriking Vikingth, who are queenth of melody and animal imprethionth. Tho letth give them a fair hearing and a warm Yorkthire rethepthion. Letth hear it for thothe Great Daneth, the Larthen Thithterth.'

Henry had expected the Larsen Sisters to be tall, blonde and beautiful. He hadn't expected them to be not only musical, but funny as well. What were they doing here?

'Oh God,' said Stella. 'They're good. Poor Tony.'

The applause at the end of the girls' act was deafening.

'Well,' said the concert secretary. 'If anybody had told me that three female Thcandinavian animal imprethionithtth would be the biggetht hit I've ever known at Thplutt Working-Menth Club, I would have thaid "Pith off." Who could follow that? Next bugger'll have to try! Will you welcome, from north of the border, that mathter of thcottith comedy, Mick McMuck, the Droll of Dundee?'

You're in trouble when you come on wearing three pink tam-o'-shanters, a very short kilt with a very long sporran, a giant kipper in your buttonhole, and a set of bagpipes on one foot, and nobody laughs.

'Oh heck,' said Henry. 'Oh heck, Stella. I'm sorry.'

'Hold my hand,' she said. 'Help me through it.'

Henry tried desperately to think of other things. He tried to imagine himself back at his first visit to a working-men's club, at Rawlaston, with Uncle Teddy and Auntie Doris, listening to Doreen Tibbs, the Tadcaster Thrush. In vain. Tony's voice broke in. 'He said, "Have you Dunfermline?" I said, "I haven't even started fermlin yet."' The jokes were even worse! He tried to speculate about the story that Tony was going to tell him. Somehow, he was reluctant to think about that. 'I wouldn't say my wife was frigid, but she thinks sex is something the ladies of Morningside have their coal delivered in. Coal. Sex. Get it? Och no, nor do I, much.' Not all of them were worse jokes. Some of them were the same jokes. Stella tightened her grip on his hand at each reference to a ghastly fictional wife. He tried to think of Hilary. All day he'd been disembodied, gliding like a ghost through the grey mist of her absence. Now, when he tried to be with her, tried to be back in bed in Winstanley Road, tried to be in Durham, all ghostliness failed him, all disembodiment was impossible. He heard Tony say, 'She smokes in bed, too. I wouldn't mind, but I don't even like kippers.' 'Oh, Hilary,' mouthed Henry. 'I love you, my darling. Let's fix the date.' It was no use. She was slipping away, because she was too real for fantasy. 'I won't say I'm unathletic but I put my shoulder out, tossing at the Highland Games. We'd only gone to Braemar for a picnic. I was tossing a salad. Salad. Tossing. Get it? Och no, nor do I, much. Mind you, I like salad dressing. It's better than the wife undressing. I won't say she's fat, but when she went swimming at North Berwick she was chased by five Norwegian whalers. Get it? Och no, nor do I, much.'

At last it was over. There was a smattering of applause. Stella sighed deeply, and gave him his hand back. It ached as the blood returned. He went to buy a pint for Tony and a sweet Martini for her. She called to him not to forget the cherry. The concert secretary introduced the 'top of the bill, that well-loved thinger from Thunderland, Arnold "Tree-Trunk" Nutley. Inthidentally, earlier today a lovely Yorkthire lath called Thuthan promitted to become Mitheth Arnold "Tree-Trunk" Nutley.' The audience applauded, and Henry had an idea for the gossip column, which was called 'Out and About'.

Arnold 'Tree-Trunk' Nutley sang 'Singing the Blues', proving that he couldn't sing like Guy Mitchell. Henry returned with the drinks. He hadn't forgotten the cherry. Arnold 'Tree-Trunk' Nutley launched himself into 'Friendly Persuasion', proving that he couldn't sing like Pat Boone. Tony returned. Stella kissed him and yelled, 'It went better tonight.' Tony nodded wearily. Henry apologized. Tony smiled wearily. Arnold 'Tree-Trunk' Nutley ventured upon 'Just Walking in the Rain', proving that he couldn't sing like Johnny Ray.

Henry bent his head towards Tony's. 'What about this story?' he said. 'It's safe to tell me now. Nobody'll hear anything with this racket going on.'

'A local publican told me, when he was pissed, that the burning down of the Cap Ferrat was no accident,' shouted Tony.

He supposed that, since Tony's phone call, he'd known that it had to be that. It was still a shock actually to hear it.

'You mean . . . my uncle was murdered?' he shouted.

'Your uncle?'

They didn't talk during the applause, which wasn't nearly as loud as the singing. When Arnold 'Tree-Trunk' Nutley burst upon 'The Garden of Eden', proving that he couldn't sing like Frankie Vaughan, Henry and Tony resumed their discreet shouting.

'It was my Uncle Teddy who was found dead in there.'

'Oh heck. I'm sorry.'

'No,' yelled Henry. 'Thank you. This gives me a chance to avenge his death. But why, Tony? Hardly for the insurance, if the owner is dead.'

'Because it was an architectural gem, I'd guess. I'd guess somebody has their eye on developing that area. I don't know how well you know it. It's very run-down. No problem, but they might have had trouble with the architectural lobby, the Thurmarsh Society, the Rundle Valley Historical Society, the South Yorkshire Georgian Society, all the freaks. So . . . whoosh . . . fire.'

They broke off for the applause. 'Cindy, oh Cindy,' moaned Arnold 'Tree-Trunk' Nutley, proving that he couldn't sing like Eddie Fisher. They resumed their discussion.

'Who told you? What leading publican?' yelled Henry.

'I can't tell you,' shouted Tony Preece.

'I won't let on,' yelled Henry. 'Us journalists never reveal our sources. And he's not likely to have seen us together.'

'His brother has,' shrieked Tony. He gave an involuntary glance in the direction of Bill Holliday.

'Bill Holliday's brother. Thanks, Tony,' roared Henry.

'Oh heck,' thundered Tony Preece.

The applause was muted. Arnold 'Tree-Trunk' Nutley hammered away at his final number, 'True Love', proving that he couldn't sing like Bing Crosby or look like Grace Kelly.

True love. Henry thought about his own true love. He still had no idea what a problem he was going to have to face in that department. The far corners of his mind were still dark, and filled with the silence of pennies that had failed to drop.

20 A Disturbing Discovery

Hexington lies seven miles to the north-east of Thurmarsh, on an exposed bluff high above the weed-knotted, pram-choked curves of the Rundle and Gadd Navigation. Seven villages and five coal mines can be seen, on a clear day, from the tower of the smut-blackened parish church. But the podgy young man who descended from the dun-coloured Thurmarsh Corporation bus, outside the Midland Bank, had no intention of climbing the 262 steps to take advantage of the view. He had four good reasons for not doing so. A thick drizzle was falling, it was pitch-dark, the church was locked and he had an urgent job to do.

He wasn't tall. His long, thick, grey-green raincoat wasn't elegant. The expression on his face wasn't fearless. And yet, there was about him a certain air of determination, for the young man . . . you've guessed it, haven't you? . . . was Henry Pratt, the Man Nobody Muzzles.

The Prince of Wales was a large, draughty, run-down Victorian beer palace, set on a windy crossroads. It had windows of opaque glass, and was topped by a round turret. It dominated the low terraced houses that surrounded it. There were two cavernous bars and a function room at the back. It smelt as if it had just dried out after being flooded.

The landlord lacked his brother Bill's charm and urbanity. Stan Holliday was a large man. His small, narrow eyes were dwarfed by his huge conk. He had slobbery lips, in which a permanent wet cigarette drooped. He had a large paunch and smelt of the morning's brandy. Twelve lank, dank, dark hairs pressed themselves into his otherwise bald pate as if seeking invisibility, yet his nostrils were a celebration of the hirsute. He smiled with his cheeks only. An ugly customer, thought Henry, except that he wasn't a customer. An ugly landlord, then.

'My name's Henry Pratt,' said Henry.

'Well, there's not a lot I can do about that, I'm afraid.' Stan Holliday smirked at his customers who, not surprisingly, were few.

'Yes. I . . . er . . . I was in a pub the other day . . .'

'Fascinating. What a rich life you lead,' said the Oscar Wilde of Hexington.

'And I overheard something.'

Stan Holliday grew wary. Improbably, his eyes narrowed.

'Oh aye?' he said.

'I wondered if I could buy myself a drink and then speak to you somewhere private,' said Henry. 'I'm from the press, but this is a personal matter.' He showed his press card.

Stan Holliday reflected, then nodded. Henry bought himself a pint. Stan Holliday led him to his office, and with mock good manners motioned him to sit in the only chair. Henry instantly regretted it. Stan Holliday now towered above him.

'Right,' said Stan Holliday. 'So what did you overhear?'

'I overheard somebody saying you reckoned the burning down of the Cap Ferrat wasn't accidental.'

'You overheard somebody saying I reckoned the burning down of the Cap Ferrat wasn't accidental?'

'Yes.'

'Who was this somebody?'

'I've no idea. Just somebody I overheard.'

'He's no idea. Just somebody he overheard.' Stan Holliday began to talk as if to an invisible wife. If she was anything like her husband, thank god she was invisible. 'Which pub was it?'

'I don't remember the name.'

'He doesn't remember the name. Where was it?'

'Er . . . right in the middle of Thurmarsh.'

'Where right in the middle of Thurmarsh?'

'I can't remember.'

'He can't remember.'

Henry tried to take a casual swig of his beer. A man's swig. It slopped all down the front of his flasher's mack.

'Right,' said Stan Holliday. He yanked Henry to his feet by his hair, and still towered over him. 'Right.' Henry had seen numerous films in which investigators had fearlessly threatened the people they were investigating. It had never been like this. 'Now listen this way. This man you don't know that you overheard in some pub you don't know somewhere you can't remember somewhere in the middle of Thurmarsh who said I reckoned the burning down of the Cap Ferrat wasn't accidental was talking through an orifice whose name I can't remember situated somewhere in the middle of an extremely unattractive cleft between two large unidentified fleshy protuberances somewhere I've forgotten not at the front of his body. I know nowt about the Cap Ferrat. I never went there. I never knew anybody who worked there or went there. And why are you sniffing round about it, anyroad, Henry Pratt, whose name I will remember?'

'It was my uncle who died there. And, if it wasn't an accident, my uncle was murdered.'

'I'm sorry to hear about your uncle,' said Stan Holliday. 'Death's very sad. It can ruin folk's lives. But it's nowt to do with me. Things like that don't happen in Thurmarsh, anyroad. Thurmarsh isn't Chicago. You're talking rubbish. Piss off.'

Henry tried narrowing his eyes. He tried glaring, as if to suggest that nobody pushed him around. He tried taking a nonchalant, man-sized swig of his beer. Then he pissed off.

On the shaking, dimly lit bus back to Thurmarsh, Henry didn't read his story, in the 'Out and About' column. He knew only too clearly what it said.

> Romance was in the air at Splutt Working-Men's Club last night. There was loud applause when the concert secretary, Eddie Simpson (59), announced that the top of the bill artiste, well-known Wearside vocalist Arnold 'Tree-Trunk' Nutley (38) was to marry Susan Ullidge, a well-known flaxen-haired hair-stylist from Mexborough.
>
> Nutley met vivacious 27 year-old Susan when he was doing a season at a holiday camp near Minehead. They plan an August wedding.
>
> What the concert secretary didn't know was that the well-known Thurmarsh comedian, insurance salesman Tony Preece (36), who works under the name of Mick McMuck, the Droll of Dundee, had also announced his engagement, to attractive Stella Hardcastle (33), a well-known blonde florist from Wath-on-Dearne. They have not yet fixed the date.
>
> Joked the irrepressible Mr Preece, 'I wonder if the third act

on the bill, the Larsen Sisters, have any romantic announcements to make!'

They didn't, but in the audience were Bill Holliday (42), the well-known Thurmarsh businessman and sportsman, and his glamorous flame-haired companion, Angela Groyne (22), a well-known local model whose successes have included three very popular calendars issued by Booth and Wignall Rolling Mills.

Their many friends have been puzzled by their on-off, on-off engagement. Well, last night Mr Holliday killed off the speculation with one word. 'Our marriage,' he declared, 'is now definitely ow.'

His first misprint since Neil Mallet had left couldn't have come at a worse time. It wasn't a good idea to make an enemy of both Holliday brothers in one day.

Israel refused to surrender access to the Gulf of Akaba and the Gaza Strip. Humphrey Bogart died. Egypt seized British and French banks and insurance companies in Cairo. There was to be no more Territorial Army training for men who'd done their national service. Henry's military career was over.

On Thursday, January 17th, there were very few buses, due to the fuel shortage and very few trams, due to mechanical failures brought about by the gradual run-down of maintenance services in view of their impending demise. Workmen were rather sheepishly removing the trolley-bus wires right opposite the stop where Henry and Ginny were waiting. All this led to conversation in the queue. Warm clouds of indignant breath rose into the frosty air.

Henry chatted to a splay-nosed man of about thirty, with receding hair and large ears, and to his spectacularly attractive girl-friend. His name was Dennis Lacey, and he worked in the X-ray department at the Infirmary. The girl, Marie Chadwick, was a nurse. They were in love. Were Henry and . . . er . . . in love? He shook his head, embarrassed, and belatedly introduced Ginny, who was polite but cool. Marie had jet-black hair and dark skin. Her mouth was small and sensual. Her nostrils were flared. Henry cast several surreptitious glances at her, to prove to himself how uninterested he now was in any woman except Hilary.

At last their tram came, and Henry thought no more of this casual encounter.

On his way to number two magistrates' court, Henry telephoned Howard Lewthwaite. 'I've found things out,' he said. 'Things I can't discuss on the phone.'

'Have lunch tomorrow,' said Howard Lewthwaite. 'There are corners of the restaurant of the Midland Hotel which are further from other living human beings than anywhere else except the morgue.'

'Funny you should mention the morgue,' said Henry.

In court – optician failed to see two red lights – Henry felt tired. In the canteen, he didn't feel hungry. In the Lord Nelson, he didn't feel thirsty. In the library, reading Colin's report of the inquest on Uncle Teddy, he felt dizzy. The fire investigation expert had found no evidence of foul play. The fire appeared to have started at the stage end of the main public room. It could have been caused by a cigarette or an electrical fault. Recording a verdict of accidental death, the coroner had added a rider about the danger of inflammable materials in public places.

By the time he got back to the news-room, Henry felt dreadful. He realized that he was sickening for the flu.

It was at that moment that Mr Andrew Redrobe's summons came.

He sank gratefully into a chair, and eyed the editor apprehensively across the neat, green-topped desk.

'The correspondence column is jaded,' said Mr Andrew Redrobe. 'Suez, Hungary, prescription charges and the folly of getting rid of the trams have been with us too long. What else have we got? The absence of facilities for square-dancing in Thurmarsh and environs! We need a major new issue. You will write a letter, a real bombshell of a letter, condemning the inadequacy and irrelevancy of what we serve up as education. You will sign it "Angry Schoolmaster".'

'Yes, sir.' Damn. It's the flu making me subservient.

'"Proud Sons of Thurmarsh". Where are your follow-ups?'

I hate the series, Mr Redrobe. 'I've been thinking about that, sir.' Damn.

'And?'

'Er . . .' I haven't been thinking about it at all. 'The Mayor?'

'A half-wit. Any other "ideas"?'

'Not at the . . . erm . . . no.'

'You've done the Tories. Have to do Labour. The leader is not a son of Thurmarsh. The deputy leader is. Howard Lewthwaite. Do you know him?'

'Know him? I'm engaged to his daughter.'

'And you still didn't . . . congratulations, incidentally . . . think of him for an article?'

'Er . . . no . . . thank you, sir, incidentally.' Damn. 'Sorry.'

'I see. How about Bill Holliday?'

'Bill Holliday??'

'All right, he's in scrap and used cars, and greyhound racing. Does that make him beyond the pale? Are you such a snob?'

'No!'

'He's a good Thurmarshian, Bill Holliday.'

And will probably crush me to death in his car dump. Great.

'I'd also suggest Sidney Kettlewell, of Crapp, Hawser and Kettlewell. A great Thurmarsh employer.'

Who refused to employ my one-eyed dad. Wonderful.

'And the one schoolmaster in this town I've any time for, because he does speak his mind. Gibbins of Brunswick Road.'

In whose class I made a monumental fart. Terrific.

Please let me go. I feel awful.

'I'm worried about you, Henry. You're not finding enough stuff on your own initiative.'

'I am onto something, Mr Redrobe. I'm onto a really big story, on my own initiative.'

'Ah! Fire away.'

'I . . . er . . .' I'm too weak to talk about it now. I want to tell Howard Lewthwaite first. I want some proof. 'I'm seeing somebody about it tomorrow. I need proof before I make allegations about people in the public eye. Could you give me a week, sir?' Damn.

'A week, then. No longer. I'm all in favour of initiative, but I don't like being kept in the dark. I don't like mavericks. A newspaper is a team effort.'

'Oh, I know. I don't want glory out of this.' Liar. 'I don't mind handing all the stuff over at all.' Shut up. You'll say things you regret. 'I just want to be sure of my facts.'

'People in the public eye, you say? I'm intrigued. I can hardly wait.'

But Mr Andrew Redrobe had to wait. Henry managed to type his letter, signed 'Angry Schoolmaster'. He managed to walk to the tram stop. He managed to undress himself and get into bed. He stayed there for more than a week.

The cold war between Russia and the United States intensified. The winter in England remained mainly mild. In Cyprus there was widespread trouble between Greeks and Turks after a Turkish policeman was killed in a bomb attack. At Cardiff Arms Park England, minus Tosser Pilkington-Brick, narrowly defeated Wales.

Every day, Ginny tried to interest Henry in food. Almost every day she sang out, with false brightness, 'Another letter from Durham!' As he began to recover, he gave her letters to post to Durham. The better he felt physically, the more his indebtedness to Ginny irked. He hoped she'd catch the flu, and become indebted to him, but she didn't. She told him that Ted and Helen had matching flu, and Gordon had it. 'He's been over-exerting himself, I expect,' she said. 'We'll see how *she* handles two households of invalids. I don't see her as Edith Cavell.'

Hilary's letters were full of incident and vitality. When he thought back to the drab, lifeless girl he'd met in Siena, he knew he should feel delighted. And yet . . . here was he, feeble and damp-haired in a tiny room that stank of his own sweat, and there was she, striding vivaciously around Durham. How long, he felt after each letter, before she tired of him, found somebody better, some gigantic student whose intellect matched his frame. So, as he waited for each letter, he grew more and more nervous. When they came, he longed to tear them open but had to wait till Ginny had gone. And always they were so full of love for him that he was reassured, until . . . until it all began again. And, because he could hardly say, 'On Monday I lay in bed and sweated. On Tuesday I lay in bed and sweated again,' he found himself forced into the sentence by sentence school of letter writing. 'I'm glad you enjoyed the lecture on John Donne. I'm very pleased Mr Tintern liked your essay. I share completely your views about Selwyn Lloyd.' Supposing she replied, 'I'm glad you're glad I enjoyed the lecture on John Donne. I'm very pleased you're very pleased Mr Tintern . . .' Supposing their love ground to a halt in bad letters.

At the end of each letter, he swore his undying love in explicit descriptions of what he'd like to do – oh god, supposing they died in a crash and Cousin Hilda found his collected love-letters, tied by an elastic band that any decent person would have reserved for jam jars.

As he began to get better, he felt deeply sexy, in that sweaty fug of a bedroom. Desperately, he listened to the wireless. The music programmes transported him back to his childhood at Low Farm, outside Rowth Bridge. Sandy Macpherson, Rawicz and Landauer, Harold Smart and his electric organ, Ronald Binge, Max Jaffa, Reginald Leopold and his players, out it poured. His childhood seemed a long way away, and he got depressed about Lorna Arrow and Eric Lugg.

The comedy programmes rolled off the assembly line too. *The Goon Show, Take It From Here, Ray's A Laugh, Life With The Lyons, Midday Music Hall* with the Song Pedlars, Barry Took, Lucille Graham and Vic Oliver. Every time he laughed, he wished Hilary was there, to laugh beside him.

He listened to everything from schools talks on the Lapps of Scandinavia and Neutralism and the Spirit of Gandhi to Jean Metcalfe visiting Vera Lynn's home, from *Mrs Dale's Diary* to an investigation into whether social mobility between the classes had been achieved in our society ('Ask Belinda Boyce-Uppingham,' he shouted. 'Ask any bloody snob.' He added, in a low moan, 'Ask me.'), from *Science Survey* on the problem of vibration to *Naturalist's Notebook*, which included a contribution on oil contamination, and a recording of a striped hawk moth, which was the best recording of a striped hawk moth he had ever heard on the wireless. And still he felt sexy. He couldn't fantasize about Hilary, who belonged to reality. That left him feeling sexy about almost everybody – Jean Metcalfe, Vera Lynn, Mrs Dale, Mrs Archer, the Lapps of Scandinavia, even Gandhi. He returned hurriedly to thoughts of Hilary.

Ginny returned halfway through the recording of the striped hawk moth, so he never heard how it finished.

'Nice evening?' he asked.

'Marvellous.'

'You met a nice man!'

'No. Gordon's still ill.' She gave him a shrewd glance. 'You're better!' she said. She sounded as if his improvement was the only blot on a splendid day.

'I wish you had met a nice man,' he said. 'You deserve one.'

'Presumably that's why you ruled yourself out of the running.'

'*Touché*.'

'You *are* better. My job is done. Good night,' said Ginny.

He *was* better. Next day, he telephoned Howard Lewthwaite, and arranged to meet him for lunch on Tuesday.

John Foster Dulles said that, if the United States became involved in a Middle East war, he would rather not have British or French troops alongside them. Only 2 out of 19 wrecks in the southern section of the Suez Canal had so far been removed by the UN salvage team.

A virulent letter from an angry schoolmaster appeared in the *Thurmarsh Evening Argus*. Its author sat in a secluded corner of the vast, scantily filled restaurant of the Midland Hotel, beneath a photograph of Stanier Pacific No. 46207 *Princess Arthur of Connaught*, passing through Rugby with the down Welshman, consisting of fourteen bogies.

'It *is* good to see you. Are you better?' said Howard Lewthwaite.

'Much better, thank you. Before we start on the main business, Mr Lewthwaite, I've been asked to do you for "Proud Sons of Thurmarsh".'

'Oh! I'd be honoured, Henry.'

The waiter handed them menus.

'Let's get the ordering out of the way, shall we?' said Howard Lewthwaite.

They studied the vast menus.

'Do you ever get criticized, as a socialist, for spending a lot on meals in public?' said Henry.

'I never thought of that,' said Howard Lewthwaite. 'I was going to order a good burgundy. I think we'd better have the house carafe. And there's not a bad choice on the *table d'hôte*, is there? I like cod mornay.' They ordered their meals. Howard Lewthwaite leant forward and said across the huge table, 'Right. What are these things you've found out?'

'The burning of the Cap Ferrat was arson,' said Henry. 'The death of its owner was murder.'

Howard Lewthwaite went white and sat very still. Henry met his glance and knew. Howard Lewthwaite knew that he knew. They held the gaze. Neither wanted to be the first to be seen to be unable to bear the awfulness of that moment. Henry's flesh crawled. His scalp itched. Hilary seemed very far away.

'You're part of it,' he said flatly.

'Not part of murder and arson,' said Howard Lewthwaite vehemently.

The elderly wine waiter brought what looked like a sample bottle. It contained what looked like a sample. He poured a quarter of an inch of wine. Howard Lewthwaite sniffed it. 'Yes yes,' he said. 'Absolutely revolting. Pour away.'

Henry raised his glass.

'Cheers,' he said. 'Aren't you going to congratulate me?'

'What on?'

'Winning the Nobel Prize for Naïvety.'

'Henry!'

How quiet the room was.

'You're a friend of Peter Matheson,' said Henry. 'You're a friend of the chief planning officer. You invite both of them to your party. You try to put me off by telling me you're convinced nothing illegal has happened. I should have guessed.'

The brown Windsor soup arrived. Those were the halcyon days of brown soups.

'How could you do it, Mr Lewthwaite?'

Howard Lewthwaite smiled. His smile was as thin as the soup. He looked older.

'Lewthwaite's is failing,' he said. 'Naddy'll die if I don't take her to live in a hot, dry climate. You're quite right. There is a development plan for the whole area between Market Street and the river. I'm not ashamed of that. It needs redevelopment. We call it the Fish Hill Complex. A gleaming new shopping centre, Henry. Thurmarsh needs it. Tower blocks by the Rundle, with grass in between. Using the river. What views. Higher than anything in Sheffield or Leeds. Mixed housing, right in the centre. A good plan.'

'Those are nice streets.'

'Henry! They're run-down. They're clapped-out.'

'They're being deliberately run-down so the poor conned townsfolk can be told, "They're run-down. They're clapped-out."'

Howard Lewthwaite didn't reply.

'All this secrecy. Fred Hathersage. Anthony Eden denied collusion with France and Israel. Do you deny collusion? Are there back-handers flying about?'

The cod mornay arrived.

'A bit of everything, gentlemen?' said the waitress.

'A bit of everything,' said Howard Lewthwaite.

Henry didn't know how he could still eat. But anything was better than thinking. Thinking about Hilary. Thinking about Howard Lewthwaite as a father-in-law.

'You feel I've let you down,' said Howard Lewthwaite.

'I feel you've let Hilary down.'

Howard Lewthwaite's eyes met Henry's again.

'You're going to suggest I drop the matter,' said Henry.

'You'll be losing that prize for naïvety.' Howard Lewthwaite smiled. His smile was as tired as the broccoli.

Henry looked across the restaurant to the table where he'd sat with Lorna. This room wasn't redolent of happy memories for him.

'You seem to be forgetting the arson and murder,' he said.

'Today's the first I've heard of arson and murder,' said Howard Lewthwaite.

'Murder of the man who took me in as his son.'

'What?'

'The owner of the Cap Ferrat was my uncle.'

'I didn't know that, Henry. Oh my God, what a business.'

'Yes. The burning of the Cap Ferrat was so convenient for you. Didn't you ever suspect it might be arson.'

'Did you?'

'I'm front runner for the Nobel Prize for Naïvety. You're a politician. Dirt's your natural environment.' No! This is your father-in-law to be.

'I think I did have a little wonder, to be honest,' said Howard Lewthwaite. 'I think I closed my mind to the possibility fairly rapidly. Something unpleasant that I didn't want to admit to myself. Can it be true, Henry? Arson, possibly. Murder? Thurmarsh isn't Chicago.'

'That's what Stan Holliday said.'

'Did he? Oh dear. In that case it probably is Chicago. Where does Stan Holliday come in?'

'He was overheard by my source, which I can't reveal, saying it was arson and murder. I challenged him. He denied it far too vehemently.'

'That's all you're going on, is it? No proof?'

'No proof, no.'

They ate in silence for a few moments.

'How's your cod mornay?' asked Howard Lewthwaite.

'Disgusting. Another sauce that should never have been revealed.'

'Look. Perhaps it *was* arson, but your uncle could still have died accidentally. I mean . . . why should anybody murder him?'

'So there's no owner of the club to pay the insurance money to. So there's no owner of the club to suspect that it was arson.'

'Your nomination for the Nobel Prize is withdrawn,' said Howard Lewthwaite. 'Will you give me a week to try and find out what I can, Henry?'

He had to agree. Hilary was coming down that weekend. He couldn't bear to spoil the weekend. But he couldn't resist making Howard Lewthwaite wait for a few long seconds for his reply. He hadn't often had that kind of power.

'One week,' he said.

They both plumped for the apple pie. Henry got out his notebook.

'Right,' he said. 'It's time to start another interview in my series, "Great Criminals and Hypocrites", alias "Proud Sons of Thurmarsh".'

'We don't need to do this if you don't want to,' said Howard Lewthwaite.

'I have to. Editor's orders. Otherwise it'll look as if he's biased towards the Conservatives.'

'He is.'

'Precisely. That's why he can't be seen to be. Mr Lewthwaite, how old are you?'

'This morning I was 49. Now I'm 93.'

'What made you enter politics?'

'I wanted to serve the Labour Party, and the wider community. My fellow citizens of Thurmarsh, I suppose.'

'No thought of personal gain?'

'Financial, no. I . . . I can't go on with this.'

'We have to. I repeat, "No thought of personal gain?"'

'Financial, no. Glory? Power? Self-satisfaction? We all seek those a bit, don't we? I don't dwell too much on motives. I prefer to dwell on achievements.' Howard Lewthwaite reached out across the table. He just managed to clasp Henry's hand. 'Henry?' he said. 'I promise you. If arson and murder are proved, I'm with you, whatever it costs. Even if it costs . . . Naddy's life. Even if it costs . . .'

Henry finished it for him.

'. . . our marriage.'

21   Dangerous Days

11,000 men were idle at Fords of Dagenham, due to a strike at Briggs Motor Bodies. Egypt announced that she might halt work on clearing the Suez Canal altogether if Israel refused to withdraw from former Egyptian positions in the Gulf of Akaba. Henry took Ginny for a drink at the Winstanley.

'There's a reply to my letter at last,' he said. 'Outraged fury, signed "Another Angry Schoolmaster".'

'Colin wrote it,' said Ginny.

'What?'

'Editor's orders.'

They sat at a corner table, surrounded by brasses and shields. He took surreptitious glances at her face, noting the differences between it and Hilary's, thus making a kind of living map of Hilary's face. It was unfair to use Ginny in this way, but he couldn't help it.

'Hilary's coming down this weekend,' he said. 'And we'll . . . er . . . quite probably be . . . er . . .'

'. . . playing bridge? You want me to make up a four? No? Having a bottle party? Fine. I'd love to come. No? Don't tell me. I've got it. Making love!'

'Oh, Ginny. No, I just thought I'd tell you so that . . . er . . . you could go away if you wanted to.'

'We never made you move out.'

'I'm not making you move out, Ginny.' There's Mr Matheson. Oh no! Supposing Howard Lewthwaite comes in and sees me with Ginny. Why did we come here? Why don't I think ahead? 'I'm giving you the chance to move out, if you want to, because, although I know sound doesn't travel up as much as it travels down, you might still be very conscious of our presence, and I know what it's like, Ginny, when you're all alone, listening to people . . . er . . .'

'. . . thrashing around in sexual ecstasy.' Ginny's eyes filled with tears. Henry handed her one of three handkerchieves which he'd brought in case of just such an emergency. She did it justice. Howard Lewthwaite entered. Ginny said, 'Thanks, Henry. I'm sorry,' and gave him a quick kiss. Howard Lewthwaite saw. Henry hurried up to the bar, to buy drinks they didn't need.

'Hello, Mr Lewthwaite,' he said, over-brightly. 'Hello, Mr Matheson. I've just been . . . er . . . telling the girl from the flat above me that Hilary's coming down this weekend and suggesting that she might like to . . . er . . . go away, so as not to . . . er . . .' He realized that Howard Lewthwaite had no idea that they were having pre-marital sex. His face blazed. Later, he'd realize that Howard Lewthwaite had been embarrassed too, because he was meeting Peter Matheson to discuss what Henry had told him.

'I've got a little story for you,' said Howard Lewthwaite. 'One of our councillors. Jim Rackstraw. He lost a champion pigeon four years ago. His prize bird. It turned up yesterday in Oslo.'

'Thanks,' said Henry. 'Terrific. Thank you very much, Mr Lewthwaite.'

When he returned to Ginny with the drinks, Henry said, 'One of the men I was talking to is Hilary's father. Do you think I could ask you not to kiss me or fondle me or be in any way physically intimate with me for the rest of the evening?'

'I think I might be able to restrain myself,' said Ginny Fenwick.

The *New York Post* attacked the American oil industry's refusal to meet Western Europe's fuel needs. Dick Francis retired from the race track at the age of 36. Denzil Ackerman took Henry for a drink in the bar of the Midland Hotel.

They sat in an alcove, on the brown leather upholstery with gold studs. Above them, the Patriot class engine was still pulling a mixed freight out of Carlisle Upperby Yard in light snow, reminding Henry that this was the corner where they'd sat with Lorna Arrow. Tomorrow he'd be subjecting Hilary to a similar ordeal in the Lord Nelson. He felt sick at the prospect. Had he learnt nothing?

'I'll be in London next week,' said Denzil. 'Interviewing glittering show business personalities so that the citizens of Thurmarsh will be wildly envious of the great world of metropolitan sophistication. I want you to stand in for me.'

'Oh! Well . . . thank you very much,' said Henry.

'This is quite deliberate, dear boy. As you know, I have private means. Not enough to keep me for a lifetime without working. Enough to keep me for what remains of my lifetime without working. I shall retire quite soon. I've found it all quite amusing, even if I haven't exactly fulfilled all my ambitions. I want to go while it's still amusing. I'm grooming you to succeed me.'

'Oh! Well . . . thank you very much.'

'You aren't made for the hurly burly of general reporting.'

'Oh. Well . . . thank you very much,' said Henry rather more doubtfully.

'You introduced me to Lampo. I'm in your debt. There are two jobs for you next week. On Tuesday afternoon you'll interview the Chief Torch Bearer of the Arc of the Golden Light of Our Lady.'

'What??'

'It's a pseudo-religious cult. A pseudo-moralistic sect. It's based in a big house outside town. Hexington Hall. It aims to protect South Yorkshire from the flood of obscenity and pornography.'

'What flood of obscenity and pornography?'

'The one it predicts is coming. And presumably hopes is coming, so that it can protect South Yorkshire from it. It's run by an ex-colonel called Boyce-Uppingham.'

'Good God!'

'You know him?'

'I know his niece. She said she had a nutty uncle near Thurmarsh.'

'Nutty's about right.'

'Is it arc as in light or ark as in Noah's?'

'I don't know. It could be either. Should be fun, anyway. And on Wednesday there's a private view of a new exhibition at the Gusset.'

'Paintings?'

'Yes.'

'I don't know enough about art.'

Denzil summoned a waiter, and ordered a pink gin and a pint of bitter.

'Use long words,' he said. 'Stick in lots of cultural references. A few exclamation marks to suggest they've missed points they didn't even know you were trying to make. It's easy.'

'Whose exhibition is it?'

'Johnson Protheroe's.'

'Who?'

'Precisely.'

'What?'

'Nobody else'll have heard of him either. So you can say what you like.'

'I won't know if he's any good.'

'It's unlikely. He's Canadian.'

'But, Denzil . . . I want to be fair to the man.'

'Oh dear. The sweet innocence of youth! Look, not only is Johnson Protheroe Canadian, but he sounds like a firm of merchant bankers. If, however unlikely, he is good and you don't spot it, I'm sure a bad review in Thurmarsh won't ruin *his* career. I'm giving you the biggest chance of *your* career. For goodness sake, dear boy, rise to it.'

Their drinks arrived.

'Try not to think beer,' said Denzil Ackerman. 'Think pink gin.'

Until he received the editor's summons, Henry had completely forgotten that, before his bout of flu, he'd promised to reveal his scoop within a week. What was he to do? He couldn't reveal it till he'd told Hilary. And he'd told her father that he wouldn't tell her until he'd found out what her father had found out.

'Sit down, Henry.'

So far so good. An order with which he was happy to comply.

'I want you to write another letter, attacking "Another Angry Schoolmaster". Sign it "First Angry Schoolmaster". This one can be really big if we get it off the ground.'

'Right, Mr Redrobe.' At last he'd get through an interview without saying 'sir'.

'It's time to find a permanent job for you, a personal niche, apart from your general duties.'

'Right, Mr Redrobe.' Henry's hopes rose. Had the neat, Brylcreemed editor forgotten?

'But first, you promised me your scoop. Fire away. I'm all ears.'

'Well . . . er . . . it involves a councillor.'

'Ah!'

'A Labour councillor.'

'Ah!!'

'And his pigeon.'

There was a long silence.

'What?'

'His pigeon. Councillor Jim Rackstraw keeps pigeons. He had a prize pigeon. His best bird. One of the four best birds ever bred in South Yorkshire. Four years ago, it disappeared. Without trace. Not a word. Not a coo. It's turned up. In Oslo.'

The editor tapped on his desk very slowly, with his silver pencil, like a sick woodpecker losing its battle for life.

'I see,' he said quietly. He looked at his watch. 'There's time to make the travel arrangements this afternoon.'

'Travel arrangements?' said Henry.

'To Norway. We'll need a complete list of the names and addresses of every single Norwegian on whom that bird has crapped.'

Henry made no reply. There wasn't any reply to be made.

'Yes, I have just the job for you,' said the editor. 'Uncle Jason.'

'Uncle Jason?'

'And his Argusnauts. It's an important job, Henry. Today's children are tomorrow's adults. Don't look so horrified. Surely you aren't going to tell me that the young man who in little more than a twelvemonth has come up with the wandering cat, the escaped canary and the rediscovered pigeon feels incapable of writing for children?'

'No, sir. Of course not, sir. Thank you, sir.'

Damn! Damn! Damn!

They were all there, seated at their corner table in that brown and secret place, that most masculine of all surrogate wombs, the back room of the Lord Nelson in Leatherbottlers' Row. As Uncle Jason entered with his pale, calm fiancée, they all turned to look, like the escape committee eyeing with suspicion the newcomer who'd been recommended as an expert in forged documents. Even Denzil was there, and he very rarely stayed over on a Friday night. Even Ginny was there, and this was the first time she'd been with Gordon and Jill since it had happened. Ginny looked brave and forbidding. Gordon looked sheepish. Jill looked defiant. Colin gave Henry a thumbs-up, as if to suggest that he already approved of Hilary. Henry frowned at him. It wasn't a question of approval.

Denzil bought a round. Hilary asked for beer. Colin nodded his approval. Henry frowned at him.

'We're discussing what the world will be like in thirty years' time,' said Ted.

'Homosexuality will be legal,' said Denzil, arriving with a tray of drinks. He spoke louder than was necessary, for the benefit of Chief Superintendent Ron Ratchett.

'Over my dead body,' muttered Chief Superintendent Ron Ratchett.

'Necrophilia may take a little longer,' said Denzil.

Henry smiled. He'd told Hilary that Denzil was outrageous, and here he was being outrageous. Then he remembered that it wasn't a question of approval, so he stopped smiling and frowned. Then he realized that this might look prudish, so he stopped frowning and smiled. Then he realized that constantly frowning and smiling looked ridiculous, so he sat very rigid and tried to show no feelings at all. Hilary raised a quizzical eyebrow.

'In thirty years' time homosexuality will be so normal that it won't even be considered odd to have homosexual priests,' said Denzil.

'And women priests?' said Hilary.

'That may take a bit longer,' said Ted.

Hilary nodded ruefully. 'You're probably right,' she said.

'The Arc of the Golden Light of Our Lady, whose Chief Torch Bearer I'm interviewing on Tuesday, seem to believe that a flood of pornography is going to be unleashed on the world,' said Henry.

'I think it is,' said Helen. 'I think in thirty years' time it'll be as compulsory for comedians to talk about willies as it's impossible now.' To everyone's surprise, she blushed. When she realized she was blushing, she went scarlet. Ted stared at her in fascinated astonishment.

'Quite right, Helen,' he said. 'Everything'll be pornographic. Even *Listen with Mother*.'

Henry bought a round. When he returned, Ted was saying, 'In thirty years' time, there'll be photos of naked women in the newspapers.' He seemed to be drawn to the subject like a mosquito to a fat thigh.

'What about naked men?' said Hilary.

'That'll take another thirty years.'

'Sex will be a subject that can be freely discussed, openly, honestly, naturally, everywhere,' said Colin.

'Surely, if sex is that free and open, men will no longer need to look at pictures of naked women?' said Hilary.

'Advantage Hilary,' said Gordon.

No, no, Gordon. You're getting it all wrong. It isn't a game, and it isn't competitive.

'Well said, kid,' said Colin. 'No more sex crimes. No more rape.'

None of them knew she'd been raped. Henry began to sweat with embarrassment. Please change the subject, he begged silently.

'What a wonderful thought,' said Hilary, so fervently that he thought she was going to add, 'I've been raped.'

'Oh dear,' said Ginny. 'I wish I agreed with you all. Your world of sexual freedom will be a world for the attractive and the beautiful.' She looked straight at Gordon and Jill. Jill, who hadn't spoken yet, blushed. Ginny relented, and turned away. 'The ugly and the unprepossessing will stand on the side-lines and ogle,' she said. 'It'll be flaunted endlessly. They'll be tormented endlessly. Sex crimes will increase.'

'How very depressing,' said Helen.

'You're all right. You're beautiful,' said Ginny, with feeling.

'I won't be in thirty years,' said Helen with equal feeling.

'Deuce,' said Gordon.

'Are you trying to excuse sex crimes, Ginny?' said Helen.

'Certainly not. I'm trying to explain them,' said Ginny. 'The British are very good at condemning results while totally ignoring causes.'

Colin insisted on buying the next round, because he'd have to rush home to Glenda soon. Hilary drily expressed surprise on learning that he was married.

'Well, time I went home to give the wife . . .' Ben glanced at Hilary. '. . . some help with putting the children to bed.'

And Colin did rush home to Glenda. Ted raised an astonished eyebrow. Henry was amazed at Hilary's ability to change things without saying anything.

A trip to the jazz club was mooted. Gordon and Jill exchanged looks and Gordon said, 'Dunkirk.' Jill looked puzzled.

'He means you should make a tactical withdrawal,' said Ginny. 'There's no need to on my account. I'm thick-skinned and hard-bitten.'

'Good,' said Jill. 'I like the jazz club.'

'Are you coming, Henry?' said Helen.

'Yes,' said Henry, decisively. 'We are, aren't we?' he added, ruining the effect.

Hilary laughed. Everyone must have seen her beauty at that moment. Henry felt proud, and then he realized that Hilary wouldn't like that, and then he didn't know what to think.

They walked down Leatherbottlers' Row into Albion Street, down Albion Street, past the *Chronicle* and *Argus* building, and turned left into Commercial Road. Henry found himself with Helen. Ted was ahead of them, with Hilary. They seemed to be chatting easily. Behind them he could hear Ginny asking Gordon and Jill determinedly casual questions about their plans. Jill was clearly embarrassed. Gordon was finding few opportunities for elegantly coded replies. Ginny sounded totally relaxed.

Helen linked arms with Henry, as they began the gentle climb up Commercial Road. 'One day when I was feverish with the flu I had a hallucination that you were there in bed with Ted and me,' she said. 'I was awfully disappointed to find you weren't.'

'For God's sake, Helen,' he said. He tried to pull his arm free. She clung on. They walked on, linked and silent.

In the jazz club, Helen said, 'Hilary's making a big hit with Ted,' and Henry couldn't bear to see her talking to Ted any more, so he went up to them, right in the middle of 'Basin Street Blues', and grabbed hold of Hilary, and said, 'I want to talk to you, darling,' and Ted hurried back to Helen, smiling, and Henry had an uncomfortable feeling that he'd been an unwitting puppet in a charade.

'How do you like Sid Hallett and the Rundlemen?' he asked.

'I've heard them before, you know,' she said. 'I'm a Thurmarsh girl. Talking of that, your series, "Proud Sons of Thurmarsh", is pretty male-oriented, isn't it? How about a follow-up series, "Proud Daughters of Thurmarsh"?'

'An excellent idea.' Desire for her swept over him. 'I want to make love with you,' he said.

'I must go and see my parents tonight.' There was applause. Sid Hallett and the Rundlemen took huge sips of beer, in unison, as if it were written in the score. They embarked upon 'South Rampart Street Parade'. 'Let's go now,' she said.

'We don't want to seem like wet blankets the first time you meet them all. You've had a bit of that effect already. Usually they all come.'

'They should go home to their wives.'

'I quite agree. But it's their life, isn't it?'

'I can't hide my feelings,' she said. 'I'm awkward, difficult, uncompromising, inconvenient. Do you want to call it off now?' She went round to them all, saying 'Good night.'

'She wants to get home before her parents go to bed. She hasn't seen them yet,' explained Henry.

They walked down Commercial Road in silence.

In York Road, near the station, she said, 'If you want a good sport, you should marry Ginny.'

'Hilary!' he said. 'I thought you liked Ginny,' he added.

'I do,' she said. 'It wasn't an insult.'

'You seemed to like Ted,' he said.

She didn't say another word. There were no kisses, that night, in Perkin Warbeck Drive.

They were on a small chain ferry, gently caressing with entwined fingers. They were crossing a placid river. Brown trout trembled against the stream. Weeds bent gently before the lazy current. On the bank, the gnarled trees were heavy with marzipan and nougat.

The ferry scraped to a halt against the chalky stones. The ferryman turned from his winch, straightened his back and

grimaced. He was vaguely familiar. He began to speak. He told
them, with blinding clarity, in less than thirty words, all the
secrets of life, of its meaning and its conduct.

He woke up. The words faded. He could hear them but not
make sense of them. He asked her if she understood them. She
wasn't there. He was alone, and last night they had parted without
a kiss.

Perhaps she wouldn't come.

She came.

'I'm sorry,' she said.

'I'm sorry, too,' he said.

'That's all right, then.'

'Not a very good evening.'

'We have to put ourselves through a bit more stress than we did
at Christmas,' she said. 'I'm not your princess. You aren't my
prince. We can't marry each other while we still seem too good to
be true.'

For lunch they had bread and marmalade. He dropped a dollop
of marmalade on her stomach, and licked it off. By the time they'd
dragged themselves from the crumpled wreck of his narrow bed it
was almost dark.

Their love was proof against the relentless rain. Darkness lent
enchantment to the shining wet streets.

Cousin Hilda was making supper. She sniffed, and Henry
wondered if she could smell sex on them. But the air was full of the
aroma of imminent faggots, and her disapproval was for the
inopportune timing of their visit.

'You should have told me you were coming,' she said. 'If it was
stew I'd make it stretch, but you can't stretch faggots. Two faggots
are two faggots, whichever road you look at them. It wouldn't be
fair to make my businessmen go short, who've paid.'

'We can't eat, thank you very much,' said Hilary. 'We're
expected at home.'

Cousin Hilda sniffed. 'You could have been expected at this
home,' she said.

'We didn't want to be any trouble,' said Henry.

'Trouble!' said Cousin Hilda. 'I suppose you're above and
beyond faggots, now you're a journalist.'

306

'Very much the reverse,' said Henry. He met Hilary's eyes and she smiled with the utmost decorum.

'Hilary and I are engaged, Cousin Hilda,' said Henry.

Cousin Hilda didn't attempt to hide her hurt, but she couldn't quite hide the delight behind the hurt.

'Oh!' she said. 'Engaged! Well! And I've never even met her before. Well!'

Henry kissed her. Then Hilary kissed her. She received these kisses as her due.

'Well!' she said. 'Mrs Wedderburn will be pleased. She'll be right thrilled. She's very fond of you.' There were tears in Cousin Hilda's eyes. She just managed to finish speaking without breaking down. 'It'll make Mrs Wedderburn's day, will this.' She hurried off into the scullery. 'All this talk,' she said. 'I'm neglecting my faggots.'

Henry's eyes were filled with tears too, damn it. And so were Hilary's. This was intolerable.

'Can I help?' said Hilary, hurrying into the scullery.

To Henry's astonishment, Hilary didn't reappear. Cousin Hilda allowed her to help. No greater compliment could possibly have been paid by Cousin Hilda. Slowly, shamingly slowly, he was beginning to realize that he'd been blessed with the love of a quite extraordinary person. He was filled with astonishing warmth and joy. He sat and stared at the glowing stove. He could hear them clattering in the scullery. He heard Cousin Hilda say, 'Mrs Wedderburn's had a soft spot for Henry ever since she lent him her camp-bed.' The tears were streaming down his face. He hurried upstairs to the lavatory, to hide this damning evidence of emotion.

Cousin Hilda insisted that they stayed. Hilary must meet her businessmen. She even offered them a cup of tea! So Hilary was introduced to Liam, who adored her instantly, and to Norman Pettifer, who tried to take a jaundiced view of her and failed, and to Mr Peters, who thought she was a fine thing and told her of other fine things to which he had become used. They sat and chatted, as the three men demolished their faggots, their mashed potatoes, their peas, their tinned pears to follow.

Oh joy of youth, it was still raining, and, as they walked to

Perkin Warbeck Drive, they were able to demonstrate again that rain couldn't hurt them.

The sight of Howard Lewthwaite brought Henry back to the reality that he'd had to hide from Hilary. How could they lose each other now, after the bonds they had forged that day? And now he made sure that the bonds were even more closely forged. He suggested that they fix the wedding date. They did. Saturday, July 20th. Nadežda cried. Sam asked if they'd had their oats that morning and had it been better than cornflakes? Henry met Howard Lewthwaite's eye and his look tried to say, 'Yes. We've made love. We love each other deeply and respect each other totally and believe our love is a most beautiful and moral thing.' Howard Lewthwaite gave him a look which might have meant, 'I understand and I'm not angry' but might also have meant, 'What on earth is that look of yours supposed to mean?' Henry gave him a look which was supposed to mean, 'Can you give me any hint regarding the progress of your investigations into the dire matter which hangs over this touching domestic scene like a thunder-cloud over the sweet cow-dunged water meadows at the end of a midge-mad July day?' and Howard Lewthwaite gave him a look which might have meant, 'I haven't found out anything definite,' but might also have meant, 'Since neither of us has the faintest idea what each other's looks mean, it looks as though we ought to stop giving each other these looks.'

'Don't mind me,' said Auntie Doris through her tears, as the wind rattled the windows of the lounge bar of the White Hart. 'I'm just a silly, feeble-minded old woman.'

'Yes, you are,' said Geoffrey Porringer. 'So shut up.'

'Geoffrey!' said Auntie Doris.

'Joke!' said Geoffrey Porringer.

'Jokes are supposed to be funny, Geoffrey,' said Auntie Doris.

Over late lunch in the hotel's deserted restaurant, she wanted to know every detail of their courtship. 'Italy!' she said. 'How romantic! And then the long quest before you met again. Isn't that a lovely story, Geoffrey?'

Geoffrey Porringer nodded and said, 'Lovely. Let's crack another bottle.'

While Geoffrey Porringer cracked another bottle, Auntie Doris said, 'Does this mean you won't come to Cap Ferrat?'

'Do you want me to come?' said Henry.

'More than anything in the world,' said Auntie Doris, who was no stranger to hyperbole.

'I'll come for a week,' said Henry, who was. Auntie Doris looked so gratified that he wished he hadn't already begun to add, 'I have to take my third week before the end of March anyway.'

When Auntie Doris went to see a man about a dog, Geoffrey Porringer said, 'She's excited, Hilary. I don't want you to think she's always like this.'

'Everything's fine,' said Hilary. 'I'm enjoying myself.'

'Sometimes when she's happy, she gets carried away, and doesn't realize how much she's drinking,' said Geoffrey Porringer.

When Hilary went to see a man about a dog, Geoffrey Porringer said, 'She's lovely, Henry. She really is. I can't get over it.'

'Don't sound so surprised,' said Auntie Doris, who always made things worse by protesting about them. 'It makes it sound as though we wouldn't expect him to make a decent catch.'

'Decent catch!' said Geoffrey Porringer. 'He's landed in the middle of a shoal of mackerel.'

When Henry went to see a man about a dog, he didn't know what they talked about, but they were all laughing when he returned, and he was a little disturbed to find how richly entertaining life without him was.

'It's a nice hotel,' said Hilary.

'How the conversation descends to the banal when I return,' said Henry.

'I'll show you the brochure, Hilary,' said Geoffrey Porringer.

'Geoffrey!' said Auntie Doris. 'Young people in love aren't interested in brochures. They've other things on their minds.'

'She's got a tongue in her head,' said Geoffrey Porringer. 'Hilary, would you like to see the brochure?'

'Very much,' said Hilary.

'You see!' said Geoffrey Porringer.

'She could hardly say, "God, no! How tedious,"' said Auntie Doris.

When Geoffrey Porringer had gone to fetch the brochure,

Auntie Doris said, 'Henry had been interceding on my behalf with his Uncle Teddy, hadn't you, Henry?'

'Well, yes,' said Henry. 'Yes, I had.'

'Until he was incarcerated in the ruins of his life's dream,' said Auntie Doris.

'I heard about that,' said Hilary. 'It was tragic.'

It could be more tragic than you know, thought Henry.

'It was, Hilary,' said Auntie Doris. 'That's exactly what it was. And at the time, when it happened, Henry, I think you felt there was a chance, didn't you?'

'Well, yes,' said Henry. 'Yes, I did.'

Geoffrey Porringer returned, waving the brochure.

'There we are, Hilary,' he said. 'One brochure.'

Hilary studied the brochure with as much interest as she could muster.

'Very nice,' she said. 'Very reasonable.'

'We like to think so,' said Geoffrey Porringer.

In the train, on the journey from a fading evening of sodden sheep to a sodium night of glistening roofs, Hilary said, 'I thought you were exaggerating, but they're every bit as bad as you said.'

'Auntie Doris and Geoffrey Porringer?'

'No. His blackheads.'

At Leeds, she caught the train north and this time she didn't turn away abruptly. She leant out of the window. He walked beside her. 'Love you,' she said. 'Love you love you love you.' He began to trot, he was out beyond the canopy, in the rain again. 'Love you,' she yelled again. He stopped right at the end of the platform, where it narrowed to a wedge. Smoke from the engine swirled around him, but every now and then it cleared and there she was, moving furiously, unashamed of love, of sentiment, of intensity, of banality, of childishness, unable to be hurt by any separation that was merely geographical. He watched until the last of the twelve bogies was invisible, and then he turned away. Rain streamed down his face. Tears streamed down his face. Never had his face been bombarded by so much water in one weekend.

President Eisenhower spoke of the 'abiding strength' of the Anglo-American alliance. Israel continued to refuse to withdraw her forces from Gaza. Canada refused to support demands for Israel to withdraw, and threatened to withdraw her troops from the emergency force unless the United Nations force was empowered to patrol the Israeli–Egyptian border and to remain to keep the peace after the Israeli withdrawal. Workers at Briggs Motor Bodies voted to defy their union and continue their strike.

'Hello, boys and girls,' typed Henry, bashing the keys angrily. 'Some of you Argusnauts are already making contributions to next Christmas's toy fund, so that less fortunate children can have a treat. Well done, each and every one of you.

'Special thanks this week for Dora Pennyweather, aged 11, who made six super teddy bears. I'm so sorry I couldn't meet her when she handed them in at our office.'

That afternoon, he interviewed Bill Holliday for 'Proud Sons of Thurmarsh'. He felt that this would make him the laughing stock of the whole town.

The dun-coloured bus growled irritably through the southern suburbs. Rows of semi-detached houses breasted the sweeping hills. Some had dark red brick ground floors and stucco above. Some had brick centres and stucco edges. Some had bay windows topped by tiny tiled roofs. Some had decorated brick arches round the doorways. These brave attempts at individuality only emphasized the sameness of it all. Towns didn't grow organically any more. They were planned by bureaucrats, and people were moved around to fit the plans. Society would pay for all this deadness, thought Henry, as the inexorable bus took him nearer and nearer to Bill Holliday, whom he was convinced was at the centre of all the dirty work surrounding the development plan.

Bill Holliday's office was a glass island in a sea of cars. In front of it, rows of used cars. What mechanical horrors did the gleaming, seemingly innocent bonnets conceal? Behind the office, on the rolling slopes of what had once been prime farmland, an alp of rust rose out of a glistening porridge of mud. The office had wide windows on both sides, as if Bill Holliday actually wanted to see all this. It had a fluffy white carpet and two soft armchairs covered in imitation tiger skin. There was a glass-fronted drinks cabinet.

'Brandy?' said Bill Holliday.

Refusals crunched round Henry's brain like old cars under a

bulldozer. I don't while I'm on duty. It might affect my judgement. I wouldn't soil my gullet with your ill-gotten gains, you murderous bastard.

He finally decided upon, 'Thank you very much.'

'Cigar?'

Ditto.

Puffing, choking, sipping, choking, at three-fifteen on a grey afternoon, Henry felt a bit of a villain himself. And liked the feeling, which was alarming. He apologized for the misprint. Bill Holliday laughed. 'Don't worry,' he said. '"Ow"! It just about sums up our engagement.' He sighed. 'She wants me for my money. The jewellery I buy her. I want love.' Love? You? Mr Scrap? The man you wouldn't buy a used car from? Love? 'People laugh when I say this, but I'm a deeply loving person. I love kids. Angie doesn't want kids. Tell you who I'd like to meet on your rag. Oops, sorry. Paper.' He roared with laughter. 'Uncle Jason. Loves kids, that bastard. White-haired old bugger, is he?'

'Yes,' said Henry. 'Yes. White-haired old bugger.'

'Grand. I'm an unashamed sentimentalist. They don't make them like that, any more.'

Henry took a deep breath and plunged in, hoping to catch Bill Holliday off guard.

'My Uncle Teddy ran the Cap Ferrat,' he said. 'You knew him, didn't you?'

'Oh aye. Angie and I went there, oh, what, must have been four times.'

'Are you sure it wasn't five?' Henry tried not to sound terrified. 'Are you sure you didn't go there once more, without Angie?'

'What?' Bill Holliday looked more puzzled than alarmed. 'On me own? I wouldn't have dared go without Angie.'

Henry had the uneasy feeling that all avenues led to brick walls. He began his interview. Bill Holliday defended his line of business. 'Folk think it's a dirty business, 'cos of t'great mounds of cars. What silly buggers don't realize is, if it weren't for my mounds, where'd cars be? Eh? All over t'bloody town. All over t'bloody Dales. Right?' He defended greyhound racing. 'When have six dogs had to be destroyed after pile-up over Bechers? Eh? Sport of kings? Piss off. Give me dogs any day.'

He refilled Henry's glass and led him to the window. They gazed in awe at the pile of rusting Fords, Morrises, Humbers, Standards, Armstrong-Siddeleys. At the top of the pile, an Austin Seven was lying across a Daimler.

'Equal, at last, in death. Like folks,' said Bill Holliday.

Henry looked at him in surprise.

'This is just a molehill, compared to what's to come,' said Bill Holliday. 'Motoring will increase tenfold. Old cars will increase tenfold. It'll be folk like me what saves the world from choking. Does the world thank us? Does it buggery.'

Henry watched a beautiful old Riley being crushed flat. He shuddered.

'How would tha like to be crushed like that?' said Bill Holliday. 'Wouldn't be much fun, eh?'

He roared with laughter.

Henry didn't.

A patrol of the Queen's Own Cameron Highlanders was ambushed by mountain tribesmen in the Western Aden Protectorate. Fighting flared up on the Aden frontier, threatened by 4,000 Yemenis. Security forces arrested 189 men in 4 days in the mountains of Western Cyprus. In Thurmarsh a crate of surgical trusses fell from a crane and nearly killed Uncle Jason. These were dangerous days.

He was on his way to catch the bus to Hexington, where he would interview Colonel Boyce-Uppingham, Chief Torch Bearer of the Arc (?) of the Golden Light of Our Lady, in the Athenaeum Club in Doncaster Road. Being early, he'd gone to have another look at the planned development area. The southernmost warehouse in Glasshouse Lane was still in use, although it was lorries now, not boats, that used its wharf. Pleased to see some life in this dying area, Henry watched as a crane slowly manipulated a crate, which contained, though he didn't yet know it, a consignment of surgical trusses for export to Portugal. One moment he was looking up into a blue sky streaked with mackerel clouds. The next moment he was watching a crate falling towards him, growing larger and larger. He hurled himself to the right, tripped and fell. The crate smashed into the pavement, inches from his head. It burst open. Wood and splinters filled the air. Surgical trusses, intended for the hernias of Lisbon and Oporto, rained down on a terrified young English journalist.

He sat up. He stood up. His heart was thumping. His legs felt weak. He leant against the warehouse wall. The crane driver yelled out, pitifully inadequately, 'Sorry!'

The landlord of the Artisan's Rest hurried over. 'I saw that,' he said. 'Tha were lucky!'

A corner of Henry's mind debated the philosophical aspect of this. In all probability, no crates of surgical trusses had fallen that day in Europe, North America, South America, Asia, Australasia, Africa or the Indian Subcontinent. The only crate had fallen inches from Henry. It could have been worse, but . . . lucky?

He accepted a large brandy on the house. As he walked away, he reflected on what a week it was becoming for large brandies in the afternoon.

He wondered which of his colleagues would have written the story that would have gone beneath the headline 'Journalist (21) crushed by surgical trusses'.

He thought of all the other things that might fall on him – decaying Georgian stone-work, disintegrating meteorites, wing-flaps off old planes, swans cut short by blood clots in mid-flight. Life was incredibly dangerous.

And then it struck him, like a falling crate of surgical trusses. The obvious fact, which hadn't occurred to him, because this was Thurmarsh, not Chicago, this was real life, not a novel, he was Henry Pratt, not a gangster. The crate had been meant to kill him. Somebody – Bill Holliday, or his evil-faced brother Stan, or both, or somebody else – was trying to rub him out.

He began to think of what might hit him by design. Packing cases pushed from attic windows. Sharp slates dropped off roofs. Bullets from hidden snipers. Meat pies lobbed from the Rundle Café. He arrived at the bus station in no fit state to conduct an interview, which might explain, though it couldn't excuse, the fiasco that was to follow.

Hexington Hall was a minor stately home, with an unimposing classical stone frontage, set in scruffy park-land. A pale, male secretary led Henry across a large entrance hall, gliding as if on wheels, his buttocks firmly clenched against the expected flood of pornography. Henry caught a glimpse, through open doors, of rooms where once the living had been gracious.

The large drawing-room smelt of damp and righteousness. Courtly ancestors in darkened oils looked down on tables covered in piles of leaflets.

Colonel Hubert Boyce-Uppingham shook his hand with surprising gentleness. They sat in leather armchairs in front of a modest fire of dead wood from the estate. The Chief Torch Bearer had short, crinkly hair, an aquiline nose, and dark eyes which glittered with intelligence, or fanaticism, or malice, or a combination of all three. Henry wasn't yet sure.

'I know your niece,' he said.

'Oh?' Colonel Boyce-Uppingham sounded as if this was so unlikely that only good manners deterred him from disputing it. He changed the subject humiliatingly, launching into his theme, not with loud military briskness, as Henry had expected, but with the more dangerous, soft, silkily reasonable tones of the man who has never doubted that he is right. 'It's only straws in the wind as yet. *Waiting for Godot. Look Back in Anger.* A French revue in which a horse "defecates" on stage.' An acolyte with acne, serving tea and a digestive, barely interrupted the flow. 'Where will it end? With four-letter words on television and the live sexual act performed on stage by the Thurmarsh Repertory Company.'

Henry looked up and saw, to his horror, right above his head, a huge chandelier.

Totally unheard by Henry, totally unaware that he was totally unheard by Henry, Colonel Hubert Boyce-Uppingham was warming to his theme. 'The military mind is trained to enter the mind of the enemy, in order to anticipate his moves. Monty did it with Rommel. That's why he beat him. That's what I'm doing.'

Journalist crushed by chandelier! Henry longed to move. He didn't dare. He was petrified.

'So I become the enemy,' said Colonel Boyce-Uppingham. 'So who am I, this enemy? I'm a greedy man. I'm an unattractive man, rejected by women. I'm a man with hatred in his heart.'

Henry looked up, at the single chain which held up the mighty chandelier. Which of them could have sawn through it? The spotty server of tea? The slinking, sliding secretary? Bill Holliday, visiting to collect an old car? He shivered, despite the fire.

'So, I will wreak my revenge on the sex that has rejected me. On the God who has given me no charm. Making a fortune as I do so!'

Colonel Boyce-Uppingham paused, for dramatic effect. Like a passenger who wakes when the car stops, Henry hurtled back to consciousness. He began to scribble, self-protectively. Reassured by this activity, Colonel Boyce-Uppingham resumed.

'I want to exploit women for money,' he said. 'I want to own and exploit "ladies of the night".' Even in the mind of the enemy, he couldn't bring himself to avoid euphemism entirely. 'I want to open filthy strip-clubs, where their bodies will be humiliated by men with hungry eyes. I want to fill the land with naughty magazines, a tidal flood of filth.'

Henry's mouth sagged open. His pencil could hardly keep up. This was dynamite. The chandelier was almost forgotten.

'Now do you see what I have to fight, why I see it as my personal mission to defeat these dark forces?' said Colonel Boyce-Uppingham.

'Yes. Yes, I do,' said Henry.

'And will you print all this, in your newspaper, to help me?'

'Oh yes! Yes, I will,' said Henry.

On Wednesday afternoon, there having been no reply to Henry's second letter signed 'First Angry Schoolmaster', Colin typed a second letter signed 'Second Angry Schoolmaster'.

The phrases rolled off Henry's rickety old typewriter. 'The Chief Torch Bearer of the Ark . . .' It had turned out to be that kind of ark. '. . . of the Golden Light of Our Lady told me, with astonishing frankness, of his secret desires.

'"I want to exploit women for money," he told me. "I want to open filthy clubs . . ."

'. . . instead of giving way to these impulses, Colonel Boyce-Uppingham is countering them by leading a nationwide fight against pornography.

'Perhaps, as the man who knows no fear can never be truly

called brave, so the man who knows no temptation can never truly be called good.'

He handed his first full-length feature article to Terry Skipton, who read it with increasing astonishment.

'He really said all that?'

'Every word.' He showed Terry his notebook. The news editor read it carefully.

'This is dynamite,' he said at last.

'I know.'

And off Henry went, well pleased with himself, to the private view at the Gusset Gallery.

His air of triumph was quickly flattened by the need to look out for falling crates. It wasn't a comfortable feeling, knowing that someone was trying to kill you.

At last he reached the comparative safety of the gallery. Safety? Man killed by falling painting. Constable lands on journalist.

The Gusset Gallery was situated next to the court house, beside the Town Hall. It was built in the Italianate style, as if it had been hoped that something of that nation's artistic greatness would rub off on it.

He climbed an impressive staircase, past the bust of Sir Joshua Gusset, liniment maker and philanthropist, past early paintings of the Thurmarsh School, some of which, unfortunately, had not been restored, and others of which, even more unfortunately, had.

The white-walled rectangular gallery was bare of furniture except for a trestle-table with a white cloth, behind which a man with a bow-tie was dispensing wine, and two wooden benches, one facing each long wall, set in the middle of the room directly beneath a skylight. Skylight! Assassin lurked in skylight, inquest told.

Men in dark suits and women in two-piece costumes with extravagant hats were standing around and talking. A few artistically attired people were even looking at the pictures.

A large lady approached him like an overdressed waterspout.

'Hermione Jarrett,' she said. She seemed to think no further explanation was necessary.

'Henry Pratt.' Two could play at that game.

'Ah!' She was puzzled.

'I'm from the *Argus*,' he said, relenting.

'Oh! What's happened to our nice Mr Ackerman?'

'He's in London.'

'Oh!' Hermione Jarrett's expression suggested that they had been unforgivably let down by hitherto nice Mr Ackerman. 'Well, never mind. You'd like a catalogue, of course.'

Her 'of course' triggered his perversity. 'Later,' he said grandly. 'When I review exhibitions, I usually like to remain unencumbered by the kind of preconceptions that titles give.'

He took a glass of red wine and tried to look as if assessing paintings was something he did every week.

There were forty-two pictures. They were modern. They were colourful. They were bold, sometimes even violent. There seemed to be a Cubist influence. They were, he thought, not terrible. But were they good? He had no idea.

He began to see certain things in certain of them. He began to see strange seascapes, with blue still seas beneath black, thundery clouds. One picture seemed to be of a barometer, with a serene, empty face set before a background of purple storm clouds. A glimmer of an idea came to him. Perhaps the pictures represented complacency, blue seas failing to reflect stormy skies, man failing to find a message on the face of the cosmic barometer. He began to see this theme all round him, but was it Johnson Protheroe's or his own? If only he hadn't so pretentiously denied himself access to the catalogue.

He listened to other people's comments, hoping for guidance. 'Look, Edgar, that's exactly the colour of our clematis,' wasn't much help. 'He's as daft as a brush,' seemed more promising, until he heard the reply, which was 'Aye, well, he would be. Red setters often are.'

Were there usually people so ignorant of art at private views? Or were these people hired hoods, with forged invitations, whose task it was to wipe Henry out?

He decided to stick closely to Hermione Jarrett, for protection. She topped up his glass, and gave him a catalogue. The pictures had no titles. No help there! He was out of his depth.

'They've no titles,' he said.

'No,' she said. 'Apparently he regards titles as the labels of prejudice. He's an uncompromising man. Of course he has been described as the harbinger of a new brutalism.'

Henry felt that he must make some reply. What reply could he make? He hadn't even been aware that there had been an old brutalism. His nerves felt shredded. He couldn't cope with all this.

'Well,' he said, 'he could hardly be more brutal than life.'

'That's not bad,' said Hermione Jarrett. 'You've been hiding your light under a bushel, young man. Well, under dear Mr Ackerman, to be precise.' She remembered dear Mr Ackerman's proclivities and visibly regretted her choice of phrase. 'Come and meet a keen patron of the arts, Mr Hathersage.' She led Henry, at a cracking pace that permitted no escape, straight towards the man who was very probably trying to kill him.

'Henry Pratt!' said the diminutive property developer. 'Greetings, young sir!'

Oh no. Another member of the 'young sir' brigade.

Like many a hostess who has solved the problem of two guests whom she doesn't like by introducing them to each other, Hermione Jarrett scuttled off with all the joy of a freed rabbit. The eyes of the two people whom Hermione Jarrett didn't like met, and Henry's blood ran cold. *Was* this man trying to kill him?

'So what do you think of them?' said Fred Hathersage.

'I think they're very interesting,' said Henry cautiously, cravenly.

'I think they're crap,' said Fred Hathersage savagely. Was his savagery really aimed at modern art, or at Henry? 'I like English painters of the old school. I'm thinking of people like . . .' He paused. '. . . Constable.'

Henry was seeing hidden meanings everywhere now. Did Fred Hathersage mean, 'Don't go to the police'?

'And Turner.'

Did he mean, 'Or you'll be turning in your grave'?

'And Sir Alfred Munnings.'

Did he mean, 'If you aren't careful, you'll end up as dead, lifeless horseflesh'?

Henry shuddered. He felt that he couldn't remain in the same room as Fred Hathersage a moment longer. He fled, back to the warm licensed womb in Leatherbottlers' Row, and just missed hearing a broad-beamed lady in an aquamarine suit say, 'It says "Toronto" upside-down on that one. How very strange!'

Next morning, before going to court, Henry typed up his review. He imagined that Denzil would approve of his intro, which read: 'If Ceri Richards is the Welsh Vlaminck, can Johnson Protheroe be said to be the Braque of Canada? Or even . . . intriguing thought! . . . her Sisley?'

He imagined Denzil nodding approval of: 'There is a series of bold, disturbing seascapes here. The seas are as blue as a de Wint door, yet the skies are heavy with the menace of thunder! Is this the *sturm und drang* of a transatlantic Klimt? Or is it a Hogarthian statement about mankind's condition?'

Henry himself quite liked: 'Another picture (a kind of *faux-naïf* Cubism of the Rockies!!) explores this *leitmotif* in an even more specific way. It shows a barometer hanging on a wall. The background says, clearly, "Stormy". Significantly, the barometer does not!'

He bashed out his final paragraph. 'If all you know of Canadian painting is of the likes of Tom Thompson, Jock Macdonald and A. Y. Jackson, with perhaps a vague notion about the Automatistes of Montreal . . . I must confess I'm shamefully vague about them! . . . then hurry along to the Gusset.'

He handed his review to Terry Skipton, with a third letter signed 'First Angry Schoolmaster'. The news editor read the review slowly, his heavily lidded eyes seeming to bore through its pathetic pretensions.

'Not bad at all,' he said.

Henry tried to hide his surprise and relief.

'Really not at all bad.'

Henry tried to hide his delight.

'In fact it's just like the incomprehensible twaddle Mr Ackerman writes,' said Terry Skipton.

'Have whatever you like,' said Howard Lewthwaite. 'Though personally I'll stick to the *table d'hôte*.'

The exceptionally mild weather was continuing, and it was

uncomfortably warm in the restaurant of the Midland Hotel. All the lights were on, for the day was grey.

'It's very difficult to prove that a fire isn't arson,' said Howard Lewthwaite. 'You can prove it is, and if you don't prove it is, you assume it isn't.'

The waiter approached.

'What is the *potage* today?' said Howard Lewthwaite.

'Oxtail, sir,' said the waiter.

'Right. Oxtail soup and I like the sound of the cheese omelette,' said Howard Lewthwaite.

'Soup for me, too,' said Henry. 'And what are the *rillettes Thurmarshiennes*?'

'Rissoles, sir.'

'The lamb chop, please.'

'They do quite a nice choice, don't they?' said Howard Lewthwaite. 'The fire people can add nothing to what was said at the inquest. All you have to go on, Henry, is one overheard comment. Heard from Hilary lately?'

'Of course,' said Henry. 'We write almost every day.'

'It's wonderful the effect you've had on that girl. Wonderful. I've talked to Peter Matheson and Fred Hathersage. We'll allow you to uncover, as a scoop for yourself, the development plans, the architect's model, the fact that Fred owns some of the property. All above board. Nothing denied. If anybody wishes to make allegations, let them try to find proof. A great story for you, Henry. We didn't want to unveil it yet, but you've been too clever for us. Kudos for you. No problems with Hilary. How about it?'

'Somebody's trying to kill me,' said Henry.

'Two oxtail?' said the waiter.

'Yes,' said Howard Lewthwaite faintly. 'What did you say?' he said, when the waiter had gone.

'I went to see Bill Holliday on Monday,' said Henry.

'Bill's all right.'

'So everybody says.'

'He's a very generous supporter of children's charities.'

'So what's he hiding? I've grown up this last year. I was interviewing him for "Proud Sons of Thurmarsh".'

'Did your piece on me well, incidentally.'

321

'Thanks. I vaguely threatened him. A threat that was pretty meaningless if he wasn't guilty. Immediately, he threatened me. And the very next day, I was nearly killed by surgical trusses.'

'Surgical trusses?'

Henry gave Howard Lewthwaite the details, breaking off as the waiter removed their plates to say, 'Mr Tintern thinks Hilary might get a first, if she works hard.'

'It could have been an accident,' said Howard Lewthwaite, when the waiter had gone.

'So could the Cap Ferrat,' said Henry. 'It isn't likely, though, is it? It's all too damned convenient. God knows, Mr Lewthwaite, I'm not brave. And I can't bear the thought of losing Hilary. But what can I do? Run away? Give up? Fine husband and father I'd make.'

The waiter returned.

'Who's for the chop?' he said.

'Both of us, probably,' said Howard Lewthwaite.

22   Black Friday

Halfway through his coffee and toast, there was a knock on his door.

'It's me,' said Ginny. 'I'm not well.'

He opened the door. Her face was pale and puffy. He felt it incongruous that a future war correspondent should have a pink dressing-gown with fluffy pom-poms.

'What's wrong?' he said.

'Prawn curry.'

'What?'

'I had a prawn curry at the Shanghai. I've got food poisoning. Will you tell Terry?'

'Right.'

She hurried off, unaware that a prawn curry might have saved her life.

There was pale, watery sunshine, but already high clouds were drifting in from the west. Dennis Lacey was also on his own.

'Is your friend ill?' he said.

'She's got food poisoning,' said Henry. 'How's . . . er . . . Marie, isn't it?'

'By heck, you've got a memory.'

'I'm a trained journalist.'

'She's gorra day off. She's changed shifts with this friend . . . look out!!'

Henry turned, and saw a black Standard Eight coming straight for them. He looked into the white, silently screaming, strangely hunched face of the driver. He dived to the side. The car missed the tram stop by inches. It just missed Henry as he crashed onto the pavement, but it struck Dennis Lacey, tossing him into the air. The car scraped along the stone wall of number 243, struck another member of the queue a glancing blow, and roared off down Winstanley Road. Somebody screamed. Dennis Lacey was lying in a crumpled heap, moaning, bleeding. The woman who'd

323

been hit was staring at her cut leg with stunned disbelief. Henry crunched across the gravel, past the monkey puzzle tree. The door opened. '999,' he gasped. A frightened woman, with her hair in a net, nodded. The house had new furniture, new carpets, a new smell, but in the few seconds before his call got through, in that dark hall, Henry thought of the teas he'd had in this house with his English teacher, Mr Quell, and his blind wife, and stale Battenburg cake. The Quells had gone to live in Worthing so that, instead of not being able to see this northern industrial town, Mrs Quell could end her days not being able to see the sea.

Dennis Lacey was rushed to the Infirmary, where he was X-rayed in his own department. 'Not an emergency already,' said one of his colleagues, as he was wheeled in. 'There would be, with Dennis late.'

Henry described the incident to the police, without letting on that he was the intended target. He'd have to tell them some time, but he wanted to tell Mr Lewthwaite and Hilary first.

He'd tell Mr Lewthwaite tonight, and go on to Durham tomorrow after work. He'd have to. There was no time to lose. He owed it to the citizens of Thurmarsh.

Dennis Lacey's only crime had been to stand next to Henry Pratt, The Man They Were Trying To Muzzle. It seemed possible that it had cost him his life.

The news-room was eerily quiet when Henry arrived at ten-fifteen. All the reporters were out on stories.

'What's kept you?' said Terry Skipton. 'And where's Ginny?'

'Ginny has food poisoning,' said Henry. 'She ate a prawn curry at the Shanghai. I've almost been killed.'

'You what?'

'A car came straight for us at the tram stop and almost killed the man next to me.'

'Why? It's not icy, is it?'

'Oh no. This was an attempted murder, Mr Skipton.'

Terry Skipton gawped at him.

'You lucky man!' he said.

'I know. A few inches more!'

'I'm talking about the story.'

'You what?'

'I came within inches of death as I saw the murder car mow down the man standing beside me. I felt the wind on my legs as the fatal mudguards brushed my trousers. Miracle escape for *Argus* reporter in tram stop rush-hour murder terror.'

'Oh my God,' said Henry. 'I never thought of it as a story.'

Terry Skipton threw back his head and laughed. Henry had never seen him laugh before. He wanted to say, 'But he was trying to kill me, you see.' He couldn't.

Terry Skipton stopped laughing as suddenly as he'd begun.

'How's the person who was hit?' he said.

'Still alive when he was taken off.'

'Ring the Infirmary and find out how he is and who he is.'

'I know who he is,' said Henry. 'He's called Dennis Lacey. He works in the X-ray department.'

'Where?'

'At the Infirmary.'

'Hospital worker's colleagues fight for his life after horror at the tram stop when rush-hour became crush-hour,' said Terry Skipton.

'His girl-friend Marie would have been with him, but she changed shifts in favour of a friend.'

'Amazing escape of Miracle Marie, the good-time girl who became a good-turn girl,' said Terry Skipton.

'Ginny would have been there too.'

'"Chinese meal saved my life," says Grateful Ginny.' Terry Skipton smiled. Henry had never seen him smile before. 'It must have been a nasty experience,' he said, much more gently. 'Now get the complete story. You have one hour to redeem yourself. Nobody need ever know about this conversation.'

He winked. Henry had never seen Terry Skipton wink before.

Barely an hour later, Henry stuck a piece of cheap paper into his decrepit typewriter and hammered away so fiercely that the letter *t* broke off. Excited by his story and by his courage in continuing to work when he'd so narrowly escaped being murdered, Henry didn't notice. He bashed out his intro: 'A peaceful ram queue urned in o a cauldron of error in hurmarsh his morning when

a car climbed he pavemen and hi   wo people, injuring one
of hem severely in he legs and ches .'

He inked in the missing letters, handed in the story, reported
the fault to the typewriter maintenance people and, as instructed,
left a note in the machine to remind them what was wrong. He
wasn't happy with the first draft of his note, which read: ' his
 ypewri er has no le   er .' He threw it away and, after careful
thought, started again. 'My machine lacks a symbol which follows
s and precedes u,' he typed. 'So please would you give my machine
a symbol which follows s and precedes u. Yours sincerely, Henry
Pra   .'

He had the front page lead, his first ever review of an art
exhibition, and a huge feature on Colonel Boyce-Uppingham. It
was practically a Henry Pratt benefit edition. He'd have felt good,
except that the better he felt, the more he felt that he didn't want
to die, and so the worse he felt.

At 3.13 his world began to fall apart. Terry Skipton told him
that an angry Colonel Boyce-Uppingham was in Interview Room
B and wanted to see him.

Interview Room B was bare and dingy, with dirty yellow paint,
four upright chairs round a nasty, cheaply veneered table, a single
light bulb with a green shade and a ribbed radiator from which the
paint was peeling.

Colonel Boyce-Uppingham was pacing up and down restlessly,
but his voice was carefully controlled.

'Redrobe's gone out,' he said, as if the editor's absence was a
deliberate snub. 'So I've come to you for an explanation.'

'An explanation?'

Colonel Boyce-Uppingham waved Henry's article in the air.
'Of this disgusting pan of festering ferret's entrails masquerading as
journalism. It's misrepresentation on a gargantuan scale.'

Henry hurried out, and soon returned with the notebook
full of someone else's shorthand notes from days gone by. He
opened it at a random page and handed it to Colonel Boyce-
Uppingham.

'"English pork is good, with leg and loin at 3s. 8d. a pound,"'
read Colonel Boyce-Uppingham. '"Shoulder of lamb is 3s. to

3s. 4d. English beef, too, is good, and offal is plentiful." What is all this?'

'Oh. You . . . er . . . you can read shorthand,' said Henry.

'"Large Norwegian herrings are a snip at 10d. a pound"??'

'Oh, I . . . er . . . must have given you my shopping notes, we do them on a Friday, how silly of me,' said Henry.

He hurried out, and soon returned with his own notebook. The colonel grabbed it.

'It's not in shorthand,' he said.

'No, I can't do shorthand.' Henry realized his mistake immediately.

'So! You were deliberately fobbing me off,' said Colonel Boyce-Uppingham with deadly calm.

'I'm sorry,' mumbled Henry. 'I think you'll find you said everything we printed,' he added, rallying. It was to prove a brief recovery.

'I don't dispute that,' said Belinda Boyce-Uppingham's uncle.

'What?'

'It's the words you didn't print that I'm concerned about.'

Fear laid her cold talons on Henry's throat. Quietly, almost gently but with suppressed fury, the Chief Torch Bearer of the Ark of the Golden Light of Our Lady explained to Henry the enormity of what he had done. He also made it clear what he thought of Henry, ironically using three of the words against which his great campaign was being planned.

Terry Skipton went white.

'You twerp,' he said. 'You bloody twerp.'

Henry had never heard Terry Skipton swear before.

Mrs Etheridge, the oldest of the copy-takers, came over from her booth with a story which had just been phoned through. She handed it to Terry Skipton without a word. Terry Skipton read it and handed it to Henry without a word. Henry read it and handed it back to Terry Skipton without a word. Terry Skipton passed it to the subs' table, where a sub-editor swiftly created the headline 'Artist fumes at "incredible" gallery blunder'.

The story that all Johnson Protheroe's paintings had been hung upside-down appeared in the same issue as Henry's review of them.

'Sit down, gentlemen,' said Mr Andrew Redrobe. Was the 'gentlemen' faintly ironical?

Henry sat opposite the editor. Terry Skipton sat at the end of the desk, facing them both.

'I've read your main lead,' said the editor. 'A good story. And a lucky escape.'

'Yes. The lad did very well,' said Terry Skipton.

Henry gawped. He'd never heard Terry Skipton give unqualified praise before. In one day he'd made the news editor laugh, smile, wink, swear and give unqualified praise. It was an achievement that would pass down in the legends of provincial journalism.

'I've had Colonel Boyce-Uppingham in here,' said Mr Andrew Redrobe. 'He's a very unhappy man. Can you explain what happened?'

'I made a mistake,' said Henry. 'I missed one vital link in his argument.'

'Do you call that an excuse?'

'No. I call it an explanation.'

'I've had to promise him a full retraction, a grovelling apology, a series of articles about his organization and free advertising. Even with all that, he may sue.'

'I'm very sorry,' said Henry.

'Why did you let this go through without checking, Terry?'

'Henry showed me his notebook. Every word we quoted was written down there at the time,' said Terry Skipton. 'And I do have to have some trust in my reporters.'

'But these were sensational admissions.'

'So sensational that I felt that, if I queried them, he might reflect on the wisdom of allowing us to print them.'

'All right. I accept that,' said Mr Andrew Redrobe. He sighed. 'Let's turn to the paintings. What excuse or explanation have you for *that* cock-up.'

'It wasn't my cock-up,' said Henry. 'It was the gallery's. All I did was fail to spot it.'

'All you did? What a wonderful story that would have made. Ridicule for the art gallery, which turned me down when I was nominated for their board, not that that's important. Intellectual poseurs pricked. The philistinism of the mass of our readers triumphantly justified. Instead of which, it's us they're laughing at. Us. Me. My paper. I'd like to hear your views on why you think I'd be sensible to continue to employ you.'

'I'm investigating a story that'll take the lid off this town and reveal a rotting heap of stinking fish,' said Henry. 'I can deliver you a scoop that'll be the envy of every provincial journalist from Land's End to John O'Groats.'

The jaws of Mr Andrew Redrobe and Terry Skipton dropped. There was a long silence. At last the editor plucked up his courage and asked the question that had to be faced.

'Is it about a pigeon?'

'It's not about a pigeon.'

There was another long silence.

'Well come on,' said the editor.

'Ah!' said Henry.

'What?' said the editor.

'These matters affect my fiancée and her family and I must tell them first. Can I have till Monday morning?'

The editor gave another deep sigh. 'All right,' he said wearily. 'You've got till Monday. Now get out.'

'Thank you, Mr Redrobe,' said Henry.

He'd made two enormous mistakes. He was a laughing stock. Somebody was trying to kill him. A man was fighting for his life, in the Infirmary, because of him. But, even on that black Friday, Henry managed to find one tiny consolation. At last he'd survived an interview with the editor without saying 'sir'.

He felt sick with tension as he rang the Infirmary. He felt as if he were asking for a bulletin on himself. Dennis Lacey had survived a major operation and was as well as could be expected. Would he live? He was as well as could be expected.

As they walked to the Lord Nelson he felt disembodied, could hardly feel his feet on the damp pavement, hardly feel Helen's affectionate squeeze of his arm in which, strangely, he could detect no element of coquetry. It was as if he were unreal, and only existed in the minds of his five drinking companions.

It wasn't a large gathering. Denzil was in London, Ginny in bed with food poisoning, Ted in Manchester on an overnight job, but they seemed determined to make up in warmth what they lacked in numbers. He'd have to leave soon, to visit Dennis Lacey in hospital, and to talk to Howard Lewthwaite. But he couldn't leave too soon, when they were all being so nice.

They vied to ply him with drinks. Helen squeezed his arm again. Gordon said, 'Small print. Small print,' and Henry sensed that it was meant to be affectionate. Ben asked him to name the grounds of all the Scottish teams, and he managed them all except Stenhousemuir. Even Jill seemed to find his company pleasant. When it was his turn to buy a round, Colin came to the bar with him, and hugged him.

'What's all this?' said Henry.

'We're all right upset because of thee.'

'You what?'

'You could have been killed today. We love you, kid.'

'What?'

'Well, I do. I'm almost crying, for God's sake. I mean, Henry, I hope you'd feel like crying if I were almost killed.'

'Course I would,' said Henry.

He hugged Colin.

Of course! He realized why they were all being so nice to him, even Jill, who had probably been told to by Gordon, on whose words she still hung even though she didn't understand many of them. It wasn't any old evening. It was the 'cheering up our Henry after one of the most disastrous days ever to befall a British provincial journalist' evening. Be churlish to leave in the middle of it. Dennis Lacey wouldn't be conscious yet, anyway, and he could see Howard Lewthwaite briefly after work tomorrow.

When the six of them walked to the Devonshire through the spattering rain, they were like six babies in one incubator, protected from the germs and hostility of the outside world.

The drink flowed. The timeless jazz rolled out in the crowded upstairs room, as if the rock-and-roll craze didn't exist.

A huge man in a bright blue corduroy suit was pushing his way through the crowds towards them. He had black hair, but his bushy black beard was streaked with grey. At his side was a delicate-looking young lady, with a round, serene face and a flat, thin body. She reminded Henry of a barometer. Both their faces were registering 'stormy'.

'Is one of you guys Henry Pratt?' said the huge man, loudly, in a North American accent.

'I am,' admitted Henry reluctantly.

'Johnson Protheroe,' said Johnson Protheroe.

Henry's colleagues, and even Jill, closed round him, shutting the door of the incubator.

Johnson Protheroe's loud voice battled effectively with the music. Sid Hallett and the Rundlemen were playing 'Basin Street Blues'. It was beginning to dawn on Henry that their repertoire was not inexhaustible.

'You're the biggest ass-hole I've ever met,' yelled Johnson Protheroe.

'Johnson!' It wasn't an easy word to invest with love, but the girl managed it.

'Listen, kid,' said Colin, grabbing Johnson Protheroe's lapel. 'Nobody calls my mate an ass-hole.'

'Colin!' said Henry desperately. 'It's all right.'

'Take your hands off me,' shouted Johnson Protheroe.

'Johnson!' said the girl. Even when she raised her voice, she was barely audible.

'Please!' shouted Henry.

'Shut up!' shouted a jazz fan.

'Shut up yourself!' shouted a second jazz fan.

'Bloody hell fire!' shouted the first jazz fan. 'I'm telling them to shut up. Don't tell me to shut up.'

'Shut up!' shouted several more jazz fans.

Sid Hallett and the Rundlemen abandoned all hope of solos and played fast and loud to overpower the disturbance. The disturbance emitted a few drowning glugs and expired. The music and the set finished, to loud applause. Sid Hallett and the Rundlemen stomped off to the bar. Henry and his friends faced Johnson Protheroe and his friend in wary silence.

331

'I never read such a load of crap as your article,' said Johnson Protheroe.

Henry's colleagues began to protest.

'Please,' pleaded Henry. 'Allow me the dignity of defending myself.'

'Oh!' said Johnson Protheroe, in a scornful mock-English tone. '"Allow me the dignity of defending myself"! Blue seas under black clouds, my ass. Those were blue skies *above* the Rocky Mountains, you cretin.'

Henry's colleagues allowed him the dignity of defending himself.

'I . . . er . . . I . . . er . . . sorry,' he said.

'The barometer that you described so vividly was a portrait of Deborah here.'

'Oh, I . . . er . . . I am sorry. You don't look a bit like a barometer,' lied Henry.

'Thanks,' said Deborah, in her low, sweet voice.

Henry's head was beginning to swim, but he managed to focus on Johnson Protheroe. 'You're right,' he said. 'I am the biggest ass-hole you've ever met.'

'What?' said Johnson Protheroe.

'It's the first art exhibition I've ever reviewed. I was standing in for our arts editor. I imitated his style. I'll never do that again in my life, especially as I happen to believe that critics should be widening the understanding of art, not narrowing it.'

'Oh . . . well . . . spoken like a man!' said Johnson Protheroe.

'I do a good imitation,' said Henry.

'Do you have football as we know it in Canada?' asked Ben.

Henry couldn't remember how they got to the Shanghai Chinese Restaurant and Coffee Bar. The evening had become a warm blur. They were all in the incubator together now, even Johnson Protheroe, who had become a harmless bear.

'Do you really know anything about Canadian artists, Henry?' he was asking.

'Not a jot,' Henry admitted. 'I looked the names up in the library.'

Johnson Protheroe's mood changed again. 'Typical bloody

British insularity,' he growled. 'Canada's full of hick towns like this full of ignorant people full of crap, but at least they know there is a world outside. Exciting things are happening back home.' He began to shout. 'Nobody here gives a damn.' Everybody pretended not to hear. 'You see!' he roared.

The food arrived. Henry seemed to have ordered a prawn curry. Johnson Protheroe's beef curry did nothing for his mood. He slammed a pile of coins on the table, shouted, 'This food is dreadful. Come on, Deborah,' and hurried to the door. He turned to face the crowded room and shouted, 'You're all ass-holes, especially Henry Pratt.'

He lurched out into the street. Deborah hurried back to their table and said, softly, 'I'm sorry. I hardly ever get to eat these days. Somebody once told Johnson that his name sounded like a firm of merchant bankers. Ever since then he's been trying to be wild and Bohemian. What an artist he could be if he didn't waste all his energies being what he thinks an artist ought to be. It's been lovely meeting you. I think you're sweet people.'

Henry returned to his prawn curry. He was ravenous.

Ben and Colin discovered how late it was. Gordon said he and Jill must be going too. Everybody said nice things to Henry. Jill even kissed him, saying 'Mmmmm!' as if to convince herself that it had been a pleasant experience.

'Ted won't be back tonight,' said Helen. She put her hand on his thigh. He put his hand on her thigh. She took his hand down towards her knee and lifted it up under her skirt. He felt that something was wrong. He couldn't remember what.

They were outside. Presumably they'd paid. How nice it was to go beautiful with a home woman.

They kissed each other. She slid her tongue into his mouth like a paper-knife. Something was wrong. He couldn't remember what.

She hailed a taxi, and it stopped. She was flushed with triumph. Taxis had been hard to come by since Suez. She'd protested about Suez. Well, not this she. Not what's-her-name. The other she. Hilary. Hilary!!!

She got into the taxi. He shut the door.

'Good night,' he said.

'What?' she said.

'Can't come back with you,' he said. 'Hilary.'

Her pert lips pouted. She went pink. She was breathing very hard. He couldn't worry about her. He turned away. He heard her taxi drive off.

He felt awful. He tried gulping fresh air but it didn't help. He dimly remembered that he oughtn't to be being careless and lurching around the town, drunk and alone. He couldn't remember why.

He slipped and fell. He struggled to his feet and hurried into a narrow alley that ran from Market Street through to Church Street. He didn't want any policemen seeing him while his legs weren't working. At the junction with another alley, in a tiny square dimly lit by one feeble lamp, a scared cat passed him, screeching. Scared of what?

Scared of the six youths who blocked his path, six youths with bleak, tense faces, six youths with bicycle chains. Maybe the idea was to beat him to a pulp, terrify him, scare him off.

He swung left into the other alley, which led to Bargates, where Henry had spent so much time in the now defunct Paw Paw Coffee Bar and Grill. Six youths blocked his path, six youths in drainpipe trousers and Edwardian jackets, six youths with knives and razors. Thurmarsh's first Teds. Today Thurmarsh, yesterday the world. So this was it. The end of twenty-one years of struggle towards a manhood dimly perceived, he was a well-nourished young man of below-average height, his stomach bore the mainly undigested remains of a prawn curry, he had drunk the equivalent of . . .

He turned, and tried to walk back the way he'd come, into Market Street. He expected to see six more youths blocking his way. There was nobody.

He walked away with a calmness he didn't feel. His legs screamed to him to break into a run. He refused. He'd only inflame their insults by showing his fear.

He began to get the feeling that nobody was following him. With the return of hope came the fullness of fear, neck-pricking, scalp-crawling, sweat-drenching fear. He had to turn and look. He mustn't. He did. There was nobody.

He heard the first sounds of battle, the swish of bicycle chains, the ring of iron boot, the scream of a razored face. They were fighting each other, not him! Relief buckled his knees. At first it seemed as if he were running in a dream, stuck fast, not moving, but then he was tearing down the alley, he was in Market Street, there was the dark drapery store. Hilary lived, he lived, life stretched before him. It crossed his mind that the day, which had begun with a story which he hadn't recognized, was ending with another one. Gang warfare in town centre. He listened to the sounds of distant battle, and scurried off as fast as his little legs could carry him.

By the time he got home, his head was throbbing and his stomach was heaving. He'd had a traumatic day. He'd had too much to drink. His resistance to prawn curry had been fatally weakened.

23 In which Our Hero Makes Two Identifications

The first oil went into the Suez Canal since the fighting ended. Henry struggled to work, unsure where his food poisoning ended and his hangover began. He was so ill that he was sent home. There was no possibility of his going to see Howard Lewthwaite, let alone travelling to Durham. He spent the best part of that Saturday in bed. We'll draw a veil over where he spent the worst part of it.

On Monday, February 11th, a mild earthquake, centred on Charnwood Forest, caused pit props to shake in Drobwell Main Colliery, brought about a fall of masonry in the remains of the Old Apothecary's House and distracted Henry from the immortal words, 'Hello, boys and girls. May I remind all Argusnauts living in the Winstanley area about a beetle drive to be held next Saturday at the home of 12 year-old Timothy Darlington. Timothy called at our offices last week with the grand total of £17 raised at a similar function, and I was very sorry indeed to miss him.'

A mild earthquake, centred on the editor's office, shook every bone in Henry's body when he was forced to admit that, due to prawn curry poisoning, he'd not been able to tell his beloved of his great scoop, and requested a further stay of what was seeming more and more like execution. A final delay of one week was reluctantly granted. Mr Andrew Redrobe also gave up over the great education controversy. There had still not been a single letter from the general public. Beneath Colin's third letter, signed 'Second Angry Schoolmaster', there appeared the message, 'This correspondence is now closed, due to lack of space-Ed.'

Later that morning, Henry was sent to get a local angle on the shooting of a major feature film.

He caught the Rawlaston tram. It rumbled out of the valley, breasted the summit by Brunswick Road Primary School and dropped down again into the smoky valley. The road swung right.

On the right was the vast, blank wall of Crapp, Hawser and Kettlewell. On the left, the tiny, grimy, cobbled culs-de-sac, among which Henry had been born.

'Paradise,' sang out the conductor.

Henry stepped off the tram, looked round anxiously but saw nobody who appeared to be about to kill him.

Paradise Lane was completely blocked by generators and film unit vans, which were almost as high as the wine-red terraces. A mobile catering van had been parked right outside number 23. Henry longed to say to the waiting technicians and extras, 'Forget your curried lamb. Never mind your plum duff. Twenty-one years ago, in that little house on which you're turning your backs, a parrot ended its life and I began mine.'

Cables snaked through the gate onto the muddy tow-path of the Rundle and Gadd Navigation. They ran along the tow-path, and up onto the elegant brick hump bridge over the cut. Standing on the bridge, among a crowd of sightseers, were Angela Groyne and the man whom Henry suspected of trying to kill him. He didn't want Bill Holliday to know he was afraid, so he joined them, but took care not to stand too near the edge.

The muddy waste-ground between the insalubrious cut and the equally unsavoury river was crowded with film men and their equipment. The lights and the camera were angled towards a man with a huge green head and tentacles, who was standing in a spring-like contraption on the river bank.

'He's a monster from outer space,' explained Angela Groyne in a whisper. 'From some strange planet or summat. 'e 'as these incredible powers, like 'e can jump across t' Rundle.'

'They've built this special spring,' whispered Bill Holliday. 'They've tried it four times. He's landed in bloody river each time.'

'OK. We're going for a take,' shouted an assistant director. 'OK. Absolute hush, everybody.'

'337, take 5,' shouted the clapper-boy.

A special-effects man operated the spring. The green-tentacled monster leapt into the air, and landed in the middle of the river.

'Bugger,' shouted the director.

'OK. Lunch. Back at 2.23,' shouted the assistant director.

'Does tha fancy a pint?' said Bill Holliday.

'Not in the Navigation. I'm banned from there,' said Henry proudly.

'Not in my company, tha's not,' said Bill Holliday, and Henry shuddered at the man's power.

And so Cecil E. Jenkinson was forced to serve Henry with a pint of bitter, and Henry was forced to drink it in the company of a man who was probably trying to kill him.

'What are you doing here?' he asked, trying to sound casual.

'Angie's in it,' said Bill Holliday proudly.

'Oh! What do you play?' he asked.

'A corpse,' said Bill Holliday. 'She plays a corpse.'

Henry shuddered, in that tiny snug heaving with film folk.

'Well, it's mainly corpses, really,' said Angela Groyne. 'There's this deadly gas or summat, so nobody can go out, but I was out already so I'm dead.'

'Two bloody great monsters turn her over and examine her,' said Bill Holliday. 'First monster says "Hey up, she's copped it," or words to that effect. Second monster says "Aye, and it's a right shame an' all because she looks a right tasty piece at that," or words to that effect.'

Henry wished they wouldn't go on and on about death.

'There's a long lingering close-up of her dead,' said Bill Holliday.

'You might think it's dead easy just to lie there dead, but it's not, it's dead difficult,' said Angela Groyne. 'You have to be right careful not to breathe in or out or owt.'

Henry managed to turn away and talk to an assistant to the design assistant, who said, 'Fabulous area, this.'

'You like it?' said Henry. 'Great. I was born here.'

'Fabulous,' said the assistant to the design assistant. 'We needed a grimy, wretched, dying earth, and a noxious outer space full of dust, swirling fog and poisonous gases. We've found every location we need within a mile of here.'

Henry bought drinks for Bill Holliday and Angela Groyne. His bladder was getting full, but he didn't dare go, for fear Bill Holliday would spike his drink.

The stuntman came in. He'd removed his head, but still created quite a stir with his tentacles and green body. His name was Freddie Bentley, he came from Wath-on-Dearne, and Henry knew that he'd got his story. South Yorkshire stuntman jumps to stardom. As he interviewed him, Henry began to feel that he'd met him somewhere before. Freddie Bentley became wary, and denied it with unnecessary fervour. And Henry remembered. Of course! Freddie Bentley must have been driving the lorry for Bill Holliday! And now here he was, in front of Bill Holliday, talking of seeing Freddie Bentley before! He might as well sign his own death warrant. Another drink appeared. Was it spiked? 'Drink up,' said Bill Holliday. Nervously, he drank up. His bladder was aching. He'd have to go.

Bill Holliday followed him. If Henry felt relieved that Bill Holliday couldn't be slipping anything into his drink, he didn't feel relieved to be relieving himself beside Bill Holliday in an otherwise deserted urinal. He half expected to feel a knife twisting in his stomach. Nothing happened. He felt a trickle of returning courage. He decided to fight back. As they returned to the crowded bar, he said, 'Seen any good trusses lately?'

Bill Holliday went pale. 'How did you guess?' he said.

'It was obvious,' said Henry.

The trade gap widened to £103.6 million. The government increased local rates in order to give councils more freedom of choice over expenditure on education, child care, fire brigades and health. The unemployment figures had increased to 382,605.

On Tuesday, February 12th, Henry interviewed Mr Gibbins for 'Proud Sons of Thurmarsh'. Mr Gibbins had completely forgotten that, eleven Februaries ago, in his classroom, Henry had been the author of a phenomenal amount of wind. Henry had mixed emotions of relief and hurt pride.

The head offices of Joyce and Sons had no record of drivers named Freddie Bentley or Dave Nasenby. Henry must have been mistaken about his old friends.

That evening, shortly before nine o'clock, the doorbell rang loudly, insistently, aggressively. He hurried out with pumping heart. Was it Bill Holliday? Or Stan Holliday? Or Fred Hathersage? Or all three?

339

Ginny hurried downstairs, in blue slacks and an off-white shirt stretched tight over her large breasts.

'Who is it?' he called, anxiously.

'Police.'

They looked at each other. He opened the door. There were two officers.

'Henry Pratt?'

'Yes.'

'We've found the driver of the Standard Eight. Do you think you'll be able to identify him?'

He had to try. Ginny insisted on coming, to lend him moral support. How could he tell her that they might not be real policemen, they could be Bill Holliday's boys? Besides, if they were, a young woman of her build might be distinctly useful.

They weren't Bill Holliday's boys. They drove to York Road Police Station.

Ginny sat in the waiting-room beside a large, square, stony-faced woman with a pile of copies of the *Watchtower*. She looked like a sculpture on which naughty boys had painted a moustache.

An officer led Henry towards a dark grey door. At the door he said, 'There's six people lined up in there. Walk up and down the line carefully. Take your time. Make absolutely sure. Say nowt unless you can positively identify the man. In which case, when you're sure, point at him very clearly, so there's no possibility of mistake, and say "That's 'im. The third one from my right."'

'What?' said Henry.

'That was just an example,' said the officer hastily. 'I'm not saying that's where he'll be. He could be fourth from your left or owt.'

'Fourth from the left is the same as third from the right,' said Henry.

The officer worked it out.

'Oh aye, so it is,' he said.

Henry felt nervous. It isn't easy to come face to face with a man who's tried to murder you. He took a deep breath, stepped through the grey door, approached the line of people, looked up and found himself staring straight into the impassive face of Terry Skipton.

Terry Skipton? Could it be? Until Friday he'd believed that

340

Terry Skipton didn't like him, but . . . until Friday! If Terry Skipton had tried to kill him, and had wondered if Henry'd seen him, that might account for his sudden change of attitude. He remembered that rather hunched, almost deformed impression the driver had made on him. Terry Skipton! But he couldn't identify him positively. And they never put the suspect on the end, did they? Better move on. He hoped none of these thoughts were visible to Terry Skipton.

He moved on. He found himself gazing into an evil, guilty face. He could hardly spend less time looking at any of them than he'd spent looking at Terry Skipton, so he had to continue to look at the man long after he knew it wasn't him.

With pumping heart he looked at the man who was third from the right and fourth from the left. Had the officer been hinting? Another evil, guilty face, certainly, but no, it wasn't him.

He moved on. Another evil, guilty face. Did all men look evil and guilty when placed in a police line-up? Would St Francis of Assissi have looked like a flasher, in an identification parade?

He moved on again, and looked into the face of the man who'd tried to murder him. A shiver ran right through him. His certainty was total. That slightly twisted neck, the white face set at a slight angle, hunched into a mass of knobbly shoulder. The sense that the man was in the car, driving straight for him, was so strong that he had to force himself not to jump out of the way.

Even though he was absolutely certain, he felt obliged to move on and examine the sixth suspect. If a man gave up his time, during licensing hours, to stand in an identification parade, it was only polite that you should take the trouble to stare suspiciously at him through narrowed eyes for thirty seconds.

He returned to the second man from the left, and again he knew. And the man knew that he knew.

'That's the man,' he said, pointing. 'The second one from my left.'

They led Henry back, out of the bare cold room into the warmer parts of the building.

'Thank you,' said the officer. 'You picked the right man. You thought I were hinting before, didn't you?'

'Well . . . I . . . er . . .'

'It's just that I'm thick.'

'Well . . . I . . . er . . .'

'Now, are you absolutely sure? 'cos in court they'll say you didn't have time to see him properly.'

'Absolutely sure. The horror of it's etched in my mind.'

'Good man.'

The officer led him into the waiting-room, where Terry Skipton was standing beside the moustachioed lady with the *Watchtowers*.

'My wife Violet,' he said gruffly.

Henry's legs began to wobble. He sat down hurriedly.

'Are you all right?' said the officer.

'Oh yes,' said Henry. 'It's just a bit of a shock gazing into the face of the man who tried to murder you.'

'Well, not murder *you*,' said the officer. 'Murder Dennis Lacey.'

'What?'

'I don't see any harm in telling you. We're arresting him. He was Marie Chadwick's boy-friend. She ditched him. Apparently she's a right tasty . . . er . . .' He looked at Terry and Violet Skipton, and the pile of *Watchtowers*, and stopped. 'Apparently he drove past there day after day, waiting for a chance to get him without getting her.'

'By 'eck, Henry,' said Terry Skipton. 'The way you stared at me, I thought you thought *I'd* done it.'

Ginny and Violet and the officer laughed.

'You?' said Henry. 'You?? No!! No, I just thought . . . you being the first . . . if I didn't give you a pretty long, dirty look it might look a bit odd when I gave the others long, dirty looks. Me think you'd done it? That's a good one!'

The police were very grateful, but not so grateful as to provide a car home. Henry and Ginny trudged up York Road and Winstanley Road. Henry ran his hand gently over her buttocks as she walked, and then he put his arm round her. He felt very sexy after everything he'd been through. He thought of Hilary, in Durham. And, in the cold, sterile hall of their house, he gave Ginny a chaste kiss on the cheek and said, 'Thanks for coming with me.' She sighed and said, 'Pleasure.' They went to their separate beds.

As he undressed, and cleaned his teeth, and clambered into his

342

clammy bed, Henry was thinking hard. The Standard Eight had not been driven at him. The gangs had not been waiting to beat him up. Of course the crate of surgical trusses could still have been meant for him, but logic now seemed to demand that it had been an accident also. After all, as he realized now, there'd been no way anyone could have known that he'd walk past, under that crane. He hadn't known it himself. Believing that it had been a murder attempt meant believing that there were large numbers of people, stationed all over Thurmarsh, waiting for a chance to kill him. In view of later events, this seemed unlikely.

And yet . . . if Bill Holliday wasn't trying to murder him, why should he have gone pale at the mention of trusses?

Henry longed for the relief of knowing that nobody was trying to kill him.

And yet . . . he also felt that he'd be a little disappointed, even hurt, if nobody thought him important enough to rub off the face of the earth.

On Wednesday, February 13th, the government announced that the Quantocks had been designated Britain's first 'area of out-standing natural beauty', and that the British Megaton Bomb, capable of destroying many Quantocks, would be ready soon.

Howard Lewthwaite walked to the Midland Hotel for lunch with his prospective son-in-law.

'Have whatever you like,' he said, 'though personally I'll stick to the *table d'hôte.*'

The weather had turned colder and a brief burst of hail pattered against the windows, disturbing the hushed serenity of that temple of starched linen.

'I've made some discreet inquiries into that crane driver,' said Howard Lewthwaite. 'He doesn't sound like a potential assassin to me.'

The waiter approached. He had new shoes, which squeaked.

'What is the *potage?*' said Howard Lewthwaite.

'Mock turtle, sir,' said the waiter.

'I'll have that, and I like the sound of that ham omelette,' said Howard Lewthwaite.

'Soup for me, too,' said Henry. 'And what's the *daube d'Irlande?*'

343

'Irish stew, sir.'

'The pork chop, please.'

'They ring the changes pretty well, don't they?' said Howard Lewthwaite. 'Are you sure they're trying to kill you?'

'I'm not at all sure any more.' He explained his reasons.

'So, apart from Bill Holliday going pale when you mentioned trusses, the probabilities are all against it,' said Howard Lewthwaite.

'But why should he have said, "How did you guess?"' said Henry.

'Ask him. Here he is,' said Hilary's father.

Bill Holliday was walking through the restaurant with what might have been the smugness of a man who knew he was appearing on cue. He was puffing at a large cigar. He stopped at their table.

'I'm not wearing one today,' he said.

'What?' said Henry.

'A truss. I'm a little better. And after what you said . . . how did you know? How was it obvious?'

'Er . . .' Henry tried not to meet Howard Lewthwaite's eyes. 'I . . . I'm a truss-spotter. I was in the truss-spotting club at school.' Shut up.

Bill Holliday looked puzzled, shook his head in bewilderment, pulled fiercely at his cigar and puffed off.

'So,' said Howard Lewthwaite. 'Nobody's trying to kill you. If you're wrong about that, don't you think you could have been wrong about all your suspicions of corruption?'

'The lorry driver who had a miraculous escape when his lorry destroyed the Old Apothecary's House is a film stuntman,' said Henry.

'Two mock turtles?' said the waiter.

'Yes,' said Howard Lewthwaite faintly.

'The haulage firm have no record of his being employed there,' said Henry, when the waiter had gone. 'He obviously came in to do that one job only. So, both the individually fine historical buildings inside the Fish Hill Complex were deliberately destroyed. So, let's talk now in the knowledge that my suspicions are not the ravings of a deluded youth.'

'It sounds as though you're determined to go through with this,' said Howard Lewthwaite.

'I have to, and I haven't much time,' said Henry.

Howard Lewthwaite raised his eyebrows.

'I told the editor I have a big scoop,' said Henry. 'I've promised to tell him on Monday after I've told Hilary.'

'I see.'

'I had to. I'd made a couple of cock-ups. He was going to sack me.'

'I see. So it's my career against yours.'

'I'd rather call it right against wrong.'

'I'm sure you would.'

'Who's for the chop?' said the waiter.

'Me, it seems,' said Howard Lewthwaite.

The waiter gave him the chop.

'No, I'm the chop,' said Henry.

The waiter muttered to himself as he hobbled away in his new shoes.

'Some of the things I'm going to have to tell Hilary – deliberately driving a lorry into an old building, arson, murder – are things you're innocent of.' He looked Howard Lewthwaite in the eye. 'You do promise me you're innocent of them, don't you?'

Howard Lewthwaite held his gaze.

'I promise,' he said.

'Right,' said Henry. 'Well, so far you've tried to pooh-pooh everything. I suggest you change your policy. I suggest you try to uncover as much evil as you can. The more evil you find in which you aren't implicated, the less important your role in all this is going to seem.'

The waiter handed them the dessert menus. Henry's hand was shaking. It isn't easy, when you're twenty-one, to talk like that to your prospective father-in-law.

They both plumped for the trifle.

'Good luck in Durham,' said Howard Lewthwaite, as they parted at the junction of York Road and High Street opposite the *Chronicle* and *Argus* building.

'Thank you. I'll need it,' said Henry.

24   Durham City

The condition of Dennis Lacey, fighting for his life in Thurmarsh Royal Infirmary, was as comfortable as could be expected.

The condition of Henry Pratt, clattering northwards through the dark February evening, was as uncomfortable as could be expected. He had to stand in the corridor. He ached with desire for Hilary. His stomach was knotted with tension. Should he tell her straightaway and risk spoiling the weekend, or should he wait until he was on the point of departure? He tried to think of other things. With his legs braced against the corridor wall he tried to read his vibrating copy of the *Argus*. Mr Gromyko had become Soviet Foreign Minister. A pilot trip through the Suez Canal by three small vessels had been cancelled 'for political reasons', presumably because President Nasser wouldn't allow any ships through until Israel had agreed to withdraw. Jenny Farthingale, aged 10, had brought two dolls to the newspaper's offices. Uncle Jason had been very sorry to miss her.

He hobbled off the train. He had pins and needles in his legs, an ache in his genitals and a yawning pit in his stomach.

'My God!' she said. 'What's wrong?'

'I've missed you so much,' he said.

She enveloped him in her warmth. She hugged him to her, on the platform, as the train snaked out towards Newcastle. So that was decided. He wouldn't tell her that night.

She'd booked them into a little pub at the bottom of the hill, in the lower part of the town, as Mr and Mrs Pratt.

'You don't mind being known as Mr and Mrs Pratt, then?' he said.

'It's the most wonderful feeling in the world.'

The landlady led them up a narrow staircase. She introduced herself as Irene Titmarsh. 'Call me Irene,' she said. 'Treat this as your home.' She showed them into a small room, which was almost filled by a huge iron-framed bed and a heavy mahogany wardrobe, which stood two feet from the wall because of the sloping ceiling. A patterned blue china jug full of cold water stood in a patterned blue bowl on a small teak table in front of the tiny, net-covered window. Curtains, carpet and wallpaper were floral, in clashing shades of daffodil, tulip and marigold.

'Will you be down for some tea?' she asked.

'Er . . . Mrs Tit . . . Irene,' said Hilary. 'This is a bit . . . er . . . my husband's in the army. He's Henry, incidentally, and I'm Hilary. He's only got a weekend's leave. We haven't seen each other for a long time. Too long, and it's so short, if you understand me. So . . . er . . . could we just have some sandwiches in our room, Irene?'

'I understand you,' said Irene Titmarsh. She had good strong teeth, but not enough of them. When she smiled she reminded Henry of several streets in Thurmarsh, and he didn't want to be reminded of them. 'I could do you two nice ham salads,' she said.

'That would be lovely, Irene,' said Henry.

'Could we have no raw onion in the salad, if you understand me, Irene?' said Hilary.

'I understand you,' said Irene Titmarsh.

When Irene Titmarsh had left them, Hilary said, 'I can't be seen in the bar. I might meet people I know, and I could be in trouble if it was found out I was staying here as Mrs Pratt. So I had to think up some excuse to explain away why we spend all our time in our room "at it".'

'Magnificent!' said Henry. 'You're magnificent.'

Her magnificence thrilled and chilled him. He didn't think he could bear to lose her.

'The only trouble is,' she said, 'if our story's to be believed, I don't see any alternative to spending a lot of time in our room "at it". Do you think you can face that?'

'I think so,' he said. 'We Pratts are made of pretty strong stuff.'

He began to take her clothes off. She was lovely in her happiness. He tried not to think how her face would look when he told her about her father.

They climbed into the bed. It was lumpy, and squeaked ominously.

'You're so beautiful,' he said. 'I suppose as a socialist I really ought to be kissing somebody ugly.'

347

'You seem to infer that being kissed by you is a privilege,' she said.

'*Touché,*' he said. 'Hilary? Anna said something very odd about you. She said you didn't undress on the beach because you wanted to spare the Italians your horrible body.'

'I thought it was horrible. I was depressed.'

'Oh.'

'And I was as thin as a rake, then.'

'Oh.'

'My God! Were you wondering, all that time before we went to bed together, what horrors were going to be revealed, whether you'd be able to cope with them? Poor darling. How brave you must have been.'

She kissed him, laughing. He wasn't sure whether she was making fun of him or not.

There was a knock on the door.

'Your two ham salads with no onion, Henry, Hilary.'

'Thank you very much, Irene. Could you just leave them outside, if you understand me.'

'I understand you, Hilary. Leave the plates outside when you've finished.'

Henry fetched the ham salads. They enjoyed themselves greedily. Then they ate the ham salads, placing tasty morsels in each other's mouths. They left the plates outside, when they had finished.

Then Hilary began to kiss him all over, slowly, with an intense expression of solemn concentration which aroused him to new heights of love.

There was a knock on the door.

'Henry, Hilary, have you had enough?'

Hilary's face appeared from under the bedclothes. She beamed and shook her head violently.

'Yes, we've had enough, thank you, Irene,' Henry said, and his voice almost broke into a laugh.

'Good night, then. "Sleep" well.'

'"We will."'

They did.

There was a knock on the door.

'Good morning, Henry, Hilary. Have you "slept" well?'

'We've "slept" very well, thank you, Irene,' said Henry.

'I'll leave your tea outside. Come down for breakfast when you're ready.'

'I don't think we'll want any breakfast this morning, thank you, Irene,' said Hilary.

At eleven-thirty Henry handed in their key and they went out into a bright, crisp world. They had an early lunch in an unlicensed café. Neither of them wanted alcohol.

They walked over Elvet Bridge and up into the dignified old university town. Hilary greeted several acquaintances.

They wandered through the stone market-place, and turned left down Silver Street onto Framwellgate Bridge. They stood in silence among the shoppers, looking along the wooded River Wear, looking up through the bare woods to the old city, the castle, the cathedral, the fortified stone houses, up on their hill, safe in the great loop of their river. And Henry knew that he couldn't tell her until she'd shown him Durham.

Dark clouds loomed up, and there were a few flakes of irresolute snow. They walked along the west bank of the river, past a wide, shallow weir, along a path of half-frozen mud, to the Prebends Bridge. All the while they had changing views of the three great grey towers of the cathedral.

They climbed towards the city. It wasn't far. The sense of height was an illusion, the great illusion of Durham City.

At last, shyly, as if the city were a woman and they were her new lovers, they entered her. They entered her by the South Bailey, and came slowly that cold afternoon towards her great heart, by the cobbles and grey stones, the dark brick and red roofs of her Georgian skirts.

In awe and silence and strange pride the unbelieving young lovers entered the great temple of God. Henry gasped at his first sight of the vast Norman nave. He squeezed Hilary's hand, as if to thank her for it. She smiled shyly, as if she had built it.

They sat in the nave, and looked up at its great ceiling. The huge, round Norman pillars, their circumference equal to their height, were strikingly carved, with vast simplicity. The clerestory and upper storey were of exquisite proportions. Three rows of

349

shallow Norman arches were built on top of each other, with delicacy and charm sitting above grandeur and power. If you looked at the arches long enough they seemed to move like waves. They were a sea frozen in stone in a miraculous moment at the very beginning of time. Man couldn't have built all this.

Hilary shuddered.

'What is it?' he whispered.

'All the beauty of the world is waiting for us,' she whispered. 'I feel so happy I could break.'

So of course he couldn't tell her that afternoon.

Darkness laid a soft glove on this godly place. The ungodly, sated with an awe that seemed in no way unnatural to them, feasted on toasted teacake and pretended to be respectable. Hot butter streamed down chins that had run with lovers' juices. Hilary told him about her friends, whom he would meet that evening. He decided not to give her his bad news until he'd met her friends, until he'd woven himself that bit more irrevocably into the fabric of her life.

He charmed her friends. He was in sparkling form. They went to a couple of student pubs. They drank slowly and sensibly, because that was all they could afford. Hilary's friends seemed delightful people. Henry tried hard not to be egocentric. He remembered their names, and asked them about their lives, and remembered what he was told. He amused them with tales of his many disasters and included, for the first time, the incidents of the upside-down paintings and the misquoted Chief Torch Bearer of the Ark of the Golden Light of Our Lady. Here, in Durham City, far from Thurmarsh, he could expiate these horrors in humour. Hilary grew somewhat wry as his charm swelled. But what was he to do? He couldn't pretend to be a Tory in order not to seem to be too good to be true. He couldn't present himself as a reactionary young man who believed that a woman's place is in the home, in order not to curry favour with these charming young women. Everything he said presented him in the light of a treasure, a find. It couldn't be helped. He was acting, yes, and yet he wasn't. He said nothing he didn't believe. He told no stories that weren't true. He tried to be quiet, but people said things to him and he had to reply. Could he help it if they found these replies witty and apt?

'That was what you wanted me to do to your friends, wasn't it?'
said Hilary, on their way back to their pub.
'What?' he said.
'Set out to charm the pants off them.'
'What's wrong?'
'Nothing. I was just a little alarmed to see you in action tonight.
You're such a performer.'
'Didn't you want your friends to like me?'
'Of course.'
'Didn't you want me to like them?'
'Of course.'
'So what's wrong?'
'Nothing.'
'Yes, it is.'
'Well . . . I suppose I'm worried because you're so social. I don't
think I can be as social as you.'
'Hilary! I don't want you to be social if you don't want to.'
'Yes, you do. You don't know it, but you do.'
'Oh God! Look. We've had a perfect day. Let's not spoil it now.'
'Yes. That's probably what's wrong with me. It's too perfect. I
thought any kind of happiness had gone for ever. Now I feel happy
beyond anything I knew was possible.'
'It worries you?'
'Well . . . yes.'
'Being happy makes you unhappy? Being unworried worries
you?'
'No! Well . . . you know those screams of the world I told you
about?'
'Yes.'
'I haven't heard them today.'
He grabbed hold of her, with violent affection. He held her to
him.
'Don't hear them today,' he said. 'You may hear enough
tomorrow.'
'What do you mean by that?' she said.
'Nothing.'
She kissed him, a little doubtfully.
'Time for bed,' she said.

351

'Just for a change,' he said.

They slipped into the pub by the side door. She went straight upstairs. He went into the bar, to ask for the key. A few late drinkers were dimly visible through the smoke. The smell of beer was overwhelming.

'Nice day, Henry?' said Irene Titmarsh.

'Very nice, thank you, Irene.'

'This is my husband, George.'

'Hello, George.'

George had ginger hair and was quite small.

'Would you and Hilary like a drink, Henry?' said George.

'Thank you very much, George, Irene. Er . . . if you don't mind, though . . . it's our last night, if you understand me.'

'You didn't have a drink last night, Henry,' said Irene.

'That was our first night. That's what forty-eight-hour leaves are like. Good night, George, Irene.'

George and Irene Titmarsh gazed at Henry's departing back with something approaching awe.

They went to bed, and gave each other great pleasure. In the morning, Irene said, 'I've left your tea outside, Henry, Hilary. Come down to breakfast when you're ready.' Hilary said, 'I don't think we'll want any breakfast this morning, thank you, Irene.'

They left at 11.47. They would never forget Irene Titmarsh, but they would never remember the name of the pub.

It was snowing gently. There was a hole coming in Henry's left shoe. They had no bed to go to. They'd seen the cathedral.

'Shall we meet your friends again?' he said.

'Would that be wise?' said Hilary. 'You'd have to charm them as much as you did last night, in order to prove that you were being charming because you're charming and not because you were trying to be charming.'

'*Touché*,' he said.

The city was touched by the thinnest covering of snow. They spent two hours in a rather dull pub, which was unfrequented by students because it was rather dull. They ate in a rather dull café. The sun came out and melted the snow. It snowed again, as gently as before. They walked, and talked, and held hands.

Hilary sighed deeply.

352

'Never mind,' he said. 'I'll see you soon.'

'I wasn't actually sighing at that,' she said. 'I was hearing those screams.'

'Touché,' he said. 'Why do I end up saying *touché* so often?'

'Because you deserve to say *touché* so often.'

'*Touché.*'

They laughed. Then she looked solemn again.

'It's already too late for billions of people,' she said. 'Their one spell of consciousness is already ruined beyond repair. Every second of happiness I have seems to me to be obscene.'

'You can't do anything about it.'

'Can't I? We'll see about that.'

'These moods of yours worry me. I'm not sure I can live up to them.'

'They aren't moods, Henry. They're truths.'

'Then they frighten me all the more. Are we never to be happy?'

'Yes. Often. Because I'm weak.'

'It's not much of a kind of happiness, that's based on selfishness and weakness.'

'It's the only kind I can offer you.'

They sat, rather bleakly, in a station buffet designed for sitting rather bleakly. They had regrettable cakes and regretted them. They shed a tear or two. Henry had no excuse, now that Hilary had herself introduced the subject of misery, for not broaching his bad news. It was a good time for it.

And it was a terrible time for it. To tell her now would be to suggest that all the loving, all the laughing, all the awe and all the charming had been an act, because he'd known what he was going to say. So of course he couldn't say it. Could the glorious memory of love among the Titmarshes be for ever entwined with the smell of deceit?

Sunday evening trains are a special breed. They're grimier than others. They're slower. Their bulbs are dimmer. They rattle more. Their heating knows only the extremes of Arctic ice and tropical greenhouse fug. They're late, due to track maintenance. Their mournful whistles are like the cries of lovesick owls. And they are full of people going from where they chose to be to where they have to be.

353

Henry shared his stifling compartment with two navvies who talked about rock-and-roll, two silent staring soldiers, a snoring sailor, a girl with red eyes and an exhausted guest preacher, who'd expected three laughs but got only one. The train juddered away from Hilary, towards his lonely flat, towards Ginny trying not to look haunted as she asked if he'd had a good time. It clanked through a hostile world, whose inky blackness was broken only by occasional lines of sodium troops and the tracer bullets of cars' headlights.

And Henry justified his silence to himself. He couldn't leave Hilary there, without him, in her final year, with her important studies, to wrestle with the knowledge of her father's corruption, of her mother's sorrow, of the collapse of their Mediterranean dream, and all because of him. Impossible. No. The time to tell her was on the first day of the vacations. Yes, that was it. The *Argus* would have to wait. It was only another few weeks. Yes, that was it. The wheels picked it up. Yes, that was it. Yes, that was it. He'd tell her on the first day of her vacations, when he'd be with her to support her, and she'd be with her family, and they could all work things out together. Yes, that was it. Why hadn't he thought of that before? He could have enjoyed Hilary's beauty, the squeaky bed, the ham salads with no onion, the great Norman cathedral, without a twinge of anxiety, without a flicker of guilt. But still, it had been a wonderful weekend. He felt more hopeful, as if his rationalization would eventually make everything all right. The train sounded faster, more cheerful altogether. They yes-that-was-itted all the way to Thurmarsh.

25 *Vignettes Thurmarshiennes*

The cold snap continued. They shivered as they waited for the tram. Ginny tried not to look haunted as she asked if he'd had a good weekend.

On the tram, he read the Situations Vacant pages. Roll Turners, Fitters, Overhead Crane Fitter required. Jig and Tool Makers wanted. Experienced Moulders needed. Spoon and Fork Dolliers and Roughers required. Swing Grinders wanted. Die Sinkers urgently needed.

On Monday, February 18th, 1957, as his confrontation with the editor loomed, Henry was losing confidence in his ability to talk himself out of this one.

But what else could he do? Could he turn rolls, fit, mould, make jigs and tools? Could he dolly and rough spoons and forks? Could he grind swings or sink dies?

He could not.

Mr Andrew Redrobe's neatness might have been an ironic comment on the state of Henry's career. 'Right,' he said. 'Fire away. I'm all agog.'

'Er . . .' said Henry.

'I don't recall ever being agogger. Reveal your sensations.'

'Er . . .' said Henry.

'It's rare that a cynical, world-weary old warhorse feels a quickening of the pulse, finds himself on the edge of his seat, hardly dares to speak lest he miss the biggest scoop of his career. What did you say?'

'Er . . .' said Henry.

'I thought you did. You've got cold feet about your story? Come on. Don't be shy. Let me be the judge of it.'

There was a moment when Henry thought that he was going to tell him. But he couldn't. But he couldn't bring himself to tell him that he couldn't.

'Er . . .' he said.

'You exaggerated?' said Mr Andrew Redrobe, in a kindly,

almost paternal tone. 'Well, you won't be the first young reporter to exaggerate. Tell me what you *have* got. I won't bite. I'm human.'

'I . . . can't.'

'What??'

'Not until after the first day of Durham University's vacations, when I've told my fiancée. I went to see her this weekend. I found I couldn't leave her, so far away from me . . . er . . .'

The editor shook his Brylcreemed head, perhaps at the idea that anybody could suffer as a result of being a long way away from Henry.

'. . . with such upsetting news as my news would be, so momentous are the implications of my story.'

Mr Andrew Redrobe leant forward. He was fully paternal now.

'There isn't any story, is there?' he said gently.

'There is!' said Henry indignantly. 'Look, I'll make you an offer, sir.' Damn.

The editor's head jerked upwards, as if his neck had struck an unseen wire.

'An . . . offer?' He didn't welcome the suggestion of a deal from one so young.

'Yes. After all, the chapel might have something to say about sacking me for not getting a scoop.'

Mr Andrew Redrobe narrowed his eyes at the mention of the union chapel. His paternal kindness was but a memory now.

'Hundreds of journalists don't get scoops every day,' said Henry. 'They aren't sacked.'

The editor's silver pencil tapped insistently on his green-topped desk. The woodpecker had revived, it seemed.

'What about your monumental cock-ups?' he said.

'You let them go at the time.'

'I'm not talking about your past monumental cock-ups.' His left eye twitched. 'I'm talking about your future monumental cock-ups.'

'There may not be any, if you accept my offer.'

'All right, then. What is this offer?'

'If I don't give you an amazing scoop, on the second day of the Durham University vacations, I'll resign.'

'Is that a promise?'

'Mr Redrobe, you have the word of a Pratt.'

The editor's right eye twitched. The woodpecker tapped on.

'The first time you kill a man is the worst,' said Mr Andrew Redrobe. 'Then it gets easier. I killed at least seven men in the War.'

It was difficult, looking at this tidy, battened-down, buttoned-up man, to imagine it.

'Sacking a man should be simple after that. And sackings there will be, if the long-term predictions for this industry are correct. So why am I so curiously reluctant to start? Is it because you look so helpless, sitting there, that it would be like guillotining a doormouse?'

Henry didn't reply.

'All right,' said the editor. 'You have till the second day of the Durham University vacations. No scoop then, and it's the sack. And I do mean it. Mr Pratt, you have the word of a Redrobe.'

The moment he knew that Henry hadn't told Hilary, Howard Lewthwaite relaxed. He positively beamed at the waiter. 'French onion soup for me,' he said, 'and I'm very taken with the idea of the haddock with parsley sauce.'

'Soup for me too,' said Henry. 'And what are the *vignettes Thurmarshiennes*?'

'It's a new idea of the chef, sir. Five tiny vol-au-vents filled with local delicacies. Black pudding, cow-heel, brawn, tripe, mushy peas. Very different. Very tasty.'

'I'll have the *chaud pot de* Lancashire,' said Henry. 'You don't think I'll ever tell, do you?' he said, when the waiter had gone. 'You don't think I've got the courage. You think I love your daughter too much. Well, I do. Love her, I mean, not love her too much. If I loved her more than any man has ever loved any woman it wouldn't be too much. And I do . . . love her more than any man has ever loved any woman. But I do also love the truth. So because I love her so much I'm going to have to tell her the truth. I'm going to tell her on the first day of the holidays. When I'm there to support her. When you're there to support her. When we're all there to support her.'

Henry felt that he could have expressed all this more elegantly, more succinctly, and that it might have been more effective if he'd been able to look his prospective father-in-law in the face.

Howard Lewthwaite topped him up with the house white.

'Supposing it comes to a clash between your two great loves?' he said. 'Hilary and the truth. Which one will win?'

Israel rejected American proposals for the withdrawal of her troops from Gaza. Britain gave the United Nations a heavily documented indictment of Greece, accusing her of giving financial and propaganda support to the Eoka terrorists in Cyprus. Charges for milk, school meals, and the NHS portion of National Insurance were increased. President Eisenhower had a persistent cough.

Walking down the busy, decaying Commercial Road, after conducting a sensational interview with the President of the Thurmarsh Friends of Fur and Feather on the catastrophic effect television was having on pet clubs – attendances at Thurmarsh Rabbit Society down 39%, Splutt Tropical Fish Society planning merger with Rawlaston Cage Bird Club, a 22% decline in entries for pigeon races oh no, not pigeons again! – he had a shock. Wasn't that man with the blackheads . . . ? He was.

Just as some fortunate people are able to live for weeks without thinking about nuclear weapons, so Henry had gone for months without thinking about Derek Parsonage.

What was the man doing, walking down the path from a severe, black-bricked, Victorian town house with rotting window frames, in front of whose sad, gravelled garden a large board announced: 'World-Wide Religious Literature Inc.'?

'Hello. Henry Pratt,' said Henry, who had no overwhelming belief in his own memorability.

Was it just his imagination that Derek Parsonage turned pale beneath his unseasonal tan?

'Henry!' he said, beaming with belated and rapidly assumed delight.

'Can we talk?' said Henry. 'I have news for you.'

'Come in,' said Derek Parsonage. 'I was only going shopping.'

He led Henry through a large entrance hall, with religious literature displayed on three tables, into his office. It was a small, plain room, with a corner of a high, elaborately moulded ceiling which had once graced a much larger room. There were two hard chairs and a desk covered in pamphlets and invoices. Behind the desk was a large photograph of a black woman with huge bare breasts being handed a Bible by a man in a pin-striped suit.

Henry sat down, paused briefly for effect and said, '"Worldwide Religious Literature Inc."?'

Derek Parsonage shrugged. 'I'm no more religious than the next man,' he said. He lowered his eyes uneasily, as if expecting the next man to materialize through the skirting board and dispute this. 'But it's a way of earning a crust.'

'What do you do?'

'We're a sort of clearing house for the world of religious publishing. Basically it's just a specialized form of import-export, with a translation service thrown in. So, what's the news?'

'The burning of the Cap Ferrat was arson. Uncle Teddy was murdered.'

'No! Henry! How do you know?'

'We never reveal our sources.'

'Arson! How? Who by? Why?'

'I hoped you might tell me.' Bitter was the taste of the shame of The Man Nobody Muzzles, Henry 'The leech' Pratt, investigative journalist extraordinaire, who hadn't even thought of looking for Derek Parsonage. 'You never suspected it might be arson?'

'No. Why should I?'

'No reason. I just wondered.'

Questions were flying into Henry's brain like pigeons coming home to . . . not more pigeons! That's all I'm good for. Henry 'All you ever needed to know about pigeons' Pratt.

'You were part of the Cap Ferrat,' he said. 'Are you being paid by the insurance people?'

'No. I sold my share to Teddy a fortnight before the fire.'

What???

'Oh . . . er . . . really? Er . . . may I ask why?'

'Certainly. It's my turn to have a shock for you, Henry. I don't want to speak ill of the dead, and I know you were fond of your uncle, but . . .' Derek Parsonage stared so fixedly at the wall behind him that Henry turned to follow his gaze, even though he

359

knew that Derek Parsonage was only looking there to avoid looking at him. He found himself staring at a photograph of a huge naked black woman with a bolt through her nose, grinning broadly as she held up a copy of *Quaker News*. 'Henry? You know your uncle told you he was in Rangoon. He wasn't. He was in prison.'

'Oh, I knew that.'

'Well, I didn't. When I found out, I was shocked. I'm no prude. Night-clubs, in my book, fair enough. But crime? No, sir. I sold out. I'd probably have made a lot more, as it's turned out, if I hadn't, but I'm glad. My conscience is as clear as a Lakeland beck.'

'Well, if you think of anything you think is even remotely relevant, will you let me know?' said Henry.

'I certainly will,' said Derek Parsonage.

As Henry walked out across the gravelled garden, Stan Holliday was entering. They looked at each other in surprise, but neither of them spoke.

Henry turned and watched Stan Holliday close the door behind him. His spine was tingling. Many things he was prepared to believe, but if that evil-faced villain was interested in religious literature, Henry was a reincarnated Yugoslavian brush salesman who could relate the whole of the Koran in Urdu under hypnosis.

A new trail was opening up. He was onto something. If only he wasn't off to Cap Ferrat in two days!

He'd lived in a house of that name. He'd been to a club of that name. His surrogate parents had often gone there without taking him. At last he was going there, at the one time in his life when it would be an annoying interruption.

The following day, all that was changed. Derek Parsonage rang him at the office.

'You said you were going to France tomorrow,' he said.

'Yes.'

'I've thought of something, which I thought I ought to tell you before you go. I suppose you're surrounded by colleagues.'

'Yes.'

Henry looked up at Ginny, pounding the keys as if she were

reporting World War Three, not a persistent smell of sewage which was upsetting market traders.

'I presume all this is top secret?'

'Yes.'

'So I'll talk in such a way that you can answer "yes" or "no". Thoughtful, aren't I?'

'Yes.'

Helen looked up from her piece on summer hats and blew him a tiny kiss. It floated among the specks of dust in a brief ray of sunshine. He grinned at her. Ted scowled, with mock jealousy that hid real jealousy.

'I thought about what you said, and I remembered something which hadn't seemed significant at the time. You remember the compère, Monsieur Emile?'

'Yes.'

Denzil looked up from his piece on theatre stars who looked forward to the spring because they were keen gardeners, and he also blew Henry a little kiss. Henry grinned.

'Monsieur Emile and Teddy had a most tremendous row. Did you hear about that?'

'No.'

Terry Skipton raised his heavily lidded eyes exaggeratedly, his news sense awakened by Henry's intensity.

'Teddy caught Monsieur Emile with his hands in the till. He gave him a month's notice. You never heard about this?'

'No.'

Gordon gave him a thumbs-up, a tribute to his brevity from the king of ellipsis.

'I heard their argument. Monsieur Emile didn't realize I was there. He said, "You'll regret this." Teddy said, "*Je ne regrette rien.*" Emile said, "So! Zis is typical. You mock a great French artiste." He was livid. At the time I didn't think there was anything in it.'

'No.'

Colin gave him a gap-toothed smile, friendly, warm, innocent of all deviousness. It made him feel wretched.

'Now that I know what I know now, I'm inclined to take a different view.'

361

'Yes.'

'Well, that's it, Henry.'

'Thank you very much indeed,' said Henry. 'I've nearly finished the article, but I'll certainly try to introduce the budgerigar side of things.' He put the phone down. 'Bloody pets,' he announced, to the news-room at large.

Monsieur Emile had said that he was planning to open a night-club in Nice. How much might he have taken from the Cap Ferrat on the night of the fire? Was it inconceivable that the solution of Uncle Teddy's murder lay not in Thurmarsh at all, but on the Côte d'Azur?

Henry packed with renewed enthusiasm.

26   The Real Cap Ferrat

The Duke of Edinburgh was created Prince Philip, a Bedlington terrier became the first dog to be successfully fitted with a hearing aid, and the Americans were permitted to defend their bases with their own guided weapons, cutting across the previously accepted practice that the RAF had sole control of British air space in war.

In the elegant, small dining-room of a small, elegant hotel in the elegant village of St-Jean-Cap-Ferrat, three people were attacking grilled sea-bass with controlled greed. How the British love fish when they're abroad.

The woman had over-painted lips and startling peroxide hair, which emphasized her age although she thought it hid it. The older man had a large nose festooned with blackheads, as if the waiter had gone berserk with the pepper mill. The younger man was short and podgy and had reverted, in these sophisticated surroundings, into a self-conscious English gawkiness which made him barely recognizable as the accomplished lover he had been in Durham.

'Teddy loved sea-bass,' said Auntie Doris.

'Could we possibly have five minutes without mentioning your first husband?' said Geoffrey Porringer, who often made things worse by protesting about them.

'Geoffrey!' said Auntie Doris, who *always* made things worse by protesting about them. 'Henry's looked forward to this holiday. Don't spoil it for him by going on and on about Teddy.'

Geoffrey Porringer dropped his knife and fork with a clatter. '*I'm* spoiling his holiday!' he said. '*I'm* going on and on about Teddy! I was complaining about you going on and on about him, Doris.'

'Geoffrey!' said Auntie Doris. 'Don't make a scene. There are Italians and Danes and Dutch here. They'll think we don't know how to behave.'

'I'm sure Teddy knew how to behave,' said Geoffrey Porringer.

'Please!' said Henry.

'Exactly!' said Auntie Doris.

'It's not me who's been mentioning Teddy every five minutes,' said Geoffrey Porringer. 'I'm well aware, Doris, that I can never hope to be to you exactly what he was.'

'Please!' said Henry.

'No, no,' said Geoffrey Porringer. 'Now it's in the open, let's have it out. I don't need reminding of my inferiority, in the husband stakes, at every turn, every bar, every café, every *pissoir*. "Teddy peed there once!"'

'Geoffrey!' said Auntie Doris.

'Please!' said Henry.

'Subject closed,' said Geoffrey Porringer. 'I shan't mention Teddy again. Teddy who? Can't remember.' He resumed the steady demolition of his sea-bass.

'It's just that coming here brings it all back,' said Auntie Doris. 'I mean, it is a fact that I had happy times with Teddy and those times still exist in my memory. It doesn't mean I'm not happy with you, Geoffrey. I am. But, I mean, if by any chance you got burnt to death in a blazing building, and of course I hope that never happens, I'd like to think that one day I might meet some man, which of course wouldn't be the same, but it'd be a consolation in my old age, and that you'd be pleased, if you could see me, which of course you wouldn't, being dead, because otherwise I wouldn't be with this other man, but you know what I mean, if I said, to my new man, who wasn't the same but was very nice none the less, "Geoffrey liked sea-bass".'

'Please!' said Henry.

In the morning, in their villa after breakfast, Henry announced that he was going for a walk. It was bright and quite warm, but heavy clouds were building up over the mountains and Auntie Doris thought it might rain. He didn't mind. At least it would be warm rain. And he had to get away from the ghost of Uncle Teddy.

He strolled along a path, between the secretive stone walls of sumptuous villas. There were brief glimpses of tiny, pebbly bays licked up by a gentle blue sea. Ahead rose the partially wooded, mainly rocky slopes of the Alpes Maritimes, their contours untouched by man except for the occasional short viaduct on one of the corniche roads. And beyond, burning white against the blue sky, were the Alps proper, the high mountains. He was here at last. He was excited. His walk proved a tremendous success in every respect except one. He didn't get away from the ghost of Uncle Teddy.

It was walking along the path towards him, gazing at the boats rocking lazily in the bay. Henry stopped, rigid. It couldn't be.

It was. The ghost of Uncle Teddy saw him. It too stopped, rigid. It went white, as ghosts should. It turned and hurried away. Henry hurried after it in his flat holiday shoes.

'Uncle Teddy!' he called. 'Uncle Teddy!'

The ghost didn't stop.

'Uncle Teddy!' he called. 'I have to speak to you. I'm here with Auntie Doris and Geoffrey Porringer.'

The ghost stopped. It turned slowly to face him. Uncle Teddy was wearing natty blue shoes, white trousers and a striped fisherman's jersey. It was a relaxed, spritely, mediterranean Uncle Teddy, the holiday version of the man Henry had known.

'Trust you to run me to earth,' said Uncle Teddy. 'Trust bloody you! How did you do it?'

'You aren't dead!'

'Ten out of ten for observation.'

'But . . . I mean . . .'

Uncle Teddy looked astounded. 'Aren't you on my trail?' he said. 'This isn't just luck, is it?'

'I'm afraid it is,' said Henry.

'Oh no,' grumbled Uncle Teddy. 'That's not fair. Are you really with Doris and Geoffrey?'

'Yes.'

'They mustn't see me.'

'No.'

'You'd better come to the villa.'

Uncle Teddy's villa, set back behind a row of colour-washed fishermen's cottages, was larger than theirs but still comparatively modest. The faint smell of last night's giant prawns still hung over it, mingling with the scents of sea and pine and thyme and the morning's fresh coffee.

It was cool and dark in the shuttered villa. A few slats of sunlight dappled the marble floor.

He followed Uncle Teddy into the marble kitchen.

'So . . . you didn't die in the Cap Ferrat?' he said.

'How long are you staying?' asked Uncle Teddy.

'I'm staying a week. They're staying two weeks.'

'Two weeks!'

'You mustn't meet Auntie Doris.'

'No. No. How insensitive to come here, with me dead.'

'You aren't dead.'

'They don't know that.'

'No, and they mustn't.' Why mustn't they? I'm a journalist. 'What's happened, Uncle Teddy? You've got to tell me what's happened.'

'So either I stay in for a fortnight or I go away?'

'Yes.'

'Bloody hell.'

'Yes.'

'Oh shut up.'

Uncle Teddy took the coffee tray through into the large living-room cum dining-room. A heavy lace cloth lay on a round dining-table, and there were six high-backed ornate dining-chairs.

'They're married,' said Henry.

'Ah.'

'I went to the wedding.'

'Oh.'

'Cousin Hilda came.'

'How is the sniffer?'

'All right. Getting older.'

'Aren't we all?'

'You look younger.'

'I feel younger. I feel rejuvenated.'

Henry stood up.

'Oh come on, Uncle Teddy,' he said. 'You're going to have to give me an explanation.'

'Why?' said Uncle Teddy, smiling.

'I'm a journalist.'

'Precisely.'

'What?'

'I may not want my continued existence to be known.'

'If I don't get an explanation that satisfies me, i.e. the truth, I'll be forced to dig. Burrow for facts. Oh come on, Uncle Teddy. You brought me up as your son. You're supposedly burnt alive in Thurmarsh. I run into you in Cap Ferrat. You can't refuse to tell me what's happened.'

Uncle Teddy remained silent.

'I know some of it already,' said Henry. He sipped his coffee. It was good.

'Oh? What do you know?'

'I know that Councillors Peter Matheson and Howard Lewthwaite and council official Herbert Wilkinson are in cahoots with property developer Fred Hathersage to buy up an area now called the Fish Hill Complex in order to redevelop it to their mutual advantage. I know the Old Apothecary's House was destroyed and the Cap Ferrat burnt down to get them out of the way.'

'My God!' said Uncle Teddy. 'You know it all.'

'Not quite. I presume somebody, probably Fred Hathersage, is paying you a good whack to a numbered Swiss bank account for the destruction of the Cap Ferrat, for which, of course, being dead, you can't claim insurance.'

'Right so far. As co-owner, Derek Parsonage gets the insurance. What aren't you sure of?'

'One. Who's the mastermind behind it all?'

'Who do you think?'

'Bill Holliday?'

'No! Bill's nothing to do with it. He's totally straight. Honest as the day is long. And if he wasn't, he's such an obvious suspect nobody'd ever dare associate with him.'

'Fred Hathersage?'

'Brawn, not brain. Fred constructs what others plan.'

'Peter Matheson?'

'Where do Peter Matheson, Fred Hathersage and Bill Holliday live?'

'Thurmarsh.'

'Where do I live?'

'You! But you're my uncle.'

'Henry, don't look so upset. You were never supposed to get fond of me. Oh God, let's have some champagne.'

367

Uncle Teddy set off for the kitchen.

'I don't feel much like champagne,' said Henry. 'It's meant to be for rejoicing.'

'Don't have any, then,' called out Uncle Teddy.

'On the other hand, I need a drink,' shouted Henry. 'If you're having champagne, it'd be less trouble if I had it too.'

Uncle Teddy returned with a bottle of champagne and two elegant fluted glasses. He opened the bottle smoothly, and poured the champagne.

'Cheers,' he said. 'Oh, for God's sake, don't look so solemn.'

'Uncle Teddy!' said Henry. 'A man was murdered so you could drink champagne.'

'Henry!' Uncle Teddy was shocked. 'Nobody was murdered! Thurmarsh isn't Chicago. I'm not a killer. Property, yes. People, no.'

'So whose was the body in the Cap Ferrat?'

'The headmaster of Thurmarsh Grammar School.'

'What??'

'His name, I believe, was Crowther.'

'You . . . murdered . . . Mr Crowther!' Was there the faintest awe alongside Henry's horror?

'No! I've told you! Nobody was murdered. He died of natural causes.'

'How?'

'Of a heart attack, while strung up by a rope from a ceiling, entirely encased in chain-mail, in an exotic brothel run by Derek Parsonage in Commercial Road, Thurmarsh.'

'Oh my God! Mr Crowther??'

'Yes. Your respected headmaster got his sexual thrills from wearing armour and being strung up on a rope.'

'You call that natural causes?'

'It was natural to him. And it's not as uncommon a type of thing as you might think.'

'But he lectured us on moral values!'

'Hypocrisy is also not as uncommon as you might think.'

'How dare he work off his guilt feelings on me?'

'Mr Crowther knew there was a risk,' said Uncle Teddy. 'It was part of the thrill. He died. Nobody was to blame for his death. We just hushed it up and used it. Well, shame if it had got out. Disgrace for his school. Disgrace for his family.'

'Closure for Derek Parsonage's exotic brothel.'

'Well yes, that too, I suppose. It really was incredibly convenient all round and I saw the possibilities straightaway.'

'But the body was identified as yours.'

'Money opens most doors.'

'What would you have done if Mr Crowther hadn't died?'

'Gone missing. Changed my identity. As I have. Much more risky, though, if people were looking for me.'

Henry stood up.

'What a story!' he said. 'Headmaster of grammar school dies strapped in armour in exotic brothel, which poses as international Bible exporters, is subsequently burnt in deliberate destruction of Regency night-club and is falsely identified as owner of said club, who's living in South of France under assumed name while Tory and Labour councillors, council official and prominent local businessman, who employ stuntman to destroy another old landmark, carry out his master plan to make fortunes out of destruction and rebuilding of large area of central Thurmarsh. I'll get an award for this.'

Uncle Teddy poured him some more champagne.

'Cheers,' said Henry. He sat down, exhausted, bewildered. 'Things like this . . . they don't happen to people you know. They're the sort of things you read about.'

'Or don't read about.'

'What?'

'You can't print a word of this, Henry.'

Henry went white. 'You haven't been drinking!' he said. 'The champagne's poisoned.'

'Henry!' Uncle Teddy shouted. 'For God's sake, Henry. I'm not a murderer.' He regained control of himself. 'The champagne is not poisoned.' He took a swig, to add force to his words. 'Delicious.'

'Then why am I not going to publish it?' said Henry.

'Because of the hurt it'll cause.'

'What hurt?'

'To Mrs Crowther and her family, who'll be deeply, deeply shocked. To me, who brought you up as my son, and will end my

369

life behind bars instead of living here. To Geoffrey Porringer, who'll discover he's married a bigamist. To Doris, who'll discover she's a bigamist and will learn that the pathetic illusion that she clings to – viz., that I'd ever have gone back to her after she'd betrayed me – is an illusion and that I have a younger and prettier woman. To Cousin Hilda, whom the family scandal will kill, in spirit if not in body. To your series, "Proud Sons of Thurmarsh", which will be revealed as the biggest load of crap in the history of British journalism. To Howard Lewthwaite, a good man doing bad things out of love, whose career will be destroyed. To Naddy Lewthwaite, who will die in a year or two in an English winter. To Hilary Lewthwaite, your fiancée, an unstable young lady who has tried to kill herself. To Sam Lewthwaite, who will be brought up in a family ruined by tragedy. For what? A bit of skulduggery uncovered. A two-day sensation. More champagne?'

'But . . .'

'I know. You have a story that's dynamite, could transform your tottering career, and you can't use a word of it. Rather a shame. Better drown your sorrows.'

Henry sipped his champagne and thought with rising shame of all the lies he'd been told, from Derek Parsonage fobbing him off about Monsieur Emile to Uncle Teddy planning a champagne reunion with Auntie Doris and . . . oh god . . . saying, 'I love you, son.'

What would he do? Would he go ahead with his story? Should he go ahead? How did you weigh the value of a general principle of truthfulness against the particular sorrows that your action would visit upon the innocent and guilty alike? He felt weakened by all these revelations.

A cool little breeze had sprung up off the sea and was forcing its way through the gaps in the shutters. Henry shivered, and took another sip of champagne.

He recognized her scent, just before she entered the room. She was wearing tight white shorts and a tight blue sweater. She carried a shopping bag in her right hand. She stood in the doorway, smiling her astonishment, as tanned as a kipper, as shameless as a cat. But he was *more* astonished.

'Anna!' he said, trying not to blush as he remembered that

night, as he wondered if she'd told Uncle Teddy about that night.

'Hello, Henry,' said Anna Matheson. 'And congratulations! I'm thrilled about you and old Hillers!'

She enveloped him in her scent and gave him an extrovert kiss, accompanied by a grunted smacking of the lips. Uncle Teddy explained how Henry came to be there, fetched a glass and poured her some champagne. She sat down, crossing her big, brown thighs studded with tiny goose-pimples. It was too early for shorts, even in Cap Ferrat.

'So, you've changed your identity,' said Henry, trying not to look at Anna's thighs.

'Oh yes,' said Uncle Teddy. 'Meet Mrs Wedderburn.'

'Wedderburn?'

'My naughty sense of humour. Alice Wedderburn was the first girl I ever did it with, behind the tram sheds. Anna will be the last girl I ever do it with.'

'Alice Wedderburn!' said Henry. 'Alice Wedderburn! She lent me her camp-bed!'

'She wasn't Alice Wedderburn then,' said Uncle Teddy. 'She was Alice Crapper. Anna drew the line at Mr and Mrs Crapper.'

There was a strangely sombre little silence. Henry was painfully readjusting his view of Cousin Hilda's friend. Uncle Teddy and Anna were reflecting on what life as Mr and Mrs Crapper would have been like.

'I got hake,' said Anna Wedderburn, née Matheson. 'You do like hake, don't you?'

'Mrs Wedderburn?' said Henry.

'We got married three weeks ago,' said Uncle Teddy. 'For the will. In case I can't keep up the pace, and have a heart attack. Yes, I like hake. Go and get it unpacked, though, love. It'll stink the place out.'

Anna went into the kitchen, with her hake.

Uncle Teddy smiled – a little sadly, Henry felt.

'Don't know if she'd stay with an old man like me if it wasn't for the money,' he said.

He went over to the window, pushed the shutters open rather violently, and looked out towards the sea.

'Doris liked hake,' he said.

27 A Day to Remember

On Saturday, July 20th, 1957, buses which ran in defiance of a strike were ambushed, stoned and daubed by strikers. Their tyres were let down, sand and grit were put in their tanks, pickets boarded buses and let off stink-bombs. Stirling Moss in a Vanwall won the Grand Prix of Europe at Aintree. The Prime Minister, Mr Harold Macmillan, said, 'Let's be frank about it. Most of our people have never had it so good.' And Henry Ezra Pratt married Hilary Naděžda Lewthwaite.

As the guests made their way into the Midland Hotel for the reception, a sharp shower dampened their hats but not their spirits.

The Sir William Stanier Room was decorated, not altogether surprisingly, with photographs of engines designed by Sir William Stanier. The buffet was as sumptuous as a socialist councillor could provide without risking his political credibility. The drink flowed with a respectful nod to the memory of Sir Stafford Cripps and to Howard Lewthwaite's bank balance. The staff dealt solicitously yet tactfully with both the wheelchairs. Henry made a nervous but charming speech. There was a big laugh when he said, 'We've even been given two pictures, neither of which we plan to hang upside-down.' Hilary's smile, as they cut the three-tiered cake, was so wide that the caption in Monday's *Argus*, 'Councillor's laughter weds former *Argus* man', almost didn't seem like a misprint.

The past contained many sorrows and disasters. The future was uncertain. No matter. For one afternoon, Henry felt royal.

Prince Hal was charming to Hilary's friends. The Duke of Thurmarsh chatted animatedly to uncles and aunts and cousins. He even revealed a common touch, saying, 'Belt up, snot-nose' when Sam said, 'I hope you've packed the soup. You'll be wanting to consommé the marriage tonight.'

King Henry the Ninth felt a particular concern for Ginny Fenwick, who had smiled bravely throughout. He was sorry when he saw that she was smiling bravely at Tony Preece, beneath a photograph of Stanier 3-Cylinder Class 4 2-6-4T No. 42527 entering Fenchurch Street with a semi-fast from Southend. She needed a good man, but not this good man, who had a good woman who needed him.

'Tony's been telling me he's got a new act,' said Ginny.

'Oh good,' said Henry. 'What is it?'

'Come and see,' said Tony. 'Bring the lovely Hilary. She *is* lovely, Henry.' There was a brief silence, during which Ginny might have said, 'Yes, Henry, she is,' but didn't, and Tony might have said, 'As you are, Ginny,' but didn't. Too late, just as Mr and Mrs Quell were approaching, Tony said, 'This sexy, well-endowed, warm-hearted young lady tells me there's no man in her life. What's wrong with our sex? Are we all blind?' He hurried off in confusion when he realized that Mrs Quell *was* blind.

Henry introduced the Quells to Ginny. Mr Quell, his old English teacher and spiritual mentor during his brief religious phase, was a lapsed Irish priest, five foot four and barrel-chested. He was ageing with dignity. Mrs Quell's porcelain face remained almost untouched by time. She told them how moved her husband had been to be invited. Henry longed to tell Mr Quell the truth about the headmaster's death. There were times when he could hardly bear the knowledge that he had been unable to share with anybody, since that day on Cap Ferrat, five months ago.

'Ginny?' said Mr Quell, just as Ginny was about to escape. 'I've been trying to describe Henry's lovely bride and her exquisite dress. Alas, our sex, the admirers of women, are paradoxically incompetent at describing them. Could you oblige me, Ginny, for Beth?'

Ginny and Henry both tried to hide their horror. 'Well . . .' began Ginny. 'She's . . . er . . . not beautiful exactly. She's . . . something more than beautiful. She's absolutely lovely.' Henry blushed as Ginny, smiling desperately, gave a generous inventory of Hilary's charms.

'You're blushing, Henry. I can feel it,' said Mrs Quell. Her husband could see the tears in Ginny's eyes. He thought they were tears of happiness for Henry.

He talked with Peter and Olivia Matheson. He had found it impossible to give the editor his scoop. He had found it impossible to hurt those he loved – Cousin Hilda, Auntie Doris, Hilary and, ultimately, himself. He had found it impossible to uncoil the tangled ropes of motive, of his warmth and affection for others, of his personal and professional integrity, of the self-interest which lay on his tangled motives like frost on a whaler's rigging. In the end he had done the easiest thing. He had done nothing. There were times when he regretted it. This was one of those times. Every corpuscle of his being screamed, 'So you've got away with it, you bastard.' Peter Matheson, knowing this, turned the full blankness of his charm on Henry. 'A happy day, Henry,' he said. 'Congratulations.' He changed gear with the smoothness of an advanced motorist. 'Such a shame Anna couldn't be here. Have you heard from her at all?'

'No,' lied Henry, terrified that he would blush. 'Have you?'

'No,' said Peter Matheson, and Henry had no idea whether he was telling the truth. Surely, having been so involved in all the machinations, he would know? But it obviously wasn't a safe topic of conversation, in Thurmarsh. 'No,' he repeated. 'We're worried, I must admit.'

'We're her parents,' said Olivia Matheson unnecessarily. She was developing pronounced crow's-feet, perhaps from wrinkling her face against her husband's remorseless charm.

'I'm a repenter of former arrogance,' said Peter Matheson.

'In what connection?' said Henry.

'In your connection,' said Peter Matheson.

'We didn't think you a good enough catch,' said Olivia.

'We'd settle for you now,' beamed her husband sadly.

'Thank you very much,' said Henry drily.

Henry 'Certified eligible by no less an authority than Councillor Matheson' Pratt set off across the buzzing, bursting room in order to speak to a former flame, Diana Pilkington-Brick, née Hargreaves. Before he could reach her, her husband swept upon him like a tidal wave.

'This isn't the time to discuss money,' said Tosser Pilkington-Brick. 'No,' said Henry. 'So I won't,' said Tosser. 'Oh good,' said

Henry. 'But,' said Tosser. 'Ah!' said Henry. 'What?' said Tosser. 'Nothing,' said Henry.

'No, I just wanted to say,' said Tosser, 'at the moment you probably don't have any . . .'

'No, I don't,' said Henry.

'I haven't told you what I was going to say yet.'

'It doesn't make much difference. Money, prospects, savings, investments, property, children, transport, you put "no" and we can fill in the details later.'

'That's why I'm sure we at United Allied General Financial Services Consultants can help you.'

'You're right. It isn't the time.'

'I know. That's why I'm not talking about it. I'm just saying, if ever in future you want to talk about it, you can always talk to me.'

'Thanks, Tosser,' said Henry, relenting. Why did he always relent?

'Small point,' said Tosser. 'I've dropped the Tosser. It has . . . connotations. Do you think you could see your way to calling me Nigel?'

'I'm sure I could, Tosser,' said Henry.

Diana had been swallowed up by the crowd. The Lewthwaites and the Hammonds were gathered round Nadežda's wheelchair, beside a frosted-glass window against whose opacity a summer shower was beating in brief frustration.

Nadežda smiled at him happily. He bent to kiss her cheek, cold even in July. How natural Martin Hammond looked in a suit. How unnatural anyone looked, who looked natural in a suit at twenty-two years of age.

'Pleasant stag night last night,' said Martin rather stuffily. He was miffed because he wasn't best man.

Reg Hammond, Martin's father, said, 'We had a good night, too. At Drobwell Miners' Welfare. They had this grand turn. Irish. He were right comical, weren't he, mother? I thought so, anyroad.' 'Right comical,' echoed Mrs Hammond, who had found that it paid to agree.

Sam Lewthwaite blushed furiously when Martin's young sister,

375

who was thirteen, stared at him. Henry was glad he wasn't young any more.

'Did anything ever come of that corruption story I put you onto, Henry?' said Martin. 'No. I tried. It fizzled out,' said Henry. 'Pity,' said Reg Hammond. 'The secret of beating the Tories at national level is to regularly expose them at local level. That's what I reckon, anyroad.' Howard Lewthwaite avoided Henry's eyes.

But, when Henry moved on, Howard Lewthwaite followed him. 'Have I lost you for socialism?' he said, looking round to make sure they weren't being overheard.

'Oh no,' said Henry. 'You were no worse than them.'

'Ah, but we have to be better,' said Howard Lewthwaite. 'As women have to be better than men and blacks better than whites to be equal in this fair land of ours. Top dogs expect underdogs to prove themselves every day of their lives.' His eyes met Henry's at last. 'Thanks for not telling,' he said.

'I didn't not tell for you,' said Henry, grammatically inelegant as usual, in the presence of his father-in-law. 'I did it . . . I mean, I didn't do it . . . for Hilary and me.'

A group of his ex-colleagues was standing beside the drinks. He approached, smiling. Helen Plunkett, née Cornish, kissed him, and Jill felt obliged to emulate her sister. She approached the task as if he were a fillet of haddock lying on a fisherman's slab, and this still irked him. Did he want to be loved by the whole world?

'Epidemic time,' said Gordon Carstairs. 'I hope you'll both be very happy,' said Henry. 'Henry's got it!' said Gordon Carstairs.

'How's Lampo, Denzil?' said Henry. 'How should I know? Ask him,' said Denzil, whose hand-carved Scottish walking-stick was leaning against a cream radiator.

'Name the wives of the English cricket team,' commanded Ben Watkinson. 'Ben!' admonished his shy, petite wife Cynthia.

When Henry moved on, Helen followed him. 'Are we going to keep in touch?' she asked. 'I hope so,' he said. 'We never actually worked anything out, did we? You've still never really seen my legs properly,' she said. 'Helen!' he said.

Ted pursued them. His buttonhole looked tired. So did he. 'Lovely wedding,' he said. 'Great girl. I'm really pleased.'

'Oh God, Ted. How could I ever have thought you were trying to destroy my career?' said Henry.

Helen wheeled away, abruptly, towards the shattered remains of the buffet.

'You're right,' said Ted.

'I didn't say anything,' said Henry.

'You didn't need to,' said Ted. 'I *should* have married Ginny.'

'We'll slip off quietly, if you don't mind,' said Mr Andrew Redrobe.

'Andy thinks his presence inhibits the journalists,' said Mrs Redrobe, who was in blue.

'Will you apply for a job on another paper?' said Mr Andrew Redrobe, his voice soaked in the infuriating, paternal kindness that he had used ever since he had become convinced that the scoop which Henry could never tell him was a figment of an immature imagination.

'No. I'm thinking of something totally different,' said Henry.

'I think that's very wise,' said his former editor.

Marie Chadwick steered the wheelchair expertly through the seething, chattering throng.

'Congratulations,' said Henry. 'It's wonderful news.'

'We got engaged before we were told I'd walk again,' said Dennis Lacey.

'Dennis! That's not important,' said Marie.

'It is to me,' said Dennis Lacey. 'People said Marie left him for me because he was crippled. She left him for love. The fact that she was prepared to marry me when she didn't know I wasn't going to be crippled proves that.'

Liam O'Reilly and Norman Pettifer were having a quick sit, in reproduction chairs with elegant curved backs.

'Grand wedding,' said Liam.

'A wedding I'd love to have seen was that of Dame Sybil Thorndike and Sir Lewis Casson,' said Norman Pettifer.

'I hope you've been talking to people,' said Henry.

'Oh yes,' said Liam. 'I had a very nice talk with one of the waiters.'

'Though of course they weren't Dame and Sir then,' said Norman Pettifer. 'Have you been to Cullen's recently, Henry?'

'No. Why?' said Henry.

'I wondered if you'd seen the cheese counter recently,' said Norman Pettifer. 'That Adrian! Hopeless. No idea.'

Violet Skipton was in purple. Henry wished that she'd shaved off her moustache for the great day, but that would have involved tacit acknowledgement that it existed. 'We'll slip off quietly, if you don't mind,' she said.

'We don't like seeing people becoming affected by artificial stimulants,' said Terry.

'I expect you think we're ridiculous,' said Violet.

'No, I suspect we're ridiculous, but I won't do anything about it,' said Henry.

The almost deformed news editor held out his hand and . . . yes, another first . . . he blushed. The blush gave a sheen of humanity to his dark, unattractive face. 'Henry?' he said. The Christian name! Another first. 'If you ever feel . . . if you ever need . . . either of you, that is . . . how can I? . . . guidance, would you think of us? Our house has an open door. Our hearts are yours. Come on, Violet.'

Terry Skipton turned away, as if angry with himself. Violet Skipton followed him for a few paces, then turned back.

'I've never seen him take to anyone like he took to you,' she said.

Baron Pratt, third Duke of Thurmarsh, was temporarily at a loss. He stood there, shorn of all pretensions, twenty-two years old and still not mature enough or good-hearted enough to fight off unkind thoughts about women's moustaches.

Lampo Davey slid through the crowd, untouched by the increasing hubbub, carrying a large plate on which his single smoked salmon *beignet* looked aggressively ascetic.

'What's happened between you and Denzil?' said Henry.

'I broke her sugar bowl. Oh dear! Tragedy. Makes *Antigone* seem like a tiff about the funeral arrangements.'

'Lampo? You aren't going to end up hurting Denzil, are you?'

'Quite possibly. Why?'

'Please don't.'

'What?'

'Don't forget I brought you together.'

'You were the most reluctant matchmaker of all time,' said Lampo.

'I love you both,' said Henry.

Diana was sitting beneath Stanier Class 5 No 45284, which was carrying a Manchester to Cardiff troop special through Craven Arms. She was enormous. The Hargreaves family stood around her. Henry bent down, and she gave him a huge wet kiss, and said she'd felt vaguely jealous when she'd seen Hilary.

'A congenial stag night last night,' said Paul rather stuffily. He was miffed because he wasn't best man.

'Did Nigel try to sell you things?' said Diana. 'Yes,' he said. 'Oh no! He's awful,' she said, but she said it indulgently. She loved Tosser! She was enormous. Mrs Hargreaves, who was as slender as a silver birch, kissed him graciously, and he blushed because he remembered that he'd once desired her, and he could see that she thought he was blushing because he still desired her, and this made him blush all the more and of course he couldn't explain. Mr Hargreaves pumped his hand as if trying to bring it back to life. Judy kissed him coolly, and said, 'I'm amazed. All this. Smoked salmon. Champagne. The hotel. That lovely church. In the north. I'm amazed.'

Nigel Pilkington-Brick, né Tosser, joined them, and Henry felt sad. Not because she was married. He wanted her to be married. Not because she was happy. He wanted her to be happy. Not because she was enormous. He wanted her to have children and, if that involved being enormous, he wanted her to be enormous. But . . . there was a Pilkington-Brick in there.

Colin Edgeley was wedged into a corner with Tony Preece's fiancée, Stella. Colin looked drunk, dishevelled and desperate.

Stella had gone to great lengths to look smart but had only succeeded in looking gaunt.

'Has Tony named the day?' said Henry.

Stella shook her head. 'Last night his act went well,' she said. 'He was pleased. He said we must name the day.' He asked her where Tony had been appearing. 'Drobwell Miners' Welfare,' she said.

'Good Lord,' he said. 'What's his new act?'

'He calls himself Cavin O'Rourke, the Winsome Wit from Wicklow. He pretends to be very stupid. He thinks it may catch on.'

'Good Lord. Stella? Go up to him now. Make him name the day, while romance is in the air.'

Stella set off, uncertainly, without confidence, towards her reluctant fiancé.

'What's wrong, Colin?' said Henry.

Colin turned his glassy, pained eyes on Henry. 'Glenda's left me,' he said.

'Oh no,' said Henry. 'Why?'

'I got drunk and stayed out all night.'

'Oh no.'

'With Helen.'

'Oh no!'

'I was so drunk I don't even remember. She said I said she had the most beautiful legs I'd ever seen.'

'Oh no.'

'Can there be any value in an experience you can't remember? Why are you staring at me?'

'Because you can make fine philosophical points when your world's collapsing around your ears. So what are you going to do?'

'Go and try and get her back. I love her, Henry. I really love her.' This discovery seemed to astound him. 'I'd have gone this weekend, if it wasn't for this.'

'Colin!' said Henry. 'This isn't important. You should have gone today.'

'And missed your wedding, kid? You're my mate,' said Colin.

'Colin! Why do you do these things?'

'I have a strong streak of self-destruction. Like you.'

380

'I don't.'

'Yes, you do. Always having disasters. Always laughing about them.'

'I only laugh at them in order to cope with them,' said Henry. 'I'd love to be a success, talking about my successes. And I will. So belt up about self-destruction and go and get Glenda and the kids and show them that you love them.'

'What's happened to you?' said Colin.

'Hilary. She's changed me. Do you know what I've become at last?' said Henry. 'A man.'

OH NO! NOT THAT AGAIN.

The hububble of noise and champagne was rising to a crescendo. They were trapped, by the wall, between the buffet and the drinks: Cousin Hilda, Auntie Kate, Mrs Wedderburn, and, nearest to the drinks, Auntie Doris and Geoffrey Porringer. Michael Collinghurst, the best man, was charming them.

They smiled as Henry approached, even Cousin Hilda. Auntie Doris was trying not to cry and ruin her mascara. Geoffrey Porringer was trying not to cry and ruin his reputation. Cousin Hilda was sniffing furiously. Even Mrs Wedderburn had moist eyes.

Michael Collinghurst came forward, touched Henry's hands, smiled shyly, said, 'Lovely. She's a lovely girl,' and then stood to one side, smiling, as if conducting, with the baton of his goodness, the symphonic variations of Henry's relations with his family. It was the first time they had met since Florence. Henry's telegram had read 'Man best my you be like I'd to.' The clerk had queried it. Michael's reply had read, simply, 'Pleasure with accept I.' Now such childish things were behind them. Henry smiled at Michael's smile and wondered if, even on this day, he had no regrets about committing himself to celibacy.

Auntie Doris hugged him, and the tears streamed, ruining her mascara, and she said, 'I wish Teddy were here to see this day.' Geoffrey Porringer twitched. Cousin Hilda sniffed. Auntie Doris, who always made things worse by protesting about them, said, 'There's no need to sniff, Hilda, just because I mention Teddy. He's still alive, you know. He's not dead.'

Henry went rigid with shock. He felt that his hair was standing on end. He heard Cousin Hilda say, 'What do you mean by that?' He heard Auntie Doris say, 'In my heart. He lives on, in my heart.' His hair subsided. His legs felt weak. He hoped nobody'd noticed anything. 'Geoffrey knows that,' continued Auntie Doris. 'Geoffrey understands that. Geoffrey accepts that.'

'Geoffrey doesn't have much choice,' muttered Geoffrey Porringer. He turned to Henry and said, 'Well done. I always knew you had it in you.'

It was the moment to be generous. It was the time to show his mettle. 'Thank you, Uncle Geoffrey,' he said.

'Oh, I say,' said Geoffrey Porringer. 'Oh, I say. Uncle Geoffrey, eh?' He put his arm round Henry. 'It's a happy day for us all, young sir,' he said.

Henry kissed Cousin Hilda. She sniffed. 'Are you having a good time, Cousin Hilda?' he asked. She said, 'I thought the bridge rolls were a little on the dry side.' Henry realized that, if she'd continued, she'd have said, 'Everything else was perfect.' You detected Cousin Hilda's praise by taking map references on the points where she had not imparted blame.

He kissed Mrs Wedderburn. 'It was right nice of you to invite me,' she said. He heard himself saying, 'One good turn deserves another, Mrs Wedderburn.' 'Good turn?' said Mrs Wedderburn. 'You lent me your camp-bed. Now your gift horse has come home to roost,' said Henry. But he knew, with a twinge of shame, that he'd invited her because he wanted to search, beneath Cousin Hilda's widowed neighbour's plump exterior, for the naughty schoolgirl who'd done it behind the tram sheds with Uncle Teddy.

He kissed Auntie Kate. She explained that Fiona hadn't been able to come because her one-legged husband was having 'one of his turns'. It was the first Henry had ever heard of these 'turns'. 'May I bring Hilary to Skipton often?' he said. 'She won't want to see a dreary, faded old lady,' said Auntie Kate. 'She will! You don't know Hilary,' he protested. By the time he realized that he should have said, 'Auntie Kate! You aren't a dreary, faded old lady', it was too late.

Michael Collinghurst, smiling shyly, bowed ever so slightly, as if laying his benediction on them all.

A waiter opened two of the frosted-glass windows, allowing the sun to stream into the Sir William Stanier Room and the cigarette and cigar smoke to stream out into the cool, tramless town.

Henry and Hilary found themselves together at last, holding hands.

'Love you,' he said.

'Love you,' she said. She looked round and lobbed a great grin across the room towards her family. Her parents smiled back. Sam stuck his tongue out. 'I haven't seen my parents look so happy since the illness,' she said.

There were moments when Henry believed that he had been utterly right not to reveal his scoop. This was one of them, until he looked into Hilary's smiling face and wished again that there wasn't this great secret between them.

'We ought to be off,' he said.

'Right. Let's step out into the great adventure of our life together,' she said.

But, before they could step out into the great adventure of their life together, a man stepped rather shyly towards them. He was vaguely familiar. With a shiver Henry realized that it was the man from his dreams, who told him, in a few blindingly simple words, all the secrets of life and of its conduct. For an agonizing moment he wondered if it was all a dream. Had he known, all along, that it was too good to be true? He broke into a clammy sweat. In a moment the Sir William Stanier Room would disappear, the late afternoon sunshine would disappear, the roar of animated chatter would be silenced, Hilary would fade into the ether, all his happiness would disappear for ever, and he'd wake up in a crumpled bed . . . where? Which part of his life was not a dream?

'I seem to recognize that man,' said Hilary.

She could see him too! He was real. She was real. He hugged her in his relief. She looked at him in astonishment.

'It's the man in my dreams,' he said.

'It can't be,' she said.

'Don't you recognize me?' said the man.

Of course! 'Oscar! From the Pigeon and Two Cushions!'

Oscar beamed.

'Nice bit of extra, this, for me,' he said. 'Congratulations, sir. Congratulations, madam.'

They thanked him. He began to gather up empties. He walked away, then turned back towards them. He had the same expression as he did in Henry's dreams. It was the expression of a man who is about to divest himself of momentous information. Henry realized that Oscar was the unlikely agent who would tell them, in a few blindingly simple words, the meaning of life and the secret of its conduct. He shivered with fear and excitement. Hilary shivered too. They clutched each other's hands tightly. Oscar came up very close to them.

'I've had this summer cold,' he said. 'It's right ironical. One nostril's completely blocked up, and the other nostril isn't blocked up at all.'

CIRCULATING STOCK
WEXFORD PUBLIC LIBRARIES

BLOCK LOAN	
BUNCLODY	
ENNISCORTHY	
GOREY	
MOBILES	
NEW ROSS	
PROJECTS	
WEXFORD	
DATE	

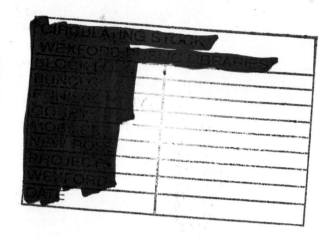

CIRCULATING STOCK
WEXFORD PUBLIC LIBRARIES

BLOCK LOAN	
BUNCLODY	
ENNISCORTHY	
GOREY	
MOBILES	
NEW ROSS	
PROJECTOR	
WEXFORD	
DATE